"Avery Cates!" someone shouted
from outside the tent.
"Come and be judged!"

I closed my eyes, a shock of adrenaline pulsing through me, quickly regulated by my limping augments. *Never a moment's peace,* I thought. The Angel we'd spotted in the street had gotten tired of waiting for me to come back out.

"We should have killed him out in the street," Remy said. But then Remy wanted to kill everybody.

I looked down at Morales. "Stay put. We're not finished," I said, and then the tent exploded silently, fluttering up into the air.

Praise for the Avery Cates Novels

"If…you watched *Crank* and thought, 'What this really needs is killer cyborgs with machine guns,' then this engaging pulp cyber-thriller will be right up your neon-lit street."
—*SFX*

"Somers just might be the genre's best-kept secret."
—Pat's Fantasy Hotlist

"An exhilarating example of powerful and entertaining storytelling." —*The Guardian* (UK)

"Fast-paced story with cool tech; well-written action scenes that drive the plot forward with perfect pacing."
—sfsignal.com

BY JEFF SOMERS

orbit

www.orbitbooks.net

THE FINAL EVOLUTION

JEFF SOMERS

orbit

www.orbitbooks.net

This book is a work of fiction. Names, characters, places, and incidents are the product of the author's imagination or are used fictitiously. Any resemblance to actual events, locales, or persons, living or dead, is coincidental.

Copyright © 2011 by Jeff Somers
Excerpt from *Equations of Life* copyright © 2011 by Simon Morden

Orbit
Hachette Book Group
237 Park Avenue
New York, NY 10017
Visit our website at www.orbitbooks.net

Orbit is an imprint of Hachette Book Group. The Orbit name and logo are trademarks of Little, Brown Book Group Limited.

The publisher is not responsible for websites (or their content) that are not owned by the publisher.

Printed in the United States of America

First edition: July 2011

10 9 8 7 6 5 4 3 2 1

ATTENTION CORPORATIONS AND ORGANIZATIONS:
Most HACHETTE BOOK GROUP books are available at quantity discounts with bulk purchase for educational, business, or sales promotional use. For information, please call or write:

**Special Markets Department, Hachette Book Group
237 Park Avenue, New York, NY 10017
Telephone: 1-800-222-6747 Fax: 1-800-477-5925**

To my Danette,
whom I regularly try,
and fail, to deserve.

PROLOGUE

HE REALLY ENJOYS THIS PART

"Tell me something," I said, easing the barrel into the soft spot on the back of his neck just below the skull. "How's someone as stupid as you get a job like this?"

He tensed for a moment, then slumped a little. "I used to be smarter."

I smiled, pressing the gun down hard while I hugged him with my free arm, feeling him up for surprises. I was alive and I felt good. "We all used to," I said. "Me, I used to be a fucking *genius.*"

I found a gun shoved down into his crotch, a battered old alloy auto with the safety chiseled off, ready to blow his balls off if he zipped up wrong. I weighed it in my hand.

"It'll go easier on you if you tell me what else you've got."

He chewed on this for a second or two. It was dark and cold as hell, the wind whipping up over the ruined outer wall of the old church and smacking into us. I stared over his shoulder at the glowing whitewashed walls, twin bell towers sticking up into the blue-black sky like broken bones. The church proper was ringed by the remnants of the old wall, a tiny, squat cottage connected to my right, the roof a vague memory. The whole world was being worn down, erased, one inch at a time, filled with empty, abandoned buildings like this. In twenty years the cottage would be gone down to the foundation. So would I.

"Nothing," he said, giving me a little shrug. "I'm just supposed to yell the alarm, give 'em some warning, anybody gets past me."

"Yell if you want to find out what your brain feels like flying through the air," I said. "Besides, it doesn't matter. We're inside already anyway. Walk me in."

If he was in the mood to be reasonable, I was in the mood to let him live. I'd killed enough assholes already. Why be greedy.

"All right," he said after another moment.

I pocketed his gun and let him put an inch or two between us, then followed him toward the church. We scraped along the frozen dirt for a few seconds in silence.

"Listen," he said quietly. "There's two guys on the first floor, right inside the doors."

I nodded. "We know."

"Let me take the slip," he said. He didn't say it pleading. He just asked, like he was asking for a cigarette. "I'll catch hell if I walk in there with you pushing me along."

I studied the back of his head. He was younger than me, but so was everyone. His head was shaved and a delicate tattoo of a spiderweb had been penned onto his skull, a blurry blue design done in a shaky hand. It glinted slightly in the cold moonlight. For a moment I considered just letting him run. My gut told me that he would just melt away and never bother me again, but I hadn't lived this long by taking stupid chances, so I sighed as if thinking about it and then I brought my Roon down on top of his head as hard as I could.

He dropped to the ground silently, and I stepped over him, glancing up at the hill that framed the church against the sky, a dome of green and brown. There was no noise aside from the crunch of my boots on the frost.

I crept forward. When I was a few feet from the big wooden double doors, they swung outward on silent, greased hinges.

"You stupid fuck," I hissed. "What are you thinking? You check your field, or you'll get punished."

"Yes," Remy said, leaning against the doorway with one of his ersatz brown cigarettes hanging from one lip. "The day you can't handle one guard who doesn't know you're coming, Avery, I'm dead anyway."

I looked him over. He'd grown like a weed over the last three years, getting broad and tall, every movement taut and powerful. He'd let his black hair grow out, hanging over his face, and he'd started a beard, a thick scum of hair that enveloped his cheeks and neck, making him look even skinnier, strangely. He dressed in black, like an asshole, but I pardoned him; he was still just a kid. And I liked him. It always surprised me how much I *liked* Remy.

"All right," I said, giving him a little slap on his cheek as I pushed past him. "Then today's lesson is, don't rely on someone else doing *their* job to keep you alive, you stupid fuck."

"Stupid fuck" had become my term of endearment for Remy.

Just inside the doors were two bodies, big guys sprawled in the sawdust poured all over the floor, a bloody mess. They were both locals, tall beefy guys, tan skin and long, dark hair tied back into tails, guns in their slack hands. Both had tiny, small-caliber holes in their heads. Remy favored big guns but he could work small if the occasion called for it. I'd taught him that, and I had a moment of weird pride, instantly soured. I stood there studying them for a moment while the kid closed the doors behind us.

"You didn't have to kill them," I said, carefully. I didn't want to prompt another speech about the military augments in his head that might explode at any moment—from decay, or stray microwaves, or an old SFNA officer with a spare remote in his pocket. I'd heard it too often. I had the same augments, forced on me by the Press Squad, but mine had been damaged. The one time someone tried to pop me with a military remote—a blackjack, the old soldiers called it—it hadn't killed me, though I wished it had, for a while. When Remy didn't respond, I sighed. "Quiet work, though," I said, looking back at him. His face was impassive, as always. He hadn't spoken for the first six months after we got out of Hong Kong, and even now he wasn't one for speeches.

"I think that was lesson three," he said, crossing his arms in front of himself. "*Noise gets you killed.*"

The church had been gutted and was just a cold shell of old wooden beams and empty windows. Up front there was a twisting set of stairs, apparently held together with wishes and good intentions, leading up to a sagging balcony that wrapped around three of the walls. I could see a door at the top of the stairs, a gleaming steel number that sported a nifty DNA-swipe magnetic lock. It didn't work anymore, of course; electricity was hard to come by in Bolivia. *Everything* was hard to come by, everywhere, since the System had fallen into a million little pieces.

"No one at that door?" I wondered aloud, walking forward and turning my head this way and that, trying to see everything, get the place fixed in my head.

"Assholes," Remy said by way of explanation. "Garces is nobody. A local strongman. I'm amazed he has a steel door instead of some glass beads on string."

I clucked my tongue. "Don't be fucking cynical, Remy. Yeah, Garces doesn't run anything half a mile away from this fucking building, but Morales is paying us a lot of worthless yen to kill him. And my intel says there should be two assholes at the front door and one asshole at the back door." I gestured up at it. "That bothers me. This lack of assholes."

"Well, there's *us*," he said with his usual flat tone.

I checked my Roon, scorched and battered but still smooth as silk—no one made guns like the old Roon corporation, rest in peace—then I took out the first guard's iron and looked it over. It was no Roon, but it looked like it wouldn't blow up in my hand, at least, so I slipped it back into my coat pocket.

"Well, let's find out what's up there."

I walked toward the stairs, thinking. Remy was right—Garces was a local boss, one of a million who'd sprung up when the army and the cops had dissolved, scattering, the System of Federated Nations getting unfederated over the course of a few chaotic months. The fact that the best people he could hire were low-quality wasn't surprising. It still felt wrong; I'd learned that when unexpected things happened, it usually went badly for you. We'd been

working so much lately, I was in practice, and in shape—
my augments, my gift from Colonel Malkem Anners
and Michaleen Garda, were damaged but still partially
functional. I still had a flickering heads-up display in my
vision, pain got washed away immediately, and when my
heart rate kicked up I got calm and clear. There was no
reason to discount my instincts.

I paused at the foot of the stairs and listened. The steps
were old wood, bowed in the center and reinforced here
and there with metal braces; they would creak like hell.
The hallway behind the door was about twenty feet long,
and there was another door that led to Garces's office. I
was standing there, judging the physics and the chances
I'd be heard when the steel door swung open and a skinny,
short man with his long black hair tied into a tight, thick
braid stepped out onto the landing.

For a second we stared at each other. "*¿Qué la cogida?*"
he said, taking half a step backward.

I put my gun on him, moving fast, my old augments
giving me an adrenaline-sick edge of speed.

"*Aqui*," I said, using one-third of my usable Spanish
and gesturing at the floor. "*Aqui.*"

He nodded, raising his hands up like an ass. Never do
anything you aren't ordered to, I always told Remy. Don't
give shit away—if someone forgets to tell you to put your
hands where they can be seen, keep your fucking hands
where they'll do you some good. He started coming down,
muttering something I couldn't quite catch with each step.
Watching him, I cheated my way to his left, and when he
was a few steps from the floor I reached out, took hold of
his ankle, and spun him crashing to the ground floor.

Remy was suddenly there, one boot on the poor guy's

neck, his massive double-action revolver pointed at the guy's head. Startled, I dashed forward and gave Remy a shove, knocking him off balance and sending him stumbling into the wall, his heavy gun making him lean. I hooked one hand into our new friend's collar and dragged him behind me as I stomped after the kid.

"Why the *fuck* do I have to always *remind* you to not just fucking *kill* every-fucking-body?" I hissed. Remy was hunched over, staring up at me from around his own shoulder, his cannon aimed at the floor. It was a ridiculously large gun, heavy and loud, but it would put a fist-sized hole in someone's chest, and Remy was attached to it despite the fact that bullets for it were rarer than clean water these days. His hair hung in his face and he made no attempt to move, to challenge me. He just stayed hunched over as if expecting a kick, and shrugged awkwardly.

"That's what we *do*," he pointed out.

"Fuck," I said and sighed, looking back up the stairs. "Maybe it would be nice to ask our new friend here what's behind that door? How many men up there?"

He nodded, slowly straightening up. "Sure, okay, Avery."

I stared at him again, my prisoner just waiting politely for our attention to swing back to him. Remy disdained caution, because Remy thought he knew how he was going to die, and thought the knowledge made him immortal in every other situation. Until his augments popped, he figured he was protected by fate. And no matter how many times I told him he was an asshole for thinking that, he was never convinced.

"Okay," I finally said, letting my guy drop to the floor and turning to put a boot on his chest and my gun in his face. "*Hola, muchacho*," I said, gesturing up the stairs. "*¿Cuantos?*"

He grinned, again putting his hands up by his face to signify that he wasn't a threat. I didn't need his hand gestures to know *that*; he'd already shown me his belly and asked me to scratch it. "*No mas*," he said eagerly. "*No mas, señor.*"

I nodded. "*Gracias*," I said, smiling back. His tan face lit up and he looked like he was going to keep talking, so I leaned down and smacked my Roon into his forehead just hard enough to knock him cold—the rusting augments in my head made such precise adjustments easy enough. I straightened up and gestured at Remy to precede me up the stairs.

"Don't be an asshole," I warned him as he slipped past me, all youthful energy and grace, sinews and adrenaline.

"We *are* here to *kill* Garces, right?" he whispered back. "We're not just going to be rude to him, call him some names, right?"

I started up the stairs behind him. As I'd suspected, they creaked and wiggled under us like it was going to be the last thing we ever did. "Shut up and keep your eyes open," I suggested. "When you have the urge to be an asshole, ask yourself if I can still beat the shit out of you. If the answer is yes, think twice."

Teaching the kid was hard work.

He reached the sagging balcony and stepped to the right, pushing himself against the fragile railing and raising his cannon. I stepped to the door and put my hand on the handle, glanced at the kid, and then pulled the door open in a sudden, smooth lunge. Remy tensed and then relaxed, shrugging.

I stepped in front of him and took lead. The hallway was made of warped wood slats on the floor and pock-marked drywall. Two doors on the sides had been boarded over crudely, leaving just the big, heavy wooden door with the shotgun slat at the other end to worry over. It made sense to limit the approaches; Potosí was not exactly a stable little city, and Garces hadn't become one of a dozen or so tiny chiefs in it through glad-handing and arranged marriages—a direct assault on his offices wasn't out of the question. If his guards weren't all local simps who couldn't be trusted to raise an alarm, the hallway would have been an effective way to bottleneck intruders and poke a gun through the slat, raking them with fire from behind the door, which I expected would be steel-plated on the other side.

We paused just outside, standing with our backs against the opposite walls, and looked at each other. Putting a finger up to my lips to forestall Remy's traditional approach of Extremely Loud and Shoot Me If You Can, I reached over and gently pressed down on the door handle. It moved easily and unlatched with a soft click that sounded like a shotgun blast to my ears. Wincing, I froze and waited to see if the door was going to explode, but nothing happened. I took a deep breath, my HUD flickering in my vision, all levels green, and pushed the door inward, stepping immediately to the left, gun out but held low.

Feeling Remy step in behind me, I took in the room. It was a nicely appointed office and almost felt civilized; Potosí was the definition of the sticks, but this place was old-school: wood paneling on the walls, a stained but thick and sound-swallowing red carpet on the floor, the opposite wall dominated by two huge floor-to-ceiling windows.

The left wall was all shelves, empty, the sunburned outlines of something or many somethings, square and all
different heights, still staining the old wood. In front of
the empty shelves was a massive wooden desk, dark stain
with deep scratches, flat and empty. Two men sat on my
side of the desk in old, busted-up, plush leather chairs,
the upholstery blistered and bursting. One was a huge
blob of a guy, pale white with dark red hair, a face made of
freckles and sweat. The other was almost as big, dark tan
and with glossy black hair spilling back over his shoulders
like a wave of ink, a thin pencil mustache adorning his
upper lip.

Behind the desk sat Manuelo Garces, who ran half of
Potosí with all the imagination and verve of a drunk piss-
ing on his shoes.

He was about my size, and ten or fifteen years younger.
He wore what passed for a nice suit in these shattered
times, and his head was close-shaved and sported a few
scabs where an unsteady hand had cut him. He was a
good-looking kid, his face round and happy, symmetrical
and balanced. He didn't look like a guy who'd come up in
the slums of Potosí, slitting throats and stealing anything
not nailed down, a guy who'd survived the breaking of the
System and the civil war that had left Potosí and everything around it for ten miles or so a scab of destruction.
He looked like a kid I would pay a thousand yen to run
messages for me.

In my peripheral vision, I saw Remy step in after me,
shut the door quietly behind him, and then step forward
and right a little, getting out of the door's way in case
someone unexpected came in. When he just stood there
with his ridiculous gun held down by his crotch, I relaxed.

The kid liked taking chances and sometimes caused trouble.

I looked at Garces. He had his hands under the desk.

"I'm not here to kill you," I said. "So don't pull that boomstick out unless you want to piss me off." Then I glanced at his two guests. "You two aren't on my list of chores today, so you have a choice here: You can jump out the window, or I can shoot you both in the head. You've got five seconds."

They both stared at me for a beat, then looked at Garces, who shrugged his eyebrows at him in the international gesture for *I don't give a fuck*. The redhead looked at me.

"We'll go without a fuss—"

"You'll go out the window," I said, affecting boredom, playing my role like I'd done a million times before. "Or you'll stay here forever." We weren't that high up—they might break a leg; they might get messed up, but the drop wouldn't kill them. If they made *me* kill them I was going to make it hurt, out of sheer irritation.

In some ways, the world was easier, now. The System didn't exist anymore—except for a hunk of Eastern Europe, where a rump of the old System Security Force hung on. Dick Marin—The King Worm—was gone. At some point the Joint Council's army had nuked Moscow into a shallow crater, vaporizing his servers. The news had already been a few months old when I'd heard it, and I'd felt nothing—which was curious. On my list of people to hate, Marin had been number three. Knowing he was gone should have felt like something.

The cops were hanging on, though. Everywhere else had just fallen to pieces. City states, small countries, a constantly changing ocean of sovereignties. Most places were run by people like Garces, gangsters who could pay for muscle to keep the peace, or by mercenaries who'd settled down with their troops. A lot of the old army officers had set up tiny kingdoms for themselves after the army had collapsed, with their units as security. It was fucking chaos, and chaos was good for business. There were no System Pigs breathing down your neck, beaming your face across the ocean, hunting you down. There were no Vids pasting your name everywhere and telling people to report seeing you. I could throw these two slobs out the windows and no one was going to investigate, no hovers were going to rip the roof off the place and dump a battalion of Stormers into the room. No one was going to care.

They still didn't move, so I shrugged and brought the Roon up, cocking the hammer with a dramatic click. That got them both out of their seats, Remy shifting gracefully to his left to keep Garces covered.

For a second we just stared at each other. Then I sighed theatrically. "If you've never jumped out of a window before," I offered, "the best advice I can give you is to take a running jump—it's easier that way, instead of leaning out in excruciating increments—and protect your head."

Red still stared at me. "You're . . . not serious."

Remy laughed, a cold, sudden snort. Remy hadn't known me back in New York, before the Plague. He knew only the new Avery. The new Avery wasn't as kind and gentle as the old.

I ticked my aim downward and put a shell at Red's feet, making him jump and yelp. The pair scampered backward toward the windows and I turned toward Garces.

"Remy," I called out. "Make sure they jump."

Garces was relaxed, a smile on his face. He stared back at me with his hands folded in his lap. At the sound of one of the windows scraping open his eyes flicked over my shoulder and then immediately back at me. He pushed his grin into overdrive and raised one hand to point at me.

"Avery Cates," he said.

I shrugged. "You're Psionic. Read my mind and shit, huh?"

Garces shrugged back as a pair of yowling screams pierced the air behind us, suddenly cut off. "You're the only *gringo* Gunner with a Bottom working around here." He ticked his head toward the windows. "You cost me money, there."

"Fuck your money," I said, easily, taking a seat in one of the busted leather chairs.

He took that in stride. "I'm guessing I'm down four men, too."

"Just two. The other two will live, unless they die of shame."

He nodded. I could see how he'd clawed his way to the bottom ladder of the post-System world. He was smart enough, and he stayed calm under pressure. "All right," he said, his accent subtle, giving his words a round feel I kind of liked, like every word was linked to the last by a thin line of silk. "Let's negotiate."

I shook my head. I had the Roon aimed at his face, my arm resting on the arm of the chair. "We're not negotiating. I just have a question I have to ask you before I transact my business. Something I ask everyone these days."

The office was damp, I realized. It smelled moldy. If I looked up at the ceiling, I'd probably find a deep brown water stain, but I didn't bother looking. Garces was a two-bit neighborhood boss—the world had tens of thousands of assholes at his level, now, shitheads who thought having a dozen big guys sending up tribute to you made you important. I'd known *really* important people. I'd been in the same room with them, made deals. Garces was a nobody, and I was about to remind him of the fact.

"By all means, Mr. Cates," he said, spreading his hands to indicate compliance. "If I can answer, I will. And then we can discuss who has hired you, and what it will take for you to go and kill *them* instead."

I didn't react. Every asshole in the world thought he was brilliant, that no one had ever had such a brilliant idea before. And there were probably Gunners who made deals like that, starting bidding wars, waking people up in the middle of the night to announce the latest bid, and would you like to bid higher or take a bullet to the face? But Gunners like that usually ended up dead sooner rather than later. The one thing people wanted in a Gunner was reliability. You didn't like to think that hiring me was just opening up a fucking auction.

"My question is, have you ever heard of men named Michaleen Garda, Wallace Belling, or Cainnic Orel?"

Garces squinted at me, cocking his head. "*Orel?* Everyone knows of Cainnic Orel, Mr. Cates. He has been dead for twenty years, I hear." He smiled. "Or do I hear wrong?"

I nodded. "And the other names?"

He leaned back in his seat. "Never heard either one."

I nodded again. I never expected any kind of shocking answer, but we'd traveled half the world since Hong Kong and I'd made it a standard thing, just asking. It was surprising what you could find out just by asking. I looked around the office. Chances were I was never going to have my revenge on Michaleen, aka Cainnic Orel, the most famous Gunner in the short, doomed history of the System, or on his lieutenant Belling. Both of them deserved to die, and I deserved to be the one to kill them, but I wasn't going to get any closer to that crawling around the wreckage of civilization killing little shits like Garces for pennies.

Wallace Belling had told me, three years and forever ago, that the fat times, as far as contract murder was concerned, were back. And he was right. I had more work than I could handle. The whole world was boiling, everyone grabbing what they could and riding the bull until it bucked them off, and the easiest way to skip your wait in line was to hire someone like me and delete a few people from the queue. I wasn't working Orel and Belling's legendary level, the Dúnmharú, a stupid fucking name that still made people lie awake at night with a gun in their hands, but I was sleeping indoors every night when most people were experimenting with a diet of dirt occasionally supplemented with their own fingers, and I was still alive, despite the odds. It was the best deal I was going to get, and every day I didn't get an interesting answer to my questions, I got happier with my lot in life.

Standing up, I pushed my gun into my coat pocket. "Nice place you got here," I said, walking toward the door. I felt good. My augments weren't as effective as they'd been when the military had first implanted them, making me feel like a kid with perfect balance and endless energy, but they kept my leg from aching and my lungs from burning, and I slept like a baby at night, just a black stretch of peace and recuperation. I spun and walked backward for a few steps, feeling light and lively. "Too bad it's going to be someone else's tomorrow."

His sudden expression of pale horror was hilarious. "You said you were not here to kill me!" he shouted, veins bubbling up under his skin. I got the impression that Garces was a screamer, when you didn't have a gun on him. That made me feel good. Screamers deserved to be shut up.

"I'm not," I said, hooking a thumb at Remy, who stood in front of the desk with his cannon held calmly in front of him. "He is. He really enjoys this part."

PART I

I

VERY HIGH ON THE LADDER

The mud sucked at my boots and splattered all over my pants and coat as we walked through downtown Potosí. I didn't know what Potosí had been like before the civil war, but Potosí today was a pimple where trash collected, a scab of a city where nothing had been rebuilt, just repurposed. It was a town of blue tarps, thick plastic sheeting laid over destroyed roofs, stretched to form rippling walls, used in architectural ways I'd never imagined. Who even knew there was so much blue tarp in the world, just stockpiled everywhere, ready to be deployed after the field-contained armaments had churned your city into a maze of rubble and bloody mud.

"Do you see him?" Remy asked without looking at me.

I nodded. The sun was incredibly bright and had absolutely no warmth; it was just a huge pale disk in the sky reflected off of every iced-over pool of water and sheet of frozen, off-white snow. The streets had been churned by a thousand feet into pudding that wanted to pull you down into the earth and hold you there, absorbing you. Some of the more enterprising people had laid down wooden slats outside their buildings, but for the most part it was just the sucking mud and a hundred assholes shoving you this way and that. Potosí had never been a big town, but it seemed empty all the time, half the old ruins unoccupied, no one hurting for space.

Even so, a walk downtown always got on my nerves.

I stopped and pretended to examine some knives on a fragile-looking cart that had no wheels. The proprietor was an extremely thin black man with a puffy white beard exploding off his face in several contradictory directions; his beard looked like a parasite that was sucking him dry. He didn't move as I fingered his merchandise, good knives that looked pre-civil war, machine-made.

"Looks like a Tele-K to me," I said, picturing the broad-chested kid in the dark black suit, trailing us by twenty feet or so.

"Does he have a mark?"

I shook my head and turned away from the cart. "Not that I saw, but I can't get a good look."

We kept slogging through the mud toward the market. "You'd think by now the Angels would have figured out that Tele-Ks don't scare us," Remy said in his flat voice.

The Angels. The fucking Angels. For years the System Pigs had kidnapped every kid who showed even a spark of Psionic ability and kept them all safely bottled up in special schools, training them to be the ultimate civil servants. Then the Joint Council undersecretaries made them into their intelligence staff, and then the whole fucking world broke and the Psionics had come wriggling up through the cracks. Half of the Spooks were just in it for themselves, bad enough when the guy horning in on your business could snap you in two from across the room. The other half called themselves Angels. They were Psionic Actives under no one's control, and they were convinced that they had been created by god to rule the world— whether they were supposed to kill the rest of us or just tell us what to do wasn't very clear. What *was* clear was that step one of their brilliant plan was to eliminate "evil men and women" by drum trial and summary execution, and I was on their list of bastards in need of some punishment. Every few weeks, one or more of the crazy bastards found me and tried to put me on *trial*.

You could tell an Angel from a regular run-of-the-mill Spook—assuming they weren't trying to squeeze your brains out through your ears while making a speech about god and evil men, which was a dead giveaway—because they liked to ink themselves up, usually on the neck right over the jugular. A Tele-K got a stylized fulcrum, a triangle with a line balanced on top, and a Pusher got a small black crow.

I fucking hated the Spooks.

"I'll handle him," Remy said, turning away. I shot out a hand and grabbed his collar, pulling him back to me.

"You stay with me and back me up," I said quietly. Remy's death wish was fucking exhausting. He thought he *knew* how he was going to die—via random augment disconnect in his brain or random encounter with former SFNA officer with a blackjack in his pocket—so that somehow made him immortal. "We'll handle him when he requires us to handle him, okay?"

Remy didn't say anything, just fell back into pace at my side with a smirk and a shrug of his shoulders. I didn't say anything else. I was responsible for Remy. If he hadn't been glued to me back in Englewood, years ago, he wouldn't have been pressed into the army at the height of the civil war. Wouldn't have had military augments sliced into his brain, wouldn't have been shipped to Hong Kong and made into a hardass, wouldn't have walked away without an official discharge, his augments still active in his skull, ticking away. Remy was on me. So far, everyone I'd tried to keep safe—few and far between—was dead. I didn't like my odds.

I thought of Glee, and had to force myself not to smack Remy in the back of the head. I *liked* Remy. I'd liked Gleason, too. It made me angry to think about her.

We walked in silence, then, between the sagging carts selling beat-up old tech and dying batteries, solar collectors, and, occasionally, tiny reactors promising near-endless energy. Such reactors existed, sure, but I doubted any of them had migrated to a cart stuck in the muddy streets of Potosí. Batteries were about the most valuable things in the world, especially if they came with solar collector hookups, and the cart had four big guys working security on it, all of them lounging around a few feet away, looking bored and sleepy. The sleepier and dumber security looked, the more I kept clear of them.

The buildings behind the carts were jagged remnants, rounded off by blue tarp and occasional attempts at renovation, raw wood rotting away again. Piles of cleared rubble popped up at regular intervals, courtesy of bombing runs by the System Pigs on one day and the Joint Council's army on the other; Potosí had switched hands a dozen times during the war. There were still unexploded shells buried in the ground or lodged in the cracks and crevasses of the buildings. Every other day someone triggered a proximity sensor and got turned into a bloody fog. Potosí was a fucking paradise.

The market was a grandiose term for a small field of semipermanent tents. Most of it was real food, pulled from the ground or slaughtered right there in front of you, a dirty, disgusting mess. Once you've seen a goat killed and cleaned in front of you, you paid whatever they wanted for the dwindling supply of N-tabs and considered yourself lucky. The smell was suffocating, the air thick with smoke, but the paths were laid out with flat gray stones that made walking easier, and everyone got out of my way as I led Remy toward the center of the field, where a bright white tent fluttered, topped by a splashy red pennant. There were two short, stocky men standing on either side of the open slit in the front of the tent, looking cold and pissed off, which was how I liked my guards. The one on the left nodded at me as we approached, and neither one twitched as we pushed past them into the tent. We were expected.

Morales was on his feet the moment I ducked under the flap, his belly preceding him, his arms thrown open. Two women holding beat-up old shredding rifles stood on either side of the flap, young girls with scars on their faces who didn't look at me once as I breezed past them.

"You magnificent bastard!" Morales bellowed, grinning. "You did it! You killed them *all*, you fucking maniac!"

Morales was a big sloppy kind of guy, a guy who was always sweaty, a guy who kept the interior of his fucking tent uncomfortably warm and his shirt undone down to his navel. He wore jewelry, thick ropes of gold and numerous rings. He was flashy and he grinned a lot and laughed a lot and when I'd first met him I'd thought he was a joke.

I put my hands up. "Try to hug me and we won't be friends anymore."

He laughed, but shifted his body and contented himself with a soft hand on my shoulder, guiding me to the large wooden table set up in the center of the tent. This was where Morales did all his business, all day, every day. He sat and ate constantly, nibbling and sipping, and a stream of folks came and went. I sat down without being asked and picked a grape from a platter. Morales wanted everyone to know he was rich, that he had juice, so he let food rot on his table every day while half the people around him were starving. Remy moved behind me and positioned himself with false casualness in a spot where he had all four of us in his sight, and leaned against a pole so his coat slid open, revealing his improbable revolver hanging low on his hip.

"Eight men," Morales said, laughing as he dropped into the other seat. "Eight men stood between me and Potosí, and now they are all dead. Garces last night. You are a genius, Mr. Cates. You have made me master of Potosí."

I swallowed the grape and decided against telling Morales what I thought being master of a lump of mud with no electricity or sewage was worth. "You owe me five hundred thousand yen," I said. "Paper notes, as we agreed." Since the cops were holding together something that resembled the System, yen remained the only currency worth anything at all. And paper was the only way to carry it around these days; even if banks still existed somewhere you couldn't touch the servers anymore, at least not in fucking *Potosí*, which must mean "nowhere" in Spanish.

Morales folded his hands across his belly, and with a

sinking feeling I realized the fat bastard wasn't planning on paying me. "Mr. Cates, you have made me a man worth having in your debt," he said cheerfully. "What would you say to continuing our partnership? I am offering you a post as my security chief. Very high on the ladder."

I sighed, picturing the tent in my mind while I kept my eyes on Morales's mesmerizing chest hair. "I would say you owe me five hundred thousand yen." I didn't tell him that the thought of staying in Potosí one more minute was about as appealing as shooting off my own foot, or that the fact that he'd had the wisdom to hire *me* instead of some drunk from the local arena didn't make him the genius he thought he was. I at least showed up with my own gun.

Morales lost his smile. Grunting, he sat forward. "Mr. Cates, I have made you a very good offer." He put the smile back, like flicking a hidden switch in his mouth. "These are hard times! Unsettled times. Here you would have the best of everything: a nice house, servants, women—or whatever it is you enjoy." He leered, and I resisted the urge to jump forward and smack him. *Whatever you enjoy* in-fucking-deed.

Morales liked keeping things polite, so I made an effort and smiled back at him. "All I need," I said slowly, "is five hundred thousand yen."

We stared at each other with our frozen smiles for a moment, and then Morales leaned back and spread his hands, closing his eyes. "I am afraid, Mr. Cates, that cash flow difficulties prevent me from paying you at this moment. However, I do not intend to, as you might say in your charming New York vernacular, *rip you—*"

I launched myself out of my chair and onto him. Behind me, I knew Remy already had his revolver out and aimed at the two guards—my only worry with Remy was whether he was going to kill everyone he met without a thought, not whether he was capable. The kid had learned all about death before I even got him back.

We landed on the dirt floor of the tent, my legs straddling Morales's swollen belly and pinning his arms. I clamped one hand over his mouth and pinched his nose with the other, making his eyes instantly bug out as he tried to roll me off.

"Listen to me," I advised softly as he bucked under me. "If I picked you up by your feet and shook you, a million yen would fall out of your fucking pockets."

Five hundred grand was about a month's survival, these days—if you lived light and weren't picky, and if you could even get people to accept yen as payment. Your chances of spending yen were better in the cities— in Potosí you could scrape together enough folks willing to take yen to get by. Any smaller than Potosí, you either bartered or you had precious metals—gold or platinum, mostly. Heavy to carry, hard to come by.

"If I pinch your nose for two minutes," I went on in a whisper, "you're dead and whatever I find in here is fucking *mine,* so think *again* about our arrangement and what you owe me. I'm going to let you think for another ten seconds and then I'm going to take my hand off your mouth, and there's a right answer and a wrong answer to the question: Are you going to pay me my fee?"

His eyes were wide and he'd stopped struggling. Guys like Morales had never encountered a professional before. They were born into a backwater like Potosí, and they thought Gunners were employees. We were the people with the *guns.* Guys like Morales, they worked for *us.*

I waited another moment and chanced a glance up. Remy had two guns in his hands, covering the guards, who both stood like newly erected statues, gaping. I stifled a sudden unwanted giggle. I should have picked up a protégé years ago.

I looked back down at Morales, whose eyes were taking on the dreamy, this-isn't-so-bad glaze of someone about to pass out. I snatched my hand from his mouth and let it hover an inch or so away as he took a deep, coughing breath.

"Yes," he gasped. "Yes, you fucking—"

"Avery Cates!" someone shouted from outside the tent. "Come and be judged!"

I closed my eyes, a shock of adrenaline pulsing through me, quickly regulated by my limping augments. *Never a moment's peace*, I thought. The Angel we'd spotted in the street had gotten tired of waiting for me to come back out.

"We should have killed him out in the street," Remy said. But then Remy wanted to kill everybody.

I looked down at Morales. "Stay put. We're not finished," I said, and then the tent exploded silently, fluttering up into the air.

II

HARD AND NOISY WAS
HIS ONLY WAY

I rolled off Morales and scrambled toward what had been the corner of the tent, hooking my elbow under the taut hemp rope, tight as a guitar string, that held the white tent fabric to the rusting stake driven deep into the frozen ground. Tele-Ks, I'd found from boring experience, basically had two attacks: They either tossed heavy things at you, or they tossed you high into the air and then let you drop. For some reason they always thought being able to do these two things gave them the advantage in a fucking gunfight.

I tried to scan the crowd quickly to find the Angel before he spotted me; Tele-Ks had to see you, or at least have a good mental picture of where you were in relation to them. Just as I picked him out, though, the world jerked under me and an invisible hand tried to toss me up into the air. My shoulder popped painfully out of its socket as I jerked upward, but I grimaced and kept my arm clamped around the rope. Ever since Hong Kong, my shoulder slipped out of its socket like it wanted to be free, and I'd gotten good at ignoring the grinding pain and just popping it back in at my earliest opportunity. I fluttered there like a piece of trash caught in the wind, and I tried to swing my gun around to throw a few ill-advised shots at him before he started pelting me with buckets or rocks or people. The fucking Telekinetics were all the same. All the power in the cosmos and the best they could do is throw shit at you.

Morales's two guards had unslung their rifles and crouched down, but didn't know what they were looking for. As I swung around trying to orient on the Angel, they both flew into the air, screeching, their careers ending more or less as expected. I spotted Remy, crawling toward me, staying low.

"Stop!" I shouted, the invisible hand slapping me into a spin. "Stay still!"

"Avery Cates!" the Angel shouted as a large rock shot past my head. "You have been judged! The world is broken! Men are vanished! The human race is barren, and we are sent to make final judgments!"

His voice was rough and throaty, a rasp. As I jerked this way and that, clinging desperately to the thrumming rope, I saw a crowd gathering behind him, eager for some entertainment in a place like Potosí. I didn't blame them. If I wasn't the unlucky bastard constantly being batted around by these freaks, I would have been pretty amused, too.

My arm burned with the effort of keeping the bulky rope pinned under my armpit, and my shoulder ached, the pain blasting into a sharp jab with every jerk. I watched

Remy crawling for another moment and then raised my arm and swung it around until I was more or less aiming in the general vicinity of the Angel, who stood there in his dark, mud-stained suit without flinching. The crowd behind him let out a rolling, chaotic roar and split into two, moving rapidly to either side of him. Fun was fun, but nobody wanted an errant bullet in the face. I couldn't get a bead on him as he tugged violently at me, trying to dislodge me from my anchor.

Below me, Remy had crawled, unnoticed, almost directly underneath. Lying on his belly, he carefully took a bead on the Angel and squeezed the trigger, but the revolver was so fucking huge it bucked in his hand as usual and all he did was tear up a spray of mud at the Angel's feet. An instant later Remy shot up into the air, getting caught in the fluttering fabric of Morales's tent. I swallowed and pushed Remy out of my mind, didn't think about being responsible for him sailing up into the air and the last moments of his life being high-velocity ones. I concentrated on the Angel on the ground, his round face and full cheeks and big, dark eyes. I brought the Roon around with a grimace and spent some seconds trying to hold a steady bead on him.

This is why, Dolores Salgado, who had once been an undersecretary, one of the most powerful people in the world, whispered in my head. She'd been dead a long time, and I was tired of carrying her around and ignoring her. *This is why we collected all the Actives and trained them. Because of this.*

He noticed what I was doing before I could get a shot off, and with a tick of his head a rusting metal barrel hosting a garbage fire sprang from the ground and sailed toward me, spitting flaming chunks of grease and sparks, smacking into my upraised arm and spinning me wildly.

When I stopped spinning, he had raised an arm to point at me.

"Avery Cates!" he shouted. "You have been judged! You have killed your fellow man! You have fomented chaos and violence everywhere you have dragged yourself! You have killed thirteen members of my order, for which only god can judge you, and it is my duty to make this arrangement!"

The Angels reminded me of the old Monks, those tortured cyborgs that used to prowl the System when there *was* a System and try and convince everyone that they had to live forever to get into fucking heaven. The Monks had generally wanted me dead, too.

Fuck aim, I thought, and shot my arm out in the Angel's vague direction, squeezing off eight shots as fast as my finger could twitch. Two or three went wide, but two managed to chew up the frozen ground at his feet, making him stumble backward. For a second, the invisible hand tugging me up disappeared as his concentration was broken, and I dropped to the ground, managing to curl up and throw my arms around my head just before I smacked down. My Roon went off on impact, and the air was suddenly filled with screams.

Head ringing, my HUD flickered, broken status reports sliding past me as the immediate pain from the impact was washed away. I rolled onto my stomach and pushed myself up. The market had turned into chaos, the crowd slurring this way and that. I couldn't see the Tele-K—he'd been swallowed by the panic—but I did see a body lying near the edge of the market, just a pair of tattered brown pants and two bare, brown feet sticking up. Nothing like an accidental kill to get the crowd stirred up.

I checked my gun over quickly, opening the chamber and dropping the clip, then slamming both home again. It seemed fine, but I'd have to strip it later. I heard a soft grunt behind me and spun to find Remy, enveloped in the white tent, fighting his way toward me in the freezing mud.

"You okay?"

He made a face. "Embarrassed."

I grinned, because I knew it would irritate him. "Move. Get in the crowd, under shelter so he can't send us into orbit." We moved to split up and I pulled up short, grabbing Remy's arm and spinning him back to me. "Try not to kill everyone who gets in your way."

He turned without a word and sprinted toward the crowd, and I trotted at an angle to him, dashing around the muddy tents. I didn't know where the Angel had gone, but I wanted him out of my hair. I didn't need him popping up with his speeches and freaky powers every time I tried to get some business done. Stepping over the corpse, I merged into the foot traffic with my gun down by my hip, my finger alongside the barrel. Things were already getting back to normal even with the poor guy still lying in the mud a few feet away—there was still a buzz of excitement, but everyone was getting back to their own business. There was no law. No one was going to come and find out what had happened, who did it. No one was coming to process the body. If he had anything on him worth stealing, it was already gone, and with that, so was everyone's interest until the shooting started again.

I stepped back onto the main road and stopped to look around. Remy appeared a few dozen feet back from me and did the same, glancing at me and then advancing across the road and into the line of carts. At least in there he'd have something to anchor himself to. Although I'd been smashed against walls over and over again, too, so there was definitely nothing stopping them from kicking your ass *anyway*.

There was a tug on my sleeve. I looked down and found half a man staring up at me. He was young, or had been, and had no legs, his midsection just ending on a filthy skid that had been designed to let him slide through mud or snow pretty easily. He held two blocks of wood in his hands for self-propulsion. His face was half normal and half a red mask of cold burns, one eye socket just a rubbery mat of pink flesh. The other eye was bright blue and glared at me with force, as if daring me to challenge him. A soldier, I decided. Someone pressed into a unit just like I'd been, but not lucky enough to get sold out of the army—if you called getting fucked over by Cainnic Orel and Wa Belling for about the fiftieth time and being left for dead—also for the fiftieth time—as *lucky*.

"I saw 'im," the cripple said in a hoarse voice. "What you got for it?"

I studied him. "I could *not* shoot you in your good eye."

His smile was the worst thing I'd ever seen. I would have paid him just to *stop*. "Naw, you won't. I hearda you. C'mon, make me an offer."

Hearda you. A deep pulse of anger went through me. That was how people got killed, especially old people like me, staring forty down and waking up every day with a new set of aches. Word got out you were soft, that you could be safely fucked with, and it was only a matter of time.

Time's what I didn't have, though; every moment made getting surprised by the Tele-K more likely, so I swallowed my irritation down.

"Five hundred yen," I said. "Paper. *And* I don't find you later and finish what the war started, one arm at a time." I leaned down, fishing a wad of notes from my coat. "And if you haggle, I swear I will tip you over right here and step on the back of your head until you stop struggling." I put some grin into it, and he blinked, reaching out with one calloused hand and snatching the bright green notes.

"Third building down from here," he said, hurriedly putting some back into sliding away. "The barber's."

I watched him make impressive speed through the mud, then looked up and over at the building he'd indicated, where someone had painted a swirling design in red, white, and blue. It was a heavy-looking building, big slabs of gray stone with the delicate carved facade still clinging to the doorway, an archway of faux bricks and tiny carvings I couldn't make out. The rest of the building was like a scar, like someone had peeled the outside off, leaving just the bones.

I put two fingers in my mouth and whistled. A moment later Remy was at my side, his revolver down at his hip, his face blank.

"There," I said, pointing. "Go around back. Count to fifty, then come in hard and noisy."

I didn't really have to tell Remy that. Hard and noisy was his only way.

He hesitated for a moment like he was going to argue,

then shrugged and sauntered down the narrow alley between the buildings.

I checked the Roon again and then held it out as I walked, finger on the trigger. I crossed behind the line of carts first and approached the door from the side, keeping my exposure low. I couldn't see anything inside the doorway. When I was a foot or so from it, I took a deep breath, my HUD fading for a moment and almost disappearing, and then took three quick, long strides and entered the building.

My eyes adjusted immediately, thanks to my old, damaged augments. I was in what had once been the foyer of the building, now sporting a single large metal chair bolted to the bare concrete floor and several scratched and dented wooden tables. A large mirror had been balanced against the wall on top of one of the tables, and the rest of the tables sported a scattering of jars and tools, brushes and razors. The floor was almost as wet and muddy as the street outside.

The barber stood behind the chair, one hand tilting his customer's head, the other holding a razor that looked like it had started out life as a thin metal file. He wasn't looking at me. He was staring at a spot on the wall above the mirror, stock-still. Standing against the rear wall, next to a closed, heavy-looking wooden door, was the Angel, hands in the pockets of his elegant coat. The second I saw him, I was enveloped in the invisible fist, unable to move.

"Fuck me," I gasped, finding it hard to breathe. "You're not going to make another fucking *speech*, are you?"

A slight smile kinked up the corners of his mouth, and he took a breath. The invisible fist tightened in one eye-popping jerk, and my HUD flickered off in my eyes.

"You have been—"

The door next to him crashed inward, smacking into him in a bit of luck I knew the cosmos would bill me for later. Remy stood in the doorway, eyes everywhere, long hair disheveled. The fist melted away and I crouched down slightly, putting three shells into the door. I looked up.

"Check him."

Remy slammed the door shut with one authoritative shove and fired his cannon twice into the crumpled form of the Angel, each shot damaging my hearing.

The sudden stillness was creepy, after that. Slowly, I straightened up and looked at the chair. The barber and his customer were gone. Then I looked at Remy and smiled. Remy stared back, expressionless, and slid his gun back into his hip holster, wiping his hands on his muddy coat.

I sighed. "C'mon," I said. "Let's find that fat fuck."

Morales was sitting on a recovered chair in the midst of his ruined tent, belly spilling out over his knees. He was smoking what looked and smelled like a real cigar, prewar. He watched us approach, with squinted eyes, affecting calm, but the sheen of sweat on his brow and the way he fidgeted told me otherwise. He was terrified, and for good reason: He probably had more muscle on tap, but they weren't here yet, and if I chose to slit his throat in front of Potosí, no one was going to stop me.

"I am glad to see you triumphant, Mr. Cates," he said with fake cheer. "Those crazy Spooks should be *opposed*."

That sounded sincere enough. I stopped in front of the fat bastard while Remy circled around behind him.

Morales cocked his head to track him for a second, then smiled at me and spread his hands.

"I was not lying, Mr. Cates," he said. "I do not have the funds I owe you."

I nodded, pursing my lips, and when I reared back and kicked him over in the chair, he didn't seem surprised. Feeling tired, I just walked over to where he was and put my gun on him, cocking the hammer just in case all he needed was some extra encouragement.

He put his hands up, the sheen of calm cheer gone. *"Espera!"* he shouted. "Wait! I have a counteroffer. I have five thousand yen in notes in my pocket. It is all I have, liquid."

I waited without moving. "And?"

He licked his lips and fucking *smiled*. "I have information you have been seeking. I can tell you where the man named Wallace Belling is. Where he is right now."

I stood there for a moment, a cold shock settling into my bones. My mouth watered and I had to blink rapidly to clear my vision. It had been *years*. I'd last seen Belling in Amsterdam, when he delivered me to Cainnic Orel—known then as Michaleen Garda—after buying me out of the army. I'd last been in Belling's *presence* weeks later, in Hong Kong. I'd been dreaming of killing them both for years.

I nodded, stepping back and clicking the hammer back down. "Deal."

III

YOU JUST HAD TO
LET HIM DANCE

I reached out and pulled Remy back. He resisted for a moment and then let me shove him down into his chair. I leaned against the bar and let my coat hang open, showing off the Roon in its leather holster. The big, hairy guy who was sweating in the unheated bar looked at it and then back at me.

"I apologize for my friend," I said. "Let me buy you a drink."

The bar only sold something mysteriously sweet and disturbingly red. I didn't know what they made it from, and didn't want to know. Our first night in Potosí I'd made the mistake of having a third.

The big guy was probably seven feet tall. Old, older than me, but still a lot of muscle. His beard was gray and black and long, tied off every few inches with bits of leather. He settled back into his stool. "All right," he said in an accent I couldn't place. "Tell your friend he should not pick fights."

I nodded at the bartender and pointed at the big guy. "He wasn't picking a fight," I said. "He likes to shoot people."

I let that hang in the air while the bartender, a skinny girl of about ten with dull, wild black hair frizzing out around her head, poured red liquor into the big guy's cup. I studied her as she worked; it had been a long time, I realized, since I'd seen a child. She looked incredibly small and new, suddenly. When she came over I handed her five hundred yen. All the bills were new and crisp.

"I need transportation, long distance," I said, holding on to the bill when she grabbed it. "You point the right person at me and there's another five hundred."

She bit her lip and nodded, eyes wide and locked on the money. Paper was still strange to me, and fucking inefficient, but it felt good to be able to bribe people again. Five hundred yen would buy her something to eat. A thousand yen might keep her alive for a week, if she lived careful. It was a good enough tip to get her enthusiasm up. I let go of the bill and she made it disappear impressively. I eyed her for a moment as she ran, barefoot on the cracked, frozen cement floor, to the rear of the bar. She probably worked the streets as a Pick when she wasn't slopping drinks in here, and she probably did well doing it.

I sat down across from Remy, who was finishing off his second cup of solvent, looking yellow and bloated, his eyes squinty. Remy was the worst drunk I'd ever known. He drank fast, like he was punishing himself, and got surly, picking fights and being nasty. He'd killed four or five poor assholes in stupid bar fights, and I'd learned that that was the whole point. That's what he wanted to do— have a reason to shoot someone. I'd had to knock him cold a couple of times just to stop a fucked-up situation from crossing over into batshit insane, but he never complained. He woke up, vomited once or twice, and seemed good to go. I looked down at my own cup, untouched. In the cup, the booze looked black, and I wanted nothing to do with it. I missed gin, but no one made gin anywhere. I missed N-tabs, too. Every time someone set a joint of meat down in front of me, I wanted to puke right onto my plate.

"Try not to piss everyone off," I said. "We've got a window before Morales gathers his troops. We don't need the rest of the town against us, too."

Remy saluted me and waved his cup in the air without turning around. I sighed.

The bar was mostly empty, just a half dozen people aside from us, four cripples who sat nursing cups on the darkened edges of the room, Remy's new friend, and a cardsharp who sat alone, shuffling an ancient deck of holographic cards that still shone bright and cheery in the dim light. There was no sound in the place aside from the wind howling through the thin walls, and not much light from the smoky oil lamps. I wondered, briefly, how come no one tried to lift anything from behind the bar with the girl gone, and then wondered why they didn't try with the girl *there*, since she looked about as dangerous as a cloud. Then I got bored and put my attention into trying to drink the stuff in my cup. I opted to breathe through my mouth and just swallow it fast. It was thick and oily on the tongue, and when I'd choked it down the burn wasn't the pleasant one alcohol usually gave me, but something acidic and sinister.

I thought about Mexico. We'd passed through it on our way to Potosí, months ago, coming south down from

Alaska and the ruin of California, which was still just a field of rubble that glowed at night. Mexico was better off; it had been largely controlled by criminal gangs before the civil war, and since the war had been under the thumb of two dozen old army units and their commanding officers, a hundred well-armed and desperate men and women who still had augments in their heads that could be controlled by their CO and his blackjack. Mexico wasn't *civilized*, but you could get things done in Mexico, and the gangs and old military units were big enough that yen was useful to them. It wouldn't be hard to run an operation in Mexico, if I could dig up the resources.

Tiny steps told me the bartender had returned, and bigger steps in tow told me my yen had bought someone's attention. I didn't turn around; Remy was still sober enough to glance over my shoulder and then shrug, letting me know it wasn't a threat.

The girl who sat down across from me was beautiful: tan, smooth skin, long, glossy black hair, an oval face with a long nose and a full mouth with nice teeth. Her eyes were a dark green and looked back at me steadily. She was wearing canvas overalls that had been patched a hundred times over a thick, gray shirt that looked warm and scratchy. Her hands were nicked by a million tiny cuts and heavily calloused, but they were folded in front of her calmly. If she was afraid of drunk men with guns, she didn't show it.

"Adela tells me you need to go somewhere," she said flatly. "Where?"

I stared at her for a few heartbeats, smiling, giving her the old attitude. It was like clicking into a groove, wellworn and familiar: *Avery Cates, Destroyer of Worlds, is not amused.* "Mexico City," I said finally. *City* was a grand term for what was left up there, but names stuck.

She pursed her lips, nodding, calculating distances and risk. She glanced at Remy, who had acquired his third cup and seemed content to stare into it, then back me. "Two of you?"

I nodded. "Probably." I couldn't think of any reason we'd acquire anyone else, but you never knew.

She nodded again, and leaned back in her chair, stretching her arms behind her and pushing her tits at me. That was probably a good negotiating trick, usually, and my smile became more natural. The girl had some brains. "My cousin has a vehicle. Four-wheel. The deal is: You provide a type V6 battery with working solar collector, plus ten thousand yen, and he will drive you there. We all provide our own food along the way."

"We?" I asked. I wondered if that was a grift, if we were supposed to stare at her tits and get all hot and bothered at the thought of her sleeping three feet away from us out in the wilderness and forget to haggle on the price. Or if she was fishing to see if we'd make her an offer to keep us company along the way. That thought made me sad, suddenly, and I made a face, waving my hand. "A working battery and a collector is gonna cost me fifty thousand yen, easy, from one of those assholes out there. That's sixty to get up there. That's fucking robbery."

She sat forward again, so suddenly I was startled into widening my smile. "Do you have a vehicle?" She waved a finger in front of her. "No, you do not. You do not like the price, you can go find someone to maybe carry you north."

Remy suddenly lashed out an arm and took hold of her

hair, yanking her head back as he set his cup on the table carefully. She squeaked in shock, but then whipped her hands up and clawed at his face, kicking the table as she twisted in the chair. If her nails hadn't been bitten down to the tips, she might have made the kid regret such a sloppy move. As it was, he had her neck bent down over the back of the chair and she had no leverage with which to extricate herself.

"Be polite," he advised.

I looked at Remy and shook my head. "No fucking need for that, dammit," I said evenly, controlling myself. He glanced at me and shrugged, releasing her and scooping up his drink casually.

She sprang from the chair, her face dark, and stood coughing. No one else in the place had so much as shifted their weight. I waited to see what she'd do: curse us out, walk away, make threats. Instead, she swallowed, pushed her hair from her face, and then slowly resumed her seat, settling herself carefully. When she looked back at me she was composed.

"Your friend should be careful with people he may be sleeping near later," she said, her voice shaking a little. "People get stabbed in their sleep."

Remy raised his eyebrows and I thought it was the closest to a smile I'd ever seen on him. "I don't sleep," he said.

I leaned forward, clenching my teeth. Fucking Remy. It was like hauling a retarded bear around with you— sometimes he got a burr up his ass and you just had to let him dance. But I didn't like it, and I saw this as a teaching moment. "I apologize for fuckhead over there," I said pointedly, clasping my hands in front of me to keep them from doing damage. Fucking *Remy*. "We have a deal." I held out my hand slowly, unclenching it with effort. I wanted to kick Remy's chair out from under him and give him a few to the ribs, but there would be a better time and place for that.

She stared at my hand for a moment, then nodded and reached forward to shake. "I am Adora. I will take you to Cristo and you can see the vehicle and discuss a deposit."

She tried to take her hand back but I held it tight. "He's a fuckhead," I said, jerking my head at Remy. "But he's *my* fuckhead. I just apologized for him, but that's all you get. If he gets stabbed, I will kill you."

She went pale for a second, swallowed again, and then firmed up, getting her face back under control. "I accept the apology," she said slowly. "Shall we go?"

She stood up, but waited for us to follow suit before walking for the exit. I smiled. I liked anyone who could look into Remy's eyes and still threaten him.

Then I looked at Remy and gave him a hard smack to the back of his head. He accepted it silently, wincing and scuttling out of reach, but saying nothing.

"This way."

We followed her through some heroic mud, the kind of dark brown stuff that made walking so much trouble you just wanted to lie down in it and be sucked into the earth. Adora was pretending to be unconcerned as she turned her back on us, but she had a blade tucked up her right sleeve. I figured some of the men she'd done business with weren't as polite as me, so I gave her a few feet of space and glanced back at Remy, who was lagging, sweat streaming down his face as he carried the battery and collector.

"Don't fucking drop it," I said cheerfully. "I just hocked everything we fucking own for that thing."

He grunted, long hair hanging in his face. Remy had wanted to just take it by force—what the hell, we were leaving Potosí anyway—and we could have; the old man running the cart had two fat guys sitting on barrels drinking moonshine for security. Remy and I would have been halfway to Mexico before those two managed to get on their feet. But the old man was just skin and bones, dried up and hanging on, and he'd wanted a fair price. Fair was fair.

We were heading toward a bleached wooden shed, a sagging collection of slats that looked ready to collapse if we made too much noise on the approach. Adora worked a rusty metal chain and padlock and threw open the warped doors, revealing a shadowy garage in which was parked a military four-wheel vehicle. I'd ridden in something like it a few times; if you didn't mind your kidneys in your throat and a few lumps on your head, it would get you where you wanted to go.

I stared at it, listening to Remy grunt and swear his way toward us. Then I looked at Adora.

"There's no cousin, is there?"

She shrugged. "Having a cousin keeps some of the creeps away." She jerked her chin at Remy. "You bought the battery; I figure you are serious."

I nodded. "We are. But serious men can't be trusted either. I've known some *really* serious men, and most of them were bastards."

She shrugged again. I liked the roll of her shoulders.

The overalls didn't give you much clue, and no one was eating well these days, but I had an impression of curves. "If I worried about every potential rapist I came across," she said, emphasizing *potential* just enough, "I would never leave the house. You have brought yen as well?"

I studied her. "Yen you get in Mexico City," I said. "Just in case you got a side business slitting throats at night."

She made a face but shrugged. "Very well. Help me push it out into the field."

I followed her into the dank interior of the shack and put a shoulder behind it.

"Why are you going to Mexico City?" she asked, breathless, after we'd pushed the heavy thing a few feet, the axle squealing.

I wasn't breathing hard; my augments still managed my oxygen supply pretty well. "We've got an old friend to kill."

IV

SORRY ABOUT THE BLOOD

"Where are we?"

Adora didn't look at me. "I don't know. We passed Panama. Somewhere north of there."

Outside the cab the world was darkness, lightning, and rain. The windshield of the car glowed a soft blue, giving Adora a vector outline of the terrain and a constant readout on the battery, our elevation, direction, and speed. The geopositional satellites were all still up there, humming along, and the last week had been like going back in time, back into the System—we were connected.

She was tired, her round face tight and her eyes puffy with strain. She sat hunched forward, her heavy overalls and thick gray shirt making her body a mystery. It had been a long time since I'd been this close to an attractive woman. I wondered how she'd managed to go this long without being molested, and then wondered if maybe she hadn't. Her hair was pulled back into a complex knot at the back of her head, revealing small, perfect ears I found strangely compelling. I tried to keep my eyes straight ahead and my thoughts off the smooth skin of her neck; even if she was interested in a roll with someone like me—which was pretty unlikely—I didn't have the time or energy for it. And I wasn't going to risk our ride. I had no way of knowing if Morales's information was accurate, but if it was, I didn't figure Wallace Belling would be in that hospital for long.

I twisted around in the safety netting and looked at Remy, who had been asleep for four days and showed no signs of waking up, ever. The interior of the four-wheeler was pretty sparse—the seats were bare metal, and the whole thing vibrated like a fluid earthquake when she put it in gear, grunting and sweating. My back ached, my legs were numb, and my eyes felt like they were glued shut. Another week in the front seat of her rolling coffin and I'd be ready to kill myself.

"He still back there?" she asked.

I looked back out the windshield. Trees, tall and slender with bushy tops, flashed by. We'd stumbled on a stretch of usable road, old and cracked but in one piece. The road came and went. Sometimes we were slurring up mud in the middle of fucking wilderness; sometimes we were bouncing through cratered battlefields with walls of fire burning eternally around us, and sometimes the skies parted, the sun shone down, and a fucking highway from pre-Unification days erupted out of nowhere, a vein of tar, and we'd bounce up onto it and suddenly everything would be smooth and easy, like the world had been built for us to drive on it.

Lightning flashed, distant. I sighed, trying to stretch. "You're not going back to Potosí, are you?"

She didn't respond. We'd been silent for so long, I thought maybe I'd surprised her. After thirty seconds or so, I shut my eyes.

"You brought only food and cash. Judging the wad, it's a lot of cash—for you. Probably every cent you've managed to scrape together. You don't bring your life savings with you on a trip."

She bit her lip. "There's nothing much going on in Potosí."

I laughed. "Sister, Potosí's a fucking sewer, but it's better than most of the world right now. At least the buildings are still standing. At least it's not irradiated—fucking Las Vegas, you can't go within a hundred fucking miles of it without being cooked from the inside out. Potosí's got something like a society—you've got trade, a social order. Fucking hell, kid. You could do worse than Potosí."

"That's fucking depressing," she said. "If Potosí is so wonderful, why were you so eager to leave?"

I opened my eyes. "People were trying to kill me."

She smiled. "And you have a man to kill in Mexico."

I smiled. "You think that's bullshit."

She shrugged. "You've got a man's gun, that's for sure. Junior back there has a gun with a fucking capital G, yes? But working for Morales doesn't mean shit. The world is filled with men who want to be hard."

I shut my eyes and tried to work the dull ache out of the small of my back. It was impossible. "Is that what I'm trying to be? A hard man?"

"You talk like one. Everything is a threat. Everything is funny and nothing is true." She shrugged again. "In Potosí a lot of people talk like that. Most are dead, now. The army occupied us, you know. For six months we had a major in charge of the town, five thousand soldiers, armor units, silver hovers in the air. They set up military courts—jokes, bad jokes, but anyone caught stealing— shot dead. Caught breaking curfew—shot dead. Don't want to sell them your...your last *fucking* cow...shot dead." She paused, her hands tight on the stick. "The hard ones, they usually didn't have anything hard to say when facing the firing line."

I nodded. "We tend to lose our sense of humor when we get executed, I'll grant you that. But I'm pushing forty, sister. Life expectancy keeps dropping, from what I can tell, and that means every year I'm that much more amazing."

She laughed, a sudden outburst of snorting and choking that was mildly disturbing. I popped open one eye and turned my head to look at her. She was shaking with sudden laughter, her whole body jerking with the force of it.

I let it drift, and she didn't say anything more. We rode along in silence for a few minutes, the rain lashing the rusted chassis, the silent lightning giving us a glimpse every now and then as the four-wheeler sailed down the road. I liked that she wasn't afraid. I was tired of people being afraid when they saw the gun, when they found out who you were. I liked being laughed at. It reminded me of New York, years ago, Kev Gatz and I crawling through the sewers and starving to death. No one had been impressed by me back then, either, and it was before the Squalor job, before London and Rose Harper and everything that came after, ruining me and then coming back to ruin what was left.

Poor Avery, a voice whispered in my head, making me jump a little.

Salgado? I thought, and waited. She didn't say anything

else. When I'd been in Chengara Penitentiary, they'd stuck needles into my brain and tried to upload me to the prison mainframe for storage, but the army had crashed the party and I'd been disconnected before they'd completed the work. Somehow a bunch of other people's stored minds had backwashed *into* me, and three of them had lasted long enough for me to get used to them talking to me. My old pal Grisha had told me those three had survived probably because I'd known them, somewhat, in real life. Dolores Salgado, former Undersecretary of the System of Federated Nations, had been in prison with me. The old bat had been important, and then she'd been in prison, and then she'd been dead, and I somehow had a copy of her in my brain.

The lightning flashed, and Adora sat forward, slowing us down. "Fuck," she muttered. "Looks like some trees in the road."

I hunched my shoulders and leaned forward too, squinting. My augments, buried in my head, sharpened my vision slightly and the darkness outside took on a pale green clarity, like my own personal moon beaming down. A few hundred feet ahead four trees, thick trunks a few feet around, lay across the road, blocking it completely at a point where sheer rocky hills rose up on either side.

She let us glide to a halt, then sat for a moment peering into the storm.

"We can't go off-road here," she said, calm and thoughtful. "We could back up a ways and try, but in this weather it might not be a good idea. I'm going to scout around a bit, see if there's any way around."

I stared at the trees as lightning flashed again, and as Adora started to squirm out of the safety netting, I put a hand on her arm, my HUD rippling in my vision as adrenaline dumped.

"Wait," I said. I felt her stiffen under my hand—it was, I realized, the first time I'd ever touched her. I took my hand off her shoulder carefully and pointed. "The trunks are cut smooth—these trees were cut down," I said. "This is a roadblock."

She looked at me, then back at the scene in front of us. "Out *here*? You telling me people just camp here waiting for someone to show up every year or so?"

I bit back some mean-spirited words, twisting around to try and peer out the back. "They've got a trip somewhere down the road, probably right where the pavement starts—it's rough and rocky there, and you wouldn't notice a pressure plate. Can run something like that off a battery for years. All it does is light a bulb a mile up the road, and the team goes into action." I looked forward and nodded. "Trust me, we're about to be killed and robbed."

"I'll back out," she said, sounding suddenly young and nervous.

"Too late," I said. There was movement out near the felled trees. I shrugged off the safety netting and heaved myself up off the hard seat in order to pull my gun. I checked the chamber and flicked off the safety, twisting my arms up to slide the gun into my shirt collar, pressed against the back of my neck, cold and uncomfortable. I twisted around and lashed a hand into Remy's face. He grunted and opened one eye.

"Trouble," I said. "Stay here and keep her alive."

He opened his other eye and raised an eyebrow. I turned and popped open the door, letting it rise up on its hydraulic hinges. I put my hands up into the pelting rain.

"Coming out!" I shouted. *They'll be behind you*, I thought. Pincered. That's how I would do it.

Hands up, I stood and stepped into the wind and rain. The door slammed down as I stepped clear. I looked behind us and saw the chain they'd stretched across the road, a heavy rope of metal. Two of them stood in front of it, just silhouettes, no guns that I could see. Guns were problematic—not the guns, which were fucking everywhere, but the ammunition, which was fucking nowhere. I turned to face forward again and decided the two behind me didn't have any barkers.

Up ahead was just one figure, but it carried a scoped weapon, a rifle of some make. The details were stolen away by the rain and the dark. Lacing my hands behind my head, over the cold butt of my Roon, I started walking forward.

"We don't want trouble!" I shouted. "We have nothing to steal!"

I was just buying a few seconds. I put my eyes everywhere as I shuffled forward, looking for anyone hiding on the edges, which would be the smart play. I didn't see anything.

"Are you fucking simple?" the woman up ahead shouted back, her accent harsh and German sounding as she pointed the rifle at me. "That fucking wagon's worth a fortune. That's close enough."

I didn't stop walking. In the old days she would have just cut me down, sprayed some bullets and hosed the four-wheeler down later. If she even had bullets; these days they were too expensive to just waste. "Come on," I shouted back, trying to keep my shoulders down and cowed, my voice shaky. "You can't—"

Without rushing, I yanked my gun up out of my collar and took two steps to my left as I got my grip and raised it up. With a squawk she let loose, the rifle spitting flares and jerking in her wet hands. I took a breath and squeezed the trigger twice, and the vaguely feminine shadow by the trees dropped without another word.

I let myself fall to the muddy pavement and I rolled toward the four-wheeler, shouts following me. I pushed myself under the vehicle and rolled to the opposite side; in the pitch dark I figured I'd disappeared, as far as the others were concerned. Pulling myself up into a crouch on the other side, I peered around, finally spying two shadows creeping up toward us, pressed against the embankment, two assholes who couldn't be sure I hadn't caught some rifle fire, and who couldn't pass up the vehicle. The battery and solar collector alone were worth the risk.

I steadied myself against the body of the car and took a careful bead; no sense in wasting bullets. I took another breath—and suddenly sensed someone behind me, a last-second wet smack of bare feet against the pavement. I ducked and someone scraped me, knocking my head painfully into the solid metal of the wheel well and rolling with a grunt onto the pavement. My vision lit up red and I sprawled on the ground, rain drilling down onto me, into my eyes and mouth, choking me.

Before I could get up, they were on me—a kid. Fifty pounds, maybe, tiny hands on my wrist, digging in nails and trying to pound the gun out of my hand. I reached up blindly and took hold of some wet, greasy hair and yanked with all I had, spinning them off me and getting a screech as a reward. I rolled away and pushed myself up in time to see a dark shape leaping for me. I swung my gun at it and clubbed it down just as two more shapes skidded from behind the four-wheeler. They slid to a halt as I raised my arm, putting their arms up as if I gave a shit. Before they could say anything, I fired twice and put them both down.

The kid was a few feet away, sniffling. Warily, I stood up and limped over to the huddled shape. My leg didn't normally bother me these days, with my implants regulating my pain, but during times of exertion the dull ache, familiar and dreadful, faded back in like a signal being picked up.

I circled around. I saw myself leaning over the kid and getting a razor in my face for my trouble, so I took some time.

"The other three are dead," I said. "You know how to work that chain?"

The kid—I didn't know if it was a boy or a girl—sniffled. I stood over it and clicked the hammer back on my Roon. It was drama, but drama sometimes got your point across.

"You know how to work that chain?" I said.

After a moment, there was one last heroic sniffle. "*Si*," a tiny girl's voice whispered. It sounded like defeat. It sounded like not eating and having no one to walk home with. As I stood there she hauled herself up, a scrap of shadow, four feet tall and nothing but bones, and limped back to the chain. I watched until she'd blended into the darkness and then pretended I could still see her. Another few seconds were measured out by cold water soaking into me and the thick chain suddenly went limp, dropping back to the ground.

I limped over to the car and the door popped up as I

approached. I slid in and let the door sink shut, sealing me in. I looked at Adora, who was staring at me, then at myself in the dim reflection afforded by the glass. I'd opened up a gash on my forehead, and blood ran down my face like ink. I'd thought it was rain. I thought of the kid, slogging home alone in the storm, nothing to show for it. Had I just saved her from three assholes? Killed her family? I'd never know.

Adora shook herself and put the four-wheeler into reverse. "Holy shit," she muttered.

I closed my eyes, hearing that wet sniffle. *Avery Cates*, Salgado suddenly whispered, sounding somehow mean in my head, *the Gweat and Tewwible, scourge of children everywhere.* "Sorry about the blood," I said, feeling empty, wanting to do some violence, break some windows. I flicked the safety back on and pocketed my gun.

V

LIKE FATHER FUCKING TIME IN THE FLESH

I missed the fucking System Pigs.

I left the door open and leaned back against the four-wheeler's chassis, feeling its warmth through my coat. I felt stiff and sticky, covered in a layer of my own sweat and brine. I rubbed my head and felt the stiff brush of my receding hair like steel wool, so dirty it was like mold growing on me. I wanted to walk around and stretch. I wanted a cigarette—a real cigarette, something pre–civil war at least if they existed—so badly my mouth watered. No matter how long I went without smoking, I wanted cigarettes, their taste and reassuring presence.

Mexico City had been pretty fucking huge, I had to admit. We'd hit the suburbs several hours ago and had picked our way through ruined streets and abandoned blocks, edging inward toward the remnants of it. I guessed twenty million people had lived here at some point. Adora estimated we still had an hour's driving through the rubble-strewn streets before we reached the small inhabited core, but the clouds had been constant and thick for days, and the battery was nearly dead. With the sun peeking out here and there, we were forced to just pull over and orient the collector to best advantage, sitting and waiting for the cells to at least read half charged. We were in a large old hangar of some sort, a big empty shell of a building with a poured-concrete floor and lots of rusted chains hanging from rigging attached to the ceiling. It was open to the air on the south side and afforded a good view of the rest of the industrial complex we'd limped into, a sad collection of warehouses with broken windows like crooked teeth and small runty buildings of gray cinderblocks and missing roofs.

I looked up and squinted at the sun. A moment later there was a scrape, distant and muffled, and I whipped my eyes back down, scanning the sun-bleached area, hand on the butt of my gun. A silver hover, split into two, lay blocking one of the roads, the army insignia still bright and clear on it. There was no army anymore, but its artifacts were everywhere.

I was afraid to leave the four-wheeler. We'd seen lots of evidence of population out here—smoke rising in the near distance, two entertaining periods of having rocks thrown at us as we raced by, fist-sized pebbles smacking into the windows like Psionic fists, and one more attempted blockade of the road, this time using an impressive amount of rusting metal junk, which we'd spotted easily in time to avoid. As Remy and Adora went out in search of water to refill our empty canteens, I'd realized that leaving the four-wheeler unattended was a sure way to have it stolen—probably by the simple expedient of getting a dozen people to lift it up and carry it away. A few years ago, the System Police had had everything under control, and I could have left the fucking thing unlocked and in gear and nothing would have happened unless the cops on duty had something against me. Now, I had to stand there, and I could feel eyes on me, hungry and patient.

I had to piss. I stepped forward and undid my pants right there. If I offended any of the bandits watching me, I figured that was an acceptable risk. I only hoped they didn't somehow manage to steal the four-wheeler from behind me while I went, or I'd never be able to look Remy in the eye again.

Behind me, the battery sensor on the dash chimed softly, indicating a charge of fifty percent—good enough to get moving. As I stood there, a wolf ambled into my field of vision, a hundred feet away, maybe, and then stopped to stare at me for three heartbeats before putting its head down and prowling back into the shadows.

It felt good, at least, to be back in a city. Mexico City didn't remind me much of New York, which was what I compared every city to—it was too wide open, the sky too big above me and the buildings too colorful, everything red and purple and green and orange. But it was better than the wilderness we'd been driving through, the mysterious fucking jungles, all wet shadows and damp hollows, vines twisting around your ankles.

Buttoning up, I turned back, half expecting someone *had* snuck behind me to steal the vehicle, and I heard Wa Belling's voice in my head, his rolling accent, all charm and venom, telling me I was the worst fucking Gunner he'd ever seen. I put one hand on the warm metal and grimaced. I was going to put a bullet in Wa's face for past betrayals. Or I intended to. Wa was an old man, but he was good—better than me, certainly, in a fair fight. He knew how to kill, and even Michaleen—Cainnic Orel himself—had said Wa was the best he'd ever seen with a gun. It wasn't going to be easy.

I stared into the shadows of the hangar and considered the possibility that this was, again, a trick. Belling had tricked me plenty of times, and his tricks were professional, done with style and attention to detail. Fuck, the man had pretended to be a completely different person for several weeks during the Hong Kong job, complete with backstory and supporting details—the man had *method*. If he was setting me up for some new hell, some new humiliation, this was how it might start: information that didn't *seem* to just fall into my hands, pointing me in his direction.

I shrugged inwardly and turned, half-expecting to see a dozen people creeping toward me in the sunlight, knives clenched between teeth, and hands curled into fists. There was no one. When people were throwing rocks at you, one man with a working gun was scary. I leaned back against the four-wheeler and pushed aside my coat, resting one hand on the Roon and letting it glint in the sun, in case anyone was watching. A scoped rifle would blow my head into a million pieces, but scoped rifles had been rare and expensive before the war, then common and easy during the war, and now it wasn't the scoped rifles that were difficult to find but the ammunition they required. Besides, if you started worrying about snipers, you might as well dig a hole and stay buried, because that sort of thinking went crazy real fast.

Movement out on the edge of the industrial park made me jerk to attention briefly, but it was Remy and Adora. It was warmer up north than it had been in Potosí, and

Adora had stripped off her heavy underclothes and now just wore the overalls, her bare skin tan and smooth, her curves strongly hinted at by the shadows created by the unveiled sunlight. Remy behind her was like a shadow in his black coat, shirt, and pants, his pale face hidden by the mess of dark hair. As they walked toward me they talked, and suddenly, about halfway to me, Adora burst out laughing again, her face contorted into a mask of hilarity, her whole body hunching and quivering with sudden mirth. A stabbing bolt of jealousy went through me, and I shook myself.

"Don't be a fucking asshole, Avery," I muttered. This was rookie shit, getting jealous of the only woman in the room. Adora wouldn't be dumb enough to start fucking one of us, anyway—that was a chip that could always be played, and you didn't play it until you had to. Not out here, in fucking Mexico City.

"Water," she said, still grinning, as they approached, and held up one of the plastic jugs they'd taken out with them.

"Clean?" I asked.

She nodded. "Rainwater. Silt had settled, mesh screening kept it clean." She shook her head. "This is the largest city I have ever seen."

I thought of Hong Kong. "I've seen larger," I said. "We should get moving."

She nodded and stepped around to the driver's side. Remy paused and stood for a moment next to me, staring off into the distance.

"She called me *forzudo*."

I didn't look at him. "Get in the fucking cab," I said, "before I break your hand."

He sketched a salute in the air.

* * *

Forty minutes later we started to see people on the streets, first as quick shadows springing for hiding places, then, slowly, as clumps of people staring at us as we sped by. I thought about Gleason, a girl I'd adopted years ago and tried to bring up, a girl I'd gotten killed. I had a bad record when it came to keeping people alive—I'd been put on the world to kill people. But I kept trying to pick up strays and teach them, and it kept ending badly.

"Where should I drop you?"

I glanced at Adora and blinked. "Slow down," I said. As we slowed to a rumbling crawl, I toggled the window in the door down and leaned out.

"*Zocalo?*" I said, trying to remember how Morales had pronounced it.

An old man with dark brown skin like mud that had hardened fast in the sun and bright white hair in a cloud on top of his head stared at me as I drifted past and extended an arm, pointing northeast.

When the buildings melted away a few minutes later and the sun hit us from the side like a bomb going off on the horizon, I first thought we'd hit a crater, some void in the city created by a bombing run, but the pavement was too regular, and I realized we were in a huge square, a vast empty space bordered on all sides by buildings.

"Shit!" Adora cursed, throwing the four-wheeler into a skidding turn to avoid the crowds gathered everywhere. The whole area was filled with people—some minding makeshift storefronts like I'd seen in Potosí, carts and wagons, walls of fabric, sometimes just marked out on the ground in chalk, others milling this way and that. Some were obviously living in the square, huddled under more blue tarp in front of messy, smoky cooking fires. Screams rippled away from us as we smashed through it all, everything lurching this way and that as we spun, finally smacking into a large metal pole that stuck up from the ground in the center of it all. For a few seconds I could feel the whole chassis vibrating under me.

"Shit," Remy said quietly over the dim ticking of the hot engine. "I thought you said this was *safer* than a hover flight."

I laughed, and then Adora and Remy laughed, too. "I've *still* crashed more often in a hover," I said, struggling with the safety netting.

Something smacked into the side of the four-wheeler, making a dull thud. A second later, two more impacts, and then a volley of smaller ones.

"Rocks," Remy said, yawning. "Guess we made some enemies by rolling over everyone."

I nodded as something big and heavy starred the rear windshield. "Up and out," I said. "We let them crowd around and pin the doors and we're fucking dead. Up and out!"

Adora was struggling with the door on her side, which was undamaged. "We can't just leave it here!" she shouted as she pushed the door open. "Do you know what this is worth?"

I put my hands on her ass and gave her a shove to get her moving. "I do not give a shit how much this rolling box is worth," I snapped, then looked at Remy, who appeared to be almost back to sleep. "Hang back half a minute," I said, thinking again I almost missed the fucking cops. "If you see a reason to do something creative, take it."

He gestured vaguely at me, keeping his eyes closed. I stared at him for a second, wanting to take a moment to educate him a little, but there wasn't time, and with a grunt I pushed myself out of the ruined car.

I stood up in the weak sunlight and drew my Roon, glancing down as I checked the chamber and slid the safety off. A crowd had already formed in a loose ring around us, angry locals shouting and brandishing some sticks and other impromptu weapons. A rock sailed past my head as I took in the crowd, looking for talent. I didn't see any, and forced myself to stand still and not flinch as another pair of fist-sized rocks came my way, missing me by inches. Nothing ruined the impression like a good flinch. It made the shitheads think they'd put the fear of them into you.

I picked one of them at random, just a guy in the front with an old table leg in his hand, raised up over his head. It wasn't far; I raised the Roon and before the crowd could even notice it and get upset, I squeezed the trigger and blew a hole in Table Leg's chest, knocking him wetly back into the crowd.

Everyone stopped moving. I looked down at my feet and cursed; I'd tried for his shoulder. There was no such thing as a safe place to shoot someone—odds were I'd nick an artery—but when it was you versus a *table leg* you had to at least *try.*

"Hey, Avery," Remy shouted from inside the car, "you don't have to kill *everyone.* You know that, right?"

Clenching my teeth, I swallowed my urge to pinch the kid's nose. I looked back up and scanned the scene. The crowd was hovering, terrified but aware on some elemental level that if they all stuck together there was nothing I could do but run.

"Repeat what I say," I said to Adora without looking at her, and then raised the gun up over my head, firing one more precious bullet into the air. Behind me, I heard Remy crawling from the wreckage, and based on the anxious ripple that went through the crowd, I assumed he had his ridiculously large gun in hand.

"I'm looking for a hospital," I shouted, and Adora shouted it in Spanish a moment later. "An old man is staying there. Rich."

A few seconds stole by, and then a handful of arms raised up and pointed to our left, where a huge two-story building stretched the incredible length of the square. The tense energy of the crowd faded away, and suddenly it was just a sagging group of people. I turned and looked the building over: red brick and tiny blown-out windows, squat peaked towers at each end and in the middle. The entrance was tiny, a single doorway in which a single figure stood, gaping at us.

I nodded and scanned the crowd again. I considered offering them something in return for their ruined merchandise and injuries, but decided against it. It would just encourage them.

"Come on," I said to Remy. "Let's go find my old friend Wallace."

He nodded and let me step in front of him, his sunglasses hiding his eyes as he watched the crowd. I had to admit, Remy *looked* fucking badass.

"What the *fuck*?" Adora shouted, and in a flash she was in front of me, all wide eyes and hands. I kept moving, forcing her to stumble backward. I was all momentum. The moment I stopped, these assholes were going to do some math and come at my back. "My *vehicle*!"

"We're done," I said, checking the Roon and letting the slide snap back into place. Adora kept tripping over herself as she squawked in front of me, but she didn't give up. I liked that. "You'll get your yen as soon as I finish here." I didn't have time. If this wasn't a setup, if Belling was really in this ancient hunk of building, he would know already I was here and be making his own preparations, and Belling was a fucking *master*. Belling had made me look stupid too often to take chances. He would expect me to creep about, to make plans and scout out the area, find allies. He would expect me to be careful, so I'd decided to just crash in, gun blazing, see what happened. I was excited; I struggled to keep an appropriately grim expression on my face.

Adora couldn't form words; she just made outraged noises as she struggled to walk backward at my pace. Just as she hit the slight lip in front of the doors and fell on her ass, hard, Remy spoke up behind me.

"We're not going to observe, map the exterior, find someone who knows what it's like in there?" he asked mildly from behind. "We're going in blind? I think that violates at least three of Avery Cates's Rules of Successful Murder, doesn't it?"

The kid was enjoying himself, but I was all momentum: I didn't slow down. I pushed past Adora and leveled the gun on the mystery man who stood gaping at us in the shadowed doorway. He was tall and thin, not very old, but had the smooth look of someone who'd been sitting on top of the pyramid back in The Day, back when the System still existed and yen meant something.

"Move," I said, "or I'll shoot you in the chest."

He put his hands up automatically, and then *he* started

walking backward as I advanced. "Wait! No! Wait!" he spluttered in English, his vowels round and his consonants clipped. "I'm a doctor!"

"The fuck do I care?" I snapped, clicking back the hammer. He blinked and threw himself against the wall of the narrow tunnel we'd entered, so I rounded on him and pressed the Roon into his belly.

"You're a doctor," I said, "so you know how a gut wound works, right?"

He nodded.

"Old man," I said. "*Old*. Like Father Fucking Time in the flesh. Guns, probably. Rich."

The doctor nodded eagerly. "Yes! Yes, of course. Second floor. Room five. Only private—"

I spun away and stormed down the tunnel. Remy was behind me like a crow, pecking.

"Avery, come on. This is ridiculous."

"If we take the time to be smart, do this right," I said, my augments still functioning well enough to keep my breathing easy even as I rushed forward, "we'll miss him. Believe me. Wallace Belling has lived a long fucking time because he's *good*. He's smart. He's fast. He's heartless, and greedy, but he's *good*." I shook my head. "If we play this smart we miss him."

The tunnel opened up into a large room with soaring ceilings. A big staircase was right in front of us, the stone steps smooth and warped from years of feet. The stairs split left and right after a flight and wound their way up; the walls behind them had once sported some colorful painting that had chipped and eroded, leaving behind a meaningless mosaic of color and water stains.

I took the stairs two at a time, my rusty old augments

pumping adrenaline and endorphins, gearing up for battle. My HUD shuddered and flickered in my vision. This was not the right way to do anything. This wasn't professional, but I knew I had to just let momentum carry me, for once. If I gave Belling a moment, he would vanish—or drop on me. The stairs snaked around and led to an open balcony that stretched the interior of the building, the remnants of a rotting, dried-up garden complete with an empty fountain laid out in front of me. I skidded to a halt and spun, eyes searching the walls for a clue, finally finding a crude wooden sign hung from a nail on the wall, indicating rooms one through three behind me, four through six in front.

Now I crept. I hunched down and duckwalked my way down the gloomy hallway, listening. The grit under my boots was loud, an endless scrape in my ears, my own breathing forming a rhythm section with it and propelling me forward. Behind me, I heard Remy arriving—the kid was pretty quiet but my gauges were in the red and I heard him behind me, instantly giving up his complaints and dropping into a covering position. Just outside the open doorway of room five, I paused to glance back at him, and he gave me a quick nod. The kid didn't like it, but he would do the job at hand. I knew that.

I let him catch up. When he was right behind me, he stood up, and I launched myself across the doorway, seeing if I could draw fire. Nothing happened, and I landed in a cloud of dust on the other side of the door with a grunt. For a second I listened again, and then looked at Remy. He shrugged at me and rolled his hand around in the air: *Hurry up.* Remy thought this was just old-school revenge bullshit, and he wanted to get it over with.

I nodded, took a breath, and jumped, landing just inside the room. I threw myself flat and rolled to my left until I hit a wall, and then I raised the Roon and looked the room over, silence crowding around me.

It was a pretty bare space, created from a much larger one some time ago with bad quality construction, the walls thin and sagging, nothing sealed, nothing permanent. There was one metal bed, rust eating at the legs and headboard, on which a thin gray mattress and a pile of dirty linens had been placed. A small wooden table was next to the bed, and a red plastic chair from a previous century against the far wall, and that was it for furniture. Two digital clipboards hung from the wall next to the bed. Sheets of paper had been pasted onto them, covered with tiny, insectoid writing. I hadn't realized anyone really could write by hand anymore.

I pushed myself up to my knees and looked around again. There was nothing else in the room. I lowered my gun.

"Shit," I muttered, hands suddenly shaking. The old bastard had fucking slipped me *again*.

The pile of linen on the bed suddenly moved and resolved itself into a thin, skeletal human being with a full head of thick, white hair. I brought the gun back up and took a cautious step toward the bed. It was an old man, stick thin and papery, his face somehow . . . off, a youthening surgery that had gone to seed, his skin sliding away from the tendons.

"Hands!" I hissed. "Show me your hands!"

A scraping sort of sound emerged, and I realized he was laughing just as he pulled his arms from under the thin blanket he rested under and held the stumps up for me. His wrists were pink and stretched lumps of skin. I looked back at his face and froze.

"Hello Avery," Wallace Belling said in a faint echo of the booming, cultured voice I knew. "My hands—my *hands*, Avery." He made a clucking noise in his throat as he raised the stumps in front of his face as if he'd never seen them before. Then his watery eyes found me again. "He *took* my hands, Avery. Mickey *cut* them *off*."

VI

JUST PLAIN OLD MURDER

"Fuck," Remy muttered behind me, stretching out the word in disgust.

I just stared at Belling. He'd been old when I'd first met him, millennia ago in London, working the Squalor hit against my will. He'd pretended to be Cainnic Orel, but Belling wasn't far from Orel's status—the best Gunner I'd ever seen live, in action. Even as an old man he'd kicked my ass plenty of times.

The man in the bed wasn't Belling. *Couldn't* be Belling. He was a dried-up old man, skinny and loose skinned, his face skeletal. His hands had been chopped off, and the angry red stumps at the end of his useless arms had healed badly and looked painful.

For a few seconds I just stared at him, blinking. I'd been prepared for a gunfight. I'd been prepared for a mind fuck; those were usually my only two choices when I met Wa Belling.

He grimaced and laboriously turned himself away,

giving me his back. He was wearing a thin white gown, and the outline of his spine was stark and clear. "Don't fucking look at me," he muttered into the wall. "You come here to fucking pity me? Just kill me. It's what you came here for."

The anger in his voice fleshed it out and matched up with what I remembered. Belling telling me I was *charming*; Belling telling me how he'd seen better.

"Michaleen did this?" I finally managed. My own voice suddenly sounded thin and distant.

"Found me in Krakow," he said more quietly, still staring at the wall, his stumps hidden from view. "I thought hiding in the middle of Cop Land was *brilliant*. I didn't have the nerve to use the augment. I was afraid of getting scrambled."

The God Augment. Memories flashed in my head of Hong Kong and the two avatars I'd thought were real people, but were just Belling and his boss in disguise. Have a technical surgeon implant that into your brain and supposedly it gave you all the Psionic powers that people were sometimes born with—telekinesis, compulsion— and some that no one had documented in the wild. Supposedly. I never knew if it worked, or how it worked, because by the time my artificial friends and I got to Hong Kong, the flesh-and-blood Belling had already been there and stolen it out from under Michaleen.

I remembered that Michaleen, in his female avatar body, had not been amused. At fucking all.

"He took it?" I asked. I didn't want Belling to roll over. I wanted him to stay with his back to me. He looked like death, and I didn't like being in the same room with a ruined man like this.

He snorted laughter. "My boy, he *took* it, with prejudice. I almost had him...I almost..." He stopped and suddenly turned back toward me, and for a second his eyes were burning and I really believed it, believed this was *Belling* in front of me. Then he deflated, sinking back into the skinny, frail body knotted up in thin sheets. "It doesn't matter. He beat me when I was nineteen, and he beat me now. And it's too late. No one will ever beat him, now."

There was a noise behind me, and I whirled to find a startled woman in a pair of often-repaired blue scrubs, carrying a plastic tray on which several brown bottles rested. She was standing in sudden, shocked stillness, Remy's gun against the back of her head, one of his long arms langorously stretched out from where he was leaning against the wall to one side of the doorway.

I jerked my chin at the hallway. "Out. Stay out," I said, and turned back to Belling.

"You never let me kill anybody," Remy said and sighed.

"You have my permission to kill yourself if you don't shut up," I said without turning. "Wallace," I said, feeling calm. "What did you mean no one will ever beat him *now*?"

My fading augments had leveled off my adrenaline, and I was in control and feeling patient. I'd been working toward making Belling regret playing me false for years, since before Hong Kong, but in my mind it had always been a fight, a challenge. Walking up to a hospital bed and putting a shell in Belling's ear wasn't revenge, it was just plain old murder.

He smiled. His smile was terrible. It was the same smug smile I'd seen a hundred times before when Belling was making fun of me with just the tone of his voice, but now there was nothing behind it. I was talking to a ghost.

You should be used to that, Dick Marin whispered in my head. I stopped myself from shaking my head to dislodge him.

"Avery, he *used* it. The augment. He had it implanted." Belling paused, licking his lips with a yellowish tongue. "And not just that: He salvaged a late-model Monk chassis and had some Techies work on it, ripping out some of the control circuitry, customizing it, and he had himself . . . converted." He looked down at his stumps. "He's not human anymore, Avery. He's something else entirely."

I blinked, everything going slow and quiet in my head. A *Monk chassis.* The Monks were the predecessors to the avatar units, developed by Dennis Squalor as the basis of his church. Squalor had killed a lot of people and forcibly converted them into Monks before I got hired to snuff him.

"Sweet hell," I whispered, imagining that short bastard in a Monk body, hydraulic strength and computer reflexes. *"Why?"*

The Monks had proven to be less than immortal; a few years after the Plague most of them were rusting hulks. But with proper maintenance, I supposed one could be made usable again. And I'd had the pleasure of being beaten to a pulp by Monks. The idea of Orel, the greatest killer in history, in one of those things was fucking *horrifying.*

"Why," Belling said, his voice flat and cold. "The idiot asks *why.* Avery, you are a stupid brute of a man. A blunt instrument. Your continued survival is mysterious on so many levels. . . ." He swallowed. "Why, Avery: Because

Michaleen is getting old. *Was* getting old." He smiled, his eyes dancing, distant. "Death comes to us all, Avery. Even *you*, you fucking roach, eventually. These last few years Michaleen could feel it creeping up on him, and it became a little project of his to stop it." He sighed. "Now he has."

I stepped closer to the bed and pulled the plastic chair away from the wall, spun it around, and sat down with its cracked back against my chest, my arms hanging over, the gun pointed at the floor. "Wallace," I said slowly, trying to sort through it all. None of my scenarios for murdering Belling had involved a fucking mercy killing. "Where is Michaleen?"

Michaleen Garda, Cainnic Orel—the same man. I'd wondered, sometimes, which one of his names was really *his*, but it didn't matter. Short little man, looked old and fat, but quick, like a dancer, and stronger than he looked. And he'd been three steps ahead of me ever since I'd decided to kill him.

I looked up as a wheezing, sawing sound filled the air. Belling was laughing at me, his corpselike body hunched up and shivering with mirth.

"Oh, goodness, Avery, I do apologize," he said, sucking in breaths that looked painful. "You're not planning to go after Mickey? Oh, my dear boy—you were no match for him *years* ago, when you were thirty years younger than him and he *wasn't* a demigod in silicone and Kevlar." He looked at me, his dried yellow eyes like smoldering coals, sick and hot. "You're no match for *him*, Mr. Cates. He's been fucking with you for so long, and you know only the half of it."

I'd decided to be patient. Years spent dealing with Remy had taught me patience, and I was surprised at the payoff it sometimes produced. I felt pretty good, thanks to my stint in the army and the augments they'd inserted, but I was an old fucking man, and I'd learned that when the cosmos let you off the Rail for a while and let you take a seat, you enjoyed it. You never knew when the next opportunity was going to come.

"Yeah, I know, Wallace. Michaleen's the fucking puppet master, right?" I smiled. "I just want to know where he is. The rest won't be your problem anymore."

His smile faded, like it was being erased by an unseen hand. "I know you've come here to kill me, Avery. And you deserve your chance, after what I've done to you—and here I am trussed up for you, a sure shot, commensurate with your abilities. And you haven't asked me why I'm here."

I nodded. "Wallace, I'm starting to get irritated, because I keep asking you a simple question and you keep giving me bullshit." I gave him my helpless face, all eyebrows up and lips mashed together. "I want to make this clean and quick, out of respect for the truly fucking monumental level of *asshole* you achieved in life. But you're making it hard."

"You are the stupidest fucking man I have ever met," he said quietly, his voice small and dry as tinder. "He's in Split. Croatia. Don't ask me where the fuck Croatia is. Look it up."

A thrill shivered through me and left a dull, listless calm in its wake. Split, Croatia. I'd never heard of it, but it was a destination. A noise out in the hall made me turn my head in time to see Remy wave me off and step lightly out into the shadows outside the room. I turned to look back at Belling. I hated him, had spent years imagining the day I'd get to kill him, but here I was and I didn't want to. He was just an old man, alone in a fucking hospital in Mexico City.

Of all places.

I frowned and stood up, clicking back the hammer on the Roon. Kicking the chair out of the way, I reached out and tugged the limp, greasy pillow from under Belling's head. He turned and looked at the wall, swallowing.

"Go on, then," he said hoarsely. "I can't fucking stop you."

I stood there for a moment. *He's been fucking with you for so long, and you know only the half of it.* "All right, Wa," I said slowly, struggling with a sudden bad feeling, a formless sense of wrong. "I'm dumb and you and Michaleen and Marin were running everything."

"Marin," he sniffed. "A fucking errand boy. Got his in the end. The world's better without him."

Sure enough, Marin whispered.

"So why are you here, since you want me to ask so badly?"

There was no sound, just a sudden, learned sensation of air molecules being pushed around, a sense that the empty space behind you had taken on mass and form—it was familiar, an old story, and I knew the ending well—despite my augments leaping into clarity, my bars going redline, and my whole body twitching, tearing muscles in its attempt to spin around, something heavy and solid caught me on the side of my head and spun me around, and as I struggled against a sudden, thick blanket of fuzzy darkness descending on my thoughts, I heard Belling's wheezing, cracked voice.

"You moron: I'm *bait.*"

VII

I THOUGHT YOU WANTED ME TO

I snapped back into consciousness, a gift from my military augments, my HUD suddenly bright and clear. The heads-up display wired from my implants to my optic nerve had gotten jarred loose or been frayed by something, and for years it had faded in and out, sometimes bright and clear, sometimes a ghost hovering in the background. Now it was crisp, and my status bars showed green across the board, though I wasn't sure how much stock I could put into their summary of me.

I sat up. I was still in Belling's room, and based on the light I'd been out only a short while, ten minutes or so. My hands were wet and cold; I was sitting in a thin pool of blood. I made my mind blank and just looked around: Belling's bed was a spreading red stain with Belling a lump of twisted sheets on top. Remy sat in the red plastic chair, staring at the far wall. Behind me and to my left a tall, tan man in a bad white suit lay stretched out, a cheap-looking small-caliber auto in one hand, a river of blood slowly leaching from him to my puddle. I'd never seen him before in my life. It was as if a hole had appeared in the ceiling and deposited him there, the perfect murder.

I looked back at Belling's body. All I could see were soiled sheets and the top of his head, the thin, perfectly white hair.

"You killed him," I said.

Remy didn't respond right away. After a moment, he said, "I thought you wanted me to."

For a second, I felt nauseous. I could feel the lukewarm blood soaking into my pants. They were thick corded pants, good for the cold and heavy as hell and forever to dry when they got wet. I felt a strange reluctance to move, though, and just sat there, breathing. I frowned. Remy should have known better. I'd talked his ear off about Belling for years, told him all my revenge fantasies in bloody detail. I wanted to reach out and slap Remy, but found I lacked the motivation.

"You know I wanted Belling for myself," I said slowly. My head felt thick, my thoughts difficult to form—I'd cracked it on the floor, I guessed. Concussion. I'd had every sort of injury possible and knew them all well, old friends. "How could you fucking just—"

"I didn't kill *him*," Remy snapped, gesturing at Belling. "I killed *him*. *He* killed the old bastard. Said something about waiting his whole life for this, and then took the gun off me and put it on the old man, and before I could do anything, fuck, the old man was dead." He shrugged. "Figgered you wouldn't want this piece of shit alive to hit you on the head again."

I followed his hand and stared at the man in the bad white suit. He was older than me and looked recently laundered, like he'd cleaned up a bit before strolling into the room and hitting me over the head. Like maybe this was the biggest day of his life, the day he got the drop on old Wa Belling, a king of the bastards who must have had an old man in a white suit waiting decades for revenge in every city in the old System. I looked back at Remy; it wasn't the first time he'd saved my ass.

Outside the room there was some low-level commotion. Nothing that alarmed me, nothing that bothered me. Familiar noises of panic, shouts, feet on the stone floors, the squeal and bark of doors being opened and shut. There was no power, so there were no klaxons or sizzling force fields or distant hover displacement. Just people running around the old-fashioned way, going batshit.

After another minute or so I pushed myself up to my feet, smearing the bed with blood as I used it as a crutch on my way up. I stood there and looked down at Belling. He seemed incredibly small, a lump of dirty sheets and blood, a bare foot poking out from underneath the bedding. My throat tightened up and I looked over at the grimy plaster wall. I hated Wa Belling, and I was *not* going to feel fucking pity for him. Not when I'd finally gotten my revenge.

It didn't feel like it was supposed to. It was all wrong. I kept picturing that foot: pale, curled inward, toes splayed.

"Let's go," I said, my voice coming out a hoarse whisper. I turned and knelt to retrieve my gun, sticky with blood, and tugged at the sheets until I had a clean corner to wipe the Roon off.

Remy was staring down at his hands. "Where?"

"Fucking Croatia," I growled, stepping over the puddle of blood and the stretched-out body. I slipped the Roon into my pocket. "Wherever that is. Come on!"

I walked out of the room and kept walking, without waiting to see if the kid was going to follow me. Out in the hall people had appeared as if they'd been hidden in little niches, set free by blood. I walked briskly toward the stairs and they got out of my way, thin people with wide eyes and threadbare scrubs on. Who was paying them? Why did they bother to come here? It didn't make any sense. Wa Belling spending his last fortune on a dirty bed in some shithole—that didn't make sense either. My hands curled into fists. At the bottom of the stairs I collided with a kid running with a pile of folded towels. He skittered away from me, hissing apologies, his eyes down. I took three quick steps and cuffed him hard on the head, sending him sprawling, a stream of high-pitched Spanish following him down to the floor. I forced myself to keep walking. I wanted violence. I didn't even know why—I just wanted to hurt someone, to *kill* someone.

I pictured Belling again, shrunken and pathetic. I'd wanted him dead, but not like that. A Gunner of Belling's caliber shouldn't have gone out that way. I suddenly remembered Michaleen in Amsterdam, the last time I'd seen him in the flesh, talking about another Gunner: *Died with a fuckin' ice pick in his throat, hands tied behind his back. Bled out over four fucking hours. No way for a killer to go.*

Adora was standing in the entryway to the building, arms crossed under her chest. My hands twitched, and I pushed them into the pockets of my coat as she stepped toward me.

"I may have found transport for us," she said quickly. "But first—"

"I know: I owe you ten thousand yen," I snapped, pushing past her roughly. "But that's all. I don't give a shit about your vehicle. *You* drove it into the pole."

She swore behind me and grabbed my arm. I clenched my hands in my pockets and fought down another urge to wheel around and hit her.

"We've got *trouble*, you fucking moron."

I stopped and finally looked up, blinking. The huge square had emptied a little, but a lot of the surly civilian population had been replaced by a few dozen men and women with shredding rifles, the tattered remnants of white uniforms still clinging here and there. And standing in front of them was a familiar ramrod-straight figure with glistening white hair and a seemingly permanent tan. A stub of ersatz cigar, rolled from some horrible plant that superficially resembled tobacco, rolled wetly around his mouth as he grinned at me.

"Well, shit," Malkem Anners said. "Mistah Cates, you and me must be linked by fate. You wanna tell me what made you think you could come inna *my* city and transact your business without tellin' *me*?"

All the fight had been shocked out of me, and I walked with Anners in a sort of numb cloud. There were twenty of his soldiers around me anyway, so all the fucked-up rage in the world wasn't going to do much but get me killed, anyway.

I turned and looked back at Remy and Adora, walking a few feet behind us. Remy was squinting down at the ground like he was hunting for bugs, and Adora still had her arms crossed under her tits, staring at me.

"How'd you end up here, Colonel?" I asked, turning back to stare at my former commanding officer, who'd sold me to Belling all those years ago. "I left you in Hong Kong, strutting around like a fucking peacock."

He laughed. "After we got shoved outta Hong Kong, Mister Cates—no thanks to you and my little deserter back there—I got reassigned to Command West. Took a drubbing for a while, but they didn't have officers to waste, so I got a command again pretty quick. I was tryin' a push south from Mexico City when we lost contact with HQ. Thought at first it was just a glitch, but... Well, fuck, that was three years ago, and I ain't heard from the Joint Council since." He laughed. "I liked it here, so I decided to stay and make it my home."

I nodded. "So you're running things here, huh?" The world was filled with assholes like Anners, ex-army or System Police or just mercenaries in the right place at the right time who discovered that having fifty men with guns and some semblance of chain-of-command discipline made you lord and master of a chunk of the world. I'd worked for some of them and had come to the conclusion that there wasn't a single person in the whole world, what was left of it, who knew what the fuck they were doing.

"I take a fifty split on everything that happens in the city," he said by way of an answer. "And I form up an execution detail when shit gets out of control. If that's running things, then I'm running things."

"What you calling yourself? Mayor? Duke?" I said, trying to cut him down a little. "I've met a few dukes."

He laughed. "You kidding? I'm the only thing people

remember to respect: I'm fucking *Director of Internal Affairs* for Mexico City, Cates. Straight ahead."

We were heading toward a decent-looking small building, two stories and painted bright white, a little bit of a space around it in the big city. Four of his men lounged against the wall, shredders on display. The guns were all in good condition, but based on the state of the rest of their equipment and uniforms, I figured Anners's men were low on everything—ammunition, body armor, batteries. The shredders were for show; if Anners's whole crew lit up at the same time I had no doubt they wouldn't have a bullet between them after twenty seconds. I was a little impressed that Anners had chosen such a modest house for his headquarters, but then I thought it was probably easier to secure against potential throat-slitters—probably the entire population. Without power for motion sensors and trip wires, keeping people out was problematic, and smaller was better. I decided it was a safe bet that Colonel Anners was not popular.

"You two stay out here," he said, waving at Adora and Remy. "No one's gonna bother you 'less I say so. Mister Cates, after you."

I clenched my fists again. I didn't have much against Malkem Anners—he was a ripe prick who'd treated me pretty fucking rotten, but after what I'd been through, that actually put him at the high end for manners. I started to get angry again, a formless unhappy rage that got under my muscles and started tugging at my tendons, making me itch. Every time I started walking, some asshole reached out to grab my ankle, and I was getting sick of it.

Inside, I was surprised to find myself alone with him in a small foyer, just an empty room with bare lathing on the walls and rough plywood for a floor. I followed him through a doorway that felt just slightly too small, crowding me as I shouldered my way in. We were in an old kitchen, the wooden floor bleached and rubbed smooth, the old porcelain sink the single largest of its kind I'd ever seen. Everything else had been torn out, leaving behind outlines on the wall and floor. It was so clean I didn't want to touch anything.

"I still got a supply of blackjacks," Anners said, crossing to the other side of the kitchen and holding up three of the small black remote controls for the military implants Remy and I still had in our heads. He turned and leaned against the wall, making a dumb show of examining the remotes. They weren't specific to any one soldier; any officer with any functioning remote could use it on any of us who'd been augmented by the army—Remy'd spent the last few years obsessed with this exact scenario. My own implants had gone sour back in Hong Kong. Remy's were still sitting in his head like a spider. "I wonder what happens if I toggle his killswitch."

My HUD snapped into clarity, my heart lurching into a jerking rhythm as all the anger rose right back up and spilled over. Anners didn't know it, but he wasn't going to fuck with Remy. When Remy had walked away from Anners's unit in Hong Kong, he'd risked summary execution via his implants just to get away from the crazy fucker, and for years I'd watched the kid stewing in terror and nightmares from his stint in the army, getting skull-fucked every ten minutes by this asshole.

No shots, I thought, my head clear, my vision sharpened by the remnants of army tech in my head. *Shots will bring every one of Anners's people.* It had been years since I'd had to do any quiet work, but there were some lessons you never forgot.

I took a step forward, keeping my hands obviously at my sides, and stalled.

"Probably nothing," I said. "I got a set of military augments, too, and I can tell you they didn't exactly use the best components."

Anners shrugged, affable. "Maybe, sure. Or maybe I press the button and he falls down dead, blood drippin' from his ears."

I wandered slightly away from him, running my eyes over the outline of long-gone cabinets and appliances on the wall opposite Anners. He hadn't brought any of his people in here with us, which told me that whatever he was about to blackmail me for was something he didn't trust his own people with.

"Go ahead," I said, keeping my voice steady and casual. "I don't fucking like the kid. He just bitches and moans all the time. Follows me around."

This bought me some seconds. Anners didn't say anything, grinding the gears. I turned slowly, keeping my eyes on the walls as if I were examining the details, drifting closer to him, and then lunged suddenly, feinting for the remotes in his hand. Surprised, he snatched his hand up into the air to hold them out of my reach, but I'd already changed direction, chopping my hand into his windpipe. Arrogance got you killed. Malkem Anners had been running things for too long.

The remotes scattered to the floor and he staggered backward, crashing into the wall, both hands going up to his throat while his eyes bulged out of his head. Reminding myself that Anners had augments in his head, too—probably better ones, since he'd been an officer—I stepped in close and kneed him hard in the groin, determined to keep him off balance and unable to gather himself. He tried to double over slightly, then caught himself and straightened up, still unable to breathe but trying to protect himself. Anners had gotten sloppy, and I imagined that having years of unquestioned obedience from people had given him some unfortunate ideas about his own invincibility. I always told Remy: Never forget you're just a shithead yourself. The only thing that separates you from the other shitheads is *knowing* you are a shithead.

I lunged in for his head, intending to slam his skull against the wall until he went out, but he managed to get his arms up between us and knock me aside with surprising force. He was a big guy, and his augments were fully functioning and giving him an added boost of adrenaline and pain suppression, letting him tear muscles and tendons with his own force and not feel a thing. I staggered for a second and recovered, coming right back at him, feinting low and then surging up inside his reach as if I was coming in for an embrace. His face had gone purple, and while his implants were compensating for his lack of oxygen he was going down fast if he couldn't get his lungs unlocked.

I decided to go old-school and just put my hands around his neck, pressing my thumbs into his windpipe, squeezing for all I was worth.

The near-silence buzzed in my ears. It was just our grunts and my whistling breathing, the scrape of our shoes on the floor, the click of his teeth as he grimaced and writhed. He pounded at me with his fists with decaying strength, and kicked savagely at my legs; then he suddenly remembered his sidearm and tried to scrabble for it, but he was getting dumb from lack of air and my arms were in his way.

His mouth hung open, making a dry sucking sound, and we stared at each other, his eyes bugged out and bloodshot, and suddenly he just let his hands fall onto my shoulders, his eyes going dim and desperate. I thought there was an element of shock in there, too, like Colonel Anners had never imagined this was the way he'd go. Not like *this*.

I let him slide to the floor slowly and released him, stepping back, my chest heaving and my arms shaking. I stumbled backward and sat down hard, panting, and just sat there staring at him. I felt fucking fantastic. All the rage was gone, replaced by a sense of having made things right. Fuck the cosmos, fuck the Rail it always tried to put me on. I made my own decisions. And Anners had it coming.

Still breathing hard, I stood up and stepped to where the blackjacks had fallen. Deliberately, I stomped my boots down onto them and put my weight into it, crushing them as thoroughly as I could. I didn't want another asshole officer to pick them up and make some other poor shits who'd been pressed back in the war miserable. I made my way slowly to the front of the house, where Adora and Remy were still standing with three or four of Anners's people. The guards weren't paying us much mind; they were watching the streets, confirming my impression that they had more to worry about from the people they ruled than anything else—and they were soldiers and didn't know you could kill a man without shooting him a million damn times. Adora stared intently at me, biting her lip, vibrating with a desire to speak. Remy, despite his darkest fear come to life in the form of Malkem Anners, was still studying the ground, silent, appearing unconcerned. Looking at him I had a sudden wave of nausea, like there was some sort of lens between us distorting the view, and then it passed.

Shit, I thought. *This is a fucking bad time for my augments to grow a tumor.* I put it on a list of things to worry about after I was dead.

"Come on," I said, trying to sound unconcerned. "We got work."

I started walking, and Adora and Remy fell in behind me. I was glad that Adora at least knew better than to assault me within hearing of Anners's men. The guards let us go; Anners had told them to wait outside, and as far as they knew I'd taken my orders from the colonel and that was it. We had a couple of minutes. When we were a few dozen yards from the little house, I turned a corner into a narrow alley with cobblestone paving that had been torn up, piece by piece, by people looking for building materials.

"We've got about five minutes to disappear," I said quietly, eyes searching the shadows and the people who hurried out of our way. "And then we've got to get the fuck out of Mexico City, fast."

Adora swore in Spanish. "What is *wrong* with you?"

I liked that. I looked at her and liked her, and gave her a smile. She turned to look at me, defiant, and then frowned and suddenly looked away. The pit of nausea in my belly spread, and my head started to pound.

"You said something about transport?"

She didn't turn around. "You said something about owing me ten thousand yen?"

PART II

PART II

VIII

MY NEW HOBBY: IGNORING THE SMELL

Hold him down. Avery, calm—I said down, you fucking desk jockeys!

My eyes snapped open, and as usual I was confused and panicked for a second, everything dark and cold and damp. My augments found some scraps of light leaking in from somewhere and firmed up some edges for me, the snaking lines of the pipes and the square, sharp corners of the humming black cubes. Something small and warm climbed up onto my leg and paused for a moment, as if sniffing the wind, and then moved on. I was getting used to the rats.

For a moment everything was unreal and insubstantial—the rough metal floor felt wrong, like it had gone soft overnight, rotting beneath me. The shadows seemed wrong, too, moving—for a second one felt almost like a person leaning over me, arms extended, and then it was gone.

I shook my head. It ached, like always these days.

I sat up slowly, careful of the pipes overhead and the general lack of space. I patted myself for cigarettes and then caught myself—I hadn't had a pack of cigarettes in years. The smell and heat crowded in on me—I'd been sweating continuously for days, boiling in my own clothes, and I imagined mold growing on my skin, fur trapping even more heat, more damp, tiny threadlike roots sucking the life out of me.

"Avery?"

Adora's voice, somewhere in the murk. Slowly, my eyes were adjusting again, and things were taking on a ghostly gray coloring, just taped-off edges in the dark.

"Whatever we agreed to pay this bastard," I said, my voice thick and phlegmy, "it's too fucking much."

She laughed. "We did not require too many details when making our deal, remember?"

I nodded to myself. We'd hitched a ride on a wagon being pulled by fucking donkeys out of Mexico City— we'd had plenty of cover; half the city was hitting its heels to get away from Anners's troops, who were busy tearing the city down around them, free from his boot heel for maybe the first time in five years. Maybe I should have stayed and revealed myself, Avery Cates, the Gweat and Tewwible, their savior. Maybe they would have been glad to see me, the man who finally killed Colonel Malkem Anners.

Donkeys. I couldn't get over it. I'd sat and stared at the gelatinous sway of their tails as they plodded along, heads down, happy to just keep pulling the fucking wagon forever. We'd have made better time except for Remy, who was suddenly allergic to walking and just complained about being tired all the time.

someone tie his fucking arms

I shook my head again. I was starting to get worried, really worried, about the headaches and the creeping hallucinations. My augments, I figured, finally corroding inside me. When I'd gone after Michaleen's avatar in Hong Kong he'd pressed my button, tried to use the antifrag settings wired into my implants to kill me, and I'd had the bright idea of sending my system into overdrive at the same moment, pushing my entire body way past its limits for the second time in a week. It had saved my life, somehow, but I didn't talk for three months and only got the use of my hand back over time—my augments never worked right after that either, and I figured I'd fried a connection or five. That made my military implants just a little better than a tumor made of metal in my brain.

I got up onto my knees and stretched as best I could, then made sure my Roon was still tucked into my pants, dry and accessible. The constant vibration buzzed up through my knees and into my chest, making my teeth chatter.

"Did you sleep?"

I sat blinking in the darkness. "I'm not sure." There had been voices and flashes—not voices like my resident ghosts, digitized brains I'd swallowed when they tried to brick me in Chengara. Those voices were just in my head, silent except to me, and I'd gotten really good at blocking them out.

Because we let you, Dolores Salgado suddenly whispered at me. A wave of light-headedness swept through me, making me reach back and touch the wet, gritty metal of the floor to steady myself.

Those voices didn't bother me—I was used to them.

"A little," I finally said, reluctant to say anything else. I was an old man, but I was old because I'd learned my lessons well. One of those lessons I'd pushed into the soft spot in Remy's brain a million times: Never reveal weakness. You hide your limps, you smile through searing pain, you never beg off, because when people smell fear they swarm you.

I squinted around the tiny space and tried my new hobby: ignoring the smell. I remembered standing on the rotting docks in Veracruz and staring at the tanker. The hugest fucking thing I'd ever seen, a slab of metal floating on the water, big enough to carry thousands. No one had seen a hover in the air for months, so I could believe this was how they were getting shit across the oceans these days, but when Javier, the broker Adora made contact with, swept his arm out and announced we were going to be traveling on the biggest fucking boat I'd ever seen in my life, I looked him over, from his old boots with the soles held on by rubber bands and the sleeve of his yellowed shirt held on with a series of rusting pieces of wire, and pointed at him.

"You're telling me *you*"—I shifted my finger to point at the tanker—"own *that*?"

Javier laughed. I could still hear him laughing. "No, Mr. Cates, I do not own the boat. But I know how to get you *on* the boat." He smiled, miming us with his hands. "You walk on, you stay hidden, two weeks later, you are in Spain."

Two weeks. I'd gone from New York in the midst of a riot to London in two fucking hours, once, in a hover.

It was funny, actually. We were in the biggest fucking thing in the known universe, but we were in the smallest possible fucking space in it, trying to be quiet like mice. Javier had come up with a bag of what appeared to be pre-swallowed N-tabs and a box of plastic bottles of water. I thought about asking him if the water would make me spend the two weeks shitting myself, but thought better of it.

"Anything happening?" I asked Adora. I couldn't see Remy, but there was only one spot in the tiny room where he could be without physically touching me. The kid had been talking even less than usual, which made him mute.

"Nothing," she sighed. "I heard the crew very close an hour or so ago, but Javier was right: They do not come in here."

We lapsed into silence. My head was pounding, as usual, and my stomach growled almost painfully—I'd gotten used to actual food, and living on N-tabs was no fun.

"He is sleeping," Adora suddenly said. "This is all he does, your friend."

I shrugged even though she couldn't see me well enough to appreciate it. "He's been through a lot. He's a project of mine."

"A project? What are you trying to do?"

I shrugged again, feeling tight and hot. "Keep him alive."

She paused. "That is not easy, in your line of work."

I let that sit for a moment. Adora had told me she was coming along because, first off, I owed her a lot of money and, second, because the System still endured, sort of, in Europe. Headless without Director Marin—good old Dick; it cheered me to think of his buried servers melting under a mushroom cloud in Moscow—and populated mainly by avatar cops who'd had their brains downloaded into bricks, it was still civilization, kind of. A few years ago I would have thought she was crazy, but I understood. The old ways of doing things still counted over there, and Adora was sick of getting hijacked every five minutes and having no one to complain to about it.

"Well—"

I paused, shutting my mouth with a click as Adora sucked in breath. Outside the rusty hatch that sealed us into our hiding place voices boomed, echoing off the steel walls. I pulled the Roon and crouched in the darkness, forcing myself to breathe steadily. My HUD flickered into life for a moment, and then faded, and a spike of eye-melting pain flashed through my skull, making me wince.

his fucking arms get his fucking arms *under control*

The voices grew louder, approaching. I heard Remy stirring behind me, creeping up to kneel next to me, and I hoped he knew enough to stay quiet. We'd never seen the crew; Javier had led us to a rusted, painted-over hatch at the rear of the tanker, had pried it open with a crowbar, and quickly led us down a maze of shafts and ladders until he'd found this little room behind an unmarked hatch. He'd cheerfully admonished us to stay quiet and out of sight, had pointed out the latrine bucket and supplies he'd set up for us, and left us with basic instructions to wait until we heard the tugboat horns that would indicate we were being guided into Cadiz. I'd paid him every yen I had left, leaving me nothing to cover my debt to Adora, but that remained the problem of some future version of myself.

My head cleared, and I crept forward the four or five steps to the hatch, my own breath beating back at me as I crouched there inches from the corroded metal. I made out three, then four separate voices, trading off with one another, getting louder as they approached. The pain in my head, like a worm growing and squirming, gave a violent wrench and I shut my eyes, almost losing my balance as the nauseous agony swept through me, and the voices swirled and got confused.

here's where I heard it
get the kid in
don't listen to him, for fuck's sake, he's a
you sure? Seems quiet now

As the pain receded, gone as quickly as it had hit me, I heard the voices outside our little hiding place stop. For three heartbeats I waited, staring blindly ahead of me, finger along the side of the Roon.

"Stowaways!" a deep, wet voice shouted. It sounded like he was vomiting as he spoke, spitting up lungs and spleens and mucus as he went. The accent was harsh, German sounding. "My name is Captain Hermann Kaufman! You are not welcome on the *Daniel Krokos!* Step out, or we will come in! And if we come in, you will be dead! We have guns!"

I let the echo of his voice ping around the tiny space a bit, thinking. Somehow we'd given ourselves away. I considered our circumstances: The hatch was small, and if thrust open they'd be faced with pitch-black darkness. Only one normal-sized person could fit through the opening at a time. With a choke point like that, I could hold off an army with nothing more than a bag of stones and patience. They could trap us *in*, but there was no way for them to force us *out*.

I cleared my throat. "My name is Avery Cates," I croaked out. "And I have a gun, too. And I'll bet I've killed more people with mine than you have with yours."

IX

THEY SAY SHE IS A
FLOATING HELL

"You okay?"

Adora was only a faint outline in the gloom, a foot or two away. I squinted at her through the pounding in my head, in time with my heartbeat, which wasn't pushing blood through me anymore, just poison. My HUD had started pulsing in time with it, too.

I scrubbed my face with my hands and tried to force myself to concentrate, to get clear. I'd tried summoning my imaginary glass shield that I used when my usual ghostly voices got too intrusive, but the throbbing pain defeated me. I didn't have time to contemplate a grapefruit in my brain, a mass of black cells gathering around my implant like spiders spinning webs with themselves. We'd been in our little hidey-hole in the *Daniel Krokos* for sixteen days, according to Adora, whose estimate I was prepared to accept. Sixteen days of stewing in my own sweat, alternating between a gnawing hunger that no amount of

N-tabs could cure and a sweaty nausea that veined its way through my body like a vine growing inside me.

The crew had kept up a steady guard outside the hatch, presumably armed, but they had, at least, taken me seriously and not tried to open the hatch and rush us. I cleared my throat and tried to take a deep breath, but the crew had done its best to make life hard on us; they'd filled all the ventilation shafts with debris and the air was stuffy and thick with our own exhalations.

"I'm okay," I said, forcing some energy into my voice. "You?"

I made out Adora's shrug. "We must escape."

I remembered a single phrase from a song. I didn't remember where I'd heard the song—my father, maybe, when I'd been a small kid, before he died and Unification and everything else. *They say she is a floating hell.* That's all I could remember. *They say she is a floating hell.* It was one of those things I'd forgotten for so long, suddenly remembered; I might have just created it, invented it.

We'd heard the tugboat horns the day before, distant. I'd expected some action after that; we were in port, and the crew was unloading its cargo, whatever it was—no doubt they wanted us off the boat before making the return trip. When nothing had happened, overnight or today, I'd begun to wonder if maybe they'd decided the easiest thing to do was just keep us buttoned up in our little room until we starved to death, skeletal corpses always being easier to debark than pissed-off, armed assholes.

"Shit," I said. "Next time someone says, here, hide in this tanker for two fucking weeks, we fucking say *no*."

can y'hear me, Avery? Avery, can you—it's

I blinked the voice out of my head as she laughed a

little, a forced noise that was more of a gurgle. She was
right—we weren't going to last much longer in this fucking disease incubator, our eyes turning white and our
watery N-tab shit slowly filling up the place. I shook
myself and forced a deep breath, then gave myself a thunderous slap on the face. Nothing hurt as much as my head,
but it did snap me up a little, so I did it again, getting on
my knees and pulling the Roon. I knew it by feel, and I
began to check it over.

"We have some advantages," I said in a hoarse whisper.
I reached out and gave Remy an indiscriminate smack to
wake the sleepy fuck up. All the kid did these days was
sleep. Another epic wave of pain swept through me, burning
off brain cells and nerve endings as it went, then passed.

"What the *fuck*?" Remy hissed, sitting up. "I said don't
fucking *hit* me."

I paused and squinted through the darkness at him,
then smiled and flashed out my hand, giving him a gentle
smack on the face like a friendly reminder.

"Stop me, kid," I said. "Until then, quit complaining
about it."

I braced myself for another convulsion of pain; they
came regularly after I lost my temper. Nothing happened
though. Remy sat there breathing hard for a moment, and
then cleared his throat softly. "What is it?"

"We gotta move," I said, putting my hand on the Roon
again. "They're obviously not going to come in after us
and if they were going to negotiate our exit they would
have opened up talks." I shook my head. "I'm thinking
they figure they can leave us to rot. So let's effect an exfil-
tration. We have," I repeated, "some advantages."

"Sure," Remy grunted. "We're dirtier. Smell worse.

We'll be blinded in full light, and we not only havta get out of this fuckin' hold, we havta get topside inna vessel we don' have any experience with." I heard him spit on the floor. "Fuckin'-easy-fuckin'-peasy."

I squinted at the kid again. Remy had gone through something when Anners had shown up; something had broken in him. I'd known Remy had a black streak in him—fuck, I'd planted the seeds of it—and he'd been a moody fuck ever since Hong Kong, but there'd been a strength in him I'd liked, that I'd been able to count on. Now something was off, and I was worried it was going to fuck us up.

"We get to pick the time," I said slowly, enunciating carefully. "They don't know when we're coming. They won't have strength out there—based on the sounds out in the corridor I'm guessing there're one, maybe two, people on guard. Once we kill them, we're lost in this fucking ship, sure, but we're three people in a boat the size of fucking old Manhattan Island—they have to find us. And you and me, kid, we've killed plenty of people—plenty of people who were trying to kill *us*. I don't know about Captain Kaufman. I doubt it, though. There's more money in murder; if he was a killer he wouldn't be crewing a tanker."

"I do not have a gun," Adora whispered. "Only my knife."

I considered her shadow for a moment. I wondered if she regretted her decision to head off for Europe and the Rump System, if she hated me. Since we'd met she'd been insulted, threatened, nearly robbed, stripped of her vehicle and ripped off of the ten thousand yen I owed her—and now she was heading into a gunfight with a knife.

I counted ammo in my head. I had fifty-seven shells, including the clip in the Roon. I was pretty sure Remy had nineteen rounds for his huge revolver; it was a slow reload but it cleared a room when he fired it. He was wrong about us being blinded by the light; our augments, I was pretty sure, would compensate fast enough.

"Okay," I said quietly, racking the slide and flicking off the safety. "Speed is the key. The hatch opens outward, and I'll bet you my thumbs those stupid fucks are standing on either side, dozing off and daydreaming of a world where they don't have to stand guard outside this hatch." I swallowed a spasm of coughs. "Adora, you're going to smash your way out. Unlock that hatch and give it your shoulder, *smash* it open and into whoever's standing to the side. Can you do that?"

hear me Avery say something if you can

She nodded. "Yes." She sounded nervous, but I gave her some slack.

"Keep moving, and go low. Smash that door open but don't wait to see what happens, keep moving and hit the floor, slide and roll. Crawl. Keep *moving*."

She nodded again and took a deep breath through her nose. "Okay."

"Kid," I said, turning to Remy. "You go out right after her. The hatch'll smash left, so go right with that cannon. Go out and try to hit someone, but fire all six rounds. Just squeeze the trigger, make noise. Just keep firing, whether you hit anything or not."

Chaos. Confusion. They didn't know how many of us were crammed in here, or how heavily armed we were. Scaring the shit out of them was the best I could do for an advantage.

"And what are *you* gonna be doin' while I'm out there makin' noise?"

I took a breath and resisted the urge to smack Remy again. "I'm out the door on your heels. I've got your flank covered," I said slowly. "I'm gonna make sure you and Adora don't get shot in the back."

"All right," he said. "All right. Then what?"

"Up. We just start moving and we go up every chance we get until we see some sky and can get oriented." I shrugged, getting back into a crouch. "Shoot anyone who gets in between us and out. Simple."

"Simple," Adora said with a snort. "Let's go. I don't care if I get shot—as long as I am shot outside this damn room."

That was a sentiment I could get behind. I was relieved, in a way—my whole world had finally narrowed down to one solvable problem: get out of the fucking room. Everything else—Michaleen, the Angels, Remy—all of it just sloughed off and left me simplified.

push, Avery

I gave Remy a slight push. "Let's go."

He muttered something but I ignored him, and he grunted his way past me in the shadows. I heard the hammer click back on his gun, and then I let Adora slip past me. She didn't smell too good anymore, but she felt delightful as she pushed by. I hadn't had much to enjoy in the last few days, crammed into this black box, and every little bit helped. I gave her a moment to get her hands on the locking lever.

"Go," I whispered, as urgently as volume would allow. "Go!"

She went. I was impressed; she yanked down the lever

and smashed herself into the hatch, sailing out into the blinding rectangle of the corridor. The hatch banged against something soft and bounced back lazily as Adora dropped down out of my view. Remy wasn't moving; I could see his slumped silhouette in the doorway and I lunged forward to give him a hard shove.

"Move!"

He grunted something and launched himself for the doorway, firing the revolver before he'd even gotten out. That was okay. It was the noise I wanted. It would have been a nice bonus if he'd actually aimed at someone, but just seeing him stumble out of the hatch, waving the gun around like he'd recently figured out what it did was good enough. He was squeezing the trigger slowly, irregular explosions of painfully loud noise that would terrify and confuse just about anyone. I balanced myself, made sure of my grip on the Roon, and pulled myself through the hatch after him, trying to stay low and move fast.

As I'd hoped, my augments had enough left in them to throttle down the sudden blindness in the bright hall to a second or so of sizzling white and then a bleached-out but workable clarity. Remy had staggered after Adora for no fucking reason I could invent, so I spun right just in time to get socked in the jaw by something really heavy, spinning my head around and making my convulsive shot go wide. I let myself fall backward, hoping Remy maybe had found his footing and might put a shot over my bow and kill the second guard, but nothing happened as I smacked down onto the hard metal floor, my teeth sinking into my tongue as my head lit up for a second with pain.

I'd had a two-week training course in pain management, though. The guard was a fat black guy in a shirt two sizes too small, as if he thought he was muscular instead of tubby. In one greasy hand he had an old-school blackjack, a piece of weighted leather wrapped around his knuckles, and he threw himself at me with it held high, meaning to smash it down on my head. It was an awesome sight as his shirt rode up with the effort, exposing his perfectly round, hairless belly. It was a target I could have hit five times with my eyes shut, and I managed twice before he landed on top of me, suddenly transformed into a side of wet, pulsing beef.

"Ah, fuck," I groaned, my gorge rising. "Ah, *fuck*." I thought of Belling. Belling had always seemed to be dressed in expensive suits, killing people via suggestion and disdain. I was always covered in blood and bile, pinned under fat guys who never bathed. It was enough to make me question my approach.

There was a moment of staticky silence. "We all okay?" I gasped, rolling tubby off of me with some effort.

push, Avery

Remy grunted. "Yes," Adora gasped from a few feet away. "What now?"

The air was torn by a piercing klaxon that didn't waver or change in any way: an ear-shredding wail of alarm.

"Fuck," I muttered, picturing Belling in his clean suits, smiling at me. We were out of the black box, at least. "We *run*."

X

IF THEY DIDN'T HAVE GUNS,
I'D BE INSULTED

The corridors were tight and filled with the steady, nerve-shredding noise of the alarm. I led the way, followed by Adora, then Remy facing our rear and making sure no one got behind us. We owned the straightaways; so far, the crew didn't have a fucking boomer among them, and I was shocked and appalled that they might have scrupled to lie about being armed.

There were multiple staircases leading to and from each deck, and at each one we had to stop cold and make sure the way was clear before I hedgehogged up, boosted by Adora so I could keep the Roon in action. The first three decks went by fast, empty and grimy, little used. I didn't know how much crew a tanker like this normally required, but it looked to me like they were running light, with the lower decks largely abandoned. As I was pushing my head up over the top step from the third deck to the fourth, I contemplated the fucking ridiculous bad luck that we'd been noticed in the first place.

As I looked up over the lip of the stairs on the fourth deck someone tried to put a boot on me and I had to let go of the railing and slide downward, colliding with

we're going to try a hot shot

Adora and sprawling to the third deck floor. Behind me I heard three of Remy's deafening shots, loud enough to hear even over the endless whine of the alarm.

"What the *fuck* are you shooting at?"

"We got a crowd," he hollered back. "Just keeping 'em back!"

"Watch your bullets!" I growled, pulling myself up and ducking up the stairs to check the way. "We can't shoot every cocksucker on this boat!"

so try to relax; the effect is not going to be

To make myself look ridiculous, I underscored this advice by putting two shells into the air straight up the stairway, making one burly-looking man with a bald head and a heavy-looking striped shirt screech and throw himself backward from the stairwell.

"Coming up!" I bellowed. "Back the fuck up!"

I grinned. Reminding myself that just because we hadn't seen a gun yet didn't mean there wasn't a gun somewhere on the ship heading our way. I had to admit I was enjoying myself. Two weeks sleeping in the dark, breathing Remy's farts and having headaches—just being able to *move* was

pleasant, which is why we had to

fantastic.

Creeping up the stairs, I took a breath and popped my head up again, then ducked down. Below and behind, Remy peeled off another two shots, and I got the impression we were in a rush to keep moving. I took a step up and sighted down the fourth deck—about four or five crew carrying heavy wrenches and pipe fittings in their hands, ten, twelve feet away. I spun rapidly and found three more creeping up the other way.

I squeezed the trigger and put one shell into the floor right in front of the trio, then spun again, putting my gun on the first group.

"Kid! Get up here and take my flank!"

I felt Adora pushing up behind me. The five in front of me were four men and one woman. One of the men, a short man with a tan, deeply wrinkled face and a yellowed beard like cake frosting on his face took a step forward, holding his spanner out in front of him like a shield.

restrain you. You're experiencing a dissociative

"What in *fuck* is wrong wit' ya, you fuckin' *blödes arschloch*?" he shouted, his eyes wide in outrage. By his accent I marked him as Captain Kaufman. "We ain't tryin' to *kill* ya!"

I put a shell at his feet, too, because I could—I felt so sharp and light, I thought I might be able to put a bullet between his eyes without even looking, just based on my spatial memory.

"That's good news," I shouted. The alarm, I had to admit, was getting under my skin like a termite and chewing on my nerves. "Because if this is you trying to kill me, it's a fail, and when people *fail* to kill me it gets unpleasant." I gestured a tight arc with the Roon. "We just want off this fucking boat. You have my apologies for stowing away."

He squinted at me, chewing his lip, but he didn't move. Remy fired again, and someone behind me started screaming like a cat in a sack.

"*Mutterficker!*" Kaufman yowled, eyes going wide. "We canna let you go!" His voice had taken on a pitiable quality I didn't like. "We fuckin' *sold* ya, and took the yen already."

I grinned again, a thrill going through me. I'd been sold like cargo so many times, it was familiar territory, but this time, for once, I still had my gun and a field of vision. I suspected this transaction was going to

break due to the Psionic's pressure, causing you to relive immediate experiences, and we have to introduce a

turn out differently than I was used to. For a moment, I imagined the cosmos had tried to put me back on the Rail, and I'd kicked a stone under the wheels and bucked myself off. It was an exhilarating thought. I grabbed onto it and decided to see how far the ride would get me.

"You sold me?" I said slowly, stepping forward and keeping the gun directly on Kaufman's face. "You sold *me*?"

He put his hands up and took an involuntary step backward, colliding with his crew and stopping short. "We— we put the name out there, an' hell, we got an offer in two hours. A decent offer." His face reddened and he found his balls again. "What the *fuck* were we supposed to do? You were stowaways! You don't have any fucking *rights*!"

I nodded. "Back up."

Kaufman pushed himself back up straight and cocked his head. "You can't shoot *all* of us, Mr. Cates."

I raised an eyebrow, still grinning. "I can't? You sure?" His crew, standing behind him, weren't convinced; I could see that. "*Back up*."

He swallowed, and for a second I thought Captain Kaufman was going to try and be a hero, but his crew started to fall back and that settled him. He didn't turn his back on me, though; he started walking backward, hands still up to show me he wasn't going to try anything. I trusted Remy to guard my rear and we started walking. Now that he was doing what I wanted, I was inclined to feel friendly toward Kaufman.

"All we want is
disruption
off this ship," I offered.

Kaufman's anxiety seemed to bloat inside him, pushing out the leathery skin of his face. He almost looked back over his shoulder, but caught himself, and a sudden idea
in order to
formed in my head. "They're here—right? Your buyers. Taking possession?"

We'd reached the next set of narrow, steep metal stairs leading up to the next deck. A bilge of dirty water stood an inch deep on the floor here, and I figured that meant we were near the main deck.

After a moment's hesitation as the crew behind him stopped moving, confused, at the bottom of the stairs, he nodded. "Ya. They came just before the alarm. We assured them it was just a malfunction."

I nodded, gesturing up the stairs with the gun. The stairs were going to be tricky, because if anyone was inclined to try for a grab of the gun that would be the ideal spot—my field of vision truncated, a third dimension I couldn't easily police introduced. If there was any talent in there, this would be where I'd find out. I didn't have much choice, though; it was up the stairs or
sever
stay in the floating hell forever.

The buyers were another problem altogether—the chances that people who would pay money to buy me *did* have guns were about one hundred percent. If they didn't have guns, I'd be insulted.

the connection

The crew began climbing the stairs, one by one. When the captain, a man who was shrinking right before my eyes, stood nervously at the base of the stairs, watching me in an agony of indecision and horror at the twist his life had just taken, I stepped back and gestured Adora ahead of me.

"Backward," I said. "Be my eyes."

She scowled and muttered a string of Spanish. Then she waved at the gun. "Are you pointing it at me, as well?"

"That depends," I said, "on whether you're doing what I tell you." I smiled. "Just

prepare yourself

tell me if anyone's trying to fuck with me as I come up."

She nodded. "I cannot wait to say good-bye to you, Mr. Avery Cates," she said, smiling a little. She was filthy, caked in a dark sort of mud that glazed her hair and stained every visible inch of her. "You are the worst thing to happen to me in many years, and that is *saying* something, *señor*." She fell into place in front of the captain as they backed up the stairs. When she had cleared the deck she looked around and then shouted down to me.

"They're all still backing away down the corridor. Oh, thank you, the fucking sun."

I chanced a glance behind me to make sure Remy had everything under control, and headed up the stairs quickly, ascending into bright, liquid sunshine streaming in through the huge plate-glass windows that lined the corridor of the main interior deck. The ocean, gray and listless, stretched away from us on all sides, and for a moment, I was dazzled just like Adora. Fresh air and sunlight had never looked so good. My HUD even snapped into clarity for the occasion, showing me mostly green status bars with a few yellowed ones here and there—but I never knew how much I could

if you can

trust the HUD anymore, with my implants rotting away in my head, gifting me with audio hallucinations and sudden, random headaches like a sweating drum of toxic waste buried in my brain. I stepped aside to let Remy come up and stand next to me, then gestured with the gun again.

"You assholes down there," I shouted. "Come up and join everyone else. Let's have you all in one place." I didn't know if there were other crew creeping about the ship, but I could *see* the fucking water. We were getting off the *Daniel Krokos* if I had to shoot everyone

Here

in my way.

I took a handful of Kaufman's shirt and shoved him. "Let's go. Where are your clients?"

I wasn't sure he'd tell the truth, but it didn't make any sense to not ask. He backed away with his hands up as I advanced on him, his eyes everywhere as he licked his lips nervously—I was starting to think Captain Kaufman had never been hijacked at gunpoint in his life, which seemed fucking impossible in the new world, without police, without government, with men like me walking around free.

we

"My quarters," he said, blinking rapidly. "Where they could be comfortable while we fetched you."

I thought about it for three steps and decided I believed him. A sign over the pair of swinging doors was in English, with arrows pointing up for GALLEY and BRIDGE. I didn't want to go to either place, but I wanted to get out into the open air as quickly as possible.

"Can you swim?" I shouted over my shoulder.

"Yes," Adora said immediately.

"Fuckin' hell, no, I canna *swim*!" Remy snarled. I blinked. Remy could swim. I'd seen him swim. He swam like a fucking fish. Before I could think on that any further, Kaufman crashed through the swinging doors and I followed him out into the warm, wet air. For a moment all I was aware of was the warm sun on my skin and the distant sound of birds. Then I was aware of the ten or twelve armed men and women waiting for us on the deck. A shaft of pain stabbed up from my neck and into my head, making me wince as I struggled to figure out who to put the gun on first. A thin, medium-sized man wearing glasses stepped forward

go

XI

ON GENERAL PRINCIPLES I'D
LIKE TO SHOOT HIM

Everything swung ninety degrees and the floor slid away underneath me and I was sitting up, back muscles screaming, wrists burning. I stared at the thin man for a second; I knew the face, but the name escaped me. He looked old, like he'd been trapped under a rock for years and only recently set free. His glasses, thin wire-frame affectations, were brand new, though, pristine and gleaming in the dim light of the tiny room.

My head was pounding.

"Take your time, Avery," he said, his accent vaguely Russian, his grammar precise and clipped. His grin was easy and confident and familiar. "We have all the time in the world, yes?"

He was wearing a utilitarian gray jumpsuit, the kind Techies wore when they had to crawl down some sump pipes to run some cable. The other three people standing in the room with us were wearing them as well, two dour-looking older women who'd spread and flattened into some-thing asexual and a tall, stick-thin Indian man with a pencil-thin mustache who leaned against a far wall eating the world's least-appetizing apple with apparent relish, his brown eyes locked on me.

In a cage on the floor, a few feet away from us, was Remy, hands locked on the bars, staring at me.

"Avery! Don't trust 'em! Get me the fuck out of here!"

The skinny old man with the glasses scowled and closed his eyes as if wishing for strength. "Someone muz-zle that dog for me, please."

For a second no one moved, and I studied the cage. It wasn't just a square of rusting iron or even a nifty cube of alloy; wires ran from it in a thick braid, and the whole thing seemed to shiver with some unseen energy. I didn't know where they were getting the power, but if I'd ever been in a room with four Techies, this was it.

After a moment, the Indian grunted and pushed off from the wall with bad grace. Sticking the apple into a pocket of his jumpsuit, he plucked a black rod from a nearby wheeled tray and stepped over to the cage. Remy squealed, his face going...blurry...for a moment as he scampered back. The Indian leaned in and studied him for a moment, judging distances and the spaces between the cage's slats, and then with one professional movement he thrust the rod into the cage. The second it made con-tact with Remy, the kid stiffened in one sudden spasm and then slumped over. He wasn't unconscious—his eyes rolled over to land on me, and he blinked slowly—but he'd obviously lost most of his upper motor functions. I made a note of the rod, and the cruel, easy way the Indian had used it.

Then I looked back at the skinny prick with the glasses. I *knew* him. I gathered myself and tried to launch myself at him, but a thick strap around my waist held me in place, and all I managed to do was make the gurney I was on jump off the floor for a second and crash back down with bone-rattling force while the two other Techies each scrambled back from me. My old friend, though, just stood his ground, watching me, and slowly extracted a crumpled pack of actual, real live cigarettes from his pocket, pulling two free and sticking them both in his mouth.

"Avery, I will give one, and you will listen to me, yes? Plenty of time for killing us later."

His name, everything about him, was on the edge of my mind. I pushed it aside and swallowed rage. "Where's Adora?" I asked.

"She is well, in another place, not far," he said immediately, producing a lighter with some sort of conjurer's trick and hunching over it, plumes of white smoke rising into the air around him. "She has expressed a wish to continue her journey alone. After we have debriefed her, we will allow this."

I nodded to myself. Good for her, I thought. Inexplicably, people always seemed to want to stick with me, and they usually ended up regretting it. I figured Adora was probably the smartest person I'd ever known. Smart enough to leave me behind, at least.

He smiled, plucking one of the cigarettes from his mouth and stepping forward to hand it to me. I snapped one arm up to take hold of his wrist and yank him toward me, but he stepped back just fast enough to evade me, and smiled.

"You do not recognize me. Yes, I understand. This will

be remedied, Avery, in a moment, believe me. Now, I will offer you the smoke again, but only if you give me your word that you will not try to break my arm this time."

I considered the odds of me breaking my bonds, the odds of the skinny Indian fellow jamming that black rod up my ass, the odds of me accomplishing anything useful by refusing, and my burning desire to smoke that cigarette. After a moment, I nodded curtly. "All right."

He grinned and stepped forward, angling the cigarette toward me so I could lean forward and take it between my lips. I straightened up, closed my eyes, and inhaled deeply. It was a crap cigarette, but it was real tobacco, old and stale but real, and my heart skipped a beat as the nicotine hit my bloodstream. It had been so long, it was like my first cigarette all over again. I was light-headed and calmly happy for a second.

I opened my eyes again and pushed the smoke out through my nose. "Why is he in a fucking cage?" I nodded my chin at the man with the glasses. "You realize that's gonna count against you, right?"

He smiled, and for a second I almost had his name, the whole batch of memories I was sure were there. Then they skittered away like pebbles, skimming along the slick floor. "Avery, we will try an experiment. Bear with me. I am going to tell you my name. I want you to let me know what happens. Ready?"

I blinked, smoke rising up between us. "Sure."

I blinked, my HUD shuddering in my vision like someone was shaking me violently. "What?"

The Techie shrugged. "You are being prevented from noting certain things about your surroundings, Avery, by a very powerful Psionic. A *Pusher*, is the term I've heard used." He took his own cigarette from his mouth and leaned against a bank of humming instruments, ashing on the floor. "Most accept the theory that such people are the result of evolution, but I have my own, controversial theory."

I rolled the cigarette around in my mouth luxuriously, trying to keep up as my vision and HUD stabilized. "What's that?"

The Techie threw out both arms and seemed pleased to be asked. "Aliens, Avery. I believe if we could sequence their genome we'd discover they differ from human DNA in significant ways. It would explain much."

He said this with perfect seriousness, and I wasn't sure if he meant it or if it was one of those elaborate Techie jokes no one understood. I sucked in smoke and tried to concentrate. "I'm being Pushed, is what you're saying. Right now."

"Right now, and for some time now, on a continuous basis," he agreed, putting his cigarette back in his mouth and pushing his hands into his pockets. The Indian fellow was lounging against a bank of instruments to my left. I realized with a start that the other two Techies had left the room at some point. "This is easily the most powerful Psionic operative I've ever encountered. Throughout your entire journey on the *Daniel Krokos*, he has kept you under his complete influence. Not just you, but your pretty friend, too." He frowned. "I am not sure if he bothered others as you moved about; it seems unlikely, but it would have made his position safer."

I didn't understand what he was talking about, so I decided to switch to a subject I could get my arms around. "You bought me."

He nodded. "We monitor the black markets constantly. We seek all manner of equipment, schematics, data cubes—so much to try and gather." He shook his head. "We do not as a rule seek out human traffickers, but we do hear names and auction details, and you, Avery—well, we have been searching for you for some time now."

I studied him, but no sense of almost knowing who he was returned. "Huh. I'm a popular guy. Who's *we*, exactly? This Geek chorus you got going here, I mean."

He smiled and looked down at his feet, amused. "You have heard of *Superstes per Scientia.*"

I nodded. "SPS, sure. So this is it?"

He nodded, looking back up at me, eyes amused. He wasn't scared of me, that was for sure. I was still tied down to a gurney, but my hands were free; I was insulted. I let my eyes drag a bit over him and thought I spotted a piece tucked into his belt right at the small of his back. A little insurance.

"SPS bids you welcome, Avery. You have grown important."

"Fuck, not again," I said, taking the cigarette from my mouth and ashing on the floor. "Being important usually means I'm in for some serious asskicking."

He smiled. "Be happy, Avery—you are among friends. I do not know what would have happened if you were allowed to remain under the influence of this Pusher, but I do not think it could have gone well. We will free you of this affliction and then we can discuss the work that must be done. There is not much time and there is not much left to save, but with your help perhaps more than we expected."

I nodded cheerfully enough. "Happy as hell, as always,

to be kicked in the balls for exactly zero pay." I put the cigarette back between my lips. "So where's this fucking Pusher? On general principles I'd like to shoot him."

The Techie laughed, pushing off from the equipment with a snakelike undulation of his thin frame. "I will show you."

He walked over to where Remy still sat and began following the thick braid of wires stemming from the bizarre cage, finally plucking one particular cord and pulling it through his hands as he walked until it led him to a small handheld device, familiar enough though I hadn't seen one operational in a while. He gestured over it for a moment, and then looked back at me.

"What we're doing here, Avery, is trying to preserve technology. Knowledge. Despite the faults of the System, it provided some stability, but now everything, as you would say, has gone to hell, and we are working to preserve what we can. As a result, right here in Spain we have what you might call a Techie's paradise, yes? Collected here is a lot of amazing tech, and we get to play with it all. There has been some wonderful work performed here these past few years, while the world shrinks and burns outside." He pointed at the cage. "For example, this. It does not have a name. What it does is disrupt the peculiar brain-wave patterns of a Psionic." He looked down at it. My HUD sharpened as I realized he was about to do something with Remy, and I fingered the material I was bound with, wondering if it would burn, how I might get free.

"Sadly, it is not very practical, as it is large, heavy, and has immense power requirements. Fortunately, though, you have brought the subject here to us!" He looked back at me, cheerful. "Thus, we can try our experiment. Thus!"

He made a dramatic gesture over the handheld and the cage suddenly seemed to vibrate, going blurry around the edges. Remy sat up ramrod straight and began to scream, a steady, unbroken openmouthed wail.

I surged against my restraints, biting the cigarette in half. I twisted and turned until the gurney overtipped, crashing me to the floor with a rattle and smacking my face against the cold cement. I didn't feel it.

"You fucking hurt him and—"

"Avery!" the Techie shouted without looking at me.

The Indian Techie leaned forward with a bored expression and jabbed his black stick against my neck, and a searing pain came and went so fast through me it might have never happened, and every muscle in my body, including my abused bladder, relaxed simultaneously.

The pain in my head swelled until I thought, well, fuck, this was it, I was going to stroke out right here. And then, suddenly, it was gone. Relief swept through me and I forgot to struggle, a cold sweat breaking out all over me. Blood, hot and salty, overflowed my mouth and onto the floor. Remy had stopped screaming, and I looked at the cage.

Remy wasn't in the cage.

Instead, it was an old man. The oldest man I'd ever seen in my life, grotesquely ancient, a tiny, shriveled person in a soiled old suit that looked to be pre-Unification, an old cut in a cheap, shiny fabric that hadn't been cleaned in a long time. He was panting, sweat dripping off his flattened, red flower of a nose, and his tiny, dark eyes were locked on me. My mind was blank as we stared at each other, and then a single thought drifted through me: *That motherfucker hates me.*

I looked up at the Techie with the glasses to see if he'd disappeared, too. He was looking down at me, one eyebrow raised in a question. I stared at him for a moment and then shut my eyes, anger and pain filling me up, making me vibrate with the need to hit someone, to strangle someone, to kill and just keep killing. I knew Remy was dead. Remy was a bloated corpse on the floor next to Belling in Mexico City, and I'd failed, again, to keep a single person alive. And I'd kidded myself that I was off the Rail, that I was calling my own shots.

Despair was like anesthetic sweeping through me. My hands shook violently, fluttering like strangled bugs.

I remembered, suddenly, being on the truck after being pressed, me and Remy and half the town. Remy up for it, helping me take on the single guard—and we had him. We could have walked away. I saw his face—young and happy. Trusting. The fucking kid had *trusted* me.

Filled with a formless, blank rage, I looked at the Techie. "Hello, Grisha," I said, my voice surprisingly calm. "Don't untie me. I might fucking kill you."

XII

MAKES ME WANT TO BE A BETTER PERSON

"He's got to be the most powerful Psionic on record," Grisha said, flicking his cigarette onto the floor as he knelt down to peer into the cage. "Certainly the most powerful I've ever encountered." He paused for a second. "It is good to see you, Avery."

I nodded absently, staring at the gnarled old man in the cage, too, thinking about Remy. Grisha had refused my advice and untied me. I tried to picture the body I'd left back in Mexico City in Belling's room. I remembered stepping over it, not even glancing down to see who'd been killed. I pictured Remy lying there, *still* there. As I pictured him, I saw Kev Gatz, gutshot, dead underneath Westminster Abbey. Then I saw R.A. Harper, staring at me after Belling slit her throat. Then Gleason, swollen and blackened, animated by Ty Keith's nanobots. I saw them all, everyone, dozens and dozens of them—people I'd tried to spare, to protect, to merely leave behind. Every fucking one of them, dead.

"I am sorry. This is a shock." He paused to cough, hard, into one hand, his face reddening. "But we must speak. There is much to discuss that involves you."

"Fuck you," I said leisurely. Grisha was barely there. In some small sliver of my brain, I wondered that he was here, that he was still alive. It was distant and vague, though, and I felt no urgency in exploring the event.

The little man in the cage stared back at me with slitted, yellowed eyes. He was about a thousand years old, and they looked like hard years. The malevolence he projected at me was like a physical sensation, and I wondered if maybe Grish was wrong about his little cage, if maybe it wasn't one hundred percent effective. He had a round head like a rotten potato, off of which his face hung in heavy white-whiskered folds like it had become detached from the bones and tendons beneath it. His nose had been broken several times and never set, his ears were red flowers blooming from the dirty, encrusted folds of his skull, his suit had once been purple and was now just dirty, and his hands were tiny, tiny things with thick sausage fingers that looked useless for anything more subtle than holding your prick while you pissed.

As we stared at each other, he spat delicately onto the floor of his cage without taking his eyes off me.

Grisha stepped over to the cage and leaned down to put his face near the old man's. "What I would like to know first," the Techie said in a wondering voice, "is why not simply *Push* Avery into helping you?"

The old man slid his eyes to Grisha and worked his lips like his teeth were sliding out of his head. He affected a stoic, calm expression, but something about the way his face never stopped moving, never stopped sucking at itself told me he was terrified.

"Can't," he suddenly growled, his voice deep and scratchy, like he'd swallowed razors. "We tried. A lot, in the field. Motherfucker doesn't take Push well. You can do it, but it ain't easy, and keepin' it up long is fucking impossible. All those *others* in his head; you'd haveta Push 'em all, simultaneously." He spat again. "But he's susceptible to *suggestion*. Takes a light touch. Subtle. Gotta get in there and really work it. Y'can fool the *eyes*, and then he sort of Pushes *himself*, see."

"Why?" I asked, standing up. "Why Remy?"

The old man just stared at me, his tiny eyes following me.

"Forgive me for putting it in this way, Avery," Grisha said seriously. "But he was incidental. This Psionic wished to stay close to you. This was expedient."

"Expedient." I wondered, for a second, about the mysterious man in the white suit. A prop, I figured. To make it convincing. One more person killed on my account. I crouched down to peer between the bars of the cage. "Let him out." I made fists until my knuckles popped, and my HUD snapped into razor-sharp clarity.

"No," Grisha said. "Avery, if we release him from the device, he will immediately be able to compel us with his ability. Come, let us talk in the other room."

"Fuck you," I repeated. "Let him out." I closed my eyes. "If he can stop me from squeezing the fucking life out of him with my bare hands, he deserves to live."

I heard the skinny Russian bastard crouch down next to me. When he spoke, it was right into my ear. His breath smelled like cigarettes and rot. "Avery, I am sorry you have lost your friend in this way. This ... Pusher wished to have access to you on a continuous basis in order to have

time to dig into your psyche gently, without being noticed.
For his own reasons he decided that assuming the identity
of your friend was the easiest way to do so. This obviously worked. It would have continued to work if not for
our intervention." He put his hand on my shoulder and I
twitched, controlling myself with effort. "There is a war
going on, Avery, and you are a battlefield. Come, let us
talk."

"No," I said, opening my eyes and finding the fucking
codger still staring at me, his mouth working like he was
chewing cud. I realized I could hear his labored breathing. "I don't care about anything aside from strangling
this piece of shit. Take your war outside, Grisha."

He sighed, and the patience in his exhalation made
me want to smack him. From what I remembered about
Grisha, the blow might not land. "Avery, for all his power,
this piece of shit is just a soldier. The Angels. You know
of them."

I nodded once. "Yes."

"You can kill him. They will send another. They will
be less subtle. Less gentle. Eventually they will pop your
mind open like a legume and scoop you out, sift through
the scattered thoughts." He leaned in again, close to my
ear. "This is not the man to kill. This is simply a tool used
against you."

Suddenly I was very tired and just wanted to be left
alone to gnaw over that day. I should have known something
was wonky, that something was off. I'd been knocked
over the head and when I'd come to, a dead body, Belling dead, and Remy not quite right. He hadn't been right,
and I hadn't noticed, or I'd been forced not to notice.
Either way, he was dead, and I kept hearing him in Hong

Kong: *You left me. You fucking left me.* I might as well have killed him myself back in Englewood, before we got pressed, for all the good I'd done him.

I let Grisha urge me to my feet and lead me out of the room. I turned in the doorway and looked back to find the short little bastard still staring at me.

The next room was the same size: long and narrow, claustrophobic. The walls weren't as covered by endless banks of electronic equipment, and were a rusty-colored corrugated metal; I realized we were in a series of old shipping containers that had been welded together into a structure. It was hot, and Grisha's fellow SPS members looked sweaty and sad in their grubby jumpsuits, sitting around an eroded wooden table that left barely enough room for people to squeeze past.

The skinny Indian immediately offered me a metal cup filled with something that I assumed was supposed to be coffee, and for a second I forgot everything else and missed the System, the good old System of Federated Nations, with a passion. It had been fucked up and dangerous and I'd done my part to tear it down, but fuck, you could get a decent cup of coffee and a real cigarette back then.

As if reading my mind, the Indian followed the coffee with a burning cigarette. I took it with numb fingers, then watched Grisha as he moved toward a white porcelain urn sitting on a simple battery-powered burner.

"So, why?" I asked thickly. All my instant anger had melted away, and I just felt tired and beaten. I'd been swimming against currents for years, and the cosmos kept ducking my head under the waves.

Grisha poured himself some coffee and then turned,

gesturing to an empty chair. I ignored him and sniffed at the coffee. I needed to know who I had to blame for Remy, who I had to go kill, and I could tell Grisha wasn't going to tell me unless I let him ramble out his whole story. And Grish was one of those oddball Techies you couldn't twist it out of. Not easily, anyway.

He sighed and leaned against the wall next to the coffee urn. I was aware of four faces on me, studying me, and I resisted the urge to look at the Indian to see if he had that black rod in his hand, if he was going to make sure I didn't misbehave.

"Our purpose, Avery, is not simply to build such fine quarters for ourselves and create toys," he began, sipping coffee and making a face. "We are a voluntary organization, and we are trying to preserve technology. These are new dark ages, yes? Civil war, the erosion of authority, the breakup of the System, Marin's destruction—you have seen the state of the world. Chaos. Fragmented culture. The complete collapse of the manufacturing base, which had been too heavily centralized and fragile under the undersecretaries. All it took was destabilization of one aspect of the chain and everything comes down, yes?"

I nodded vaguely. "It's a fucking shit storm out there, sure."

Grisha smiled. "Yes, apt: shit storm." He shrugged. "We are here to save what can be saved, in hope that when the world stabilizes again we will not have to rediscover everything, yes? But it is not just technology we find ourselves protecting, seeking." He paused and looked around at his fellow Techies. "Avery, do you know when the last live human birth was?"

I blinked at him. "What?"

"The last time someone had a baby," he added through a spasm of damp-sounding coughs. "That lived."

I frowned over my mug, which smelled like something you'd describe as coffee if you'd never smelled coffee before in your life. "You mean aside from me?"

It was an automatic joke. I didn't know why I'd said it, or where it had come from.

Grisha smiled. "Six years ago. This is the last confirmed live birth in *the world*, Avery. It is possible, of course," he continued with a wave, "that due to the breakdown of communication lines and scientific work that we have merely *missed* every report and simply not observed the teeming thousands of newborns mewling everywhere. But it is more likely that for some reason, as yet unexplained, the human race has simply gone sterile."

I thought back over the last few years. A lot of my attention had been taken up with not being shot in the face, but I could not recall any young children. No one under six, that was certain—plenty of dirty-faced preteens itching to steal your wallet or swarm you in an alley. Yeah, plenty of dirty-faced moppets like Adora's sister, learning to drink at nine and looking fifty by the time they were thirteen, sure. But no babies.

Then I remembered Remy, and stopped caring. There was a boulder jammed in my chest, blocking every thought and making my head throb with ebbing blood.

"Dying. We are dying, as a *race*, Avery. As an organization, SPS is split in its preferred response to this crisis. Some feel we should be putting our dwindling resources into trying to solve the problem. I and others believe that time has past, and we are seeking to salvage what we can."

I let my eyes crawl around the interior of the container, feeling tight and buried, cooking alive inside this metal box, with Grisha's calm, jolly voice droning on and on. I needed one fucking piece of information from him: Where to go, who to hunt, who was responsible for Remy. I wanted to launch myself across their stupid fucking salvage table and toss my hot coffee in his eyes and push the cigarette into his forehead until he squealed, then ask him politely what I needed to know. Except Grisha wouldn't squeal, and his three friends would pull me off him, and then I'd find myself tied down to a gurney again.

So I listened.

"We are sadly reduced. We cannot fabricate things. We are forced to work with whatever we find—components that can be cannibalized, re-used, re-programmed. We are good at this. But we have no more capability of genetic research, of even primitive reproductive science beyond forced breeding—which was, I am ashamed to say, seriously considered. But we are facing the extinction of the human race. Any possible escape route must be considered."

Aside from the table and the coffee, the room was filled with crates with obscure labels. Some of them had been torn open, a yellow fuzz of packing material spilling out like guts, looking scratchy and hot. On the other side of the table was another door, tightly shut and barred on the inside, and off to the side in the dark corner was a tall, narrow crate, on which sat my Roon and three spare clips.

"Happily—though we are not unanimous on the happiness of this thought, I confess—this world is littered with technology we might use to preserve the intellect and culture of the remaining humans, such as it is. Happily, we do already have a great number of high-quality intelligences filed."

Reminding myself not to stare at things you wanted, I dragged my eyes back to Grisha. It was remarkable how unchanged he was. Face still narrow, eyes cheerful, stupid fucking glasses. "Filed?" I asked, feeling dumb and slow.

"Avatars, Avery. The human race is slipping into the dark night, yes? One day the last of us dies, what is left? We can digitize intelligences, but someone must be out and about, for maintenance. We had designed our world for arms and legs; we must have them. Avatars, Avery. The whole world is *littered* with avatar shells, most damaged, but many usable with some repair. The civil war left us with a supply, you see. We have been collecting them, preparing the way. Most are simply irradiated, which will not matter once the rest of us are all dead!" He shrugged, planting the cigarette back in his mouth and toasting me with his coffee. "As we die, we process people, and at least there is a remnant of us to carry on." He shrugged his eyebrows. "Also, we can choose who to salvage and who not. Leave the bastards responsible for the mess behind."

I glanced at the gun again and took an easy step to my left, making as if to claim the empty seat next to the Indian Techie. "The human race is dying, and you want to stuff us all into *avatars*?"

"What choice? Every day, thousands of us perish—natural causes, people like you, bad fish—leaving us reduced. Time is running out quickly. When the patient is bleeding, you apply tourniquet."

I nodded as if I gave a shit and was processing everything carefully. "And this has *what* to do with me, exactly?" I said carefully, trying to guide him where I wanted him.

He sighed, standing up. With an easy motion, he set his coffee down on the table, stepped over to the smaller table, and picked up the Roon and clips, turning and holding them out to me.

"Before you hurt someone," he said, cigarette waggling up and down. "For fuck's sake, Avery, you are not a *prisoner*. I have full confidence you will choose to help us.

"There is one problem with using the avatar stock: All are tied to Director Marin's old network." I groaned inwardly. Richard Fucking Marin. Everything had gone to hell the first day I'd met that artificial bastard, and here he was still haunting me.

I'm hurt, Avery, his ghost or imprint or whatever whispered in my head, like he'd been doing for years. *Your friendship has meant the world to me. Am I really destroyed in real life?*

"Marin now exists only as a scatter of atoms floating through the atmosphere." He sighed. "The avatar models are all System Police, and all are tied to an annual signal from Marin's private key. This to prevent mutinies, you see—if Marin cannot send signal, the whole avatar network shuts down. Marin was destroyed right at the end—near a year ago." He shrugged again. "This means all the avatar stock we have collected—as well as every System Pig still walking around in Europe, trying to hold the sand castle together—will shut down and be totally inoperative in about three months." He picked up his coffee and spread his arms. "So you see: problem."

I nodded, checking over the Roon. "Your confidence in me makes me want to be a better person, Grish," I said. "But I'm still waiting to hear why my friend was killed and why a fucking Angel has been pushing his fat fingers into my head for three fucking weeks." I racked the chamber and clicked off the safety. "And then maybe you could explain why I shouldn't go back in the other room and make that piece of shit's head explode."

Grisha nodded as if this were a reasonable request he'd been expecting. From what I remembered about Grisha, maybe it was; he was a Techie, smart and skilled, and he was someone who could blow your head off and not flinch. He was probably the most dangerous bastard, one on one, in the whole damn world.

As I moved back toward the front of the room, he moved with me on the other side of the table. None of the other Techies moved, but they didn't get out of my way, either.

"Marin was, you know this, a digital construct. A scan of the once-flesh Cal Ruberto, made into a god. He had programmed limits on his behaviors—this you know also, as your first interaction with him was designed to create a scenario that allowed him to elevate his security status and disable some of those restraints. The Joint Council knew enough to fear Marin when they created him, Avery, so they not only set up these limits, they programmed him to have override codes. In case he slipped his chains." He waved the coffee around. "If there had been a functioning Joint Council when Marin pulled his stunt with you, this code would certainly have been used. It was not, obviously, and until recently the code itself was thought to be lost. It was not lost."

Without warning, he took three quick steps and put himself in front of the door leading to the second container and put one hand up in a placating gesture. In honor of the friendship we had, I kept the Roon aimed at the floor and stopped for a moment, clenching my teeth.

"Avery, it is firmly established that *you* know where this code can be retrieved. With Marin's override, we can disable his safeties on the avatar network and utilize the avatar stock safely."

I opened my mouth, thought better of it, and then frowned, all thoughts of what I'd been doing gone. "That's fucking insane, Grisha. I don't know where Dick Marin's fucking *override* codes are."

You don't, Dolores Salgado whispered in my head, and I froze, my heart pounding. *But I do.*

XIII

THAT IS ... UNFORTUNATE

I imagined Salgado walled up in a cell, behind inches and inches of old brick, her voice barely audible, muffled. Then I looked at Grisha.

"Step aside," I said slowly, keeping every muscle under conscious control to stop myself from leaping for his throat. "I am going to kill that fucking thing in there." The Pusher had killed Remy. I couldn't change that, but I could make him wish he hadn't.

Grisha smiled sadly and shook his head. "Avery, I do not imagine I can trade body blows with you. I have seen you work. But you cannot be permitted to kill that man until we have debriefed him. Until we have debriefed *you*."

I heard the scrape of a chair behind me, and ticked my head slightly. "Tell your friend with the cattle prod he's not going to touch me."

Grisha didn't say anything, but his eyes moved over my head and he shook his head just slightly. He looked back at me and shrugged. "I am not moving, Avery. You will have to attack me."

I swallowed with difficulty; it felt like I had someone alive in my throat, clawing its way up. I couldn't bring anyone back to life. I couldn't go back ten years and do everything differently, but I could kill the fat old bastard in a cage in the next room. I could kill him so hard it left a fucking mark, and it was all I wanted to do. The Angels. I didn't need Grisha to draw me a fucking picture. I was sure the Russian had info I could use—he always did—but I didn't need it that badly. I'd find them.

"Grish—"

With a sudden jerk of his arm, he dashed his lukewarm coffee into my face.

"Avery, *listen*. We are not talking about your wounds, your losses. Hell, we have all *lost*. Do you imagine you are the only person who has survived a global war? The only person who has fought and killed?"

I stood there in numb shock, coffee dripping off my face. Grisha had never done anything like that, and I didn't know how to react. He shook his head. "You cannot be this *arrogant*." He tossed his empty cup to the floor with a savage disdain that made me hesitate. "This is not about you. The whole world is dying, Avery. The *whole fucking world*. You *will* not be allowed to derail this process for petty revenge."

I wanted him to *move*, to let me past, but I found I could not lift my gun against Grisha. We had been through a lot, and he had been a true friend, back in Chengara and afterward, even if he had tried to kill me once. For a second or two we both just stood there, and I could hear the harsh rasp of my breath in and out of my nose.

I looked down at my hands. "Fuck, Grisha," I said slowly, begging. "I don't fucking *know* anything."

I heard Salgado—a whisper in my head, silent and clear, years ago, back when I was being tortured in Chengara Penitentiary for information I didn't know *then*, either: I *know that Marin did not suspend* all *of his programmed overrides. I know that there are bare-metal panic codes built into his design. I do not know the overrides myself. But I know the identity of the one person who* does.

The person who *does,* I thought.

I looked back up at him, and for a moment we just looked at each other, and I felt my shoulders roll. I couldn't fuck with Grisha. He'd never done me wrong, and I could not ignore that.

"Salgado," I said.

He nodded. "Salgado." He reached up and put a hand on my shoulder. "I am sorry, Avery. We must intrude upon you again."

"Dolores Salgado," the Indian Techie, named Lokprakash—who everyone wisely called Lok—read from a thick hard copy. I hadn't seen so much paper in years. "Original undersecretary, originally serving under Councilman Cavendish. Prior to Unification, she was retired." His accent was English, bitten off with cheerful relish, as if words were fun. "She served as undersecretary for the Australian Department and generally got good grades, right up until Marin arrested her under authority of the Emergency Stabilization Directive, colloquially known as the Monk Act, as it was issued during the Monk Riots that followed the collapse of the Electric Church." He looked up at me and *winked*. I resolved to break his nose at the earliest opportunity.

I was not secretary, Salgado suddenly said in my mind. For years she'd been mostly silent, hiding, and now she was ready to talk and showed no signs of stopping. *I drew my salary from the State Department, but I was no damn diplomat.*

"Those were the days, yes?" Grisha suddenly interjected, shaking with suppressed coughing. "When there were such things as formalities like official directives?" He sighed, swallowing phlegm and bile. "Civilization."

We were all seated at the tight wooden table, and I'd finally accepted a cup of coffee, which sat in front of me like regret in lukewarm liquid form. I tried to concentrate, but I kept seeing Remy, thinking back on it. Trying to see where I should have anticipated a trap, protected the kid. Belling telling me he was *bait*. The old bastard still clinging to some hope that he'd come back, get back on top— that he'd survive. Otherwise he might have tipped me off. Belling and I weren't friends, and I'd come there to kill him, but we were both *professionals*.

"She was processed through Chengara Pen and never heard from again, but so were several thousand other people, not to mention the people who churned through the other five EOT installations Marin had built around the world." He paused and cocked his head. "There may be cold iron under those prisons with thousands of human minds burned onto them, come to think of it."

I shook my head. "My impression was they uploaded as fast as they cracked us open."

Lok leaned forward slightly. His hair was long but stiff and slightly curled, standing up from his head in a glossy black wave that shifted gently like grass when he moved. "So, you were really there? You really got seventy-nined?"

I cocked my head and squinted at him, duplicating his own expression, and then I leaned forward, slapped both hands onto his head, and smashed his face down onto the table. He bounced up and back, ending up sitting perfectly straight and staring at me in complete shock for a moment while his nose sent out a thick stream of dark blood.

"Avery!" Grisha shouted, his tone almost amused. "You are among friends, you animal."

I pointed at Lok. "That's for the rod, back there," I said, leaning back and extracting one of the cigarettes they'd been good enough to give me and sticking it between my lips. It was like I'd never gone several years without smoking. "That's today's lesson: You cattle prod someone, you better keep them down." I smiled as Grisha handed the still-stunned Lok a rag. "Be happy, comrade. We're even now." I picked up the communal lighter from the table. "You done with the history lesson?" I looked around. "I've got Dolores Salgado in my head, yeah. Years ago she told me she knew about Marin's codes, sure. I forgot, because people kept shooting me and arresting me and pressing me into the fucking army and I always had better fucking things to do than worry about Director Marin. I got processed. Or almost processed. They got, like, eighty percent of me, and I got a head full of psychic backwash." I lit up and sent a plume of smoke into the air. "Only three of them still talk to me, though." I decided not to mention Marin or Squalor's ghosts; this bunch might get excited and gang rape me on the floor if those names started floating about. "You want to tell me why the Angels decide to stop trying to execute me and send a Pusher to kill my... kill my friend and follow me around?"

Lok, holding the rag to his nose, half stood, swayed a little, and sat down heavily. I watched Grisha, who was clearly in charge. He looked at Lok and sighed, then looked back at me, his pinched face cheerful behind his stupid glasses.

"They know, somehow, of Salgado inside you. They realize that even if you were a man who submitted to torture—and all men have a breaking point, Avery—that you likely do not even know the information they seek. There is a theory that Salgado would feel all your sufferings if you were handled correctly, but this is theory. They might torture you until death and still get nothing useful, if she is walled off and impervious to your own sufferings." He smiled. "They believe a prolonged exposure might yield results. Subtle Psionic pressure over weeks or months might reveal to them what Salgado knows, or allow the Pusher to access Salgado directly. They did not count on your propensity for being kidnapped and sold on the black markets, however."

I shook my head, sucking in smoke. "She doesn't know the codes. She knows who has—or had—them." I shrugged. "This was years ago, and just about everyone who was alive years ago is dead now, I think." I winked at Lok. "Or will be soon, eh?"

"That scans," Lok said, his voice muffled by the rag. I'd knocked some of the insane cheer out of him, at least, and I was impressed that he was still conscious and able to speak. "These codes would have been created when the Joint Council was still conscious and in control. As an undersecretary, she would not have clearance for the information. This likely emboldened Marin; he probably thought *no one* had his overrides. No one still alive."

We sat for a moment, quiet. A smog of cigarette smoke had filled the container, making everything hazy. Grisha cleared his throat and sat forward. "Avery, have you asked her?"

I blinked. I'd spent years trying to shut the fucking ghosts up, to keep them at bay. The idea of purposefully asking Dolores Salgado a question seemed...crazy. I stared at Grisha for a moment and then closed my eyes, taking a deep drag on my cigarette.

Well, Dolores? I know you can hear everything. You got anything to tell me?

She didn't respond for a moment, and when she did she was loud and clear, like she'd been living in my head, a turtle in its shell. *You won't like it, Avery.*

I don't like anything anymore, Dolores, I thought. *Just tell me who has these fucking codes so I can get on with it.*

If you thought about it, you'd guess, Avery. It's Garda, of course. You didn't think he was just an assassin, *did you?*

For a second, I went calm and cold. Without effort I slammed down an imaginary glass shield, trapping Salgado outside, giving me a second of perfect silence. Michaleen Garda. Otherwise known as Cainnic Orel, the legend. Otherwise known as the last person I was going to kill before shuffling off.

I opened my eyes. "It's Orel," I said. "It's Canny Orel."

Grisha nodded, frowning. "Orel," he breathed, coughing once, twice, and then breathing again, leaning back. "That is...unfortunate."

                         * * *

I found Adora outside SPS's cluster of interconnected shipping containers, leaning against one of them and smoking, staring off into the distance. She'd cleaned up a little, her face and hands were free of grime, but her hair and clothes were almost pitch-black, hanging off her with greasy weight. She was as beautiful as ever, though, her still, calm face all delicate lines that somehow came together into a perfectly asymmetrical pattern, a fine mouth pursed to blow smoke into the air, her green eyes slitted in the light.

When I was close, she turned and smiled at me, her face opening up and turning bright. She reached out with one hand and squeezed my shoulder. I found that after being pressed against her chastely for weeks on end, her touch was comforting.

"Cigarette?" she said, holding up a case. "They are rich with them here. I did not smoke much before, but this is my fourth one in half an hour. I am dizzy."

I shook my head. "They gave me a bunch, too."

She frowned down at her feet. "I am sorry about... about your friend. For all of it. I—"

"Wasn't your fault," I snapped. I didn't want to talk about Remy.

"What will you do?"

I leaned against the wall next to her and pushed my hands into my pockets. "What I came here to do."

She snorted. "Kill everyone."

I nodded. "For starters."

She tossed her cigarette away and pushed herself from the wall, shoving her hands into the pockets of her filthy overalls. My arms jerked spastically as I almost reached out to touch her, pull her back. I didn't know if it was just being cooped up with her for so long, or if she was the first woman I'd met in a while who wasn't a murderous robot or cyborg, but I suddenly didn't want her to be anywhere but next to me.

In the end, though, I held my arms tightly against me and said nothing. She took three steps and stopped. She didn't turn around.

"I go north," she said. "Toledo. My people are from there, back in the mists of time."

I nodded, thinking back on our long evening in the *Daniel Krokos*. "I remember."

"I think I would see it. Perhaps you will come find me when you are finished."

I smiled at her back. "You'd want me to?"

She started walking again. "There is no one else left."

PART III

PART III

XIV

YOU GET AROUND

"Try not to kill this one," Grisha complained, flicking his cigarette to the street even as he pulled another from behind his ear and placed it between his lips. "At least not immediately, yes?"

"We got what we needed from that ancient piece of shit in Cadiz," I said easily. Grisha had been complaining for a week about shooting the Pusher. His grousing had gotten familiar and I almost enjoyed it, the way he sawed on and on about things you couldn't change. It was like rain. You just took it for granted and forgot it was there. "You're lucky I gave you three days."

He grunted in dissatisfaction. I got the feeling Grisha didn't get disobeyed too often these days. He liked to sigh on and on about how SPS was a communal organization without a leader, but Grish had four Techies who followed him around like puppies, and I'd seen him snap his fingers and bring some serious resources to bear. I'd been everywhere over the last few years, and there were whole cities, whole regions where no one had any control, where things were fucking chaos. Grisha and SPS had _resources_. First there had been the efficient and kind of satisfying torture of the old Pusher, who'd squealed like a pig with just a _tiny_ Push, terrified at finding himself, for the first time in his life, without his usual power to make assholes like me dance. Grisha had produced some nightmare-inducing devices, applied with a clinical and emotionless efficiency that was worse, somehow, than the devices themselves. There'd been a ragged-looking black box with several thick cables sprouting from it like some terrible plastic and silicone plant, each terminating in a copper clamp that was attached to the old fuck's _head_ in various places, and which made him just scream and vibrate while Grisha stood over him, smoke leaking up in a thick stream from his mouth and nose. There'd been a small, shiny black capsule inserted into the old Pusher's ear, making his eyes bug out, blood streaming suddenly from his nose. He hadn't screamed that time, but that had been worse, because I got the feeling he _wanted_ to but _couldn't_.

There'd been four-wheelers to take us from Cadiz into Italy. There'd been more SPS members to act as muscle and lookouts. There'd been yen when yen was being accepted, and there'd been barter when that was the best they could do. Grisha snapped his fingers and things got fucking done. I hadn't seen much of that recently, and found I liked it.

"We know, what? That he does not know what an Angel is. He had no mark, yes. That he works for the remnants of the SSF." He laughed humorlessly. "I am thinking, good, this is good. We will ask him who his contact is with the System Pigs. We will get details. Perhaps he knows things we do not even know to ask about! I go into the room and there is Avery, there is a dead Pusher, and there are no more questions."

I shrugged, picturing Remy on the floor of the hospital in Mexico City, picturing me stepping over him. "What was he going to tell us, exactly? The cops want Marin's override codes because in a few weeks their avatars are going to shut down and they'll hibernate until the fucking sun swells up big and red and eats this fucking hellhole. That's easy."

Grisha grunted again, irritated, but let it drift. He'd developed a stoop, moving with the slow, oiled grace I remembered but bent over, his shoulders up and his head low, hands perpetually in his pockets. Getting old, I figured. Apparently that's all anyone was doing—those of us the old Monks used to call *meat* just aging away, and even the Avatars in the world had an expiration date just a few weeks away. He'd developed a little cough, too, a wet-sounding gurgle that punctuated every other sentence. I stole a glance at him as we moved along opposite sides of the square, the sun beating down on the top of my head; he was just strolling, hands deep in the pockets of his jumpsuit, glasses glinting in the light and cigarette bouncing in his mouth. It was like one eternal cigarette, always there.

I looked across the square again. A group of fat, shirt-less old men were sitting outside a dilapidated old bar, fanning themselves and shouting simultaneously in Italian. It was a tiny little town, a speck; one second we'd been bouncing along in the four-wheeler Grisha had summoned out of the thin air, thick brush and ragged-looking trees everywhere, and the next we'd been creeping up a shadowed, cool stairway, emerging into a tiny village of faded stone buildings that looked like the System had forgotten about it. A few dozen feet from the group, a man in a showy white suit sat alone at a tiny table, a small cup of what was passing for coffee these days steaming in front of him. His suit looked light and cool, but was wrinkled and grimy, stained. He was just sitting there with his eyes closed, hands folded peacefully on his belly, but that didn't mean anything.

I looked around, scanning rooftops and balconies, places I'd put lookouts and snipers if I were going to sit in the middle of an open square drinking fake coffee like nothing could touch me. The town was all pale, yellowed stone and red slate roofs missing tiles, half crumbled. But you got the feeling the buildings had been half crumbled for a thousand years, unchanged. The central square was big and roomy but once you stepped off you got trapped in narrow, winding little roadlets; Grisha had Lok and four other members of SPS, each armed with oddball single-action rifles they'd scrounged from somewhere, positioned at several of the side streets, but we couldn't man the entire square.

As we approached, the old men stopped talking and looked at us; I wondered if their silence was a signal to our guy that someone was coming. I'd been in Italy before, but it had been a different world: damp, buried by water, everything salty. This little scrub of a town was dry and warm, everything dusty. An old monastery overlooked the square from a mild hill rising up behind us, looming.

We walked past the group, and when we were a few dusty feet away from the man in the white suit, he spoke up.

"You must be lost," he said without opening his eyes.

"Because no one in the whole history of the world has ever come to Fiesole on purpose."

I froze for a second, my hands in the pockets of my coat, which had been cut to let me pull my gun directly from the hip holster I'd started to favor. "I know you," I said without thinking, amazed. "I've seen you before."

He was made of a melty red plastic, his skin scaly and angry everywhere. His hairless head was a mass of scarred tissue and rippled, ruined flesh, and he was the cop I'd met in Hong Kong when I'd been there hunting the God Augment, the one organizing resistance to everyone, the one who told me he'd be King of Hong Kong before it was all over. He opened his eyes and looked up, grinning.

"Avery Cates," he said. "Holy *shit*, you get around."

"You have met?" Grisha said. One thing I liked about Grish: He never felt the need to pretend he knew more than he did.

"Couple times," the cop said, grinning. His teeth and eyes were startlingly white and clear in the midst of his ruined face. His hands were gloves of twisted, scorched flesh, too, and I felt itchy and painful just watching him as he picked up his cup of coffee just to show us how unconcerned he was. He sipped his coffee with his eyes on me. "What's the matter, Cates? Don't recognize me? You did have someone else on your mind when we met." He set his cup down and extended his scaly hand. "Horatio Gall, former major, System Security Force."

I was surprised into a smile. "*Gall*," I breathed. "You were in Venice, working bodyguard for that old asshole." Slowly I pulled my hand from my pocket and reached out to take his; it was dry and hot, which was probably my imagination. "You took a bomb there."

He nodded gaily, indicating his face with the other hand. "Ain't that the fucking understatement of the century. Don't worry, I don't hold grudges. That little incident clarified things for me." He took his hand back and raised it into the air, gesturing at the silent group of old men up the street. "That's why I'm sitting here in my own skin, instead of a silicone robot."

There was movement behind us, and I whirled to find three of the fat old men hauling another table and two more chairs over to us from the interior of one of the two-story buildings along the square. They moved silently, leaving behind another two steaming cups and walking away without a word or glance our way. The fucking System Pigs—even burned-up, resigned ones like Gall—never fucking changed. Everywhere they went, they put under the boot.

Grisha and I looked at each other, and then he shrugged and sat down. "You have expected us, then?"

Gall nodded. "Just for the last few hours. You were spotted bouncing along in one of those wheeled vehicles." He shrugged. "I don't have satellites and wireless power anymore, men, but I've got fifteen old coots who call me *padrone* and who can sit on a roof with an old sniper scope and give me a warning." He spread his hands. "Okay, Fiesole has about thirty residents and one business, which you're sitting in. So you didn't come here for the wine, which tastes like fucking vinegar, or the food, of which there isn't any, or the sights, which you just saw on your way in. So," he said and spread his hands, "you came to see me."

I shrugged at Grisha, and he plucked his cigarette from his mouth as I shook one of my own out. "We need to make contact with the SSF, the police, up in Berlin. We do not have any routes of communication with them anymore, and even entering central Europe is a chancy thing." He pointed his cigarette at Gall. "I understand you have maintained some presence within the SSF."

Gall grinned, his white teeth shocking. "You speak English like you learned it from a mime, pal. *Presence.* I was Marin's attaché, for fuck's sake. Every cop in the world reported to *me.* Of *course* I still have some people. Besides," he said and sat forward, suddenly conspiratorial, "I'm not the only old badge who didn't like the whole avatar business, who cut ties and ran—or tried to. There's a bunch of active duties up north who tried to run and got caught by Marin's murder machine before they could. We share a mind-set, you know?"

I leaned forward. "So you can help us get in touch."

He nodded. "Can help, yes. *Will* help, maybe. Despite our deep and ancient comradeship, Mr. Cates, as men who have been fucked by Dick Marin, I have to be crude and ask you what's in it for me?"

Grisha cocked his head. "Mr. Gall, this is not some heist scheme, or an assassination for yen."

Gall winked at me. "This is gonna be good, huh?"

"Mr. Gall—"

He held up his hand. "Look, I've dealt with SPS before—I know you fucking Techies. Everything is for the greater good. Everything is to save the world. I don't *care.* You want me to make introductions, give me a reason."

I was on the verge of leaning forward and giving my old friend Gall a *reason*, but Grisha surprised me by burping a harsh laugh and putting a hand on my chest like he'd foreseen my near future. "Mr. Gall, I do not believe yen will be worth anything this time five years from now, so you would be welcome to as much of it as we can find."

Gall grinned again, lowering his hand and picking up his cup to toast us. "Now that's more like it. Paper?"

Grisha nodded, picking up his own cup and holding it up. "Naturally."

Gall opened his mouth, but behind us there was a sudden commotion, all the old men shouting in Italian. Grisha and I leaped to our feet, but Gall just sat for a moment, then shouted something back.

"What?" I snapped, pushing my hand into my pocket and palming my gun.

Gall grimaced. "Angels."

XV

YOU GOT MY PERMISSION
TO SHOOT THE LOT

"How many?" Grisha demanded, jumping up and signaling his people with a single, brisk flex of his upraised hand, the sort of confident gesture some people just came to naturally, people who assumed—always correctly—that they would be obeyed immediately, and without question. I'd known a couple of people like that in my time, and I'd never been one. People always argued with me; I usually had to hold a gun to their heads to make things happen, or inflict a few flesh wounds.

Gall shouted something, and the old men—busy carrying their tables and chairs from the street into one of the small buildings along the north side of the square—shouted back in a jangly chorus.

"Five," Gall announced, picking up his coffee, tossing its contents to the cobbled street and tucking the delicate white cup into one pocket while producing a huge, chrome-plated auto from another. The monster gleamed in the sun and looked big enough to kill elephants. It still wasn't as big as Remy's huge revolver, and that made me picture Remy again, crumpled on the dirty floor of Belling's room. I spun to fix the layout of the square in my head, thinking that the Pusher who'd killed Remy maybe wasn't an Angel, and had been working for the cops. But the Angels were Psionics, and they would do, for now.

The north side of the square was a row of attached buildings, weathered and dark; the south was a bigger building set back from the street; either direction led to the crush of buildings that was this town. A good place to get lost, and if there were more Angels than Gall's men had spotted, it was likely they'd be filtering through the narrow, dim streets, sneaking up on us. I didn't think that was likely, though; I'd never seen more than a few Angels in one place. The world was dying, says Grisha, and manpower was an issue for everyone.

That meant northeast—the town sat on a hill, and there was a sheltered, hidden approach a half mile away, leading up an ancient stone staircase from the valley below. Anyone could creep up that way and be on the main road of the town before we knew it. Once on the main approach they'd be exposed, and if we could risk getting close we'd be able to pick them off pretty easily, but the moment we were seen, either we'd be in the air courtesy of the Tele-Ks, or we'd just shoot ourselves in the head courtesy of the Pushers.

"Cover," I said, spinning back to Gall and Grisha. Lok was leading Grisha's four troops at a run from obscured alleyways. "We have to get out of sight."

Gall nodded. "Follow the old bastards into the dining room, fellas. We own that building and it's got windows on three sides."

We all started trotting toward the building, Lok and the other SPS people falling in with us like they'd been trained to do it their whole lives.

"Seems like," Gall said, breathing hard as we ran, "every time I see you, someone is trying to kill you, Cates. Isn't it supposed to be the other way around?"

I laughed—I couldn't help it. It *was* fucking ridiculous. "You live as long as me, things start to skew around, you know?"

As we gained the dark rectangle of the building, Gall stepped aside with his old System Pig reflexes and covered us with his shiny gun, eyes bright white in the setting sun of his face. He grinned, not looking at me as he scanned the street. "Tell me about it. You know how many meetings I took in Old New York about you?"

I pushed into the building and a second later Gall was in behind me, pulling the door shut with a boom that shook the walls and lowering a thick metal bar across it.

"Up," I said, running my augment-brightened eyes over the cluttered first floor, which contained the disorderly pile of chairs and tables and nothing else aside from dust and a few scattering rats. The house had been retrofitted with an escalator at some point, which had flattened into a slide when the power had disappeared. "Forget the door, we'll post at the stairs."

Grisha was ahead of me, impatiently gesturing his people to the old escalator. Lok made it up with impressive speed, and by the time I'd reached the bottom I was watching Grisha's ass wiggle its way up. I did my best to look professional as I ascended, but my boots kept slipping and I ended up having to half crawl my way onto the second floor, ears burning, and I popped up angry, spinning

around to look over our little team as Gall cursed and
screamed at his personal bodyguard of fat old men with
no English, each one huffing his way up the old escalator
like their heart rates hadn't been this high in fifty years.

"Anyone has a heart attack," I shouted at Gall, "push
'im down the slide." I turned to Grisha's team and eyed
their long, slender rifles. "Who's fastest on the reload?"

They hesitated, all five of them looking at Grisha, who
was checking over his handgun, a perfectly serviceable
old Hamada. When he glanced up to find them all looking
at him, he frowned.

"What the fuck are you all waiting for?" he pointed at
me. "This man has *died* before, and here he stands. Do
whatever he tells you to do."

As one, the five Techies looked back at me. After
another moment of hesitation, Lok and a short, extremely
hairy man whose beard was inches away from achieving
sentience raised their hands.

I nodded and pointed. "At the top of the slide. Don't
hesitate—anything bigger than a rat moves down there,
shoot, reload, shoot again. Pour it on as fast as you can until
you don't see anything anymore. Don't *wait.* If they see you,
fix you in their minds, they'll have you. Try to anchor yourself, because if it's a Tele-K, you're going for a ride."

They both blinked, but then pushed through the crowd
to take position, and I gave Grisha credit for at least having people with half a brain under him.

"The rest of you, on the windows. Stay low. If your
head pops up, bad things are gonna happen to you. Try to
stay out of sight and only take shots that make sense."

I spun and looked at Gall's geriatric waiters. They had
immediately crowded against the far wall, away from the

windows, which gave me some hope that they weren't as genetically retarded as I'd feared. I looked and found Gall peering owlishly out a tiny triangular window in the center of the room.

"These guys of yours got anything to offer?"

Gall shook his head. "They're useless. If I'd had time to think, I would have pushed them out the windows. You got my permission to shoot the lot if they get in the way."

I nodded and edged back toward the windows, angling my head carefully, trying to glimpse the square outside without exposing myself. For a few minutes we all just crouched in the sweat-thick air of the second floor, breathing hard and stretching our necks for any hints.

This is what happens, Dick Marin decided to whisper in my head at that moment, *when the Psionic population is left to its own devices. That's why we snatched every one of them we could find off the fucking streets.*

I blinked and resisted the urge to remind Dick that he was dead, that the imprint I'd somehow acquired back in Chengara was probably the last vestige of him left in the universe.

"How far were they?" I hissed in Gall's direction.

He shouted something over his shoulder and one of the old men shouted back. "Five minutes, he says."

"Then where the hell are they?"

"We are here."

I spun around, crouching low with my Roon on the group of old men across the room. One of them had spoken, the voice deep and smoked, old as sin. They were just the same group of men who'd been sitting out on the street, muttering in Italian, but this voice had a distinct, clear Creole accent.

"What the fuck?" Gall snapped. "One of you fuckers speaks *English* and you never thought to tell me? I ought to shoot you all right now."

One of them pushed his way to the front of the pack. They were all swarthy, short men with broad chests and distended bellies, their faces leathery and sunworn. This one was maybe an inch taller than the others and had a jaunty strip of red cloth tied around his neck.

"I have Traveled from t'outside into t'is body," he said, his accent lazy and fat. I had a sudden memory flash, back to Hong Kong, to a girl with glowing blue eyes apologizing because she'd been *hacked*. But that had been someone with a fistful of tech implanted into her brain on wireless networks, hacked by Techies the same way circuits had been hacked for decades. This was an old man who'd lived his whole life in a tiny village, who'd probably never even heard of SPS or the Angels. "I have come to talk to Mr. Cates before we begin hostilities."

"This is new," Grisha said almost conversationally. His tone of awed calm told me Grish's geeky bones had been rattled by this new phenomenon, and I worried for a moment that if he had to make a choice between saving my ass and destroying some new species of Psionic he wouldn't make the wrong choice.

"Who are you?" I said, my voice coming out phlegmy and cracked and making me flush a little in shame. "Every time I've met you folks before, you've tried to kill me."

The old man ticked his head to look at me. "I am the Angels. You may call me Mikhail. Yes, you have been condemned."

Marin giggled inside me and repeated something he'd said to me before, long ago: *I'll be judge, I'll be jury, said*

*cunning old Fury. I'll try the whole cause, and condemn
you to death.*

"There has been a reconsideration of your case, Mr.
Cates," the Angel said through the poor old man. "I am
here to negotiate your pardon."

XVI

YOU'RE GONNA HAVE TO BE MORE SPECIFIC

I smiled, not feeling anywhere near amused. "My *pardon*?"

The old man didn't smile. His fellows were staring at him like he'd turned into something hairy and growling, and I wondered briefly if they'd end up slitting his throat just to be safe later. After a moment he spread his hands in a slow, deliberate gesture that was epically *wrong*, like every tiny muscle adjustment had to be beamed over from a short distance away. It was like watching a stop-motion video of someone spreading their hands.

I suddenly wished fervently that he *never* try to smile. I wasn't a strong man anymore. Something like that might break me.

"Mr. Cates, you have access to information—we were not aware of this before. You have access to information—"

I put the Roon on him. "Too fucking late. I already *accessed* that information, and shared it with my friends."

The old man glanced at Grisha for a second, and then

back at me. "Mr. Cates, the members of SPS are *not* your friends, whatever they may tell you."

I nodded. "I've led a lonely life."

"Nevertheless," he said as if I hadn't spoken. "We still have a deal to proffer. You have informed SPS of the location of Director Marin's override codes. They intend to use these codes to clear the SSF networks of auto-shutdown and anti-mutiny routines, making it possible to load organic consciousnesses into old avatar stock, yes?" He nodded, a dozen individual ticks of his head, as if I'd answered. "We cannot delete information from the world easily; this we have learned to our regret. So we have another proposal. No doubt you are now working with SPS to organize the discovery of these codes?"

This time he paused and stared at me, as if expecting me to confirm this. "You're running out of time, buddy. I'm easily bored these days."

If they thought there was anything we could discuss that would keep me from going after Michaleen, that would stop me from forcing a conversation with that old bastard, they didn't know a fucking thing about me.

"Mr. Cates," he said in a firmer, faster voice, "we are schismatics within our own order, and have been ejected. This is because despite your history of violence against your own species, of callous disregard for human life and your ongoing affinity for the very technology that has brought us all down low, we are prepared to lift our sentence of death from you. For this, we ask that you abandon your path. Men of your…talents are rare in these days. You have proven this in surviving our attempts to bring you to god's eternal justice."

God. I didn't hear that word much anymore. It reminded me of the Monks.

"Aid us in preserving the override codes," he said with a straight face. "Prevent their use. Use your talent for violence and intrusion, your disregard for human life in the service of god's ultimate plan for us, and you will be spared judgment. We will then also pledge to defend you, to honor your service. You alone in the world will be allowed to live out his years to their natural extent." He paused and blinked in that bizarre stop-motion way, and I wondered why in fuck the Angel pulling this poor asshole's strings would bother to *blink* for him. "Until you die, of course, Mr. Cates. We cannot make deals for *god*, after all, and you will be forced to answer for your crimes then, if not now."

I stood there with my gun on him, staring. A deal. The Angels had just offered me a fucking *deal*. I tried to think of how many of them I'd killed over the last few years— eight? A dozen? Now all I had to do to earn their fucking *pardon* was work for them. Everyone thought I was just there to do their dirty work. The Angels, Grisha, fucking Canny Orel in his little god suit in Split. I was just a fucking windup toy—point me in the direction of things you wanted destroyed.

Avery Cates, Destroyer of Worlds, huh? Dick Marin whispered, sounding amused.

"Mr. Gall," I said evenly, keeping my eyes on the old man. "Can you spot these motherfuckers out there?" I didn't know anything about this neat new Psionic ability—whether the old man could survive it or if he'd just fall over, vacant, when the Angel abandoned him, or what the range was on popping into other people's skulls, but I was willing to make a little side bet with the cosmos that it wasn't far. I was also willing to bet this little trick of Traveling required some fucking concentration. I could barely remind myself to breathe and walk at the same time, so I couldn't imagine how hard it was to Push yourself into someone else's body and do anything else at all.

I heard him moving behind me, breathing heavily and grunting as he struggled to peer out the windows without exposing himself to any Tele-Ks that might be spotting on the windows.

"Sure, sure, I see 'em," he said after a moment. "Three ugly bastards in dark suits. One woman in the middle, tall, long salt-and-pepper hair, standing there with her eyes closed."

"Do me a favor and throw some bullets at them." I nodded at the old man. "Tell god this," I said, and pulled the trigger, aiming for his feet and chewing up the floorboards.

The crowd of old men scattered, screeching in Italian, and there was a scream, suddenly, in the near distance, and then the roar of half a dozen guns being fired simultaneously behind me. I vaulted over the railing and landed awkwardly on the escalator, managing to avoid a fall by taking a handful of splinters off the makeshift railing, and skidded onto the floor just as the front door was torn open, framing a tall, skinny figure. For a moment we stared at each other; I couldn't see his face, which was bathed in shadow, but I somehow had an impression of dumb shock.

"You don't have to be fucking psychic," I said. The figure took a step toward me, raising his hands, and I fired three times, making him dance and jig and fall in toward me, landing on his face. People who didn't try murder on a regular basis usually thought they were inventing everything right there on the spot, like some sort of murder prodigy.

As I stood there congratulating myself on being a genius, something huge filled the now-empty doorway, and my HUD suddenly sharpened up, my laboring augments kicking in. Everything slowed down just a tiny bit; I shifted my weight and launched myself to the right just as a large crate crashed through the door, widening it by a couple of inches and shattering on the floor. I landed on the gritty floorboards and rolled until I hit the front wall, where I braced myself and pushed up into a crouch. The gunfire above me was still being poured on; there was a clear pattern as a thunderous roil of shots would trail off to a single *pop-pop-pop*—the rifles having their say, and then Gall emptying a clip while they reloaded. Gall had said just three, and I'd nailed one, but Psionic Actives were worth a dozen assholes.

"The world is dying, Mr. Cates!" a woman's deep voice shouted from outside, the same round Creole accent the old man had sported—our Traveler, I decided, giving the term a capital letter. "You know this. In fifty years, there will be no one left, only the sullen monuments of arrogance we leave behind. We are here to bring meaning to these final years of humanity, to judge those who have ensured its destruction. You cannot prevent this extinction, no matter what your friends in SPS have told you. If you try to derail god's plan, he will simply find a new route."

Hell, I thought. *Why is it that the crazies always find god, and always talk so fucking fancy? Any theories, Squalor?*

The ghost of Dennis Squalor, who'd founded the

Electric Church and been the world's first digital intelligence, remained silent.

"They want you to *protect* Orel, Mr. Cates," she went on. "They wish you to find him and collect him, and then he will make a deal, and he will *live.* They will grant him protection in return for the information he possesses. These are your *friends.*"

Another rain of bullets from above, and I duckwalked over to the doorway and leaned out carefully, trying to spot our Spooks. I wanted to kill them with my bare hands, feel the bones in their necks snapping, see the terror in their eyes. I wanted them to feel what Remy had felt, shot while I lay there unconscious. I wanted them to feel what Gleason had felt, being eaten alive by tiny robots, bloating and swelling as her body was devoured. I wanted them all to feel it. I wanted *Michaleen* to feel it. It seemed like Michaleen had been in my life forever, since before I was born. I'd been hearing the name my whole life, and I wondered, suddenly, if it had truly been a coincidence that Wa Belling had showed up in London all those years ago, claiming to *be* Orel and inserting himself into my Squalor operation.

The cosmos didn't do coincidence. There was a Rail.

The square outside looked exactly as it had, empty and dusty. I could see only a chunk of it in front of me and off to my left, a disorienting slice of the world, but if I leaned out farther to get a better view I'd more than likely be in the air. I stayed still and forced myself to breathe, trying to will my HUD to stop flickering and either disappear or at least stabilize. Patience, I would have told Remy: Patience kept you alive. When you had the urge to run, to blast away, to throw away ammo, take a breath and wait.

And Remy would have said, Fuck it, I can't die this way.

As I crouched there, a medium-sized woman with red, almost unnatural-looking hair streaming behind her ran across my field of vision and ducked into the large building across the way. I could just see her white shirt in the dark doorway almost directly across from me, but I had no shot while I hid behind the wall. I saw myself squaring around to take a bead on her and being sucked into the air, sailing gracefully until I smashed into something ungracefully.

I turned and looked at the Spook facedown on the floor, a big guy, broad in the shoulders and sporting the same shade of unbelievable red hair, his black pants damp with piss. I grunted my way back from the doorway and hooked the cuff of his pants with one hand, pulling him slowly toward me. When I had him out of sight, I slid my arms under his shoulders and pushed to my feet, pulling him up with me, my knees popping and back screaming. When I had him up in front of me, I settled the weight in my legs and staggered toward the door, staying out of the line of sight until the last moment. With a grunt, I surged forward and swung myself around into the doorway, letting go of the corpse just as it was pulled away from me.

The dead Spook jerked up into the air and I put myself into motion, my augments smoothly dumping adrenaline and endorphins, allowing me to hit top speed in three strides, holding the Roon out in front of me. As I ran I aimed at the white patch of her shirt, the gun made steady by the curious focusing of my augments, and squeezed the trigger three times. With the third shot the patch of white shirt disappeared, and the corpse hit the ground in front of me.

I dropped and rolled, smacking into the stucco wall hard enough to make my HUD blink off for a moment. In that flash, I thought I heard Remy, somewhere inside me like the other ghosts.

Stop, Avery. Don't.

Then it was gone, and I shook my head, trying to clear it and get my focus back. I jumped to my feet and took a breath, leaping forward to land in the doorway, my augmented vision adjusting to the darkness immediately. The Spook was on the ground, her chest a red bloom, her eyes staring.

I had myself in my nostrils. I smelled like someone else's piss.

"Next time you decide to make a charge, Avery," Grisha shouted from behind me, the crunch of his boots approaching, "perhaps warn the people shooting indiscriminately at the ground, yes?" I felt him get close, and then he was standing next to me in the doorway. He stood there for a moment and then he clapped me on the shoulder.

"The third one, the leader, has run," he said.

I turned and holstered my gun. *Stop, Avery. Don't.* I replayed Remy's voice in my head. Something fist-sized had appeared in my throat, and I wanted to punch Grisha in the face.

Gall was coming up behind him, scowling. "You shot at Carlo, goddammit," he groused. "Why the fuck'd you do *that*?"

"I've shot a lot of defenseless old men," I said gruffly. "You're gonna have to be more specific."

Grisha held up a hand to stop Gall's approach. "Avery, you have made the right decision. These people, these

Angels, have only their own twisted agenda. We are trying to salvage what is left of this world."

"The world is a fine place and worth the fighting for," Gall said. "A wise man once said."

"We have an agreement, then," Grisha said so seriously I wanted to laugh, at him and the rest of SPS, their pretensions to saving the human race. We were unsavable, I knew. "You will get us into SSF-controlled Europe and make introductions."

"Sure, I'll get you in touch with an old pal o' mine," Gall said. "Mr. Cates, I believe you know her, too."

I stared at them both, and nodded, then turned back to look at the dead Spook in the shadows. "Tell her to bring Mr. Marko. For laughs."

I didn't say anything they might take for agreement. I had my own plans.

XVII

I HEAR I MIGHT ACTUALLY OUTLIVE *YOU*

"The border's tighter than my ass," Gall said in his easy, booming way. "Which is pretty fucking tight. The cops who are left thought they were hunkering down to preserve the System for the Second Coming of Marin or something. Now they're starting to figure out Marin ain't coming, that the *Shutdown* is coming, but they're still grinding the gears and walking the wall." He shrugged. "They don't know what else to do."

Everyone had cleaned up nice. Gall was still a crispy fritter of a man, everything about him hot and red and scaly, but he'd gotten himself a clean suit of light pink that matched his general skin tone pretty well, making him look like a big clown. Grisha had changed out of his grubby overalls and into a snazzy suit that looked about twenty years old, based on the style and the sheen of the worn fabric, and he'd pulled in a dozen more people from SPS, quiet men and women who did anything Grisha told them to with a speed and dedication that meant they either were terrified of him or thought he was a genius. Maybe a little of both.

It was fucking madness outside Berlin. Grisha had come up with more four-wheelers and we'd made decent time north, the roads getting better and better as we drove until, finally, about thirty miles south of Berlin we'd clambered over a pile of rubble and bounced onto the widest highway I'd ever seen, in good shape, too. The roads hadn't been maintained for decades, sitting out in the weather, ignored while people sped over them in hovers, but they'd been sitting there, waiting, like the world knew we'd all come back to the roads eventually. Most of them had been torn up at some point, by bombs or weeds poking up through cracks an inch at a time, but long stretches were still usable, as long as you didn't mind the taste of your kidneys in your throat. We'd hit speeds that reminded me of hover rides, complete with constant low-level terror and the urge to always know exactly where your safety netting was. That had been great for six hours or so, and then we'd hit the camp.

It was a tent city, if you wanted to be generous with the word *tent*. I saw the blue tarp familiar to me from Potosí everywhere, stretched and folded in ingenious ways that gave me hope for the future of humanity no matter what Grisha said. It was a huge settlement, thousands of people crammed onto a rubble-strewn area pressed up against the fortified border the System Pigs had set up, straight across the road like it wasn't even there. We pulled up, secured the four-wheelers with thick, rusty chains through the axles, and started walking.

The border was just an overpass the cops had barricaded with two burnt-out hover hulls overturned to block the road, guns mounted on the bridge stretching perpendicular to the road above, a mass of pissy-looking officers gathered at the choke point where they scowled and, I assumed, interviewed people who wanted in.

"Why is everyone camped out here?" I asked the ex-cop. The world was filled with abandoned real estate; you could have a mansion somewhere if you wanted it.

"They want in," Gall said. "They don't know any better; they think the System is their best choice. Sure, there's power up there, some order maybe, but it's all fucking *cops*. The cops don't need a bunch of mewling assholes to watch over, now that they don't have Marin's programmed requirements to protect and serve and all that pushing them along. They need slave labor to keep the gears turning and they need every Techie they can get their hands on to work their little autoshutdown problem." He laughed, a bitter cough. "These assholes are trying to get *in* because they think there's yen up north, work, jobs, safety. There's work, all right, but that's about it."

I shook my head, staring around. I knew these people. I'd never met them, but I'd walked around the streets of New York with them. I'd been knocked around by System Cops with them. I'd plotted to kill, beg, and steal with them. And here they were, begging to get back *into* the System, or whatever scraps of it were left. I fucking hated them for it. They didn't know the world was dying—or maybe they did, who knew? But they could have been trying to make something better. To *do* something.

I was doing something. I was going to do plenty.

Rough avenues had been carved in the camp, forming muddy pathways, and we picked our way through the throngs. People sat outside their crappy tents and stared at us, people jumped up to run in front of us, begging, people looked at our clothes and our boots and scowled, hating us on sight. I knew exactly how they felt, but it was strange to be on the receiving end. The world had turned and suddenly I was rich, I was powerful—and they hated me. And with good reason.

My HUD sharpened in my vision as my heart rate kicked up. I felt that acidic boiling in my belly, the sense that violence was on the horizon. Gall walked with the rolling, stick-up-the-ass gait of the seasoned cop, certain he would not be touched simply because he didn't *wish* to be touched. Grisha strolled with his hands in his pockets, chin on his chest, oblivious, his team mimicking him like they thought his posture was going to save them. I fought the urge to turn and look behind us, certain that a huge crowd of angry people was gathering at our backs.

And I thought, *Shit, this* is *just like the System!*

Nothing happened, though. We slogged our way through the camp and came to a wide, central path, just as muddy, but someone had taken the time to line each side with stones. It led directly to the barricades, and the System Pigs doing border duty watched us with their fake, plastic eyes as we approached. They were all officers, dressed in nice suits that looked a little worn, a little tattered on the edges. They were all men—if you could consider avatar bodies made of silicon and circuits to have a sex—and each wore a broad-rimmed hat, a hip holster under their jacket, and a battered-looking Roon 1009, a shredding rifle slung over their shoulders. As we approached I looked up at the big swivel guns mounted on the overpass, and then back down at the cops staring at us. The entry was only wide enough for one person, and no one was going to move those hovers easily, even for a Tele-K. Forcing your way into Copland wasn't easy.

Feeling their eyes on me, probably uploading my face and running an optical facial recog scan through their servers, I wondered why anyone would *want* to force their way in. Then I thought about the mud I'd just skated through, all that piss and sweat and shit and blood pumped into the earth by people living under blue tarps, and it almost made sense.

The cops didn't speak, or pull weapons, or anything. They just watched us until Gall turned and gestured for the rest of us to stop a few feet away. He spun around and continued forward, holding up his hands and saying something that made the cops laugh. Then he leaned in and had a whispered conversation with one of them, who I assumed was the station chief. Watching them, I was amazed all over again at the avatar tech. These were robots, with quantum-state hard-drive brains on which a fucking program that had been *them* was operating at clock speeds. They looked human. Their skin moved right, their eyes shone right, and they had all the nervous tics and weird tells of a person. But they were fucking androids, connected to a network in the air, constrained by programming and destined, according to Grisha, to shut down in a few weeks, just go dormant and sit there for eternity, rusting.

Gall nodded and turned back to us. The cop he'd been speaking to straightened up and resumed practicing to be a statue of a System Pig.

"He's sending in my message. Shouldn't be more than a few minutes."

"Sure," I said. "She's probably got about twenty-five of herself running around in there, doing her chores."

It took twenty minutes, and when Janet Hense emerged from the shadows behind the barricades, she looked exactly like I'd last seen her, fighting the civil war in Brussels, snapping out orders and handing me a bomb disguised as an old Monk. And back then she'd looked exactly like she had the day she'd left me for dead in Bellevue back in Old New York. And I suspected she'd look exactly the same fifty years on, and maybe forever.

The cops manning the barricades straightened up when she emerged. I noted the five pips on her collar, and had no fucking clue what that meant. Last I'd seen her she'd been a major, four pips and everyone had run away from her like she could order executions without filling out the paperwork. Now she'd been promoted past that, and I didn't know what rank that was. She was a short, tiny woman with skin the color of light coffee, her dark, straight hair pulled back with a minimum of style. She paused and ran her eyes over us, not pausing or reacting in any way when she saw me. Then she stepped forward, and I noted with professional detachment the way the cops on the line stiffened up, put hands on their rifles, and looked in different directions. I guessed it wasn't often a ranking officer stepped outside their green zone, this close to the shitkickers.

"Horatio," she said, almost smiling. "It's good to see you. You look fucking terrible."

"Janet," Gall said with a nod. "I wasn't sure you'd be so happy to see me."

She nodded. "We need everyone we can get, Rache. There was an amnesty issued a few months ago, asking every officer to come on back, no questions asked."

Gall cocked his head and grinned. "Funny how that happened after you couldn't build any more units, huh?"

For a second, they stood there in perfect silence, perfect stillness. Then Hense turned to look at me. "Fucking hell, Cates, you're a fucking weed: You can't be killed."

I winked. "Someday, Janet. You just got to keep faith. Although I hear I might actually outlive *you*, in a sense."

She didn't like that. She stared at me for another few seconds, chewing something sour, and then spun away, walking toward the barricades.

"These people are with me," she announced to the cops guarding the entrance to what was left of the System of Federated Nations. "They are at liberty and anyone who fucks with them will be *erased* from not just his unit but the fucking *server* itself. Pass the word."

The cops said nothing and stared anywhere but at her as we approached. I kicked up a little and caught up with her.

"Every time I see you," I said, grinning, "you've moved up in the world, Janet. What are you now? God?"

She stared straight ahead. "What do think?" she said, and then turned to look at me. "I'm Director of Internal Affairs."

XVIII

WE JUST FIND PEOPLE TO PAY US FOR WHAT WE WERE GONNA DO ANYWAY

Berlin was the cleanest city I'd ever seen.

It was so clean my skin itched as we rode along its wide, empty streets in a huge version of the four-wheel vehicles Grisha seemed to have an endless supply of. These were cleaner, slightly larger, and clearly marked with the stars and globe of the SSF, and appeared to be Droids, driving along without anyone at the controls. We all sat in rigid silence, packed into the back, driving along at a stately pace so slow I would have considered it impossible according to my understanding of the physical laws of the fucking universe—we might, I thought, be going backward.

Jammed between Grisha and Gall, I was suddenly conscious of how bad I smelled.

"What are you waiting for?" Hense suddenly snapped at Gall. "This *is* the fucking meeting. I don't have time for anything formal."

Gall grinned, his rubbery face demonic. "Don't look at *me*, Janet. I got paid to set up a meet. This is *their* gig."

He pointed at Grisha. Hense looked at him for a withering second and then turned her dead eyes on me. I did my best to stare back, circuitry for circuitry. Hense always made me feel like I was beneath her.

"You're working for *Techies* now, Avery?" She made the word an insult. I forced myself to grin at her, my tongue poking into the gaps in my teeth.

"Gunners always work for ourselves," I said. "We just find people to pay us for what we were gonna do anyway."

She squinted a little at me. "Last reports we had on you, you had an apprentice."

Cold water splashed through me. I went still, and I forced myself to keep staring back at her despite the urge to look away. Remy flashed through my mind—he'd been an asshole. Complaining, morbid, disobedient. He'd refused to learn a fucking thing and he got in the way every time I planned something out, and I'd let him get clipped right under my nose.

"He's dead," I said, my voice flat. I swallowed and stayed silent, and after a moment she looked at Grisha.

"Grigory Baklanov, born Arkhangelsk, interred Chengara Penitentiary presumed dead on site. Obviously not dead, as you are the founder and current leader of *Superstes per Scientia*, aka SPS. SPS is listed in SSF servers as an Opposition Group."

Grisha nodded, affecting a tiny little bow in the cramped quarters. "And you: Janet Mitchen Hense, ostensible age forty-three, currently occupying what looks like Gen-Four Squalor Series Two nonbiological individually controlled deployment unit, also known as *avatar*. You are Director,

Internal Affairs, System of Federated Nations Security Force. You have thirteen avatars with your imprint in the field, and you have not long to live." He shrugged. "So to speak."

Another second of thick, oppressive silence, and then she nodded. "Why am I talking to you, Mr. Baklanov?"

He nodded back. "We have mutual problem, mutual solution." He smiled. "We are both mortal."

Her nostrils flared, and I distracted myself from my pounding heart and clenched fists to ponder the fucking programming and resources that went into getting an avatar to do that. Why? What the fuck was the point that Janet Hense be able to flare her fucking nostrils?

"And the solution?"

"Former Director Marin's override codes. We know where they can be found. We need SSF's help to get to them."

She cocked her head slightly. "Why?"

Grisha paused, gauging, I figured, how much it was safe to give away. I leaned forward. I knew Janet Hense, her type. She was going to get more out of us somehow, and she knew more than she was letting on.

"You know exactly *why*, babe," I said, and her visible clench at being called *babe* made me happier than I'd been in a long time. "Orel—Michaleen Garda, whatever his real name is—has the code. He's holed up in a uranium museum you assholes created during the civil war, so any carbon-based life forms get within ten miles of it, they start to melt." I shrugged. "We need an assault force that can withstand radiation levels like that." Belling had told me Mickey was in Split, Croatia. If the System Pigs didn't know that, I wasn't going to tell them.

"We estimate dose of approximately seven Gy," Grisha added without looking at me.

Outside, somehow we were back in the wilderness: trees zoomed past us, green and brown and red blurs. We were still on a wide, paved road, but it was as if the big, empty city we'd been in had melted away. A hazy feeling of confusion infused me; for a second I almost panicked, my heart lurching in my chest. Then my old augments kicked in and a sense of calm filtered through me.

"Garda," Hense said, looking out the window. "Fucking *Garda*. That makes sense." She continued to stare out the window for a moment, and then turned back to us. "I don't have access to Garda's SSF file. It was single-copy-only on Marin's local server and it got turned into mulch along with him. But I know he wasn't just some random Gunner."

In my head, Dolores Salgado suddenly spoke up. *Random? Michaleen was there from the beginning. The Dúnmharú didn't take jobs. They took assignments—all designed to push Unification. That man* made *Unification happen, by the simple expedient of murdering anyone in a position to oppose it.*

I blinked her away. "He's fortified," I said quickly.

"Wired up in modified Squalor Series One," Grisha inserted. "And the Londholm Augment. Which he uses to Psionically compel a security staff that dies off at an alarming rate."

Hense was unreadable. She settled back into her seat as we emerged from the trees and into a cleared circular driveway in front of a big, domed building. The dome was just a skeleton of bare metal, but the rest of the building looked to be in great shape. Several other four-wheelers had been parked in front of it, and the open space crawled with System Cops in their fraying suits and heavy overcoats and other people, all wearing gray uniforms, all engaged in manual labor of some sort. A group of men tugged an ancient cart along the road, sweating and straining to haul whatever was under the heavy canvas sheets. Half of the four-wheelers we passed had two or three people working on the engines and the solar panels, faces blackened from grease.

"No Droids, huh?" I said to the window.

"And not enough vehicles or power," Hense snapped, sounding irritated. Her irritation lifted my spirits. I felt like if I could irritate Hense, I could do anything. "Where is he, then?"

"No," I snapped back, turning to look at her. "Not until you commit." Garda's location was our last chip. I wanted to be there, to be put within reach of that short bastard or whatever he was now. And Grisha didn't want the System Pigs to get the override codes without him there to supervise.

I exchanged a quick glance with the Techie, and he winked at me. I had to admit, I *liked* the crazy fuck, and I was glad we were working the same angle for the moment.

"Avery will be acting as Taker on this," Grisha said. "We take him, and we extract the information from him and share it with you. We need SSF to breach outer defenses, help get our team inside."

The vehicle rolled to a stop, but Hense sat there for another moment, her eyes swiveling from me to Grisha. "Taker. Avery Cates has never *taken* anyone he could kill. He's a fucking savage. His type is one of the reasons I tested into the SSF, Mr. Baklanov. He hates Garda, has a personal vendetta against him. And you wish me to believe he will *take* Garda instead of shooting him?" She cocked her head. "Assuming you can even get him next to Garda without he himself dying of radiation exposure. Seven Gy will take about twenty minutes before he's on his knees puking blood."

"We have rad suits that can withstand such exposure for perhaps an hour," Grisha said, leaning forward. "We must work *together*, Director Hense. Are we different species? Perhaps we are. But we are species on the brink of extinction, both." He leaned back again. "We offer you a way. But it must be our way."

She shook her head. "I arrest you, and search radiation zones—preserved settlements with lethal-dose ionizing rad levels. I find him without you."

Grisha shrugged his face, pulling the corners of his lips down. "Yes. Maybe you even find him before your automatic shutdown routines kick in. Maybe you go through a dozen false leads and then time runs out, yes?"

She continued to stare. Without transition, or any movement on her part, the doors to the four-wheeler popped up, letting in the brisk Berlin air. "I will have officers as part of the extraction team. Cates can be your *Taker*, but I will have hands there to keep him on target."

Before I could say anything, Grisha nodded. "Agreed. Yes. But they will follow Avery's orders. Avery will be lead on the extraction team."

I closed my eyes, feeling the gentle rock of the chassis as everyone struggled to unglue themselves and exit. I didn't like any of this. If he were here, I would have told Remy to always exit a vehicle last; if there was an ambush waiting, let someone else take the brunt of it. And then I would have told him to also always know your exits, so you don't get trapped inside. And then he would have nodded and yawned and asked me if I had anything alcoholic to drink stashed away somewhere.

I opened my eyes and shook myself. I had work to do. I pushed myself along the oddly comfortable upholstered seats and pulled myself from the four-wheeler; Hense and Gall and Grisha were already on the huge stone steps leading up into the building, which stretched away majestically to my right and left. Some weak, watery sun had poked its way through the clouds, and the sensation of open space felt strange and oppressive.

One of the poor assholes in a gray uniform, similar to SPS's jumpsuits, stood in front of me. His head had been shaved to a pink, round ball, and he squinted at me with a dopey, ludicrous grin on half his face.

"Hullo, Avery," he said.

I looked back at him, and after a moment a shock of recognition hit me. Without his bloom of hair, his stupid glasses, and the extra thirty pounds, I would not have recognized Ezekiel Marko under most conditions.

"Zeke," I said, giving him a grin, for a moment everything else forgotten. I had a soft spot for Mr. Marko. Then I frowned. "You used to have better fashion sense."

His whole round head turned crimson, and his face folded up. It took me a moment to realize that good old Zeke Marko was fucking *livid*.

"I've been assigned to be your technical liaison," he said. Then he paused and looked over my shoulder, his eyes squinted. "I made my way south after we crashed, and did okay for a while. Then I got caught between a press unit for the army and the police, and I chose what I thought was the lesser evil." He indicated his uniform with a sweep of his hands. "I'm a fucking indentured servant here, now. Because I got burned and ran, they don't trust me to put me in an avatar—which I'm glad for—but they need people like me to work on their little problem." Suddenly he looked back at me, and I was shocked at the sustained anger and directness of his gaze. The Marko I'd known had been a timid little shit, worming his way through life. "Don't help them, Avery," he whispered, leaning in.

I blinked. "What?"

"Let them all go dormant," he whispered, his eyes jumping around nervously. "Every last fucking one of them."

XIX

YER GONNA NEED MORE GUNNERS

"If this is what they're calling booze," Gall said, "I haven't been missing much by way of fucking *civilization* by staying out in the cold."

We all stared down at our glasses with a mixture of dismay and embarrassment. When our minder, a blank-faced, skinny captain named Mehrak, who never smiled or reacted in any way to anything we said to him, had told us there was liquor to be had in Berlin even Grisha had gotten excited. Mehrak had been assigned to escort us around the city, and he'd taken us to a grand-looking restaurant on the other side of the big forestlike park we'd ridden through, directly across from ancient, rusting rail tracks. The place was staffed by unhappy-looking workers in the gray uniforms—slaves, basically, who'd been brought into Berlin one way or another and implanted with a chip that set off alarms if they strayed too far outside the city limits. The cops swore they'd set them all free once things settled down, but I knew as well as they did that things never settled down. Not that much.

The menu consisted of three items: potato stew, bread hard enough to commit murder with, and potato liquor. The greasy sheen on the stew made me gag, so I'd contented myself with a tall glass of cloudy booze, which turned out to have been made from dead rats and old cheese, based on the taste.

Once convinced, Hense had proven almost eager to cooperate, which made me nervous. She'd hammered away at everything, pushing for advantages and control, which was to be expected, but she'd *bargained*, instead of dictating, which meant either she was in a weaker position than we suspected, or she was playing us. Since she was right in the middle of a long line of people who'd fooled me, and badly, in my life, I wouldn't have been surprised. In the meantime, she'd agreed to put what was left of the SSF at our service. She'd even agreed to let us keep the actual location of Michaleen's fortress, where he was incubating or molting or greasing his hinges or whatever, until the last minute. Either she was desperate, or we were going to get brutally fucked in the end.

Either way, a drink had sounded about right.

I raised my glass. "To the end of everything," I said. "And about fucking time."

It was a strange moment. It felt calm and almost happy, like everything was draining out of the world and leaving a brief moment of static before it all went black, and suddenly Horatio Gall and Grisha felt like my friends. Some of the other tables in the place were filled by gray-uniformed workers—on breaks, I guessed. They stared and kept silent. I figured the fact that Hense had issued orders to let us keep our weapons didn't make us seem too friendly.

"Fuck you," Gall said, chuckling as he winced his way into a sip of his drink.

"Nothing ends," Grisha said with a faint smile. "There are just new ways of doing things."

Mehrak said nothing. He stood a few feet away with his hands in his pockets, his sunglasses on to ward off any attempt to engage him. He was an avatar, of course, but he looked like he'd been quick and nimble as flesh and blood, the sort of cop who would chase you into places you didn't expect to be chased into.

"Besides," Grisha said, suppressing a cough after his swallow of deadly booze, his whole body shivering, "that is why we are here, to make sure things continue."

A group of workers emerged from the interior of the restaurant, each bearing two glasses of booze in dirty hands. There were three of them, one man and two women, all middle-aged and tired looking. Thinking that if they actually drank both I'd be in some personal fear of them, I watched them pause awkwardly when they saw us, and then sit down at a table behind me.

I looked back at Grisha. He sat easily, studying me with a frown. He was the most competent man I'd ever met. Not especially talented in many ways: not the best shot I'd ever seen, not a brilliant inventor, nothing like that. He was just a collection of pretty fucking good at everything rolled into one person. I never would have pegged him as someone wanting to save the world.

"You think of your friend," he said suddenly. He held up his glass, smiling archly. "He would have enjoyed this?"

His kindness made me angry. I thought of Remy, again, saw him going inside and demanding a jug of this acid, getting into a fight when they said no, getting hauled away and beaten up somewhere, then crawling back to where I was, bruised and scabbed, not sorry. Never fucking sorry.

I'd never had friends. Running with snuff gangs in Old New York as a kid, tossing a handful of dirt into some dandy's face and knocking him down, fifteen, twenty sets of hands invading every possible pocket in seconds, ripping everything free and then running through the twisty old streets—you kept whatever you got your hands on. No sharing. If you wanted something someone else got their hands on, you had to take it. I hadn't had some worn-down old Gunner showing *me* the ropes, some old man to make jokes about death with. I'd learned everything on my own. My first job gunning, I didn't even have a gun yet. Guns were expensive. Knives you could make out of shit you found, sharpened pieces of soft metal, plastic. No one showed me *how*. No one listened to me bellyache for hours on end about my hard deal, how I had metal in my head, how I'd been abandoned.

Friends made you weak, and weak made you dead. I looked weak to Grisha, I thought, the Russian fuck laughing at me, really. Of course he was. I'd laugh at some old asshole misting up over one particular dead body in a long road made of dead bodies.

I thought about smashing my glass into Grisha's face, finally finding out just how tough he was. I thought about telling him to fucking mind his business. I thought about telling him I kept seeing Remy in my mind, staring eyes empty, hands curled into stiff half fists, that I'd had hopes for him, of finally teaching someone something useful. I thought about drinking off my entire glass in one gulp and seeing what happened.

Instead of all that, I just looked away. "Yeah, he would have."

"It is not your fault. That old man was the most powerful Pusher I know of. You had no chance."

"Fuck you," I said before I even thought it. "I'm forty fucking years old, give or take. I've *survived*. I know better. Turning my back, relying on him, letting that old cunt Belling distract me." I kept staring off into the distance. "I've been fucking pushed and pointed for *years* by Michaleen Garda. Cainnic Orel. Whatever his name is. Years. Who knows how long—I'm so fucking stupid it might be from fucking *birth*. And along the way, anyone I tried to keep fucking *alive* got killed. I could keep us here a month just talking about the people I've killed, or let be killed." I laughed suddenly. I didn't feel it; it just crawled out of me. "I'm motherfucking *death*, Grish. You spend enough time with me, you're dead." I laughed again. "Shit, for a while during the Plague, that was the literal fucking *truth*." I was glad I'd put my glass down. My hands were clenched so tight I would have crushed it, slicing my hand to pulp. "Fucking cops, Grish," I said. "They hired the Pusher. Put him on me. *They* killed Remy. And here I am, working with them, showing them my belly."

I didn't have to look to know that Grisha and Gall were exchanging a lingering look of alarm. I'd been on the other end when someone you were working with suddenly started to bark. You saw all your plans go out the window. You saw all your investment wasted, and you started thinking about cutting your losses and getting a new partner. I blinked my eyes rapidly a few times and took a long pull off the glass, resisting the urge to pound the table, and looked back at them.

"The translation is: Fuck you," I said.

Grisha narrowed his eyes at me a moment, then nodded. "Yes, fine." He pointed at me. "You have a chance *now*, you self-pitying asshole," he said slowly, steadily. "You are concerned about those who have gone before? Save those who are *still here*." He leaned back again. "We need you, Avery. You have a skill set and experience no one else in the world has anymore. We cannot simply advertise for world-class assassin, intimate experience with legend Canny Orel preferred. And we cannot pursue petty revenge. We also cannot choose our partners."

Anger made me lean forward until the table bit into my belly. "So what, I'm just one of your fucking *resources*? I'm—"

"Avery!" he shouted, slamming his hand down on the table. "*Yes*, you are fucking *resources*. I *do not have any to spare*, and I have no fucking *time left*. No one does. Get that through your fucking thick, selfish skull. Am I using you? Yes! Poor Avery. Poor, poor Avery. I am *using* you to save the human race from extinction." He sat back, staring at me. "I make no apology. I also do not play games. I do not lie to you."

I realized I was on the edge of my seat, my muscles quivering, ready to launch myself forward. For a second all I could hear was the blood rushing in my ears, and then—someone was clapping.

Directly behind us. I turned, and the three people at the table behind me were staring at us, just a foot or so away.

The woman right behind me was smiling at me, clapping her hands in a deliberate, steady rhythm.

"Oy, this is a fine scene, innit?" she said, her eyes on me. "The great Avery Cates, bawling and trembling. And you think yer comin' after *me*?" She looked past me at Grisha. "Yer gonna need more Gunners."

XX

I KILL *EVERYBODY*

I experienced one of those rare moments of total, paralyzing shock—I couldn't make it fit in and make sense. The woman wasn't my age but wasn't young, her reddish hair dry and bristly and mixed with gray, her complexion stained red with gin blossoms—she'd lived hard. She was smiling at me in a relaxed, confident way, but I'd never seen her before in my life. This was a fact. There was no wiggle room in it.

"What?"

She cocked her head the other way and smiled. The smile was vacant and terrifying—there was nothing in her eyes. They had rolled up, showing just the whites, and vibrated slightly. Behind her, her friends stared in puzzled agitation.

"Keep up, boyo. That's always been yer problem, Avery. Yer good at dealin' the cards, sure, sure, but you bet like a drunk sailor on shore leave, heavy and blind."

A thrill shot through me. *This was Orel.* I thought of

the old Italian man in Fiesole, and a second later I surged up, tearing the Roon from its holster and swinging my arm around, intending to shoot her in the face and find out how much pain you could cause a Psionic when they'd Traveled into another body. As I put the gun on her, though, I hesitated. She *wasn't* Orel. She was just a vessel he'd forced himself into, and for a split second I hovered there, thinking I couldn't just shoot some poor bitch who'd been drinking herself to sleep because of her shitty life a few seconds before, fucking unaware of what a *really* shitty evening was.

As I stood there, the woman, eyes still twitching in their sockets, leaned back suddenly and smashed her glass into my head. A bloom of cold and hot spun me around and I shot wild, then let my momentum carry me into a spin out from behind the table. She'd been *fast*, and as I spun back and brought the gun up, orienting myself, she had somehow leaped up onto her table and launched herself directly at me.

All I saw as she sailed through the air, my augments working to speed up synapse response, making everything seem slower, were her wonky eyes, all white, little hints of pupil skimming the very tops. She had that same crazy smile on her face as I fired twice, hardwired habit, her stomach exploding into a spray of blood just before she crashed down onto me.

"What the *fuck*!" I heard Gall shout.

I shoved the squirting, twitching body off me and surged up onto my feet, blood dripping from my face where a flap of skin had been carved open. Gall, Grisha, and even Mehrak had guns in their hands, tables and chairs rocking gently where they'd been flipped over to clear some space.

"Well, shit," I started to say breathlessly, and then the man who'd been sitting with the redhead stood up.

"Yer gonna have to be faster than *that*," he said as his eyes rolled up into his head just like hers had, "if yer goin' to come after *me* when I don't have this kind of fucking *lag* to deal with."

Four guns barked almost simultaneously, and finally everyone else in the place realized they were in trouble, chaos breaking out with shouts and screams, tables and chairs flying as people ran for cover. The man was short and fleshy, a huge belly pushing the structural integrity of his uniform to its limits, but he dived and rolled on the ground like a pro, all four shots trailing him like an invisible tail swishing behind him as he moved.

"It's Orel!" I shouted, moving in a wide arc sideways to keep him in my light cone as he disappeared behind a wall of overturned tables.

"Canny Orel's five hundred years old and the size of my thumb!" Gall shouted back. He and Grisha were mirroring me in different directions, all of us crouched down and moving slowly, circling around the cluster of tables where the man had hidden himself. The air was cold, and in the distance I could hear the whine of four-wheelers—the SSF responding to shots fired in their precious little city. After all my life spent craning my neck up at Stormers dropping from above, the System Pigs had been swatted from the air at last, having to roll toward trouble on four wheels. The world really was ending.

"Trust me!" I shouted back. I didn't know what this meant—how close did he have to be to just take over someone's mind? How hard did he have to concentrate? Was he ten feet away, comatose with effort? All I knew was that in some sense he was *here*, and when I'd shot the old man in Fiesole his Psionic "handler" had screamed in pain. I wanted to make Michaleen hurt a little.

These poor assholes are just bystanders, Dolores Salgado suddenly complained in my head. *You're going to hurt* them, *and they don't deserve it*.

I gritted my teeth. The fat man surged up from behind the tables and threw his glass at me with sudden, savage ferocity. My HUD spiked sharp and clear in my vision, all the bars flashing red for a second as I twisted myself aside, the glass sizzling past my ear. I snapped the Roon up and had it on him for a second, but hesitated, Salgado's voice pinching me in the ass, and he dropped back down to the ground with a cackle.

"Sweet hell, Avery," he shouted in another voice but with the same fucking Gaelic accent. "You're afraid of killin' innocents *now*? After the damage you've done?" He laughed. "You kill *everybody*, boyo. It's your damn *calling card*. Even the orphans and castaways you try to train, you end up killing."

"Fuck you," I hissed before I'd realized what I was doing. My head throbbed and my ear felt like it had swollen to about three times its size. My HUD had a flashing yellow cross in one corner, indicating that its first-aid routines were not working, and I was on my own as far as pain and infection and bleeding went. "I took care of the fuck who did Remy."

I cursed myself immediately. You don't fucking talk. You don't give shit away to people. No matter what it was, it was a way *in*, and you couldn't afford that. If Remy had done it I would have slapped him in the head and told him to learn to shut up, and he would have smiled and told me it didn't matter, because he didn't have any secrets, or any heart.

The man suddenly just stood up. He just suddenly appeared, white eyes and slack arms. I put the gun on his chest but didn't fire, Salgado's words in my head. "Fuck, that Pusher did a number on *you*, eh? The *fuck who did Remy*, huh?" Grisha and Gall had circled around behind him, and we all stood there like assholes, unsure what to do with an unarmed man who was, for the moment, Cainnic Orel. "Well, shit, this's a test run. Let's see what I can *do*, eh?"

I felt…something. A brush, a feather against my thoughts. I knew the feeling—a Psionic Push, though I was used to a rougher and more invasive sensation. This was like someone was tapping on my thoughts instead of sledgehammering them into mush, and I twitched in response.

"Are you okay, Avery?" Grisha called, eyes flicking to me.

I nodded slowly, the butterfly sensation in my head suddenly swelling up like mist and filling my thoughts. And then my legs went out from under me and—

I saw it all in quick flashes. I was there. I was there and I was there, watching and being watched, like I was hovering around on the edges. Everything happened in jerky cuts, like frames had been removed from my memories. I knew, somehow, that I was being manipulated, that someone was doing something to me, but I also knew, somehow, that this was not a trick. I'd been there. The room felt exactly the same: dry and dirty, the grit under my boots, the smell of Belling rotting away in the bed, the sound of distant business as the hospital tried to function around us, the crowd gathered outside, angry but afraid to follow us in.

I saw the old gremlin, the Pusher. He just stepped into the room. He didn't say anything, or hold up his hand in some wonky bit of stagecraft. He just walked in and Remy and I and Belling, we all went still, frozen. The gremlin chewed his gums as he walked, his mouth in constant motion, glistening and pink. He breathed heavily through his nose, unhappy with having to move.

He looked at me and I raised the Roon; it was practically in Remy's face. The kid didn't react, just stood there staring at the door, frozen.

The gremlin grunted. I pulled the trigger. A small hole appeared in the back of Remy's head, and with a spray of blood and bone and snot and teeth his face exploded on the other side, and he crumpled to the floor, silent.

The gremlin grunted. I spun to the bed. Belling just stared, unresponsive, eyes wide and mouth open. I fired twice, moving the gun precisely in between, and Belling shivered and went limp.

The gremlin huffed and grunted his way into the room and looked around. He smelled. He hummed tunelessly to himself as he wheezed around, and then he took up a spot near where Remy had been standing, leaned down, and retrieved Remy's huge, ridiculous gun. Standing up again, his face was bright red. He turned to spit on the ground and nodded to himself.

"A'right," he whispered, eyes jittering everywhere. "Le's get this shit going."

* * *

opened my eyes.

The sky over Berlin was gray and cloudy and looked cold. I thought of the yellow, burning snow we had in New York and I wondered if it was the same here. Everything looked empty and clear up to the clouds, the whole world just a crystal, an hourglass, and all of us slowly shaking out of the top to the bottom, getting sucked under.

I sat up. I felt fine, physically. Kev Gatz used to give me a headache when he Pushed me. Even that old bastard Bendix had left me feeling sick after he'd shoved my brain around, but this felt like *nothing*.

I felt like nothing.

Someone was crying nearby. I sat up, a cold sweat breaking out all over me. I still had my gun in my hand. Squinting, I looked around. Grisha and Gall were kneeling in the spots they'd been in, the worker between them. The fat worker was crumpled on the ground, bawling, shaking with his arms wrapped around himself. Grisha looked up at me.

"Are you well, Avery?"

I nodded, pushing myself to my feet. I saw the back of Remy's head, the spray of blood against the wall.

Grisha looked back at the worker. "He dropped at the same time you did," he said. "He began wailing. I think whatever... possessed him has passed."

I nodded. I saw my gun almost touching the back of Remy's head. I stepped around the toppled tables just as a trio of four-wheelers screeched to a stop on the edges of the restaurant's open area. The worker looked up at me, his face a red, rippling mask of horror. Tears streamed

down his face. Michaleen had been in him, had *pos
sessed* him.

"Whatever happened to him," Gall muttered, "it wasn'
enjoyable."

I looked at the worker. I saw a tiny wound appear
in the back of Remy's head, like an editing trick. For a
few moments, the worker had been Michaleen. Mickey
hadn't made me kill Remy, but he'd made me *remember* it
And this guy had *been* Mickey. Had *been* Cainnic Orel.

I raised the Roon in one fluid motion and shot him
twice in the face. Grisha and Gall scrambled back on
their elbows and asses, cursing, and behind me I heard
the familiar sound of a multitude of guns being drawn. I
stared down at the worker, a dark pool of blood growing
around his ruined head.

I heard an old ghostly voice mocking me: *You are not a
Bad Man.* I *am a Bad Man.* Through the numb heaviness
that infused my torso, my head, I felt a terrifying, black
regret. I'd shot an unarmed civilian in the *face.*

I was shaking, suddenly. Without being asked, I let the
Roon slip from my hand and put my arms up into the air.
Something like a ball of mud had formed in my throat,
and my eyes stung.

"Avery!" Grisha shouted, surging to his feet and stepping over to me with purpose. I braced myself for the blow,
the crack to the skull that would send me to my knees, and
he raised his gun into the air, but paused. "Avery," he said
in a suddenly controlled, tight voice. "You did not have to
kill that man."

I nodded without looking directly at him. I saw
Remy's body, crumpled on the floor of that hospital. I saw
myself stepping over it without a glance. Then I dragged

my eyes to Grisha's, because he deserved to be looked at. I saw a spray of blood and bone and snot and teeth. He flinched.

"I kill *everybody*," I said.

I felt nothing.

XXI

THINK OF ME AS AN EXECUTION

Mr. Marko gave me a curt nod as I joined him on the steps of the big building being used as SSF headquarters. Everyone called it by a German name that sounded like they were clearing their throat, but I just called it Cop Central out of habit. Behind us as we ascended the steps, Berlin was a cauterized wound, empty and filled with echoes. There were only a few thousand cops and workers in the whole fucking city. Only about twenty thousand cops left, period, according to Grisha, whose ultracompetent estimate I was prepared to accept. I felt all that empty space behind me, cleaned up and whitewashed, all the shitkickers kept outside, pushing against the edges.

"How are you, Zeke?"

"That depends," he said quietly, "on whether you're going to go crazy and shoot me in the face today." I clenched my teeth and my hands stiffened in the pockets of my coat, twitching toward the slits in the lining that gave me access to the Roon. But I just swallowed it. Mr.

Marko had come down in the world. The old model would never have said something like that to me. He would have been too afraid.

"Who was he?" I asked, deflating, all my sudden anger pooling at my feet, wasted. I saw his face again, twisted and tortured. Poor sap got sucked into Copland and then got shit on by Cainnic Orel. I tried to tell myself I'd put him out of his misery, but now I saw *his* face instead of Remy's when I closed my eyes.

"Guy named Murray. Didn't know him well. Worked in the mechanics pool. Not well liked." He looked at me. Marko without his ballsy halo of hair was just a freakishly round kind of person—his head and torso were like concentric circles of flesh. "You got everyone terrified, and the scuttlebutt is Hense wants to cut you loose."

"Let her try," I said, twisting my head to the right until my neck popped with a satisfying crack. "What about what we discussed?"

He nodded. "Sure. I'll take care of it. So, you do something for me, then."

I took a step in silence to let him know I was thinking on it. "Go on."

"Get me on the team. Going in after Orel. Make me your tech support."

I let that hang for a moment. I knew Marko—or I'd known him. But if he still had Marko's brain, he'd be good to have around, and I realized, suddenly, that I'd gone days now interacting with the Techie without once wanting to slap him, or call him names. We were walking in a comfortable way, old allies. Having him around would be...good.

"All right," I said. "Want to see your work first-hand, huh?"

"I want to get the fuck away from fucking cops."

I remembered him, plump in his nice suit, staring down at his holographic ID in the Rock, horrified that it had gone an angry red. I wondered if I'd destroyed Ezekiel Marko too. "Hell, Zeke," I said quietly. "What happened to you?"

He shrugged. "I got arrested."

"He's unstable. He'll be a liability."

Hense was so angry she almost had an expression on her face. I sat next to Mehrak, who appeared to have been instructed to stare at me with one hand on the grip of his gun tucked into his shoulder. I thought about showing him a little trick that ended with his trigger finger broken, but wondered if you could *break* an avatar's finger.

Grisha scowled. "Yes? You have Gunners on your payroll? People experienced in finding targets and eliminating them, analyzing security fields, allocating resources, being able to pull the trigger when the time comes? You have resources to *burn*?" He shook his head savagely. "He killed a worker. A worker who, under influence, had just *attacked* him. So fucking what, Director Hense." He tapped a finger on the table. "I will repeat it since you have suddenly become a champion for human life: *So fucking what*. I do not have resources to burn. Avery is our lead on this."

We were seated around the most civilized conference table I'd ever seen. It was made of stainless steel, gleaming and scratch-free, apparently made out of a single sheet of metal that had been beaten into shape. The room was too small for it, though, a windowless square of drywall that had us all crowded against the walls. It was the sort of room that kept the peace, because there wasn't enough elbow room to swing a good punch.

She pointed one tiny hand at me. "He—"

"Given the System Security Force's well-documented stance of valuing all human life," I said, spreading my hands, "I officially apologize for killing one poor bastard in your fucking *kingdom* of poor bastards up here." I put a smile on my face, hard and plastic but the best I could do. "Especially since I know you, Janet, have never lined a bunch of skells up against a wall and shot them all in the head just because you had an appointment to get to, or any shit like that."

I gave her a wink. For a moment I thought she was going to dive across the table and try to twist my head off.

Grisha smiled at her. "This is your opportunity to go your own way on this project, Director Hense."

I loved Grisha. This was why we had held back Orel's location. If Hense already had that, she'd have cut us all loose without a moment's hesitation and gone her own way. Now she'd burned off even more valuable days working with us, and was in even worse shape regarding her looming deadline. We had her under our thumb, and Grisha, as horrified as he'd been with me in private, was putting the screws to her like a pro, following the first rule of a criminal partnership: You never throw your partner overboard unless it was an absolute necessity.

Hense looked down at the table and folded her hands in front of her. For a few seconds she just sat there; I guessed she was conferring with the rest of her, all the other avatars of her in the field, as well as her primary; within Berlin they still had power and signals in the air. When she looked up at us, she was suddenly all calm and happiness again. "Very well." She swept a hand in my direction. "The floor is yours, Avery."

I looked at Grisha. He'd told me that Hense by virtue of her promotion was now bound by some of the same programming limitations as Marin had been, and thus was bound to honor deals made in her official capacity as director. We were about to find out if he was right. His glasses caught a glare from the lights and looked like two white circles on his face. He nodded once at me, and for a second I felt a sudden, powerful affection for Grisha, tinged with regret for putting him in a position where he had to defend my competence. Then I took a deep breath and pushed everything else aside. I was Avery Cates, and Avery Cates did not get all blubbery even when he'd fucked everything up, even when people died for his mistakes. And everyone in the room was watching me for signs of weakness, for any evidence that killing poor fucking Murray had been crazy instead of brutal, that I was unhinged instead of cold-hearted.

I had to sell cold-hearted. Luckily, I had experience with that.

I stood up and opened my hands; Grisha tossed the tiny remote at me and I snatched it from the air with augmented dexterity. I held it in my palm and gestured, and a holographic image, a flickering, faint blue, appeared in the air over the table. It was a ruin, a faint square outline with a few surviving structures. Newer buildings, some also ruined, had been built inside and outside the old walls.

"Diocletian's palace," I said. "Split, Croatia. Yeah, I never heard of it either until a few weeks ago. Big old place, turning to dust, and the city around it was turned into a big cloud of radiation during the war—half an hour, tops, I'm told, without a level-four rad suit and you're puking your kidneys up."

"Orel is protected in a standard Monk chassis," Grisha said. "They were designed to withstand such conditions." He smirked. "Dennis Squalor was a genius, yes, but a paranoid man as well."

I gestured and the hologram telescoped down, piercing the earth. "The basement is where he'll be. The topside is ruins and cheap structures that don't give much protection. Underground is thick stone, more or less preserved. Easy to defend entrances, hard to get anywhere bombing it—he's pretty safe down there." I shrugged, and gestured again, and the hologram zoomed wildly out again and swerved south and east, showing another set of ruins like a long, narrow bridge disappearing into the ground. "This was the water supply back in the land before fucking time. What it is right now is a small way into caverns that lead to the basement of the palace, big enough for a small party to worm its way in."

"He may have set up security perimeters out that far," Grisha said. "We cannot know."

I shrugged. "He may have dragons and unicorns guarding the way, too. What the fuck difference does it make? This is where we go in. You land a shitload of System Pigs on the shore, rain 'em down from hovers since you got a fleet still operational, you make him feel your presence. I take a small party in and try to sneak up on the old fuck."

"And take him alive," Grisha said immediately. "Yes?"

I nodded, scanning the room, my plastic smile in place. "That's the plan. You get creative and get the code from him, and then I get him *back*."

There was a second of silence. Hense had taken her seat and now sat like she was a real human being, hands steepled under her chin. Mehrak, who I realized I'd never heard speak a word, still sat with his hand on the butt of his gun, making no attempt to conceal the fact that he was ready to shoot me in the head at a moment's notice. Marko was staring down at the tabletop, frowning, his hands limp in his lap, and Gall appeared to be asleep, mouth open, head back.

"Cainnic Orel is guilty of treason," Hense said slowly. "Whatever arrangement he had with Marin or—or the fucking Joint Council—is null now. We will arrest him, interrogate him, and he will be in our custody."

I shook my head. "Think of me as an execution, Janet," I said. "You can write a memo and make it legal if you want, but part of the deal is, I get him *back*."

She smiled, leaning back. The smile was instant and so insincere it hurt to look at her. "There are more *parts* to this deal than I could have imagined, Avery." She gestured at the hologram. "We know where he is. So why do I need *you*?"

I looked at Grisha. He looked down at his hands as if vaguely embarrassed. "This is a calculated risk, Director," he said quietly. Hense's eyes shifted to him. "We suspect that, as a first-generation avatar, you are programmatically precluded from negotiating in bad faith."

I smiled again. "In other words, you're fucking bluffing, and wasting my time. We have a *deal*."

Another long moment of stuffy silence. Hense dragged her eyes from Grisha to me, and then she sat forward. "You have requested Mr. E. Marko as part of your team. Mr. Marko, do you have any objections?"

He didn't look up, but his face took on a comical expression of exaggerated surprise. "*Now* she asks if I have fucking objections. No. I'm a volunteer."

Hense nodded, no hint that she'd just lost a ploy or was irritated in any way. The weird thing was, avatars were designed to be human, and several had fooled the hell out of me. This *was* who Janet Hense was, or had been—cold, controlled, and no fucking fun whatsoever.

"Mehrak will continue to liaison on this, so he is also part of your team," she said, standing up. "I assume you wish to keep the numbers small, but I insist one more representative of SSF interests be included."

I shrugged. I'd expected her to hand me a dozen System Pigs to deal with. Just one more felt like a gift.

The door opened and a well-dressed, short, compact woman with long black hair pulled back into a severe bun entered. Her suit was a deep, velvety blue, and it looked like it would have been expensive back when you could still buy suits and didn't have to make them yourself from old leaves and bits of wire.

She was Hense's exact double, and as I watched, they both cocked their head at me, in perfect sync.

"You can't be trusted, Avery," they said together. "So I'll be there to *supervise* you."

PART IV

PART IV

XXII

HERE WE ARE, AND *WE* ARE SO SPECIAL

I'd forgotten the nauseating whine hovers made when they were in the air, the feel of violent humming under your feet, the freezing cold inside one when you were high up and moving fast. For a second I could imagine the past few years hadn't happened: I hadn't assassinated Dennis Squalor, setting off the Monk Riots and indirectly causing the Plague; I hadn't been arrested and put in the same yard as Cainnic Orel; there hadn't been a civil war that destroyed everything. For a second I could imagine we were all back in the System. I'd been arrested again, and I was about to take a beating over something in a Blank Room in New York, and Kev Gatz would buy me a few glasses of gin at Pickering's when I was tossed out again.

It was oddly pleasant, imagining that fucking hellhole of a world again.

I'd come up in the world. I was sitting next to a tiny window in a fairly luxurious hover—it had nice seats and some effort at climate control, although the seat fabric was torn and the stuffing was spilling out of them, the walls were scorched, and ugly metal plates had been bolted over damage in several areas. The windows were thick and cloudy, but afforded you a vertigo-inducing view of the world below, looking so peaceful for a fucked-over globe filled with people like me, roaming around free. My only friends in the world were three avatar System Pigs— one of whom was Director of Fucking Internal Affairs, the new Queen Worm, or at least a copy of her—the founder and leader of SPS, an ex-cop who'd once been the second-in-command of the entire SSF back before they decided to go forcibly digital, and a Techie who'd once been a midlevel success in the SSF. Aside from Grisha, it was all-cop, all the time.

There wasn't much conversation. We'd spent a few days more in Berlin's weird, ultraclean bubble, gathering what-ever intelligence we could muster—which wasn't much, and mostly supplied by Grisha and SPS, since the System Cops were pretty fucking useless, as a rule, outside their own narrow borders these days—and figuring out details. Rad suits for the extraction team, weapons and ammo for the assault, hovers to get everyone in position, electro-magnetic pulse trips for me for use against... well, Orel officially, but Mr. Marko had been nice enough to amp them up beyond specs for me. If the cops I was suddenly surrounded by became troublesome, the EMPs would knock them out temporarily.

I'd used the EMP trick once before on a Monk, back in Newark, prepping for the Squalor job. They had a wonky range and their effectiveness depended on a lot of factors. If it worked on Orel in his modified Monk body, I still wouldn't be out of the woods; the EMP might take down his circuitry, but I didn't know if that would knock his organic brain unconscious. Still, taking his guns away from him seemed like a good start.

A voice, all treble and static, screeched into life around us.

"We're currently ten minutes out from designated landing zone. Please follow safety protocols."

No one paid any attention. No one buckled their seat belts or took hold of the safety netting. No one double-checked the door seals or made sure all the crap we were lugging with us was secured. There was no point.

I looked out my tiny window and squinted down. After a moment my old augments kicked in and my vision zoomed down a little, bringing the strip of land we were approaching into sharper focus. After another second, though, my vision swam a little and my extra focus disappeared, leaving me just an old fuck squinting out a window. Croatia looked exactly like every other spot in the world. It had once been a country, I'd been told, before Unification. Maybe it was a country again, now. No one knew. I assumed the scab of red-roofed buildings on the coast was Split, and I tried to pick out the palace, but it had been subsumed into the city itself and I couldn't spot it, even though I'd seen plenty of renderings over the last few days.

It looked like a model of a city, mountains rising behind it, blue ocean stretching out in front of it. It was hard to believe it was deadly to step into, hard to believe Canny Orel had buried himself there, like a spider, waiting for everyone else to die so he could pick through the graveyard.

Grisha, who'd been sitting next to Marko having what

appeared to be a friendly conversation about molecular shred constants, whatever that was, stood up as if he'd never been in a damaged, crashing hover in his life and strolled over to sit with me. Hense glanced up from a huddled conversation with her bodyguard/attaché, who looked like a young-looking girl named Digby, all tight blond hair and rosy eyes—but since she was an avatar, who knew what she really was, inside. Maybe she'd been an old man before being tinned, or a black woman.

"This is the last of it," Grisha said. "Amazing, that we are here."

I frowned. "The last?"

"The last of our combined strength. The last strength anywhere, I think. The last time we will see hovers in the air. The last time anything like authority," he said and reached out his arm in front of us, making a claw with his hand, "stretches out its power to try and order up the world."

I stared at him. "Are you fucking drunk?"

He smiled at me. "Avery, don't you realize how many people in history have thought themselves so special that the universe had chosen *them* to witness the end? Of the world, of civilization—call it what you will. And they are all wrong. Yet here we are, and *we* are so special. The world ends; we are here to watch."

I smiled again. "You *are* drunk."

He laughed, an easygoing roll of laughter that was shockingly relaxed and *normal*. Grisha sounded like a man who'd spent the last few years growing vegetables in his garden. "Avery, based on my own intelligence sources, the SSF has committed *all* of their remaining strength to this operation. They very rightly believe the recovery of Marin's override code—and thus recovery of their own autonomy—is worth applying every bit of their last strength. Every avatar unit, every hover, every bullet has been committed." He shrugged. "If they fail here, if they are smashed against the rock that is Canny Orel, there will be nothing left in the world that resembles *order.*"

I thought about Blank Rooms. I thought about Chengara, and Dick Marin's flash grins when he was telling you that this particular unit didn't have the authority to prevent your execution. I thought about snuff gangs and cops in beautiful silk suits kicking the shit out of you in the street.

"That," I finally said, "is a fucking shame, isn't it?"

Grisha laughed again. After a moment, I couldn't stop myself from joining him. This was what it was like, I thought, to have narrowed everything down to the essentials: revenge, survival, whatever. No one in the hover with me had any ulterior motives. We were all fucking pure, for once.

The tinny voice crackled through the crank air again. "Uh, Director Hense, to the cockpit."

Everyone glanced over at Hense, who looked up, hesitated a moment, and then stood, smoothing down the utilitarian black coat she wore over the SSF field uniform, which resembled the old Stormer kit except it was black, her five silver pips shining in the dull hover interior lights. Without a word she stepped through the hatch and disappeared up front.

"Not good," Grisha said in a tone so serious I immediately laughed. After a moment, Marko joined in, and the three of us hooted deliriously for a minute while Mehrak and Digby stared in robotic confusion.

We were still catching our breath when Hense re-entered the cabin.

"Emergency protocols," she said tersely. "Pack everything up tight and check weapons. Prepare for evasive maneuvers. Digs, priority message the rest of the convoy."

Digby nodded, her pink-and-white skin too perfect to be believed, and then did absolutely nothing, sitting there staring while she worked her internal circuits.

"What's up, boss?" Gall said, suddenly shaking himself out of a doze. "We hit Croatia yet?"

Hense nodded, consulting a tiny handheld that lit her face up in a purplish light. "We are. We're being prevented from landing, though."

We all sat forward in a moment of comical synchronicity. "Prevented?" Gall asked, bunching up his puckered face into a frown. "What crazy shithead is left out there who thinks they can trade body blows with *you*?"

Hense didn't look up. "A crazy shithead named Dai Takahashi," she said.

XXIII

EVERYONE WANTED TO HIRE ME ON

"Get Berlin," Hense snapped at Digby. "And find out why in *fuck* we didn't know this asshole had set up camp here. Find out if he's on Orel's payroll. Find out *anything*. Then find out who gets their fucking server space wiped."

Through some magic, Digby suddenly looked five years old, as if her avatar shell had some advanced capillary response simulation.

I looked out the tiny window again, but couldn't see anything. "How in hell does he stop you from landing?"

Hense didn't look up at me. "By finding all the possible landing zones within a few miles of Split and mining them, parking burned-out tanks on them, mounting whatever big guns they still have, and offering antiaircraft screening. By generally being a pain in the ass when I don't have the resources to spare to turn Dai Takahashi into an outline of ash burned into the rock."

Dai Takahashi. I'd never met the man, but I'd heard plenty about him, and I'd been within a mile of him in

Hong Kong all those years ago, when Orel and Belling had been having fun making me look like an asshole. He was just one of a million ex-army officers who set up their own private little army during the civil war, renting out their troops and materiel to anyone who could pay. When everything just sort of fell apart, guys like him and Colonel Anners found themselves the only thing resembling authority within a hundred miles, and most set themselves up as tiny little kings. Five years ago the System Pigs would never have allowed that shit to stand, but the System Pigs weren't what they used to be.

I remembered hammering out a deal with his girl with the funky glowing eyes, and I looked over at Hense, who was talking in a low voice as she gestured violently at her handheld.

"Director," I said, giving it a little grin to remind her that I didn't give a shit that she'd taken over for Dick Marin. She held one finger up and didn't stop speaking or look at me. I pushed a smile onto my face. "*Janet*," I said loudly.

She considered just ignoring me again, but then obviously thought better of that strategy and looked up from her handheld to stare at me, still talking quietly to someone either in the cockpit or a million fucking miles away, probably shitting diodes out their aluminum ass at the tone she was using.

"Tell Takahashi I want a meeting."

She kept talking for a second or two, and then without transition raised her voice. "What?"

"Tell him Avery Cates wants a meeting."

Hense just stood there again for a long moment, staring at me, her dark face blank. She was terrifying, this tiny, doll-like black woman with glossy, stiff-looking hair.

I didn't know if she was communicating with a dozen of herself like Marin used to do, holding seven conversations simultaneously—though Marin used to just seem insane when that happened, instead of terrifyingly calm—or if she was grinding a decision tree through her chipset brain. I remembered her leaving me for dead in Bellevue: *I am a woman who keeps her deals. I see no reason to kill you, Avery. Because the Monks will almost certainly do it for me.* She'd been pretty fucking calm *then*, too.

"Why," she finally said, cocking her head to the side like she was listening to someone else, a gesture that reminded me so strongly of Dick Marin I shivered in sudden recognition, "would I do that, Avery?"

I tried to cock my head at a complementary angle. "Tell him we had a deal in Hong Kong and he fucked me over, and I have a complaint to register." I nodded assertively. "Tell him he *owes* me."

She kept staring at me. "Does he?"

I shrugged. "Nope. But he's a reputation whore," I said, thinking back on my conversation with his employee with the glowing eyes. "He'll want to defend himself."

Gall laughed, loud and off center. "Shit, takes one to know one, huh?"

We got permission to land one hover way outside of Split in the middle of fucking nowhere. We got a tight approach and a stern warning to make no alterations to the flight plan. We descended gently into a flat, open area that had once been cultivated fields, still squared off and obvious from the air despite the scum of brush and new, wild growth that had crept up. The landing was easy, just a slow glide down to the ground; I didn't even realize we'd made touchdown until the displacers cut off, leaving us all in a throbbing silence.

Hense crossed to one of the open seats and sat, all without taking her eyes from her handheld. "We wait," she said before anyone could even ask her. "When Takahashi arrives, Cates and Mehrak go. No one else. Avery, keep in mind you are not authorized to make any deals. Since you have a prior relationship, you can open the conversation with this piece of shit mercenary. You can bring his demands back. But you can't *agree* to anything."

I sketched her a little salute as I stood up. "Sho, boss, sho." I gave Mehrak a slap on the shoulder as I moved toward the bay hatch, an entire side of the hover, designed to let dozens of Stormers shimmy down to the surface on silver wires. "C'mon, asshole. Let's go out there and tell the man in charge we aren't authorized to do shit, and so we're just wasting his time."

It was cool and damp, and my boots sank an inch or so into the ground when I jumped from the hover's bay. I stood for a moment, looking around—from ground level it looked more like sparse wilderness than slowly collapsing fields—and started walking. Mehrak stuck to me like we were tethered.

"Where are we *walking* to?" he asked. These were more words than I'd ever heard him speak. His voice was a pleasant bass, deep and smooth. He could have worked for the Vids, back when there'd been Vids.

"There's another clearing just a bit this way," I said, fixing the image of the area from above in my head. "He'll most probably want to be out of sight of the SSF hover just in case." I looked over my shoulder at him and almost laughed. He was staring in dismay at his beautiful shoes, now encased in thick, black mud. "We're on his turf, so we came crawling. That's the problem with the System Pigs. You never give in to the practical considerations."

"Fuck" was all he said.

The next clearing was just a thin scrub of trees away, although every branch wanted to scrape me raw as we pushed our way through. The other side was almost identical, just long grass and deep mud, a few big rocks to spice things up. I made for the approximate center, and Mehrak followed me, cursing under his breath the whole way.

"You got orders to put me down if I do anything crazy?" I asked without looking at him, just scanning the horizon. I could see dark, thin smoke not so far off.

"Yep," he responded immediately, without any hesitation. "But I'm also supposed to take the long view of what *crazy* means, darling."

I smiled. Honest cops amused me. I could hear the roar of ancient engines, and a second or two later trucks burst into the clearing. They were old, rusty hulks from another century, rubber tires and retrofitted internal combustion engines with solar panels mounted on the hoods. The smoke was burning lubricant, I figured, and wondered if these old pieces of shit were one-time-use kind of vehicles—you drove them until they seized up, then you piled into the next one and hoped it made it the rest of the way.

Four trucks in total, each crammed full of people, each person armed to the fucking teeth. The trucks did a slow ballet around us, puking black smoke and grinding the mud into a lathery froth, and I guessed about a hundred shitkickers, all with knives and sidearms, rifles on their backs and in their hands. Most wore the remnants of the old army uniform, the weird, flowing white fabric—it still gave me the willies to think about it next to my skin— though some looked like they'd probably been slitting throats and shooting people for profit right up until Takahashi rolled into town one day with a better offer.

I wondered how much ammo they had left. I guessed they each had a handful of rounds for their rifles and probably nothing at all for the handguns. And they were probably under strict orders not to shoot without a really good fucking reason.

The trucks ground to a halt and the engines went dead immediately, filling the air with just the gentle clicks and taps of cooling metal. None of the men and women in the truck beds moved or said anything. After a moment the doors on one of the trucks popped open, and two people descended from the cab to approach us. One was a tall, thin black man in a nice suit of gray clothes, his collar popped and his necktie fresh and colorful. His tight curls were cut close to his round, small head, and his eyes glowed a soft blue I remembered from Takahashi's other assistant, Mardea, dead back in Hong Kong.

Walking just slightly in front of him was a kid, the tallest, thinnest kid I'd ever seen, dressed head to toe in black skintight leather—leather pants, leather vest, leather jacket, leather gloves. He wore a pair of flashy sunglasses and his long, perfectly straight and perfectly black hair hung in greasy strands around his face. He was a handsome kid; his clear, tan skin, high cheekbones, and long, sharp nose gave him a nice symmetry. As he walked, he gestured continuously at a large handheld, about as big as one of his own hands, and didn't look up at us even when he came to a halt a few feet away.

"Mr. Cates," the black guy said, smiling in a way that was somehow *precisely* polite, without edging into friendly or sliding back into hostile. "Mr. Takahashi's time is valuable. He recalls dealing with you in Hong Kong. He regrets that you feel he has not lived up to your agreement, but he feels strongly there are reasonable objections to your statement of injury. He would also like to point out that he lost a very valuable employee and did not receive payment on the bargain in any event." He raised one eyebrow, again in a precisely calculated way—lower or higher, I decided, would have conveyed the wrong impression. "However, Mr. Takahashi respects you. You are famous for your ability and your honor. Thus he has agreed to this meeting."

The kid just kept gesturing, all his attention on the handheld. I looked at him and then back at his man.

I stretched it out a little, letting my eyes roam, my augments sharpening my vision a little. I fixed on the details. The people in the truck, now that they were stationary and I could get a good look at them, were a mixed bag: Some of them were watching me with the alert, careful look of someone trained to it, but some were dozing, or staring with the unblinking look of fucking terror or stupidity. Some were holding their rifles—a mix of newer shredders and some old stock like SPS had used in Italy—with obvious familiarity and comfort. Others looked like they would shoot both their feet off before figuring out where the trigger was.

The trucks were in worse shape than I'd thought at first, and I could smell something chemical and sweet in the air—fuel, I decided. Exactly what, I wasn't sure.

I looked back at Takahashi's man, still giving me polite, his eyes still glowing. But I wondered if he was hooked up to anything. It was possible to run a private net off solar generators and your own booster dishes, but that was expensive and difficult and wouldn't have much range anyway. I decided he wasn't getting any signal from anywhere. The eyes just glowed.

I nodded my head, trying to match his dry approach. I didn't even look at Takahashi himself, who was frowning at the tiny screen of his handheld, his long, elegant fingers working the gestures so quickly I wondered how he held onto the small square of hard plastic. Takahashi obviously thought he was above things like conversation and paying attention to known contract killers. Then I noted his lack of even a sidearm, and I took a breath and started lying.

"It was my understanding that I was under Mr. Takahashi's protection when we made our agreement. I was attacked just seconds later and no attempt to secure me or my party was ever made."

The kid suddenly looked up, fingers pausing for a moment. A fucking reputation whore. People were always glad-handing me about my stellar *reputation*, but I knew it was just polite bullshit. I'd known assholes like Takahashi before. They thought it all meant something, and they were fucking prickly as shit about theirs.

Takahashi looked back down at his handheld and his man spoke again.

"Mr. Takahashi regrets this misapprehension. You had reached an agreement *in principle*," he said smoothly, glowing eyes creeping me out. "But you had not transacted your business, and thus no responsibility was transferred to Mr. Takahashi. He regrets this, and wishes you to know he would have very much liked to have worked with you in Hong Kong. It would have been an honor." Suddenly the black man grinned widely, his whole face unfolding into glee like a flower. "In fact, Mr. Takahashi would like you to know that if your current commitments allow for it, he would be happy to make you an offer for service in his organization, at a very high level."

I thought back to Morales. Everyone wanted to hire me on.

I gave a stiff, overdone bow. "Tell Mr. Takahashi, when you fucking see him next, that I regret I cannot accept his generous offer to go sit in the mud and jack off for the remaining couple of months we all have left. And that I accept his fucking apologies concerning Hong Kong."

The kid looked up sharply again, stared at me for a moment, and then as one he and his man turned and walked back to their truck.

"You always take the piss out of people who have a hundred guns pointed at you like that?" Mehrak whispered.

The trucks all started with a roar and a huge belch of black smoke. I turned my head to look at Mehrak, who was pin-perfect from the ankles up, and a slop of mud from the ankles down. "We're under *par-lay*," I said, remembering the word. "That stiff asshole wouldn't even use harsh words as long as we're negotiating with *honor.*"

As the trucks spun around us, heading back toward the woods, Mehrak and I both turned and started slogging our way back to the SSF hover.

"You didn't really want to talk to him, darling, did you?" Mehrak said quietly, maybe with a note of unexpected understanding.

I shook my head, pulling out my pack of cigarettes and shaking two loose, holding them out to him without thinking. "Nope. Just wanted to get a look at him and his people. We were never going to make a fucking deal with that asshole. He's been a tiny king for too long, too used to getting his way, being bought off instead of run off." I shrugged, putting both cigarettes between my lips. "I'm going to have to just kill him."

XXIV

IF YOU WERE PAYING ME, I'D TELL YOU THAT COSTS EXTRA

What are you up to, you crazy bastard? Dolores Salgado whispered in my head. *You've been too calm. I'd say you've been "happy," but I've never seen that before so I don't have a frame of reference.*

I looked around at everyone and tried to imagine a shrug for her. *It helps to have a reason,* I thought back at her.

"Bring up that image," I said. Marko started to move, then hesitated, looking at Hense. She looked like she had something furry and sour stuck in her throat. After a second or two she nodded, and Marko gestured at the table. A sharp image of the area around Split popped into the air. I gestured and it zoomed down to a close-cropped view of the city and a crescent of wilderness around it.

The translucent map lit up the modified hover bay in an eerie green glow. Hense ruled a kingdom that was pretty much a few dozen hovers parked ten miles southeast of Split on a wide black sand beach, seawater lapping up against everything in this maddening, endless rhythm. Each hover had a big, bulky solar panel spread open on top like glass wings, but there hadn't been much sun, and I wondered how far each brick would get. We scuttled across the damp sand from hover to hover taking emergency meetings, the System Security Force a fucking bureaucracy to the last.

At night it freaked me out, because none of the fucking avatars needed light. It was pitch-black, with everyone moving around easily. My own augments stuttered, sometimes bringing the night into perfect clarity, sometimes leaving me nearly blind.

"Looks like Takahashi's bedding down here," I said, pointing at a large clearing north of the city. "It's clear of the radiation bloom and gives him old-road access to most of the rest of countryside. You can see his truck yard over here, and these are tents. The possible landing areas are also visible here, here, and here, and you can see his mining operations pretty clearly. Takahashi owns the immediate area."

"Working for Orel," Hense said.

I nodded. "Sure. The old man's not stupid—he knows someday someone comes after him. Step one's gonna be setting up camp outside the city, so he gets Takahashi to secure his ass. So if we're going after the old man, first we have to take Takahashi out of the picture." Hense opened her mouth and I talked right into it. "In years past, Director, I would have pegged the SSF for shoving a fleet of hovers right into his groin, a real scorch-the-earth, damn-your-own-casualties kind of operation, just so you could piss into his skull and show the world that no one denies the System Pigs *permission to fucking land*, right?"

I waited until she tried to talk again. I was enjoying

being Janet Hense's boss, whether she realized our roles or not. "But you *can't*," I shoved into her open mouth. "This is your wad, and once you shoot it, you've got nothing left. You spend it wiping Takahashi off the map, you've got nothing left to take on Split. So this is *my* problem, then."

Glancing left, I saw Grisha hiding a grin behind his hand and a burning cigarette, and I threw him a wink. He was crammed between Marko and Mehrak in the tiny space, looking yellow and sweaty.

Hense waited me out for half a minute, holding back as I grinned at her. "We don't have time," she finally snapped, biting off the words like they were bits of leather in her mouth. "Recon, intel gathering—there isn't *time* to plan another operation."

Her voice was absorbed by the dense, soft soundproofing that lined the interior of the hover, just dying a foot short of me and sinking into the floor. The SSF couldn't mount a raid on a two-bit warlord because they didn't have the fuel and bullets to spare, but they still had kick-ass soundproofing on their hovers, which seemed like yen fucking well spent.

I shook my head. "We don't need time. I go tonight. I don't need anyone, but you can send Mehrak with me if you want."

Mehrak scowled at me. "Brilliant. Thanks a fucking *lot*, you knee biter."

I remembered Orel telling me that even if you could be rebooted from cold storage, no one liked dying, and I extended the middle finger of my right hand in his direction.

Hense leaned forward and put her skinny stick arms onto the table. "Avery—"

"I have everything I need," I said. "Takahashi's fronting. He doesn't have ammo; half the guns he brought with him

yesterday were props. He doesn't have manpower; half the
fucking *people* he brought yesterday were fucking *props*."
I held up my hand and began ticking off fingers. "He's
been operating since before the war ended—that's a long
time for a warlord to hold his crew together out in the cold,
Janet. He's got solar panels bolted to his trucks, but they're
not connected—he's running those trucks on fuel, ethanol
most probably. He brought a hundred fucking *props* with
him to meet little old *me*." I closed my hand. "He's fronting. He's weak and he's trying to fool us to hold us off. I
can get in there, slit his throat, and get out without breaking
a sweat." I glanced at Mehrak. "Well, maybe a little sweat
if I have to drag your boy behind me like a lead boot."

Mehrak leaned back and flipped me an elegant finger
right back. I was starting to like him, avatar or not. Which
wasn't good for him. Everyone I liked was dead.

Hense was shaking her head. "We don't want quiet.
We don't want slit throats in the night." She studied me,
chewing a rubber lip. There was so much unnecessary
programming in the avatars it was stunning, sometimes,
when I noticed shit like that. Then she leaned back suddenly. "We need noise. If you cut him down in the night,
we still have a huge number of fuckheads with guns in our
way. We need to chase them off. We need them to feel like
the universe just kicked them in the head. We need them
running for their fucking lives into the forest."

I winked. "Sure. If you were paying me, I'd tell you
that costs extra."

"Hold up."

I turned to find Marko, Mehrak, and Grisha following

me. The sun was hidden behind a scum of gray clouds, and the air smelled like salt, a constant, endless pushing wind of it making any movement aside from the one the cosmos wanted difficult, exhausting. The three men didn't look right together. When I'd first met Grisha he'd seemed like a typical Techie—a skinny fuck with fake glasses and a perpetual squint. So had Marko. Marko had gotten dark, but he was still just a Techie, a little round at the middle and his hands twitching like they were gesturing at a handheld all the time. Now Grisha looked like someone I would have taken a meeting with back in New York, someone who would have *hired* me, and argued the price. Mehrak was all cop, all the time, smooth and smug and self-assured behind his shiny square glasses. The three of them didn't fit.

"Hello, Avery," Grisha said as they caught up with me. He offered me a cigarette with a breathless smile. "That was an excellent presentation."

"I'd hire you, dear," Mehrak said with a grin, his eyes on Grisha's offered smoke. "Shit, I miss cigs."

I looked them over and slowly accepted the cigarette. "All right," I said, turning to resume my walk to the beach. "Let's hear the pitch."

We walked in silence for a moment or two, and then Grisha cleared his throat. "Avery, you are...too fucking calm."

I lit my cigarette and climbed a dune, the glittering black sand crumbling under me and making it a slow job. My damaged augments moderated my breathing and circulation, still doing that much for me. "Too *calm*?"

Grisha's breathing was like a chainsaw, heavy and wet. His cigarette dangled from his lips as he talked. "Just days ago you were killing random strangers. Now you are humming happy songs and planning a side operation with gusto, like nothing happened these past few years." He twitched his hands up. "It is disturbing, especially as we plan to accompany you."

I stopped and spun. Marko was right behind me and squawked in surprise, stumbling back and then falling over, landing on his ass in the damp sand, arms splayed out behind him.

"Fuck, Avery!" he hissed under his breath.

"You're not coming with me on Takahashi," I said, looking at Grisha.

Grisha smiled, smoke rising slowly around his face, the damp twilight reflecting in his glasses. He'd never once seemed concerned I might hit him, in all the fractured time I'd known him. "Yes, we are, Avery. I do not mean to insult you, but you are a very important resource, Avery. We must take steps to ensure your safety."

I took the cigarette from my lips and spat tobacco. My teeth ached. I had several molars missing, but I was used to that. Now my whole jaw ached with my pulse, like someone was going to punch me so hard in the future it reverberated backward in time. Grisha and I studied each other for a few seconds. He was on the balls of his feet— his arms were lazy and hung at his sides easily, and he was grinning at me, but I knew that if I dived forward and tried to get my hands on him he'd spin away and give me a good shot in the kidneys. If I pulled my gun he'd surge forward and clamp both hands on my wrist, forcing me to aim at my feet. Grisha was trying hard to look relaxed. When people worked at looking relaxed, my experience was they were ready to break your fucking neck.

"My safety, Grisha?"

He shrugged, giving me a crooked smile. "We have one shot at this, Avery. One shot at saving what is left, before we go gentle into that good night, yes?"

Mehrak turned toward the breaking waves and muttered, "Rage, rage against the dying of the light," in a low, singsongy voice. "I miss getting shitfaced, too, if anyone's wondering. End of the fucking world, and I get to face it sober. *There's* justice."

"As I said: Your calm is disturbing, Avery," Grisha said, stepping forward a half step and putting a hand on my arm. I tensed, and then forced myself to relax. Grisha was not going to stab me in the belly with a shiv. If Grisha decided to kill me—and I could think of plenty of scenarios when that might come to pass—he would come at me from the front, with a word of warning. "Do you understand that you represent our last maneuver? You go up against Orel, your winning or losing determines whether the *entire human race* withers on the vine, fades from the universe. Yes? It is you." He shrugged, releasing my arm. "I must be sure you make it to go after Orel. And I must be sure you understand that you *must* take him alive."

His eyes were locked on mine. They were bloodshot and watery, dull brown, surrounded by an intricate spiderweb of deep smile lines. His glasses were just thin panes of glass in a wire frame; the frame was rusted and had stained his nose a dull red.

I kept my eyes on his. "I understand," I said. I didn't say anything else.

XXV

OOH, LOOK, AVERY'S TRYING TO THINK

"Mr. Marko," I whispered as loudly as I dared.

Marko stopped and turned to look back at me. He'd toughened up a little, I could see, but he was still kind of tubby, and moved slow and loud. It was a wonder the Markos of the world had survived long enough to push their genes into the pool. He was letting his hair grow back, and it sat on his head like a frizzy cloud, a shadow of the proud sculpture that had once rested there, which wrapped down the sides of his head to combine seamlessly with his beard, which in turn grew down his neck like mold. He was fucking made of hair.

If Glee was still alive, if I hadn't let her die, she would have said, *Ooh, Avery is judgmental. Avery is blind to his own fucking* horrifying appearance.

"Hang back. You're tech support on this little mission, just in case Takahashi has a surprise in his rusty little pockets."

Marko scowled in the bright moonlight but let the three of us move past him. We'd been dropped about ten minutes west of Takahashi's main camp and had been hoofing it in costume, each of us wearing the grimy, mix-and-match military clothing I'd seen all of Takahashi's people wearing when we'd met, each of us with a rifle slung over a shoulder. We'd emerge from the darkness and just blend in—even if he was blustering about his troop strength, Takahashi had too many people on this detail for a couple of new faces to be noticed. If challenged, whatever language was being spoken we didn't understand, and Mehrak, Grisha, and Marko were my cover: The idea was to keep me moving, no matter what.

If Remy was still alive, he would have hissed into my ear: *You're breaking your own fucking rule, man. You haven't done the recon. You don't know* shit *about what you're going to find here.*

I didn't need to. Takahashi had come out of the new army, and I knew how he'd set up his camp: He'd be in the middle. There'd be clear lanes of foot traffic toward it. If there was power to be had, his tent would have it and it would very likely be lit up like a fucking beacon in the night. Takahashi probably had a core of people who were trained and experienced and loyal, but he was infected with shitheads. That had been obvious from our meeting. Either they were conscripts plucked from the local shitholes or they'd been offered some hazy bounty in the future for a year of service or something like that—but they were either too low quality or too untrustworthy to get working guns. That meant that if alarms got tripped, our strategy would be to make noise. Stir shit up. When an armed camp didn't have cohesion and discipline, it was pretty fucking easy to turn it into chaos, and chaos was my friend.

If Glee were still alive, she would have said, *Oh, Avery's all chaos theory and shit. Avery is fucking* chaotic. And I suddenly thought of Adora, who would have smiled and asked me if I thought I was so much more disciplined.

The edge of Takahashi's camp was a garbage dump, a few dozen square feet of cleared ground piled high with plastics, animal bones, and twisted, scorched chunks of metal. I stared at the bones and my stomach flipped, the rusty rounded ends, the bits of flesh still clinging to them here and there; it was fucking disgusting. It smelled pretty ripe—they were using the area as an open-air latrine, too, I guessed, my boots sinking into the mess two inches deep.

I could see tattered tents and the familiar blue tarp just a few dozen feet beyond. I turned and signaled to Grisha, Mehrak, and Marko, the three of them glowing blue in the moonlight and looking pretty much like a trio of worn-down mercenaries. With a nod from each, they drifted off to the left and right, putting some space between us.

From above, the camp was a fairly clean layout of concentric circles, travel lanes spiraling around. Takahashi had been here long enough for everything to take on a sheen of permanence: The lanes between the tents were packed down and lined with stones. The cook fires—fucking cook fires, like something out of an old Vid—had complex structures for hanging pots erected over them, and the mercenaries lounged outside their pathetic shelters with an easygoing familiarity. This was home.

As I walked between them, I could feel eyes on me. I kept mine straight ahead. Marko, Mehrak, and Grisha were fanned out in the midst of the tents, matching my stride but weaving their way through the fields, hopefully unnoticed. If Remy had lived, I could have told him to not look at anyone, to just keep his head up. Looking at people you were trying to walk past was a sure way to get them to say something to you. The trick was to act natural, to keep up some business.

I turned my head slightly and spat onto the path.

My heart kept stuttering in my chest, which was new. It would beat normally, then suddenly pause for a count of two, then slam back into a steady rhythm with a lurch. It wasn't bothering me, physically, so I ignored it and blamed it on my rusting augments, which had never been meant for long-term deployment anyway, much less long-term deployment after blowing through the termination sequence unsuccessfully.

It was quiet. There was a murmur of conversation, and occasional shouts in the distance, but in general the camp felt calm and peaceful, a semipermanent city that had settled in. Considering the state of the rest of the world, I figured Takahashi hadn't had to deal with too many armed groups at his level—if you had troops and guns and some sort of control over them, you did like Anners and created a little duchy for yourself, or you took a big-ticket job like Takahashi and spent your days guarding Canny Orel's ass. You didn't roam the wilderness wasting lives and ammo on pointless fights. Takahashi's little private army felt flabby and sleepy to me as I walked—just a sense. I didn't *know* anything. I had no raw data. Just my gut telling me the hunting was easy around here if you didn't mind a little radiation in your meat, and these fucks had had nothing to do for years except occasionally intimidate a few civilians on a raid. They were soft.

If Remy had lived, he would tell me I was being an

asshole, thinking I had some magic gut that told me shit without needing any actual facts.

I kept the image of the camp from above in my head as I walked, hearing my feet cracking twigs and pieces of glass embedded in the soft ground. The air smelled like fifteen kinds of smoke and fifty kinds of burning flesh, and my stomach rose up again. I loved N-tabs, and dreaded the day they would say, *Sorry, Avery, you ate the last ones yesterday. It's fucking charred animal meat for you from now on.* I didn't give a fuck about the animals. They tasted like death and I wanted to throw up every bit of them I ate, was all. With N-tabs you were always hungry, but I'd never thrown one up, not once.

I looked to my left and saw Marko and Mehrak threading their way around tents. I looked to my right and Grisha was close to the pathway, and he jerked his chin at me in greeting, a cigarette burning between his thin lips.

I looked straight ahead again. Having competent people felt good and was a nice change of pace. It was eerie, the soft voices all around, the smoke hanging in the air, the soft snaps and pops of my passing. I felt like a ghost.

As the pathway curved to my left, bringing me more or less in direct line with what I'd assumed was Takahashi's tent—larger than the rest, in better shape, roughly in the center of the camp—I spotted a trio of women coming toward me. They were all short and tiny, but all three had leather ammo belts crisscrossed on their chests, sidearms on their hips, and rifles slung over their shoulders. Something about their gait and the fact that they were wearing precious ammunition told me they were probably old hands on Takahashi's detail. I looked at them for a few seconds, obvious about it, and when they glanced at me, I nodded. If Remy were here, I would have told him that when someone was staring at you already, ducking your head and trying to be invisible was a sure way to be noticed in a bad way. So you get yourself noticed in a neutral way. These women ran into new shitheads they'd never seen before every day, and it was better to draw attention away from my three friends in the shadows.

As we drew close together, the one nearest me looked and chucked her chin at me. Her dirty-blond hair had been hacked short in a violent way, and her face was deeply lined and covered in dirt. The whites of her eyes seemed bright and pure, though. She came up to my shoulder.

"They heavy tonight, brother?"

A surge of adrenaline ran through me and I thought rapidly, imagining Glee taunting me: *Ooh, look. Avery's trying to* think.

I took a chance—there were only three right answers, anyway; yes, no, and fuck if I know. If Remy had been standing next to me, scowling, hungover, and pissed off, I would have told him that getting paranoid was just stupid—there was no reason for them to suspect anything, so just bluster your way through.

"N'bad," I muttered, grinning and trying to project "dumber than dirt." Then I decided to get a little creative. "Got a smoke?"

She snorted as they passed me. "Fuck, grandpa, you find any smokes, you kick 'em up like everyone else, yeah?"

I snorted back and kept walking. My ragged heartbeat thudded in my ears as my adrenaline crashed, leaving me jerky and shivering. I looked up, and Takahashi's tent was straight ahead. Four men stood outside the flaps, rifles in

their hands, but they didn't seem particularly alert or concerned. They chatted with each other, looking around and
keeping their eyes open, but not exactly keeping fucking
army discipline about it.

The tent itself was just a fucking tent, though it was
made of good strong canvas and was pegged securely into
the ground, with heavy-looking logs sunk into the soft
earth on top of the pegs to stop anything or anyone from
just pulling the tent up. There was a hard shell of some
kind that the tent was erected over, too, which had shown
up on the SSF's scans as metallic alloy and most probably
was a bullet-resistant shielding, so just spraying the tent
with bullets wasn't going to get me very far. I pictured
Takahashi with his fucking handheld and figured that if
they had any sort of network up over the camp, he would
likely be able to summon assistance pretty fucking quick
if I just ducked inside the tent and tried to shoot him in the
face or some other equally complex bit of genius. When
thinking this through after my meeting with the man,
I'd known I needed to get him the fuck out of his tent,
and I needed to convince him to not pull the alarm—or
I needed *everyone* to pull the alarm.

When I was still a few dozen feet away, I angled to
my right and, without the guards paying me any mind, I
stepped off the path into the field of tents. I looked around
and caught sight of Marko and Mehrak, and we raised
a hand into the air in acknowledgment. Then I looked
and found Grisha a few feet away, and we did the same.
With a nod, I reached into my pocket and brought out the
plastic bottle of accelerant, flicked the cap off with my
thumb, and began spraying down the tents around me. It
was almost silent, just a drizzle of liquid, and I moved fast

from tent to tent while Grisha and Marko and Mehrak did the same, dancing and spinning in the darkness.

When I had about a quarter of the bottle left, I crept up on Takahashi's tent from behind and doused it heavily, using every last drop. I brought out my lighter in one hand and my Roon in the other, clicked off the safety, and turned to find Grisha in the shadows. When we saw each other, I nodded. A second later, tents started lighting up, a sudden orange bloom of light everywhere all at once.

I counted to ten and then flicked the lighter into flame. When it was a healthy, steady yellow in my hand, I tossed it onto the tent, which immediately burst into a thick carpet of fire.

I didn't pause to admire it. I put the Roon down by my hip and moved around the cone of fire I'd just created. The camp was erupting into chaos as people fled their burning tents and shouted in the night. If they were following the plan, Marko, Mehrak, and Grisha were angling around to cover me as I approached the front of the tent, where three of the guards had taken off to investigate the fires. I took a bead on the fourth, a tall black man who held his rifle with a modicum of experience, and whose scalp popped off his head in an almost comical way when I shot him. As he dropped I stepped quickly over to where he'd been standing and matched his position and posture, just staring out into the night.

Then, with shouts and gunfire suddenly filling the night, I waited.

It didn't take too long. Even with his bulletproof shielding, he couldn't stay in the tent; he'd be cooked. A minute or so after I'd killed his guard, the kid emerged calmly from his burning tent, a satchel under one arm, his handheld in another. He took two steps into the night and paused, standing right next to me as he scanned the camp, watching tent after tent burst into flame. For a second I just studied his profile, wallowing in the sense that I commanded the universe, that I could keep him standing there as long as I liked. Then, almost regretting the necessity of shattering the moment, I raised my Roon and shot him in the ear. He dropped to the soggy ground soundlessly, and I paused to put two more shells into him before stepping quickly back onto the main pathway and crossing to the other side.

Mehrak found me first. The fires had spread pretty well, with tents blooming up one after the other, and Takahashi's men were already a fucking mess, shouting and running, no one in charge. As I converged on the avatar, we were both shoved and pushed by people running just to run.

"I lost your little friend," Mehrak said in his clear, distinct accent.

I nodded and we started walking south, toward our predetermined rendezvous a mile out. "I told Grish to keep an eye on him. He'll probably show up carrying Marko on his back."

Mehrak nodded. "Nice work, this. Didn't think a pro like Takahashi would go up this easy."

I nodded. "He was ready for a war, for an army trying to dislodge him." I holstered my gun, the heat of a hundred fires beating against me. "He wasn't ready for dirty fucking pool. He wasn't ready for me."

XXVI

NOT AS MANY PROBLEMS AS BEING TURNED INSIDE OUT BY RADIATION

When Grisha found me in one of the empty hovers on the beach, he paused for a moment in the hatchway and burst out laughing.

"You look like a piece of spoiled fruit," he said, stepping into the hover, followed closely by Marko and Mehrak. The three of them were apparently my best friends in the whole world. Everywhere I was, they went.

I was sitting enveloped in the heavy, bulky rad suit Grisha had supplied to me, except for the headgear, which lay on the filthy, muddy floor of the hover next to me. It weighed about the same as a planet, was about five thousand degrees, and smelled like the last guy who wore it had melted and been absorbed into the weird, coarse fabric of the lining where he'd continued to rot on a molecular level. I had a canteen of the terrible German liquor they'd had in Berlin and I'd been drinking from it for two hours. My head pounded in time with my heartbeat, and my mouth was filled with sand.

I raised the canteen up and waggled it at Grisha as he approached. He made a face.

"Fuck, Avery, you stink. What will you do when you have to piss?"

I winked. "The question should be, what *did* I do when I had to piss."

He laughed again. "You are a fucking animal, yes?"

I tried to shrug, but the suit was too heavy. It appeared to be a single piece of strange, gray material, seamless and stretchy. There was one slit in the back you stepped into, which mended itself magically when pressed together. When you put on the helmet it sealed itself and somehow generated an air mixture, though I couldn't see any kind of tanks.

Grisha knelt before me as the other two inspected the bay for seats. This was one of the old drop hovers, used to dump Stormers on our heads. There was no furniture, aside from narrow benches along each side, and the interior was a mess of damp sandy mud. Mehrak was wearing a spiffy, old-fashioned suit, complete with vest and gold links on his huge white cuffs, and he stood there pondering the muck with an expression of total confusion on his synthetic face. Marko was back in Techie scrubs and after a second's hesitation just sat down. He seemed to have gained an inch of hair overnight.

"How is the weight?" Grisha asked, studying the suit.

"Like I'm carrying *you*," I said. He reached out and took the canteen and tilted it back into his mouth. "It's hot, doesn't bend well, and the headgear gives me about an inch of peripheral vision."

He nodded, grimacing as he swallowed and held the canteen over his head. Marko leaned forward and took it. "Yes, about what was expected. You foresee problems?"

"Fuck *yes*, I foresee *problems*," I said thickly. "But not as many problems as being turned inside out by radiation."

Marko dissolved into a paroxysm of spluttering coughs, holding the canteen out and away from him like it had bitten him. After a moment Mehrak shrugged and plucked the canteen from his hand and just held it, looking, for a moment, incredibly sad. I thought about never drinking again for the rest of fucking *eternity* and felt sorry for a System Cop for maybe the first time in my life. For a second I had drunk tears welling up in me, and I swallowed with heavy, bitter effort. I was not some fucking kid plotting his first-ever rat-cart takedown with some other snot-nosed orphans still wondering if Mom was coming back to claim them.

Grisha stood, turned, and sat down next to Mehrak without even considering the filth factor. Grisha was fucking practical. If the only seat was filthy, well, you sat in filth. "He will be in Monk chassis. Stronger than us, faster. More precise with aim. Reloads on the weapon will be nearly instant. Then he will have his mental abilities, the God Augment. He will Push us. He will pick us up and fling us about."

I laboriously raised a heavy arm to waggle a thick gloved finger at him. "He isn't Pushing *me*, if that cunt back in Spain is to be believed. Said it took time and planning to keep me under. And if he's stuck with original Monk issue, those guns jammed like nothing I've ever seen. But don't forget his new fun little thing, *Traveling*. He'll pop into Zeke and make him turn on us."

Marko blinked and straightened up, his hairy face red

and damp under his whiskers. "Why me? Fuck, he might do it to *you*."

I started to shrug amiably, but Grisha shook his head and spoke first. "No. Avery . . . Avery's brain is fucked up." He threw a smile at me as he fished cigarettes out of his pocket. "No offense, Avery. After Chengara, his brain was fundamentally changed. He should have been erased, like everyone else who went through second-pass version of AV-79 Amblen processing, but he was not. His brain . . . *re-wired* itself. Accommodated Salgado and . . . others, repaired itself." He reached over and claimed the canteen from Mehrak. "I doubt Orel *can* 'travel' into Avery. If he does, he may not find what he expects."

I remembered Marin, far away and long ago, telling me, *Now you, you're from imprint one. Imprint one scans out at one hundred and fourteen percent complete. Which is, of course, impossible.* I wondered how I always remembered shit like that so perfectly, every word, exactly. He'd been trying to brain fuck me, of course, to convince me I was an avatar unaware of himself, but I wondered if the data he'd been using had been real—rule number one of lying to someone was to use as many facts as possible. It made your lie seem real. If Remy had lived, I would have leaned over and told him that, and he would have opened one eye, then reached out for the canteen and gone back to pretending to be asleep.

I came back to myself and winked at Marko. "See, Zeke? Has to be you. I'll apologize in advance if I have to shoot you."

Marko stared at me, then looked down at his muddy shoes. "Fuck," he whispered, stretching it out into one long noise.

I wondered if I'd be able to stand up on my own with the suit on. I thought I probably should have considered that before getting shitfaced on the floor. My vision seemed to have waves in it, and when I shut my eyes everything started to spin, so I opened them again.

"We go tomorrow, yes?" Grisha suddenly said, looking at Mehrak.

The cop glanced at Grish and then nodded. "Assuming we get a full day's sun to charge up the panels, yes. The panels only supplement the fuel supply, though, running electric motors alongside the solid-fuel cells—we have only enough overall juice, assuming a full day's charge, for one long-range trip with full weapon activation. But, yes, tomorrow." He looked at me, raising a jolly eyebrow. "Unless you think we ought to give princess here—"

"Avery will be fine," Grisha said decisively. "He drinks professionally. Take the canteen with us and let him hydrate." He looked at me. "You are ready, yes?"

I nodded and tried to give him a thumbs-up, but my arms were too heavy to lift, so I just nodded as assertively as I could manage.

Mehrak's expression was bland and unconvinced, but he shrugged. "Bricks in the air before dawn, darlings; the assault hits half an hour later, drawing whatever muscle the old man's got around the palace. He's got a surprising number of people working security around the palace. They die off pretty fast, but people keep streaming in."

"Pushed," Marko suggested quietly, scratching at his neck beard.

Mehrak waggled his brow. "Maybe. I've never seen the Pusher could maintain hundreds of people like that over a period of fucking days, weeks."

Marko snorted. "That old fuck traveled with his *brain* to Berlin from Split and took over a series of poor fucks," he pointed out, sounding admiring. "I think it's safe to say this is a new kind of thing for you to wonder about."

I laughed. "Shit, Zeke, you got mouthy."

I almost said, *I'm gonna miss your fucking stupidity*, but stopped myself. No reason to state the obvious about Mr. Marko's chances of surviving me.

"So, we will go at the same time, find our sewer hole, and begin infiltration," Grisha said. "By the time we attain the main part of the underground complex, our friends the police should be in full swing, drawing Orel's forces and, hopefully, attention up and out." He made a fruity little flapping gesture with his hand, and I started to laugh a little. I felt pretty good, despite being sick to my stomach, way too old, friendless, and sitting in a urine-soaked rad suit so heavy it was smothering me by increments. I felt at peace. Tomorrow, I thought. Tomorrow I avenged everyone, every*thing*.

"What if he has a reserve of people down there?" Mehrak said, frowning. "We can't assume he'll be rattling around down there alone."

Grisha shrugged. "Regular people, we do not worry about them. We have Avery. We have *ourselves*." He paused and glanced over at Marko, who seemed absorbed in his own fingernails. Then Grisha nodded firmly. "Ourselves. Orel should worry about *us*, not us about his slaves."

Mehrak raised an eyebrow, seeming amused. "And when we run into the glorious Mr. Orel himself in his golden jumpsuit? When he starts tossing us around and making us see visions?"

Grisha nodded. "I have some surprises for him. SPS has not been idle, and we have done much research into the Psionic active."

Surprises, I thought murkily, my head swimming. And then, as my vision folded up on itself, I chased that with *me too*.

XXVII

A MOMENT OF CRAZY

"Light goes green, you bend your fucking knees! You put both hands on the guide clip! You do *not* fucking hesitate!"

The cop had been a real bruiser in his flesh life—a big, red, round face, a thick neck with cords that stood out and big, buggly eyes, bloodshot and genetically outraged. He'd been yelling since birth, I figured, and had been assigned to drop-ship duty because it was the only place in the world where his congenital volume made any sense.

The wind was fucking intense, tearing at us as the hover moved through the air, everything vibrating, the rhythm of it drilling up through my feet into my body, moving my organ around and making my teeth chatter. I was strapped to a harness made of wires so thin and nearly invisible I could not believe it would hold me on the way down. I was about to find out what it had been like for all those Stormers through the years, waiting for roof charges to pop and blow the top off some dive and then plummeting down on their thin, silver wires, seeming to appear out of fucking nowhere. There was no time for us to make an overland approach—we had to be inside the palace on a schedule, so we had to jump out of a fucking hover. I didn't care. I hadn't come this far for the cosmos to kill me this way.

That had been Remy's line, that certainty about your fate. I'd always thought he was a self-pitying asshole for it, expecting him to one day just wake up and be over it. Maybe he'd just learned it from *me*.

The cop smacked one of his mitts against the big light bolted to the side of the bay, protected behind a metal grate. "Light goes green—"

"Say it again and I'm pulling you down after me!" I shouted back over the howling wind. "What am I, a fucking recruit? *Shut up.*"

The cop popped his eyes out at me, and again I was amazed at the artistry involved in the fucking avatars. Then he smirked and clapped his hands together, mimicking washing them, and snapped them apart as he backed away from the open bay. I translated that into *Fuck if I care if you catch a crosswind and get broken in half, asshole.*

Behind me, Grisha leaned forward to shout in my ear. "Light goes green, you bend your fucking knees!"

I tried to stay pissed off, but I burst out laughing. I was going to miss Grisha.

We were wearing the radiation suits already, of course, and in twenty minutes mine had become intolerably heavy, pushing me down relentlessly, squeezing my lungs. They'd been fitted with hip holsters on each side; in the right I had the Roon, oiled and cleaned. In the left I had some random automatic the cops had handed me, no personality. We each had a shredder slung across our chests in a precise way that would make it awkward as hell to quickly deploy but difficult to shake off accidentally as we hurtled downward through the air. I'd found a small pocket along one thigh of the suit where a large old hunting knife fit nicely; I wasn't much of a knife fighter, but a lot of times people saw the guns and forgot there was any other kind of weapon in the world, so a knife was sometimes a nice surprise to have. The pockets of the suit bulged with ammo, and if we didn't have enough between us to kill everything within a mile radius we were fucked to begin with, so it didn't matter.

"Put on your helmet!" Grisha shouted. "One minute!"

I took a deep breath and raised the heavy helmet up and over my head. It seemed to pull down on my arms as I let it settle onto my shoulders, sealing itself to the suit. There was a moment of suffocation, and then some chemical reaction began sweetening the air and I could breathe normally. My vision was hampered, but I was comfortable enough despite having another twenty pounds to lug around. I was already sweating, and my heart was still doing its weird little fluttering thing.

Fuck it, I thought. *Light goes green, bend your fucking knees and quit complaining.*

Out in the distance I could see the flashes and smoke of the main assault, drawing attention and letting the cops vent some of their frustrations. It was beautiful—the explosions and streams of Stormers raining down on their silvery lines, silent and distant, like a Vid being played with the sound off.

The light turned green.

For a second I was frozen. The green light meant bend

your fucking knees, grab onto the clip, and push yourself into the open air, but *fuck* the ground was far away. I was sweating like a stuck pig, and I was jumping into airspace that would cook me from the inside out if not for the suit. I stood for a second staring at the green light, mesmerized.

Jump, dummy, Dick Marin whispered at me.

I didn't bend my fucking knees; I leaned forward and grabbed the guide clip and then kept leaning forward until gravity reached up and plucked me from the bay. There was a moment of crazy when I didn't have a center of gravity and just whipped this way and that, and then everything settled down and it was exhilarating, just gliding down through the air. I couldn't hear anything because of the suit, and I couldn't feel the wind pushing against me; the sensation was like floating with purpose, and for a few seconds I forgot about everything else.

Then I glanced down and thought, *Oh shit*.

The ground came up so quickly I made a squawking noise of surprise, suddenly remembering, vaguely, something about going into a crouch while still in the air and letting go of the guide clip at a precise moment. Then I smacked down hard, bouncing once, the impact absorbed partially by the thick, almost-armor-like material of the radiation suit. I skidded along the rough ground for a second or two and then crashed into something unyielding and came to a sudden, ringing stop.

Almost directly in front of me, Marko managed a perfect landing, dropping onto the ground and into a shuffling run, the silvery wire snapping back up just like I'd been told to expect. His momentum took him a few feet and then he stopped himself and knelt down, like taking a bow. A few moments later, Mehrak, wearing standard Stormer

Obfuscation Kit scrubs instead of the rad suit, hit the ground with similar grace, and when Grisha smacked down like a load of wet shit I was fucking happy, and I watched him roll like a rag doll with something approaching satisfaction. Even the perfect landing Hense's doppelganger—also in standard issue Stormer kit—managed when it landed couldn't ruin the moment.

Marko stepped over and reached out a gloved hand. My earbud sizzled into life. "You okay?"

I let him haul me up. "Peachy. Hitting the ground at a thousand fucking miles an hour is a tonic, you ask me."

"We had mandatory training," Marko said, sounding almost apologetic. "Even the Tech Associates. This was my fifteenth drop."

"Two hundred forty-nine," Mehrak buzzed in. "Two hundred thirty-three live in the field."

"Compare manhood later," Grisha panted in my ear, "and someone help me up. There is no *time*."

I spun around, taking in the scenery and picturing the aerial images. "This way," I said, breathing hard already in the heavy, hot suit.

It was hard to believe the whole area was dangerous—everything looked normal, natural. It was easy to think that the rad suit was a joke, that Hense was trotting along behind me with her endless fission energy hiding a smile as she imagined me sweating and straining under its weight. I had a crazy urge to just shed it, to peel it off and feel the cool air on my skin.

Hense's voice buzzed in my ear. "You ready for him, Cates?"

I smiled inside my humid little world. "Tell me something, Janet: Do you hear yourself? Are you just whispering to yourself constantly? Are there, like, forty echoes of your own voice in your head?"

"This unit is off-net, Avery," she buzzed back, static making her sound thin and distant. "We didn't want any signals getting noticed. I'm independent."

I thought about that. Independent. Fuck, I'd thought I was independent for years, but I was on the Rail, being pushed gently into increasingly terrible things. And I didn't even have circuits where my brain should be, hardwired with who knew what. I didn't have an automatic shutdown routine if my insane leader somehow got shut up for a few weeks.

We were in the right area, but I couldn't see the entrance to the sewers. I spun around, feeling constricted without proper peripheral vision, and finally spotted a big clump of rocks too squared off and too precisely piled to be natural. These turned out to be the edge of near-buried ruins, big slabs of worked stone fallen over onto itself, exhausted. I climbed into the midst of it and followed the outline of the stone, finally finding a sloping indentation into the earth, lined with faded, moss-eaten stone, leading down into darkness. What was left of some previous System, I thought. Some other King Worm had built this, then died, and it was still here, being swallowed an inch a century forever.

"Right here," I breathed.

I waited for everyone to catch up, clambering over the stones and swatting low branches out of their faces. Marko and Grisha were like nimble foam men, all bulk and shapeless material but somehow still able to bound from toe to toe, balanced and easy. They all gathered around the hole and paused, staring down into it.

"Fuck the hazard pay," Mehrak said as melodiously as ever. "This is the worst assignment I've ever gotten."

"Duly noted," Hense snapped. "Now, in. Mehrak takes point, Avery and me in the middle, our two Tinkers in the rear."

"Careful," Grisha said, sounding out of breath but amused. "Parts of avatar can still be broken. You might trip down there in the dark."

Mehrak shrugged. "If I do," he said, "don't recycle my chassis for one of your crunchy geeks, promise?" Without waiting for an answer, he plucked his sidearm from its holster and with a glance around jumped down into the darkness. I gestured on my helmet's built-in light and jumped in after him before Hense could issue me any more instructions.

It wasn't a very far drop. I landed easily on a brick floor and immediately stepped aside to let the rest follow Mehrak and me. We were in a tight little tunnel, big enough for us to walk in single file along its damp, slippery stonework. It graded down a few feet but then appeared to level off to a subtle downgrade, pitch-black aside from the trickle of sunlight from the hole and the thin light Mehrak and I were throwing around. I was just thinking that it was going to be a painful procession with Hense at my back barking orders when a shadow moved up ahead.

"Get down!" I shouted, my own voice buzzing in my ears with feedback. Mehrak dropped to a knee instantly, his gun coming up in time with my own. For a moment, we were statues, trembling with the desire to pull the trigger and make some fucking noise.

"Oy, don't fuckin' shoot," a woman's voice called from the gloom. "I'm comin' on up to ya. Don't fuckin' *shoot* me."

The shadow moved again, creeping up toward us, slowly resolving into a tall, thin woman with bright red hair, an unpretty face but a nice body, shown off to good effect in her skintight pants. She wasn't wearing a lick of protective gear, and as her face resolved in the dim light I instantly knew why.

"Fuck me," I said, straightening up. "Mara."

She stopped a foot or so beyond Mehrak's reach and put her hands on her hips. "Ach, Avery, you know better'n anyone here there's no-fucking-body named *Mara* in this world. If you don't recognize yer old pal Cainnic, or a version o' him anyway, then t'hell with you."

"Avatar?" Hense hissed from behind us. "Of *Orel*?"

Mara's eyes flashed over my shoulder. "That's right, sister. An' I come bearing the fucking flag of *truce*."

I licked sweat from my lips and wished fervently I could wipe it from my eyes. "Why's that, asshole?"

Mara's face smiled sweetly, transformed, for a second, into a pretty woman. "Because I've gone fucking batshit insane."

XXVIII

SOMEONE WAS TELLING ME A STORY ABOUT BEING KNOCKED ONTO THE GROUND

I raised my gun and took a half-lunging step forward toward the avatar, looking just like the familiar young girl with reddish hair, a flat, angular face, and long, graceful-looking limbs. "This was a poor fucking day to find me and taunt me, Mickey," I said as she scrambled backward from me, slamming up into the ancient, smooth stone of the tunnel. I pushed the barrel into its nose. "A poor. Fucking. Day."

"Cates!" Hense snarled behind me.

"Avery!" Grisha shouted, breaking up into wet coughs. "Wait!"

I paused, my own breathing through my nose sounding impossibly loud in my ears. My HUD, inexplicably bright and shiny in my vision again, reported that my core body temperature was rising, but still well within tolerations. I flicked my eyes to my left out of habit, getting a good look at the shadowy interior of the rad suit's helmet. I forced myself to dial it back a little, and I eased my finger off the trigger.

"Say it fast," I said. The Mara avatar had its hands up by its ears, its tits thrust out at me, but its face was smiling.

"Avery," Grisha said, his tinny voice like a tiny Russian Techie was standing in my ear, shouting. "If this is a *copy* of Orel, it may possess what we need."

"Too fucking easy," I heard Marko mutter. "I've been on trips with Cates before. Too fucking easy."

I looked back at the Mara avatar, which was still smiling at me. I pushed the gun into its nose a little harder, but it just raised its eyebrows. I put my thick gloved finger up against the helmet approximately where my mouth was, and Mara winked.

"No," I said. "He's too smart for that. He wouldn't take the risk those codes would be out in the wild." I smiled at the avatar, even though it couldn't see my face. "Orel wouldn't trust himself."

Without warning, something heavy crashed into me, knocking me down. In the rad suit it felt distant, like someone was telling me a story about being knocked onto the ground. I flopped my arms, trying to roll over onto my belly, but something stamped down on my wrist, pinning me to the ground. I looked up at Hense, looking incredibly tiny and light, like she was made of loose twigs, and I tried to roll my arm free, but it was pinned to the floor like I'd been nailed down.

"Talk," she said to Orel. "Make it quick. I can't stand on his fucking hand all fucking day. You have one minute."

I reached awkwardly to my left and eased my second gun out of its holster, but suddenly Mehrak appeared between me and the director, his legs planted on either side of my belly, his own sidearm aimed at my helmet. He smiled a little and just shook his head. "Sorry, darling," he said softly, like he was kissing me good night.

"I appreciate yer time…Director," Orel said in Mara's rough feminine voice. I wondered if there had ever been a real Mara, whether she was long-dead or scratching away somewhere. "I know this is…surprisin', and Avery's never been good with surprises."

Hense didn't move a muscle. "That took ten seconds. You have to do a better job of managing your time."

His smile spread across the girl's face. "Aw'right." He pointed one delicate finger at Hense. "I'm offerin' you a deal. I've gone fuckin' crazy. I popped that piece of junk into my head, and it was downhill from there." He spread his hands in a slow, graceful way, a con man's gesture, smooth and totally believable. "I'm offerin' you *me*, on a fucking platter. All I want in return is a pardon. All I want in return is, you let me walk, no hard feelings."

Hense nodded. "But I don't need to make any deals. I have *you*, now."

For a second, Mara's plain face rippled with surprise and unease, and I was glad in my heart.

"Here's *my* deal," Hense said slowly, taking her time and, I would swear, enjoying herself. It all felt theatrical, too wide, too ripe. "We're taking you. We're calling off this mission and hauling your ass back to Berlin, where we're going to feed you into the mainframes and suss out what we need." She leaned in slightly. "And then when we've settled our problems, we'll come on back for the real you."

She sold it—I was even terrified of her, that tiny little dark-skinned woman with the fussy hairdo and the perfectly cut clothes, the soft steady voice and the unblinking eyes. Then Orel snapped Mara's face into a wide grin again. He didn't have any of the real Orel's artificially stimulated Psionic powers, but he was still irritatingly sure of himself.

"Marin's codes, huh?" The avatar barked a laugh. "You 'n me, we're in that boat together. Because Av'ry's right. That crazy bastard edited *that* out of his imprints. He edited a lot out." Another laugh, this one harsher, Mara's flat face getting red in another astounding example of avatar programming. "You imagine it? Brain salad surgery on *yourself*? He's fucking far gone."

Hense didn't move. "I don't believe you," she said in a precise way that hinted at all sorts of violence.

Orel laughed, crinkling up Mara's face in a way that evoked the old man's wrinkled round head perfectly. "Yeah? You got the juice to take a risk, box me up, and check me out and then come *back*?" He shook his head. "You ain't got the *slack*, Director. The good news is, yer wrong. I don't have your fucking override codes. *He* deleted them from me." He spread his hands again, an actor on the stage. "I'm in th' same boat, girly. I'm on the same fuckin' network." Mara's face turned dark again. "That fuckin' bastard sets me to be his lackey, rattlin' around this fucking *basement* for months. He's gone barkers."

Hense didn't move or speak for a moment. "How do I know you're actually Cainnic Orel?" she said, and I knew she was taking his deal. He was right; the cops didn't have the fuel, ammo, or functioning avatar units to make another assault on Split, so we had to proceed with the plan. She would, I was pretty sure, screw him and take the avatar back to Berlin anyway after they'd grabbed the main event, just in case. But I figured Orel had about as much experience with the System Pigs as I did, and so he must expect to get the screw from her.

Mara's face bloomed into a wide smile as Hense turned to look down at me. "You've spent time with this old asshole," she said evenly. "What do you think?"

Mara turned her spotlight smile on me, burning me through the rad suit. Mehrak adjusted his grip on his gun as if he expected me to go batshit. I closed my eyes and let myself relax, soaking in my own fucking sweat twelve feet underground, time slipping away. If Remy had lived, I would have told him that you had to pick your moments. That sometimes you had to accept you were temporarily on the floor with Janet Hense's boot on your wrist and Mehrak's gun in your face.

"Back in the yard, you told me you knew somebody, Mickey," I said. "Who was it?"

A second of pure silence, and then Mara's obscure brogue. "Yer dad, Av'ry. I told you I knew ole Aubrey."

I nodded. "That's him," I said. I opened my eyes and looked at Mehrak. "I'm getting up," I said. "Okay?"

He hesitated a moment, and then stepped back. "Okay. Behave yourself."

"Fuck you."

Hense spun her foot off my wrist and watched me stand up. It was a ridiculously difficult process, like I was enveloped in odd gravity imported from some other planet, and everyone just watched me huff and puff my way through it. When I'd finally gotten to my feet I holstered my gun, and Hense turned back to Orel.

"All right, we have an understanding. I want you—the *real* you. Alive. You can help with that?"

Mara's cheerful face nodded. "Sure, sure—I put myself in charge of the fucking security around here. I kin walk ya right *in*."

Hense nodded, all business again. "And in return?"

Orel pushed off from the wall and shot Mara's cuffs. "In *return*, Madam Director, I want you to shoot that fucking *thing* that used to be me *dead*, and I walk. That's all. That ain't me anymore. *I'm* me. You shoot that freak show dead and I walk. That's it. That's all I want."

Hense nodded immediately. "Agreed."

I made fists with my heavy, gloved hands. I would have told Remy that any deals made that fast were worth the air they were breathed in. I kept my mouth shut.

With a graceful little bow, Hense waved Orel on. "Take point, we'll follow. Any *hint* that you're walking us into a trap, I will give the order to open the shredders on you, and I will take your fucking core out and bring it back with me to hook up to virtual storage, where I will set the server for *perpetual fucking torment* before we go offline, you understand?"

Orel put Mara's hands up in supplication. "Sure, sure—I told you, Director, I'm in the same boat. I *want* you to get those codes. I *want* to stay alive. Awake. Awake an' alive." She took a few steps down the tunnel and then turned, looking down at the floor and scratching the avatar's nose—I could again picture Mickey doing exactly that. "There is one more stipulation to our agreement, Director."

Hense paused, cocking her head. "Yes?"

"There's another avatar of me creepin' around down here," Orel said, turning away again. "It gets dead, too. There's only *one* o' me. Ever."

XXIX

IT DOESN'T LOOK LIKE A *PLEASANT* FORTY MINUTES

"We're gonna run inta some resistance," Orel shouted as we followed. "Soft."

I shouldered my way past Mehrak to get right behind Mara's avatar. It walked like a girl: sinuous and graceful. Behind me, I heard Grisha speak up.

"Hense, this is a mistake. You trust this? If this *is* Orel, do not trust him. If this is someone *pretending* to be Orel, do not trust him."

"Duly noted, Grigory," she snapped back. "Now back off or I order Mehrak to back you off."

Grisha snorted. "Your monkey boy may *try*, certainly."

"Fuck you," Mehrak said, sounding jovial enough.

The tunnel was widening and getting damper, my little visor steaming up and staying one water droplet ahead of the rad suit's mechanisms. I stayed on Orel's heels, and after a second or two he turned Mara's head slightly to look back at me and smiled.

"Uneasy, Av'ry? Sure, sure, you always have been. Uneasy in your soul, in your mind."

"How many of you are down here?" I asked. "And what do you mean by *soft* resistance?"

"Just the one other o' me," he said, turning his head away and holding up one of Mara's slender fingers. "Same avatar model. Same imprint. Prob'bly also hopin' to make the same deal with the new director back there."

"You always knew the fucking angles, huh, Mickey?"

"More than you, sure," he said cheerfully. "But I'm behind th' eight ball on this one, pup. I told ya: I went fucking *crazy*. Don't recognize myself, an' here I am trapped in this fuckin' cesspool. First sign I'd gone off the deep end was movin' inta this fuckin' ghost ship."

Speaking with Mara's light, feminine voice, he sounded like someone in charge, like he was giving us a tour of this narrow tomb. As we walked, the ground shook gently under our feet, a ceaseless, distant thudding from the System Pigs' assault on Split. Dust sprinkled down from above, making my vision muddy.

I reached out and put a fat glove on her shoulder. "And the *soft*?"

He stopped suddenly and turned to flatten Mara against the wall. "There's the *soft*, Av'ry."

I looked past him and saw them, and had an instant flash to Bellevue Hospital, with all the victims of the Plague staggering to their feet. They had the same noodly way of walking.

A few hundred feet away, there were people. About twenty of them, crowding into the tunnel. They looked more or less like regular people, aside from the running sores on their skin, the deep bluish bruising, the thick trail of blood leaking from their eyes and noses. They didn't look bothered by any of it, though; dressed in regular clothes I'd seen in a million slums and downtowns, without any protective armor at all, they limped toward us, lugging old-fashioned-looking rifles they held diffidently, like they'd never been shown the right way, or been shown and didn't care.

As I stared, the two in the lead, a broad-shouldered man with a nose that looked to have been broken at least three times and a square-shaped older woman with a bowl haircut, slowly seemed to focus on me, staring as if seeing another human being for the first time. With blood dripping from their noses, they each raised their rifle in a weird, slow motion. I stared back, transfixed. It was like they were miming, pretending to move. It didn't feel real.

When they fired, I just blinked. The floor of the tunnel in front of me poofed up into a tiny cloud of dust. Then again. It was impossible that people moving so slowly could hurt me—avatars blinking by faster than humans could manage, Monks moving at clock speeds, sure. This kind of slow-motion murder was just playacting.

"Cates!" Hense shouted from behind, blocked by Orel and me. "What's happening up there?"

Orel, in Mara's silicone body, snorted. "*He* did this right away. He moved into this fucking graveyard, and people started showin' up. Pushed. You kin only Push someone you kin *see*, but he figured out a neat trick: He could Travel into someone, someone he'd picked out already, someone he could keep in mind. He could Travel into that poor shit over an' over again, and Push people hard *through* that person." He shook Mara's head almost sadly. "So he's been poppin' into some poor bastard's head in the outlyin' villages and layin' the Push on a dozen people at a time, forcin' 'em to show up here and do 'service.' "

The two in the lead fired again, clips suddenly popping up and out from their rifles and fluttering through the air, and again a spray of dust went up around my feet.

"Cates!"

I kept ignoring Hense.

"That ain't me," Orel said through Mara's mouth as he stared ahead at the shuffling group of bleeding people. "I don't mind crackin' a few eggs to get what I want, Av'ry, but this shit is just fuckin' *cruel*. They wear out fast 'round here. A few hours, sometimes a day. They keep doing what they're told until they can't do it no more, and they don't complain. Just bleed out and suddenly fall over. The fucking place is littered with corpses, just people fallin' over, dead." He shook his head again. "Ain't *me*."

I raised the extra sidearm the cops had given me; I'd lost the Roon when Mehrak had blindsided me. The two people hadn't made any move to reload; they were sort of standing there, eyes half-mast, mouths open, bloody bubbles forming as they breathed laboriously in and out, as they melted under the invisible sun of Split's radiation load. I took a bead and fired twice, managing two head shots that sent them down like wet sacks, revealing three more right behind them. The one in front was a skinny young kid, his shirt soaked with sweat and blood and hanging open to reveal a bony, concave chest turned into a swamp of scabby sores.

Just people fallin' over dead. I reached out and took hold of Orel's avatar by the collar of its leathery coat. "It's fucking *you*, all right," I hissed, and pushed it in front of me. "Move. Take some bullets for me, cocksucker."

Orel spun around and started walking backward as I advanced. Two more of the weak popping sounds of those old rifles being fired, but Mara's face remained calm and I couldn't tell if he'd taken some rounds for me. I looked over my shoulder. No one had moved to follow me.

"Stay back!" I shouted. "I'll give the all-clear!"

They couldn't do any good anyway; the tunnel was too constricted here. I looked back at Mara's grinning face— she suddenly twitched, taking an unlucky bullet. I hated it. I hated the face, because it had led me all over Europe on a fool's fucking errand and tried to kill me, in the end. I hated the intelligence animating it because it was Michaleen, Canny Orel, whatever his fucking real name was, and I could lay just about every bad thing that had happened to me in the last ten years at his feet, somehow.

"You're in charge of security down here," I said, unclenching my teeth with effort. "What the fuck does that mean, exactly? *That's* your fucking security?"

Mara twitched again at the crack of a rifle, but kept smiling. "We could keep you inching along at a snail's pace for *years* in this tunnel, Avery, with just fifty goons with rifles. Did you think we wouldn't cover the old aqueduct? Hell, boy, of *course* we covered the tunnels. Aside from me and my twin and the incredible melting assholes behind me, we got charges laid to collapse an archway or two, close off the access in case y'get too deep in." He rolled Mara's eyes upward. "We're about twenty feet from one right now."

He was being fucking chatty, but I didn't have time to wonder about that. The tunnel was widening out slightly, not enough for a second person to walk alongside me. The stones were getting larger and the ceiling was rising up. Behind Mara's tall frame I could see an archway, and beyond it a much larger space—the basement of the palace. The rhythmic thunder of the assault on Split was stronger, making the floor twitch beneath me.

I looked back at Mara's face. "At the entrance to the basement proper," I said, and she nodded, looking like she'd just eaten something delicious. Fucking overconfident motherfucker. I wanted to change that expression. For once in my life I wanted to make Canny Orel *blink*, wanted to make him wonder if it had been fucking smart to poke me with a stick over and over again like he had.

"When we get there," I said carefully, keeping my gun on Mara's face, "go left and stay out of the way."

"They're innocent folks, Av'ry," she said, still smiling, cocking her head. Fucking with me. "Y'gonna kill 'em just 'cause they're in yer way?"

"They got about forty minutes left to live, from what I can tell," I spat back, adjusting my grip on the gun. "And it doesn't look like a *pleasant* forty minutes. Putting them out of their misery's a better way to put it."

We cleared the archway into the basement proper, each of us ducking down to avoid the low transition, and then Orel leaped to the left and pasted Mara's body against the sandy off-white wall of big, head-sized blocks. I took a half step back and ducked down a little; there was a log-jam of about five people, all with the empty eyes and slack mouths of the Pushed. I'd seen it often enough—hell, I'd *been* Pushed often enough—to recognize it.

I hesitated for a second, horrified. They were all bloody messes. Big yellow-blue bruises bloomed on their arms, on their necks and faces, their hands—everywhere. Blood leaked in watery rivulets from their noses, the corners of their mouths, their fucking *eyes*. They didn't blink, or wipe it away. They aimed their rifles dully and stared, momentarily confused because I'd crouched down below their line of sight. The Pushed didn't think too well; they only had the instructions they'd been given to work with.

"Go on, Mercy Killer," Orel said jovially. "Put 'em down."

My left eye twitched with a sudden wish *I* was Psionic, so I could twist his avatar in pieces, so I could bash it against the walls until it shook apart, until I could make him feel his mind coming apart like the pieces of a machine. Then I duckwalked forward three steps, pushed the lead guy's rifle aside, and stood up an inch away from him. I put the barrel of my gun against his forehead.

"If you can hear me," I said in a low voice, surprised at myself, "I'm sorry."

I squeezed the trigger and the fucking cop-issue hand-gun jumped more than I liked in my hand, and the guy's head exploded, splattering me with blood. I had to imagine it was warm.

His body dropped softly to the floor and into a weird kneeling position, the rifle still clutched in his hands, and the other four simultaneously fired into the tunnel behind me. I heard someone shouting curses back in the shadows, and I realized I was on the clock. I stood up and spun around, backing up to put all four of them in front of me, and squeezed off four more rounds, dropping them one after the other. They made no noise; they just slid to the floor like they were finally free to relax a little.

I looked up at the archway we'd just come through, Orel standing next to it with his arms up in a perfunctory way, like he was humoring me. My augmented eyes clicked in, sharpening the scene, and I could pick out the thin, almost invisible wires leading from a rusted-looking pressure plate up into the ceiling of the tunnel we'd just emerged from. I straightened up and stepped forward, carefully avoiding the soft, cooling bodies around me.

"Damn, boyo, you sure are—" Orel started to say, laughing.

"Fucking *hell*, Cates—" Hense somehow bellowed from deep in the shadows of the tunnel.

I took the last two steps with a little hop, reached out, and slapped the pressure plate as hard as I could. There was a quick, blue flash, a tiny *snick* sound like glass breaking, and then a low, annoying whine that started rising in frequency.

"You fucked, Cates?" Orel hissed, suddenly bounding from the wall and knocking into me. As we hit the floor there was an explosion, and my HUD snapped into clarity to show me my audio status bars turning an angry red. I let Orel's heavy momentum carry us along the floor for a foot or two, then bent my knee and caught us on the heavy rubber tread of my rad suit's boots, taking hold of Mara's thin shoulder and letting her roll us so I was on top. Then I jammed the barrel of my gun into the soft fake skin under Mara's chin.

"Just twitch, you cocksucker," I said, panting inside my helmet, "and I blow your circuits all over the floor and I won't *give a shit* because I've got a spare *you* down here I can go deal with, all right?"

Orel raised Mara's delicate eyebrows and rolled her eyes to look over at the collapsed tunnel and then, with exaggerated care, to look down her own face at my gun. Then he looked back at me.

"All right, Av'ry," he said slowly. "All right."

I smiled, hoping he could see it through the helmet. "Good. Because the only fucking person you should be fucking making fucking *deals* with down here," I said quietly, "is fucking *me*."

XXX

THERE'S A LOT OF *WE* IN THAT SENTENCE

The basement was a huge series of rooms studded with thick, heavy-looking columns and low, rocky ceilings. It felt strangely open and airy, though, as if the stone were made of something less substantial, like it was really smoke and light, an illusion. Every now and then shafts of weak light stabbed downward from holes punched up to the floor above us, giving my augments something to work with and keeping the space from complete darkness.

The place was crowded with Orel's *soft resistance*, both alive and dead. Some *long*-dead, burst-open corpses turning into blackened pools on the stone floor, flies and maggots—apparently unconcerned about radiation—swarming in thick clouds and rippling layers. The ones still alive weren't even all armed, and they patrolled the basement with a sleepy-eyed unconcern, often looking right through us and letting us pass without seeming to see us at all.

"What's the fucking point of these poor assholes?" I asked Mara's back, ramrod straight, her hips swaying gracefully as she walked in front of me. "They're fucking useless. *Soft* doesn't even begin to describe them."

"They need orders, Av'ry," he sang back over his shoulder. "They're Pushed, which takes away some o' their *initiative*, y'see. They'll take an order from me or my twin, or that freak show who used ta be me." He paused for a few steps. "They'll take an order to shoot you down now, if I give it," he added. "They're stiff, so you'd like as not manage longer 'n I'd like, but by sheer weight o' numbers they'd take y'down."

That was Orel giving me the word, letting me know that if I'd surprised him for a moment, he still had me in the vice, and not the other way around. I was playing along. I was willing to play along with whatever he decided to throw my way, because each step brought me closer to the real Orel, the flesh-and-blood brain inside an old Monk chassis. I could pretend anything for the duration.

I kept my shredder aimed at Mara's back and eyed the half-dead victims around me. "Looks to me like I could just find a nice dark corner and wait for them all to bleed out."

Mara's laugh was the same humorless, harsh bark I remembered from Hong Kong. I wondered if that had really been her laugh, or if this was a translation error, Orel being filtered through Mara's audio circuits. The laugh cut off suddenly. "So, exac'ly what *kind* of deal are you proposin', Cates?"

I scanned the immediate area as best I could in my sweaty prison, keeping myself just out of reach behind Orel, the shredder braced against my shoulder. The

Pushed folks kept drifting past us, mouths open, rifles up. Every third or fourth one had no rifle and just held their hands up in front of them like they were in a dream, a dream in which they were chewing off their own tongues, pushing their own eyeballs out of their sockets. The explosions topside were louder, and each one was followed by a lingering groaning noise, like the ancient stones above us were being slowly worked loose from their moorings. My HUD was faint and hard to read, but a bunch of status bars were inching into yellow; the rad suit might be keeping me from cheesing out like Orel's Unluckiest People in the World, but it was suffocating me.

"You put the real you in my pocket," I said, "and you get to be the one and only Canny Orel again," I said.

He chuckled. "Some'tin tells me you ain't lookin' to freight me out of here for study, Av'ry. You lookin' to double-cross dear Janet? 'Cause in my experience she's not someone I'd advise *crossing*."

"You know Hense?" I was just making chatter as we moved. If Orel wanted to talk, that was fine. I kept my eyes open and ran through my limited inventory as we walked.

"I worked with *everyone*, Av'ry. She's an old hand," he said casually. "I remember when she came up right outta the testing dorm. We'd just elevated Ruberto and formed the fuckin' cops to begin with, and she was the first star."

I nodded mechanically, then focused on Mara's back suddenly. "There's a lot of *we* in that sentence, Mickey."

He laughed. "You ought to ask yerself: Why does Cainnic Orel, if he's just a fuckin' Gunner, have Dick Marin's *override codes*?" Mara's shoulders rolled in a shrug, but he didn't turn around to look at me. "They said, make

Unification happen. So I made it happen. I made it happen by murderin' every single motherfucker who was in a position t'stop it. Then they decided they needed a security force to keep all the shitkickers in line—so much for peace on earth and all that high-minded jumbo. They were already beginnin' to split and spit at each other, and some of 'em—this was the Joint Council, still, but the undersecretaries had plenty of juice to throw around even back then—didn't trust me anymore. So I had nothin' to do with the cops."

We were headed toward a shallow, dark staircase leading down farther into the depths. The crowd of Pushed was getting thicker, and I couldn't avoid pushing through them like moving through tall grass. As I followed Mara, two of them just paused as if suddenly remembering something and fell down, a noiseless slump they were never getting up from.

"Then the cops scared the balls off of 'em. Salgado, especially. So they wanted a Big Dog to keep the pack in line, and so they made Marin. I had full access to everything. I just downloaded the codes, covered my tracks, and got that robot's overrides, but shit, they were fuckin' *useless*. They basically didn't do shit except under certain specifically shithole situations. You had to drop a house on the King Worm before his system would accept any sort of override instruction."

I put the shredder on Mara's back. Even though this was just a digital copy of Orel, it felt good to think about pressing the toggle and turning his avatar to a fine mist, just for that split second of panic and surprise I could imagine in his fucking spider brain. I pictured that short fuck dickering with Salgado, with Marin, all of them, moving people like me around like pieces on a board so they could feel *safe*.

"You were, what, their attack dog?" I said.

"I was their *facilitator*," he snapped, jerking Mara's head to glare at me. "Those fucks had everything—money, power, and shit. But they didn't know how to get anything *done*. That's where I came in."

Mara laughed again, the sound absorbed by a sudden swell of cracking, groaning noise from above. Ten or fifteen feet to our left, the ceiling caved in with a bloom of dust, making the floor shake and crushing three or four of the Pushed under big slabs. I swung the shredder around and crouched down as two plump, round figures dropped to the floor where they promptly toppled over onto their backs and waved their stiff arms and legs around helplessly. I squinted through the dust and gloom: radiation suits.

I started to stand up, and then there was a gun pressed against the side of my helmet.

"You're slippery, gorgeous," Mehrak said amiably enough. "But that is why we have trackers in the rad suits. Don't move, please. And drop the shredder."

Hense stepped around from behind me, looked over at where Grisha and Marko were struggling like baby turtles to regain their footing, and then turned to face me with her hands on her hips. Her face was bland as always, though I imagined I saw a haze of frustrated anger there, making her blurry.

Mehrak gave me a tap, and I let the rifle slide from my hands to the floor.

"You have broken our contract, Mr. Cates," she said. Her voice reminded me of Bellevue, of her telling me she wasn't going to kill me because there was no need to waste the fucking bullets. No matter how tiny she was, or had been when she'd been alive, I never doubted for a second her rise in the System Security Force. It had never occurred to me to doubt she'd been promoted to take Marin's place as Director of Internal Affairs. Janet Hense had been born with a stare that made tough assholes look at their shoes. "You tried to fuck us." She cocked her head. "As we're in a state of emergency here and I am the ranking officer here—I am the ranking officer *anywhere in the fucking world*—I'm invoking SSF Charter Rule 3."

I blinked. "The SSF," I said slowly, "has a *charter*? What rule discusses summary executions in back alleys, 'cause I'd like to chat about *that*."

Hense actually smiled. It was hideous, and I wished she would stop. "Actually, that's also Charter Rule 3."

"You can't field trial him," Mehrak said, sounding surprised. "We don't even know what happened."

Hense's face went still again. "Captain, did you just instruct me about what I *cannot* do?"

"I—"

She cut him off. "Captain, invoking Charter Rule 3— which I am within bounds to do despite your *opinion*—I find you guilty of insubordination."

The gun in my ear went slack. "What the *fuck*?" Mehrak almost whispered, the first time since I'd met him that he'd sounded shocked or surprised.

She's the slippery one, Marin whispered in my head. *She had to make a deal with you to get Orel's location, but now you've broken your end by going after Orel alone, which she can interpret as you going to kill an SSF asset. So she can cut you loose.* I had a sudden, clear memory of Marin—one of him, anyway—underneath Westminster with me: "I am programmed to obey all Joint Council resolutions, standing orders, and enacted laws, in both spirit and letter, so I cannot directly harm a citizen of the System or act directly against a certified religion."

Faster than I could track, even with my augmented vision, Hense drew her sidearm, took a bead over my shoulder—impossibly precise, *impossibly* quick—and fired twice. I twitched away, spinning around and putting my back against a column. Mehrak slid a few feet, crashing through the Pushed and knocking them over in weird, static silence, his head turned into a white and silver flower, coolant spewing onto the dry floor.

I looked up, and Hense already had the gun on me.

"Avery Cates," she said in a clear, steady voice. "In my capacity as an officer of the System Security Force under the instruction set of the SSF Charter Rules, I accuse you of treason against the System of Federated Nations in that you have planned to destroy an asset deemed vital to the survival of the System of Federated Nations."

She fucked you, Marin whispered in my head. *She's bound by the same fucking rules I was, and she waited for you to act so she could fuck you.* Bizarrely, Marin began something close to *singing: I'll try… the whole… cause…*

"Invoking Rule 3," Hense continued, Orel's barking laugh filling in the thick, dusty air behind her, "I hereby field trial you and find you guilty, and condemn you to death."

"About fucking *time*," Orel sighed.

XXXI

I WENT FOR SOMETHING MORE *EXCITING*

I stared at Hense, my mind stuttering like it had tripped over something. As I stared, she cocked her head quizzically, shrugged slightly, and pulled the trigger. All she got was a dry click.

"Jammed," Orel said, leaning against his own column.

"I know it's fucking jammed," Hense snapped, cracking the auto and peering into the chamber.

"What the fuck is going on?" I said, moving my head enough to spot the shredder on the floor at my feet. I glanced back at Hense, who was frowning down at her gun, then at Orel, who winked at me. I knew I couldn't take on Hense physically; avatars were too strong, too fast. But a shredder made us all the same size. I didn't care that much what was going on, really. My own priority hadn't changed, and it had nothing to do with whatever dirt these two artificial people were trying to do. But if Remy were still alive, still following me around like he was this close to having something better to do, I would have told him that people liked to talk, and if you were in a tight place it never hurt to try and let them do it. "Are you fucking *partners*?"

Orel barked Mara's rough laugh again as Hense cursed and began what looked like a very professional breakdown of her standard-issue sidearm.

"Naw, Av'ry, we ain't *partners*. Janet hired me to do a little wet work for her not so long ago, and now I'm just hanging around waitin' on her to tell me if we still have a *current* deal or not."

"You give me Orel Prime, and you can walk out of here as Michaleen Garda and do as you please," Hense said immediately, concentrating on her gun. I pictured the area of the basement we were in, the paths through the columns, the crowd of loitering Pushed who hovered around us like breathing speed bumps, giving myself low scores for grace and speed in my smothering rad suit, and decided a run for it was a suicide mission.

"Yer gonna need more than jus' little ole *you* to take on that crazy asshole," Orel said. "The old Monk units aren't as classy as these newer avatar issues, lass, but he customized it a fair bit, and the bones are just as strong, just as fast. And then there's the slug o' wires buried in his brain, which *you* helped him get."

Hense shook her head distractedly. "I've got another team on its way. They haven't breached the main entrances yet, so they're working their way back the way we came in."

"She helped you get the God Augment," I said, looking past Hense at the spot where Grisha and Marko were still struggling to right themselves.

"Payment," he said. "I didna need any more fucking *yen*,

so I went for something more *exciting*, follow? Besides, it was a big order. I told her rubbin' out Marin wasna' like walking up to some mope on the street and puttin' one in his ear—Marin was the *cloud*. He was multithreaded. I tol' her, you want Marin dead, I'll have to figure outta way to drop a nuke on his head." He made Mara's face wink at me again. "An' that *costs*."

"You're lucky I don't drop a nuke on *you*," Hense snapped, inspecting the barrel of her gun with one digital eye. "Because *this* bullshit is not what I expected."

Mara's face bloomed into amused horror. "Poor *you*. Not my fault you didn't see the possibilities. Not my fault you didn't know the protocols. You said y'wanted Marin gone; I made him gone. Y'said y'wanted to be director; well, you're the motherfucking *director*, ain't you, Janet? You didna know about the hardwired *rules* y'have ta follow now, Marin's instructions set imprinted over your own, too fuckin' bad."

"I didn't know I'd have to come back here to crawl up your ass for *override codes* to stop me and every other cop from going to *sleep*, Michaleen," Hense snapped back. "*You* knew. You might have mentioned it."

Orel shrugged. "Wasn't part of the deal, lass. You wanted Marin—an entity the size of a city, as heavily defended as anything, requiring the resources o' half the fucking System to be gone. I made him *gone*. The rest is up t'you."

Hense nodded, snapping the gun back into one piece. As she racked the chamber, Marin suddenly began whispering to me.

Tell her you're invoking Charter Rule 3, Subarticle 54, he said in my thoughts.

I blinked, and started to formulate a silent reply to the ghost in my brain, but Hense swung the automatic up at me, so I just opened my mouth: "I'm invoking Subarticle 54!" I said quickly. "Charter Rule 3, Subarticle 54."

Hense went absolutely still. Two pounding, staggering heartbeats went by and she did absolutely nothing.

She's bound by my instruction set, Marin whispered. *It was programmed into the role of Director of Internal Affairs to make sure I couldn't make any power plays. Took me years to engineer a few things to give me some leeway. She hasn't had years.*

Leeway. He'd forced me into assassinating Dennis Squalor and taking down the whole fucking Electric Church, starting the Monk Riots, and leading directly to the Plague that killed half the System, all for his eternal State of Emergency and fucking *leeway*.

"You're claiming to be a protected SSF informant," Hense said slowly, grinding out the words. She was shaking slightly, the gun held unerringly on my chest. "I-I-" she stuttered and then shook her head once. "I need a badge number."

Can't help you there, chum, Marin said. *I haven't been connected to the SSF databases in years. Wait—try 649-215208-40-293-38.*

I repeated the numbers as they appeared in my thoughts. I knew where the shredder was, the position it had landed in. I imagined myself diving to the floor for it, coming up with it dead-on Hense and toggling a burst. Then I imagined myself doing that wrapped up in heavy, damp burlaplike material. The endings of those two thoughts were different in grim, unhappy ways.

"You're claiming to be *Richard Marin's* protected

informant under Rule 3, Subarticle 54," Hense said
slowly, biting off the words like her CPU cache was
maxed out, passing data through a bottleneck. "We have
a valid certificate of termination on server for Director
Marin, so—"

Tell her she cannot invoke Rule 3 because she is in vio-
lation of Rule 3, Subarticle 1.

"You're in violation of Rule 3, Subarticle 1," I said
quickly, before she could finish declaring Marin dead.

Again, she went still. I heard Orel rasping out one of
Mara's scratchy laughs, but I didn't look at him. If he
decided to knock me down, take a part in this, I was dead
anyway.

"You are claiming I am *not* the ranking officer in the
situation," Hense said robotically, like she was forced to
speak the words due to some deep magic programming in
her avatar brain. "Identify the ranking officer."

I didn't need to wait for my ghost to speak again.
"Director of Internal Affairs Richard Marin, badge number 649-215208-40-293-38," I said.

Say: I am his duly appointed representative under
provision 901 of the Charter.

We're just stalling, I thought, repeating the words.

Feel free to invoke better ideas, Avery, Marin said
easily. *I'm fighting for my life, too, here, you know.*

Hense shook herself again. "As it has been established
that a valid Termination Certificate is on server for Director Marin—"

Try invoking Rule 234, Subarticle 43. When she asks,
tell her your citizenship revocation statement exists only
in physical form and must be authenticated before fur-
ther action can be taken.

I said it, repeating the words as Marin whispered them, but when Hense once again locked up for a second or two, processing this new piece of gristly bullshit, I launched myself forward, crashing into her and knocking us both to the floor, where I bounced, once, and rolled over onto my belly, taking hold of her hand with both of mine just as she squeezed the trigger. The shot sounded distant, like someone shooting in another room.

She was moving immediately, pushing me off fast and easy, like I weighed nothing. I held onto her gun with both fat, numb hands and she whipped me this way and that, trying to shake me off, and squeezed the trigger again either out of reflex or hoping to tear my rad suit open, let the invisible knives in to fuck with me. Then she whipped me back around again. I planted my feet, squeezed as hard as I could, and when she tried to pull me back, her hand slipped from the gun, leaving it awkwardly clenched in my gloved hands.

Before I could process this tiny victory—I was so fucking unused to victories, tiny or otherwise, that I goggled at them when they did arrive, like a tourist from misery—she crashed into me bodily, knocking me to the floor, the gun squirting from my hands like a living thing and arcing through the stuffy air to smack into the bleeding, sweating head of one of the Pushed. Then it disappeared onto the floor and their feet, and Hense had me by the helmet, raising me up off the floor, pulling my visor close to her face, which had darkened into a shade of crimson I'd never encountered before.

I put my fat hands on her tiny waist and tried to twist her off me, but she just ignored it and slammed my head down onto the ground as hard as she could. I didn't feel the stone, but my head pinged back and forth, smacking into the hard metal interior, making my HUD light up bright and clear for a second and then start flickering, as if the augments in my brain had been knocked loose.

I reached up, going for her eyes, but she released my head and smacked my hands away. She was *strong*. I was breathing hard, sweat streaming down my face inside my wearable prison, and she looked like she could roll over and take a nap whenever we finished.

I feinted for her face again and then went for her belly. Her hands flashed up to block me, and I got a good shot in, knocking her backward. I surged up, something tearing in my belly, and finally got my hands on her throat, squeezing for all I was worth.

"Hell, Mr. Cates," she said, sounding almost bored, "you can't *strangle* me." Almost casually, she broke my grip, taking each of my arms by the wrist and bending them back. I let out a screeching kind of noise, certain that tendons had snapped in my arms, red pain licking up into my chest. She flipped me off her and, with a kick that knocked the wind out of my lungs, sent me hurtling into the Pushed, who obligingly went down like pins, giving me a soft, near-vertical landing. I pushed myself back to my feet and spread my legs a little. Hense was still standing just a few feet away, her hair a little mussed but otherwise untouched. She took one step toward me, making me wince as I tensed up, and then she paused for one second and dropped to the floor in a loose heap.

Behind her and a little to my left, Orel did exactly the same thing.

I stood there, panting, my visor steaming up with my own exhalations, and slowly another plump rad suit waddled into my field of vision, holding a small electromagnetic pulse device in its gloved hands. Slowly, Mr. Marko turned to face me, and then actually waved.

"What," I gasped, wincing, "took you ... so fucking ... long?"

He shrugged. "I couldn't stand up."

XXXII

THE ONLY THING MISSING IS THE SOUND OF HIM LAUGHING AT ME

Legally, Marin whispered, *that is to say—on the SSF servers—there are two people. One's named Cainnic Orel and is one of the most wanted men in the System, accused of everything from theft to treason. The other is named Michaleen Garda, and aside from some minor offenses and a Hold Order issued on him a few years ago that landed him in Chengara—Hold Orders not requiring any actual evidence or even formal accusation as long as they're issued by the director—he's a legitimate citizen of the System. So Hense's instruction set will allow her to let* Garda *walk away, but any entity she regards as* Orel *she'll have to either arrest or destroy.*

I don't fucking care, I thought back, stepping over to Marko.

"Thanks, Zeke," I said, putting a hand on his shoulder. "You just saved my fucking life." I almost felt bad.

He nodded. "I *did*, didn't I?"

I shifted my hand from his shoulder and gave him a light slap on the helmet. "The moment's over." I turned away, searching the crowded floor for my sidearm and my shredder. "How long will they stay out?" I said, looking from Hense's avatar to Orel's.

Grisha staggered into my field of vision, his rad suit covered in dust, holding his auto on Mehrak. "Standard warm reboot of core systems in ten, fifteen minutes," he said, his voice faded and wrinkled by static.

I nodded, spying Janet's gun on the floor. Shoving aside a group of docile, bleeding Pushed I reclaimed it, checked the chamber, and walked over to where Hense lay crumpled. I stared down at her for a moment; she looked like some girl off the street, tiny and frail, like someone had stolen up behind her and sandbagged her, taken her credit dongle, and run off. Her eyes were open and staring, her face slack. She looked dead.

I leaned down and put the gun about four inches from her face and squeezed the trigger three times, getting sprayed with the weird, warm mixture of fake blood and white coolant I'd come to expect from avatars. Then I put a shell in her chest and belly, too.

"We've got to move," I said, turning away. "She's got dozens of herself, and at least one is going to be heading down here with a backup team of digital gorillas to put us out of our misery."

Somewhere, one of the Pushed let out a long moan. It went on and on, stretching out and slowly rising in pitch until it was a wet scream.

"Avery!" Grisha said, shouting and sounding breathless. "Think for a moment. Surely Orel—the primary—has heavy security. Your differences with Director Hense aside, we will need the manpower she supplies."

I turned to look at him. "My *differences*? She was going to execute me right here. Put me down like a dog—which she wanted to do weeks ago but couldn't because of her fucking *programming*. And now that she's found a loophole, you think we can *trust* her?"

The scream turned into a series of screams, and I realized it wasn't alone—a few more of the Pushed had joined in, filling the room. They sounded like they were drowning in themselves.

Grisha didn't move for a moment, and then he put one gloved hand on top of his helmet, rubbing as if he could feel his shaved scalp through the thick material. "I want a cigarette so badly I am close to removing this helmet, fuck the instant death," he said. "You are right, of course." Then he whirled. "What is with *screaming*?"

I turned away, purposefully holstering my gun as I looked for the shredder. Grisha, I knew, wanted to be sure the override codes were secured, one way or another. The success of the mission was all that mattered, and I didn't doubt that he'd sacrifice me in an instant if he thought he had better odds with Hense and her dwindling army of avatars. I didn't want to put a bullet into Grisha, but I would if he made me. If I did, I'd lose Marko, too, I figured. Marko had hardened up a little, but I doubted I'd be able to shoot someone he regarded as a member of the *team* and still rely on him to help out.

I'd have to run with Grisha as far as he was willing to go, and then cut him loose.

As I studied the ground for my shredder, I kept Grisha in my peripheral vision as best I could with the fucking helmet in my way, with my own sweat condensing on my visor, my own fetid air congealing around me inside the rad suit. The noise was getting hard to think through, between Mehrak's low groaning and the Pushed's rising screech.

And then, right in front of me, one of them blinked his bloody eyes and looked right at me. He was a kid, sick-skinny and covered in bleeding sores, his arms still locked in position to carry a rifle he'd lost long before. His hair was white and black, falling out in clumps, and his eyes were like two dull coals, just red with a speck of blackness in their center.

Without warning, he sagged forward and grabbed onto my suit.

"Dita," he whispered so quietly my augments and the suit's microphone barely registered it. "Where is she?"

I staggered backward in surprise, bringing my auto up in shock, and he slid off me, hitting the floor and staying there. I looked around. Half the Pushed in the room were showing signs of life, of awareness. Orel's Push was wearing off, and all these people had just graduated from Unluckiest Fucks in the World to Unluckiest Fucks in the *Universe*.

I spun and barreled my way toward Grisha, who turned instantly to put his gun on me.

"We've got to go," I said, loud, but trying not to shout. I needed to be persuasive. I needed to be reassuring. "We've been fucked with."

Grisha kept the gun up, but studied me through the muddy visor. I had faith in Grisha. Grisha was a thinker, and he would give me the seconds I needed. "Avery, we must proceed."

I shook my head. "We've been *fucked*, Grish. Orel's not here. *He's not fucking here.*" I gestured in the air. "Look at these poor shits. They're waking up. The Push is fading. He Pushed them and then he left—he wasn't here when we dropped." I curled my free hand into an involuntary fist. "He's somewhere else."

Grisha turned bodily to take in the room. "It may be," he said slowly.

"His avatar sure seemed to know to expect us," Marko put in. "It was sitting down here, waiting in the tunnel."

"Fuck," Grisha said in a flat, low voice. Around us, more and more of the Pushed were dropping to the floor. The ones with any strength left began screaming immediately; others just writhed there, getting slower and slower, like fish plucked suddenly from water. "Fuck!" He turned again, fast, but kept the gun down by his hip this time. "How can we be *sure*? Avery, the future counts on *us*. How can we be *sure*?"

I holstered my gun and began fishing in my suit for the big hunting knife I'd brought along with me. "I've been on the dangling end of Orel's pole before," I said. "I know how it fucking feels. The only thing missing is the sound of him laughing at me."

"Fuck!" Grisha shouted, lashing out a leg and kicking a body on the floor, then stumbling backward as his center of gravity went wonky in the heavy suit.

"It was too fucking easy," Marko said, waving his arms. "I *knew* this felt too fucking *easy*!" I decided to let Marko rant. I didn't have time to remind him that he didn't rank high enough to have unsolicited opinions.

Abruptly, the explosions and shaking from above stopped.

Knife and gun in my hands, I stormed over to where Mehrak was lying on the floor. "Marko!" I snapped. "Help me!"

He jumped and then scurried over to me, slipping on the sweat and blood and crashing into me in a kneeling position. I steadied him with my gun on his shoulder as I pulled the knife from its hiding place with my free hand.

"Go over to Orel," I shouted, putting my auto in Mehrak's face. I fired twice, then pushed myself up and put two more shells into his chest and belly, making sure. Who the fuck knew where they might put a brain in these tin men. I dragged myself, breathing hard, over to where Marko stood over Mara's avatar, hands hanging limply at his side.

"That was—" he started to say, but I shoved him aside and stepped over to where Orel's avatar slumped, eyes open like Hense's. Without Orel's personality it was just the image of a tall, plain woman, reddish hair in curls around her face. I knelt down and yanked on her feet to straighten her out, then took hold of Marko's shoulder and yanked him down with me. He fell into a kneeling position, squawking in protest.

I pulled out his hand and pressed the knife into his glove.

"What are you doing?" Grisha shouted at me.

I ignored him. Time was closing in on us—another avatar of Hense was on her way, System Pigs in tow, and even if she believed me that Orel had played us, she'd already decided I was expendable.

The noise level kept climbing and the slow, drugged shuffle of the dying bastards around us was herking and jerking into an alarming flurry of jagged movement. The

Pushed weren't in any physical condition to be a threat, but a couple dozen warm bodies could slow anybody down, and some of them did still clutch their rifles, assuming Orel had even bothered to give them ammunition.

I tugged the shirt under Mara's jacket down, exposing her white neck. I looked up at Marko. "I want the head," I rasped. "You're the trained technical associate."

"Aw, *fuck*," Marko muttered, leaning down and tracing his chubby fingers along Mara's neck. He was murmuring something softly as he worked, reciting specs from the avatar designs.

Suddenly Grisha was looming over me. "Cates, there is no time for souvenirs—"

"I'm done following that bastard around, playing by his rules," I said, lungs burning. I watched Marko take the knife with a precise, strong grip that hinted at competence and certainty, press it against the avatar's fake white flesh, and begin *sawing*. Coolant oozed everywhere like sap, slow and cold. "I'll bet you he didn't manage to erase *everything* from this avatar. I'll bet you he doesn't want lowly old Avery to have it. I'll bet you he comes after it." I grinned. "This time, Orel's gonna come find *me*."

PART V

XXXIII

SHEER DETERMINATION AND WILLINGNESS TO HURT

"Three hundred and sixty-two cigarettes left," Grisha said.

"In the world, probably," I said, shivering uncontrollably. The fire we'd built three weeks before and had kept going continuously was huge, but it seemed to offer no heat whatsoever. "Time to quit."

"Quitting is easy," he said, smiling as he knelt down, putting his hands out to warm them and leaning forward with a cigarette in his mouth to light up. After a second he leaned back, exhaling smoke into the air like he was making clouds. "I have quit many times."

I didn't remember it so cold. Or so flat, and so empty. You could still see the basic outline of the buildings, and about half the wall was still standing, sand creeping up on both sides, catching the moon now and then and glinting like a beacon in the distance. The silence was complete. When the fire died down and Marko and Grisha and the others had gone below, all you would hear was the wind, the sky above crystal clear and filled with stars.

I held out my hand. "Give," I said. Grisha snorted, amused, and handed over two cigarettes. I settled back into the weird little seat I'd made in the sand and stuck one behind my ear, the other in my mouth. I didn't bother lighting it yet. Grisha was getting cagey with his cigarettes, and I could see the near future when he would simply refuse to give me any more.

A few hundred feet straight ahead of us the tail end of an old SSF hover jutted straight up into the air. In the daylight it was charred and dented, more than half-buried, a permanent sculpture in the middle of fucking nowhere. At night it looked sleek and shiny, the firelight playing off of it giving an impression of infinite possibilities, thousands of shadows. I'd been staring at the hover for days now. I was pretty sure I'd seen it crash, in some alternate universe thousands of years before, when I hadn't had any metal in my brain, when Remy was alive and far away from me.

If Remy had lived, I'd have told him that patience was the most important thing a Gunner could learn. Canny Orel was legendary for his patience, for waiting in rooms for days just to get the drop on a mark, for pretending to be an entirely different person for weeks, for months. Any asshole could score a cheap gun or a good knife and walk around like a hard case, calling himself a Gunner, and maybe even get someone equally stupid to pay them to kill someone. If they didn't learn patience, if they didn't learn to wait for the right moment instead of charging in, stoned out of their minds and convinced sheer determination and willingness to hurt would carry them through, they usually died fast.

And Remy would have said, "Shit, Avery, I put up with you, don't I? I know all about fucking *patience*."

The world *felt* empty. Grisha had called home to his SPS troops and gotten a hover to us in fifteen minutes, skimming easily through the chaos in Split. The System Pigs were embroiled in an assault on Diocletian's palace that proved to be tougher than they'd anticipated, because the Pushed topside had been given clear instructions to resist and didn't let minor things like gunshot wounds slow them down. They fought until they bled out, and then someone stepped up from behind them and took their place. The cops actually took losses. The SPS hover had gotten us to Spain in decent style, back to Grisha's people. Even there things had felt wide open and loose, like my every step had an echo that had been muffled before.

Sitting down next to me with a grunt, Grisha glanced past me at the old crate I'd set up as a makeshift table, shook his head, and settled in, smoking contentedly.

"How many N-Tabs?" I asked.

"About a thousand," he said immediately. Grisha's competence was startling sometimes. "Mr. Marko has determined baseline survival can be maintained with a half a tab each per day, assuming adequate water. Which we cannot assume, as we have found no source of fresh water yet. Please do not ask me how much water we have left on hand."

I nodded. Half an N-tab wasn't much, but I'd done worse. I'd done worse in this very spot.

We'd made no effort to be stealthy, making a lot of noise on our way from Spain. We'd stolen what we needed, often at gunpoint, and I'd used my own name everywhere, obnoxiously. Not that it mattered, I didn't think—Orel could certainly track us electronically if he had some power to draw on and a functional satellite in the air. But everywhere you went these days there was old tech, abandoned, rusting, useless, so you couldn't make any assumptions. I wasn't taking chances.

"Why here, Avery?" Grisha said suddenly.

I didn't answer right away. I felt small in the hugeness of the world around us, suddenly, comfortingly certain that I was too tiny to really matter, that nothing I did was going to nudge the cosmos this way or that. I was off the Rail, I thought. I'd jumped the tracks and I was skittering down a steep incline, scraping myself off on it, eroding myself on the way down, but at least I was choosing the path.

"I wanted someplace familiar," I said, leaning forward with some difficulty to light my cigarette in the flames. I wanted New York, but New York was gone. There was nothing familiar there anymore. "I wanted someplace where I would know where I could put my back, where I could grab some cover. I wanted someplace empty so I wouldn't have to worry about collaterals." I waved my hand around. "There's no fucking place on *earth* more empty and familiar than Chengara Fucking Penitentiary."

The underground complex was still usable, depending on your definition of the term. The topmost level was a wreck, bombed to hell and invaded by sand. The old elevator shafts were sturdy enough and the lower levels were clear enough and stable enough to use as shelter. I didn't like being down there, both because it reminded me of them shoving needles into my brain, that moment when hundreds of voices had poured into me, screaming and chattering, and because I didn't want to get trapped down there. Shelter could become a tomb if someone got the drop on you.

"Familiar, yes," he said sourly. "I remember it well,

also. I did not realize it could be so *cold* here." He sent another plume of smoke into the air. I heard a commotion from my right, but didn't bother lifting my automatic from where it sat on the ground next to me. Grisha had brought two dozen grimly silent men and women, all our age—fucking old—and all wearing the plain gray jumpsuit that was kind of an SPS uniform, but I'd come to recognize Marko's thunderous entrances into any situation; if he didn't have a knack for tech and a kind of unquestioning obedience I admired, he would have been nothing but a lethal weak link in any operation.

"But it is good choice," Grisha went on, studying the coal of his cigarette, which inspired me to finally light mine. "Defensible. Wall still in place, mostly, which is both good and bad—masks approach but gives us protection from long-range attacks. Wide open so we can keep watch and no one can sneak up on us. Underground bunker that has proven to withstand aerial assault, plus it gives us movement under the ground." He nodded. "With the tech we have wired, and the sun that never fails us out here, we are in best possible position." He snorted. "Except for *not being here*, best possible position."

Marko lumbered up to us, bundled up in several layers of clothes. His beard and hair were growing back nicely, and at a startling rate. The man was like the God of Hair. He tossed a pack of cards into my lap, their old holographic suits dead and pale. "What are we playing for?"

He'd asked us the same question every night for a week. "I've still got about five million yen in dormant accounts," I offered.

Grisha snorted. "Five million digital yen is worth as much as this sand here. We might as well play for sand."

"You're just pissed you don't have any yen in dormant accounts," I said mildly, sucking in smoke. I couldn't remember how the old cigarettes, the pre-Unification ones, had tasted. These seemed fine, but I thought the old ones had to have been better, even as stale and dry as they'd been. "This is just grousing."

Grisha nodded. "We play to see who digs the new shithole," he said amiably.

"Fuck," Marko muttered, sitting down. He glanced at the crate next to me and made a face. "Why not just hand me the shovel, then? I never fucking win."

Grisha leaned over and placed a hand on Marko's shoulder, his face serious. "You do not wish to be pitied, Mr. Marko. If we let you win, we would not respect you."

"Digging shitholes, on the other hand," I said immediately, "is a sign that we cannot possibly respect you *more*."

There was a moment of silence, and then Grisha solemnly picked up the cards and began shuffling them. I tried to pinpoint the odd feeling I had—peaceful, but amped up, like I was jonesed about something and perfectly happy to do it. Like I knew, for the first time in forever, exactly what I was doing and how it would all end up. Me dead, certainly—but that was, for once, part of the plan. Nothing bothered me, and I didn't even want to twist Marko's nose. I liked Grisha; I even liked Marko. I was fucking *happy*.

"How do you know, Avery?" Grisha said, frowning down at the cards in his hands. "How do you know he will come? And how do you know he will not just wait until we are dead?"

I shrugged, flicking the stub of cigarette out into the

desert. "He can't stand to think I've got *him*, a version of him. His mind. It's driving him crazy, because I'm not supposed to win on any level. You can't beat Canny Orel. It's not allowed. And I've got *him*—his thoughts, his memories. He can't risk us digging in there, finding out his secrets. And he won't wait because he's been a fucking god for only a few months. He's not used to being forever, and waiting for us to die is just too fucking *long* to wait."

Grisha nodded, then glanced over at the crate. "What do you say, little head?"

We all glanced over at Mara's head, wires snaking from her neck into a humming black box Grisha had produced, its power meter glowing a pale green in the darkness. It appeared to be asleep, eyes shut, mouth slightly open, but as we looked it popped one eye open and flashed it around at us.

"Och, you bet your ass I'm comin'," Orel said. "And sooner rather than *later*."

XXXIV

UNCOMFORTABLY CLOSE, AND THEN GONE. USUALLY DEAD.

The sun hadn't changed. The wind was freezing, but the sun was hot, though the overall temperature wasn't nearly what I remembered. I'd been in Chengara only a short time; I must have missed the winter out here, which was almost fucking pleasant.

Grisha didn't agree. For about the thousandth time he straightened up from where he'd been sweating and wheezing over a tiny black box he'd half buried in the sand, and squinted up at the sun, cigarette dangling from his lower lip. "Fucking sun," he groused.

I rubbed my damp head, the rough fuzz of hair warm to the touch. "We could be underground in the shadows, but you insisted we had to walk the perimeter and check the security systems." I scanned the flat, almost featureless horizon. Spread out around the old prison were small groups of Grisha's people, all of them huddled over similar spots, fussing with wires and boxes. "What is this shit, anyway?"

"Motion sensors," he grunted, leaning down again. "Self-charging, though the cells are getting saturated and only hold a three-fourth charge at best. There are not many of these types of cells left."

I nodded absently. "You think motion sensors will keep Orel out?"

"No, Avery, I think they will *warn* us when he arrives. That is all." He flicked open a tiny little handheld that began buzzing and chirping as he passed it over the box. "Unless you are a fan of having your throat slit in the night."

I shrugged, letting my eyes roam the bright, cold landscape. "Not usually, but there have been times when it probably wasn't the *most* horrifying option."

He snorted. "Of course, we are still going to be dealing with a...creature that can affect objects with its mind, dominate your will, Travel into your body, *and* shoot at you. I have brought as many Psionic-related security devices as I could, but we have no way of effectively fighting Orel, if he does come."

I nodded. "He's coming."

He snorted again, and then paused. "Avery," he said, and I looked down at him. "Do not tell Mr. Marko this. He is terrified as it is." He looked away suddenly. "I would... protect him. If it were possible."

I studied Grisha. I'd never considered anything personal about him; partly because the time I'd spent with him had generally been bullet riddled and terrifying, and partly because it had never occurred to me that there *was* anything personal about Grisha. He was a machine.

After a moment, I nodded, grinning and looking away again. I wondered if I shouldn't cut Marko loose, give him a dozen N-tabs and a canteen and send him on his way. He'd been useful during the trip and getting us set up at the prison, but keeping him around now seemed fucking cruel. Marko had never actively tried to fuck with me, and I couldn't hold his general air of physical incompetence against him. Besides, Marko and Grisha were the closest things to friends I had left.

I wondered about Adora, what she was up to. We'd been cooped up in a ship's belly for weeks, in the dark, our noses up each other's ass, and then she was gone. It seemed as if everyone I'd known was like that—there for a while, uncomfortably close, and then gone. Usually dead.

Something on the edge of the world caught my eye. My augments, wheezing and chugging, zoomed my vision as much as they could manage, and I stood there staring out into the desert for a while.

"I don't think we're gonna need this shit, Grish."

Grisha cursed unintelligibly, all consonants and spit. "And why is that, Avery? Has Orel the power to dissolve into mist now?" He sighed. "I would not be surprised, honestly."

"Nope," I said, pointing at the tiny dots approaching from the distance. "Someone's coming."

"You've got a fucking organization," Marko said. "You've got people. Why do we have, like, a dozen fucking people in the middle of fucking nowhere? We should have a *battalion* here."

"All that would be is ammunition for Orel," Grisha said testily. "He had dozens, hundreds Pushed simultaneously in Split. If we had a *battalion* here, it would quickly turn into the Fighting Orels." He shook his head. "We tried it the way the cops wanted, and it did not work. This is *our* way."

I snorted. "*My* way is usually me tricked into committing suicide. I didn't know there *was* another way."

We were watching the group approaching, about a dozen people in long black coats and sober suits that must have been hot in the sun despite the cool air. They were *walking*, and since there was no indication otherwise I was assuming that they'd walked *across the fucking desert*. If that was true, chances were they were going to drop dead the second they stopped walking, so I chose not to worry too much about them.

"What about *us*?" Marko demanded. "Won't Orel just control *us*?"

"You, yes," Grisha said, smiling faintly. "Avery's brain is damaged beyond use. My own brain is made of steel."

I turned and scanned our little camp one last time. Grisha's mopes stood directly behind us in a ragged line, looking tired and slightly pissed off, their single-action rifles slung over their shoulders. We'd disconnected the avatar head and hidden it away; we didn't need Orel shouting things at inappropriate moments, and I didn't need people knowing more about me and my situation than necessary. Though I suspected that people locating you in the middle of a fucking desert, *on foot*, indicated that your personal security measures were, perhaps, not quite up to snuff.

I watched them walking from under my own eyebrows, the sun making everything white and filled with glare. We hadn't been idle. These were definitely Spooks coming toward us—no one else had such consistent and terrible fashion sense, and no one else walked around looking like a dozen brothers and sisters of exactly the same fucking age. Lucky for us we'd been working hard to defend the camp *from* a Psionic. I tapped the switch plate under my foot lightly, making sure I was positioned correctly, and lifted one hand to shade my eyes as I checked their distance, scanning the ground for my reference point, an old ammo locker the SSF had left behind, a well-preserved green tub once filled with shredder rounds.

Spooks could fuck with you at a distance, of course, but I'd learned to rely on their tendency toward speechifying.

If you could pin people to the wall with your thoughts, you'd get used to captive audiences too, Marin whispered at me. I could almost imagine that digital bastard grinning at me.

Shut the fuck up, I thought back, still feeling ridiculous thinking at the ghosts in my head, even after all these years. *I can't have someone I* liked *trapped up there? All my friends, dead, and you're still gassing at me.*

You never had any friends, Avery, he said crisply, and fell silent.

"Is this shit going to work?"

Grisha grunted. "Yes, Avery. In the middle of the desert using scavenged equipment and running power from degraded cells I can absolutely guarantee success. Also, we have tested this equipment on exactly three Psionics, including the subject you brought to us. Who we could have tested further if you had not killed him."

I smiled and started to say something back, but noted that the group had drawn up more or less even with my marker. I mashed my foot down on the switch, putting all my weight on it to be safe.

Instantly, and with a jangling, screeching noise I quickly upgraded to my least favorite noise ever, a metal cage erupted from the loose, sandy ground around the newcomers, staggering upward about ten feet before it stopped, shivering and crackling. It had caught one of the Spooks on one edge as it rose and she hung there, squawking, for a moment before overbalancing and falling inside with the rest of them.

Grisha glanced down at his handheld. "We have about five minutes," he said. "Then batteries are flat."

"Shit," I muttered. "Are we sure it worked?"

"We are not in the air," he said, looking up at me. "I am not trying to strangle you."

"All right then," I said, stepping forward. "That's a good day."

I walked out toward the cage, which looked like a bunch of hastily welded metal, junk left in the desert to be eroded one atom at a time. The men and women inside its perimeters had been talking to each other in loud whispers, gesticulating, but as I drew close they stopped suddenly, as one, and stared at me with their spooky, big round eyes. I noticed that each of them had red, rubbery scars on their necks—exactly where Angel marks would have been if they had not been burned or cut out.

I stepped up just outside of arm's reach, primed to be flung into the air. Then I unslung the shredder from my back, toggled it active, and as the soft whine of the rifle filled the thin, dry air, I looked them over. All kids, all with clear, round faces. They all seemed to be concentrating on me very hard, trying, I figured, to do what they usually did with threats, what they'd done with threats their whole lives: take charge of them, effortlessly, with just a thought.

"We've got about three minutes," I said. "When my associate back there tells me to, I'm going to kill you all. So if you've got something to say, say it now."

As one they looked at the rifle, and then back at me. One girl, softly pretty with round, red cheeks and a helmet of brown hair not even the winds out here seemed able to touch, stepped forward the inch or so allowed to her. "How have you done this?"

"Fuck if I know," I said. "My associate says that Psionic Actives broadcast a specific brainwave pattern, identical in each of you. He says that by pushing an opposite pattern *into* you, the waves cancel out and you are effectively neutered." I turned my head slightly. "That about right, Grish?"

"Yes," he said simply.

I looked back at the girl. "Okay. So there you go." I gestured at my throat. "You were Angels."

She nodded, squinting at me. "We were. We are schismatics."

I nodded, pursing my lips and estimating the time remaining in my head. "The Angels were pretty easy to understand: They wanted to kill me. I'd been judged."

She nodded again. "You are judged. But we believe you can yet be forgiven."

Schismatics, I thought. It was fucking amazing. Even as the world wound down, going still, all the assholes in the world were hard at work making everything more complicated, and more complicated, and then even fucking *more* complicated.

"So you're not here to kill me, is what I'm hearing," I said. "That about right?"

She nodded, once, grim and still.

I looked randomly to my left and squinted at the horizon. "Assuming I believe that shit," I said, looking back at her and cocking my head. "Okay. You're not here to kill me. So why *are* you here?"

She blinked, once, placidly. "To help you kill Orel."

XXXV

THEY'LL HAVE HIM DANCING AND JUGGLING

I looked up as Grisha entered the room and I held up my hand, feeling tired. I'd expected him to come berate me, and I wanted to cut the conversation down to a minimum.

"I know what you're here to say. I didn't agree to their terms. But we could *use* a team of Spooks against Orel, couldn't we?"

He nodded, throwing up his hands and beginning to pace around the ruined lab. The lower level of Chengara was only accessible via a service ladder in the old elevator shafts, a ladder that shimmied and vibrated under your weight, groaning with rusty horror as you descended. The lab was nothing like I remembered it, although when I'd come to I'd been filled with voices and hungover from having drugs and needles and who knew what else shoved into me. The walls were scorched, and the equipment and furniture were shattered and bent. Flaking brown stains mottled the walls and floors, old blood the only sign that anyone had ever been here. I wondered about the lack of remains—no bones, no old clothes. Just the occasional bloodstain. I wondered if the System Pigs or the new army or *someone* had a team that came around these old battle-fields and took away the bodies, the wreckage of destroyed avatar units. After everything I'd seen, it wouldn't surprise me.

"They are here to *destroy* him," he said, pacing. "They are here to *prevent* us from gaining the access codes. Not to aid us. *Not* to aid us."

I nodded, keeping my mind blank. "We use them. We point them at the things we wish to control, and when we have him down, we step in between Orel and them."

He looked at me, his tight, careful face judging. "You think we can control them? Psionics?"

I shrugged. "You think we can deal with Orel without them?"

He nodded, once, firmly. "Yes. We have a plan."

"Sure, but they give us a *much* better chance of success, Grish." I blinked. "Wait: You left Marko up there alone with them?" I laughed. "Shit, they'll have him dancing and juggling."

He shook his head and looked down so I wouldn't catch the slight smile that played across his face. I felt like I was walking a tightrope, trying to keep Grisha hanging on. It was exhausting. I kicked at a spent shredder clip, empty and crushed by some long-gone boot. It skittered across the metallic floor and hit the far wall, making a tinny noise. It was difficult to believe I'd been in here years before, getting my brains scooped out.

I stood up and stretched. "C'mon. Let's walk the line and make sure we're ready."

"You are so sure he will come," Grisha said, falling in behind me as I squeezed through the broken doorway and out into the hall.

"And soon," I agreed. "I've been in the same room as Orel only a few dozen times, and half the time I was with him I thought he was someone fucking else. But I know him. He's a fucking spider, and knowing I have a version of him, can poke in there and find out anything I want—it'll eat at him. He can't have that. He doesn't want me finding out what he's afraid of, what he did when he was a kid, who he fell in love with, the last time he cried like a fucking asshole, whatever state secrets he might have neglected to erase." I shook my head. "He can't have it, Grish. Trust me."

Grisha fell into silence behind me as we moved through the dark, moldy hallway and toward the elevator shaft. A huge number four still caught the dim light, painted onto the wall in the tiny elevator lobby, the opened doors revealing a yawning black rectangle where an elevator had once ferried the SSF staff in and out of their little sausage grinder in the belly of the desert. I was calm. I'd expected to be angry, to get worked up from being back in Chengara, but I didn't feel much at all. Everything had narrowed down to a point: getting Orel within arm's length, on my terms for a change. Not me chasing after him, not me being lured along by phantoms and avatars, but him, coming to me, where I could watch him approach and pick my moment. Everything else had fallen away.

We rose slowly up the shaft, one hand over the other, Grisha panting behind me loud and damp. He was more bent over than he had been before, more hunched, his face crisscrossed with new wrinkles. I figured he could feel the end of the line coming, too. The world was petering out, and we were dancing on the final stop.

I gave him a hand up out of the shaft, back into the shallow, sand-filled basement level that had been blown open during the army's raid on the prison all those years ago. The cold wind hit us immediately, cutting through everything I had on and making me shiver.

"This is our retreat," I said, loudly, competing with the wind. "If we get into trouble, we head down into the cave. Single point of entry, no way for him to see us or reach for us with his mind unless he comes down. We take potshots at anything that tries coming down." I pulled out one of the tiny disc grenades Grish had been able to provide; we each had a dozen or so stuffed into our pockets. "Hell, we can toss your grenades into the shaft if he gets that far."

"If we *get* into trouble?" Grisha said, shaking his head with a smile.

The sand had banked against the western wall of the old guards' quarters under the main complex, and we were able to scramble up back onto the flat ground on the surface. The moon was huge and white, making everything look colorless and frozen. Half the old cinder-block wall of the dormitory was still standing, sand halfway up one side as it traced a straight line for a few hundred feet and then veered at a right angle to the east, going another fifty feet or so before ending in a jagged jumble of blocks and shiny shrapnel. We stepped around to the sheltered side of the old dorm, littered with the twisted wreckage of the old bunks and other junk that had blown there, spent clips and random equipment the cops and troops had dropped.

"This," I said breathlessly, my HUD flickering my vision, the status bars pulsing with my heartbeat, "we can use to break line of sight. That motherfucker might be a demigod, but he's got to *see* us. He can't toss us into the air or latch onto our minds if he can't see us." In the corners were neat piles of ammunition for the shredders as well as our autos, which we'd swapped out so we were all carrying the same caliber. "We reload here, too. We keep *moving*, no matter what. You blow your clip, you keep moving, you duck in here, you reload."

"Our new *friends*," Grisha said, out of breath but managing to sound sour anyway. "Where are they?"

I was already walking, angling my way back to the open air of what used to be the yard, still marked off by the ruins of the old wall. One of the corner towers still stood, creaking and shuddering in the wind. I jabbed a finger at it as Grisha struggled to keep up. "Three Tele-Ks and four Pushers," I said. "None of them Travel—fucking never heard of such a thing. Two of the Tele-Ks in the tower. They're up there now, half a canteen of water and ten N-tabs between them. They're the strongest but they're not certain of the range they can do anything effective at. The rest are on their own. They're mobile. The Pushers will try to break the three of us out if he gives us a nudge, and the last Tele-K is just basically going to put him in the air as much as possible." I smiled. "Where are your people?"

Grisha grunted and gestured vaguely. "Sniping. They are out in the sand, in shallow digouts with scoped weapons." He coughed wetly. "If they receive a signal from me they are also to try and swarm him."

I nodded. I finally spotted the old ammo locker, now a dull and drab gray. The rattling cage Grisha had brought in pieces from Spain and assembled had been retracted back into the soft ground, hidden from sight and ready to leap up again, fresh batteries attached to the apparatus, the best batteries we had left, which Grisha thought might give us seven or eight minutes of juice with the cage pulling from them.

"We herd him here," I said, standing in the spot where the cage would be when triggered and throwing out my arms. "They throw his own shit back at him—throw rocks at him, put him in the air, Push him, if they can. Your people shoot at him. We keep him dancing. Marko's gonna be in the old basement with one of the old rifles. He's a shit shot, but I just told him to stay low and out of sight and harass the motherfucker, put shots at him as much as he can. You and I, we're mobile. Take cover, displace often. Throw shots at him as much as you can. Don't take chances—he's a Psionic. He sees you, you're in for suffering."

Grisha nodded, hands on his hips, studying the ground at my feet. "We herd him."

"Marko's got the switch plate. The second Orel's standing here, he mashes it, and we're done."

"He will have one shot," Grisha said slowly. "If he mistimes it, if Orel manages to skip free before he is trapped, that is it. We will be done." He nodded to himself. "This worries me."

I nodded. "Sure. You think you should be in the hole, taking potshots and pressing the button?"

He nodded. "I do. But you are right: I am better with a gun than Marko, and I am better in the field. It is the stronger disposition of resources to have me out here." He sighed, starting to cough. "We will just rely on Marko's judgment."

For a second we both stood there, silent, pondering the horror of that statement.

"I told them all to wait," I said. "To let him get close. Don't waste bullets on a distance shot, and don't try anything fancy when he's too far to do anything."

"The Tele-Ks should take a chance if they see one," he said, spinning around to look at the crumbling old guard tower. "They might pluck him up and land him on this spot before he can do anything."

I shrugged. "Maybe. He's a smart old bastard, though. He's gonna be expecting tricks from us."

"Yes," Grisha said flatly. "He is a god now, yes? Does *smart old bastard* cover it?"

I tapped my head. "He's still got the same old brain."

Grisha opened his mouth, then paused. Clipped to his belt, the small handheld connected to our motion detectors was buzzing and flashing an angry red that was bright enough to light up his face from below, making him demonic. He glanced down at it, then back up at me.

"It's a feint, you know," I said, turning to scan the dark horizon.

"Yes," Grisha said, and I heard the snap of his auto being racked. "But he is here."

XXXVI

YOUR PROBLEM IS YOU THINK YOU'RE SPECIAL

We had no lights. Suddenly, after weeks of travel and days of preparation, days of thinking about this moment, days of staring at Mara's decapitated head and listening to Orel's ghost crack wise and insult me, I wished to fuck we'd thought of fucking *lights* out here in the fucking desert at night.

Grisha had disappeared instantly, on the move, and I dropped down onto my belly and studied the night around us. My augments tried to brighten up the night and had plenty of moon to do so, but I couldn't see any movement. He was out there. Thundering around in his heavy, nuke-powered Monk chassis, he was within sniper range. My heart thudded in my chest. All I could hear was the wind.

Somewhere, out in the darkness, I heard the rippling crack of a rifle shot. A moment later, a distant scream, rising and fading—someone being plucked from the ground and sent sailing, about to smash down onto the ground.

Grisha's people were tough as old leather, in general, but they weren't trained for this shit. No one was.

I stayed on my belly and worked my way back toward the remaining dormitory wall. I had to assume he could see me, unlikely as that seemed. I made pretty rapid progress, scraping along, the sound of the sand beneath me and my labored breathing seeming loud and amplified in the cold night. About halfway there, a stray cloud drifted between us and the moon, and the old prison was suddenly in near-total darkness. My HUD was bright and clear, everything working perfectly for a change, and slowly my vision brightened as my augments soaked up every bit of light left and focused it.

When I reached the wall I pulled myself behind it and sat up. Sheltered in the old dorm space where Marlena and I had sat and smoked and fucked, I checked my auto and carefully pushed myself out around the edge of the wall, inch by inch, trying to be *part* of the fucking wall, unnoticed and unnoticeable. I reached into my pocket carefully and found one of the tiny earbuds we'd shared out and pushed it into place.

"Grisha?" I whispered. "Marko?" I didn't bother raising any of the Spooks who'd come to fulfill their bullshit religious destiny, or any of Grisha's people. I hadn't learned anyone's name anyway. I figured they would all be dead soon enough, and I didn't need to put more names on my list of people I'd fucked over by my mere presence. At any rate, they weren't listening to me, and I wasn't listening to them.

"I am at foot of tower," Grisha rasped into my ear. The way the sound bloomed and died in my ear was strange, the complete silence and the crackle and hiss of individual words with so much dark silence between sentences. "I see nothing."

"I'm where you put me," Marko hissed, sounding like someone was standing on his balls. "I'm *freezing*."

I ignored him, keeping my eyes on the move, looking for any clue.

He might circle back behind you, Marin whispered in my head.

I shook my head and caught myself. I didn't respond. Orel hadn't come here to sneak around and do some old-school Gunning, wearing us down until we fucked up and he got one single, perfect shot. He'd come to make me feel the wrath of the new god. There would be fucking taunts, and he'd play with us, make us understand that he would have let us go, he would have let us live out our measly little lives in peace, but we had to go fuck with him.

A single shot, small and wet like a firecracker, plinked in the distance, immediately swallowed by the silence.

"Rafeal is dead," a man's voice, calm and monotone, whispered in my ear. I didn't know who the fuck Rafeal was, or had been, and I wasn't interested.

"Grisha, you getting any more buzz?"

"Nothing, Avery," the Russian replied in a hushed voice. "No other motion detectors have been triggered."

He's fucking with us, I thought. *He's going to have us jumping at shadows.*

He's got you jumping at shadows, Salgado hissed. *What a waste. So much yen poured into this place, so much tech and blood and sweat. And they used it for a brain-suck operation, and we bombed it to hell. And now an arena for you and Orel. A waste.*

Dolores, I thought, keeping my eyes open and moving,

I regret to inform you the one positive I can take away from having Canny Orel's gun shoved up my ass is that I will never have to hear your thoughts again.

"Hello, Avery."

Marko's voice in my ear. I went still, putting my eyes on the ammo locker marking the location of the cage and tried to be aware of my surroundings, all around me, picturing the layout of the prison, the approaches to my position. "Hello, Mickey," I said quietly.

"Interestin' band of morons you've assembled here, Avery," he continued in my ear, in Marko's voice but with Orel's patterns.

"C'mon, old man," I whispered. "Come try me. Quit hiding."

"Avery?" Marko's voice again, but once again with the original-issue accent.

"Move, Mr. Marko," I hissed. "Displace. Keep your assignment in line of sight but move. You're spotted."

"Yer problem," Grisha suddenly spoke in my ear, loud and with Orel's accent, "is you think you're special."

I threw myself into a roll, thinking, *The fucking bastard can see us all.* I spun myself out and around the wall, flopping onto my belly and crawling rapidly through the sandy dirt until I was on the other side.

"Marko," I whispered as I hauled myself along the wall, breathing in more sand than air. "You find yourself a new spot?"

"Yeah," he whispered back. "Fuck me, that was fucking *horrible.* I'm—"

"Do *not* fucking tell me where you are," I hissed. My lungs were burning and my mouth was full of grit. Sweat was streaming down my face as I crawled despite the cold. "You still have a line of sight?"

"A line of—oh. Yeah, I got it."

"Shit, I'm not even going to kill these poor bastards," Orel barked in Grisha's familiar voice, flat and lifeless without the accent. "I'm goin' to *spare* their miserable brief little lives and let 'em crawl around a little more. I'm gonna show up at their fuckin' funerals and give the fuckin' eulogy. Here lies some asshole. Avery Cates tried his best to get 'im killed, just like every-fucking-body Cates ever met."

I found the far edge of the ruined dorm wall and peered around it. I could see the depression that was the bombed-out basement of the old complex, the sandy soil coasting downward toward the elevator shaft. I figured Orel was out in the darkness behind us, and I needed to feint out, grab his eye, and get him coming to *me* before he managed to put me in the air or Push me.

Seconds ticked by. I listened to the wind and stared into the dark.

"Grish?" I whispered.

There was a soft cough, and then a deep breath. "A-Avery?"

He sounded normal again. "You okay, man?"

He didn't respond for a moment. "I am...okay, Avery. It was like...like someone *worming* into me. I could *feel* it happening, being...pushed aside."

"Displace, Grish," I whispered back. "Don't sit there. He knows you're there."

"Yes to *that*."

I forced myself to pick a spot on the horizon and study it, clearing my mind and just letting instinct and the primitive wiring of my head lead me. He was a god, maybe, but he was still a tired old man, deep down, and tired old men—even the great Canny Orel—made mistakes. Fuck, I was living proof of that.

"Hello, Avery."

I froze. The voice was right behind me.

XXXVII

RISING TRIUMPHANTLY FROM THE TRASH BIN OF HISTORY

It didn't sound like Orel, his raw, wide brogue and the nasally, creaking way he had of enunciating. It was the flat pitch of the old Monks, devoid of anything like curiosity or detail, something a computer had decided approximated a human voice. The words were sucked dry and vanished by the cold wind, and a second later it was like he hadn't spoken at all. If I stayed still and kept my eyes straight ahead, I might pretend it had never happened.

My HUD flickered and went dim.

"You stupid bastard," he said. I judged him to be about five feet behind me, a little elevated. I raked my eyes over the scene in front of me; I didn't want to turn and provoke him. If he wanted to stand there and do his little demigod routine, let him waste the time. The ground sloped down into the basement, the elevator shaft a dark blob of nothing at the far end. I didn't see Marko or Grisha, or anything else that might be useful. I fixed the location of the cage in my mind, ahead and to the left. Get him there and hope Marko was awake and paying attention.

I wouldn't beat his digital reflexes. I wouldn't get the drop on him. But trying to was the only play I had. I sucked a slow, deep breath in, gripped my automatic loosely, finger on the trigger, made sure the safety was off, and whipped myself around.

Instantly, the Monk soared into the air with a strangled squawk. I'd barely caught a glimpse of it, so familiar— a shiny new model, the face bright white in the moonlight, the eyes just dark circles where I knew tiny, delicate cameras clicked and ticked for eyes. He was wearing a heavy longcoat that spread out behind him in the wind as he sailed upward, his white hands and face soon all I could see.

I just sat there and stared up for a second. I thought at first he'd put himself up there for an attack, but as he twisted and rolled in the air I realized one of the other Tele-Ks had put their hand on him.

For a second I just stared, blood filling my head like pus into a wound and muffling everything. He looked so tiny and peaceful, like a satellite a thousand miles above us, so far away he couldn't possibly hurt anything. He twisted and spun in the air, struggling against the invisible fist he'd been caught in, and I found the sight mesmerizing.

There were shouts in the distance drifting through the dry, chilled air. I spun around, catching sight of figures in the near distance running toward me—Grisha's people, rifles in hands. They swarmed past me without even a second glance, took up positions ringing the general area, set themselves on their knees, and took aim up at his tiny little figure...and then did nothing. They sat there with rifles fixed and just stared up at him, afraid to accidentally kill him if they started to fire at him.

"Fucking hell," I muttered, slamming my Roon back into its holster and pushing myself into a staggering jog at them. The closest one was a grizzled old woman of forty, her face a permanent red mask of weather and booze. As I stepped up to her I took hold of the smooth barrel of her rifle and gave her a playful shove that sent her tumbling to the sandy ground, the gun tearing from her hands. I took a second to look the ancient stick over and checked the chamber, wrapped the shoulder strap around my forearm to get it out of the way, and lifted it up. Through the scope Orel looked ridiculous, a tiny Monk fluttering in the air like he was a kite, a piece of plastic. I guessed our Tele-K was trying to put him on the ground where our cage was buried and Orel was pushing himself in the other direction. Taking a deep breath, I decided to change the rules of the game, and I squeezed the trigger as I exhaled.

Behind me, as if I'd set off some sort of alarm, there was a rumbling noise, vibrations shooting up through my legs.

I ignored it. Racking the action again, I glanced down at the blond woman to make sure she wasn't creeping back to get her revenge on me, then concentrated on the fluttering figure in the air and squeezed off another round. I started to turn my attention back to the blonde, but a sudden earthquake beneath me and an ear-splitting, groaning noise tearing through the thin air made me spin around. I stared for a second; the old half-buried SSF hover was tilting and vibrating, shifting this way and that in the crater that held it upright. I turned to glance up at Orel, who was twisting and fluttering, one black arm stretched out toward the ground.

I snapped my head back around just in time to see the hover slowly disgorge itself from the earth, the ground shaking hard under me. Sixty feet of alloy and plastic, intact displacers along its belly each weighing a ton, a ton and a half. Years of sandy soil caked around it after an impact that had buried it twenty feet into the crust. And it jerked and tugged upward in loud, shaky spasms, the metal groaning as it bent and tore under the stress.

Suddenly it popped free, snapping up into the air. Everything seemed to go still. The hover stopped and hung impossibly in the air for a second, huge and heavy and weightless. If not for the complete, dense silence you could have believed the hover had spontaneously shaken off years of rust and decay and ignited its displacers, rising triumphantly from the trash bin of history. I turned in time to see the tiny figure in the sky twitch.

With a tearing noise of rending metal, the hover flicked into motion, accelerating suddenly toward the guard tower. The tearing noise deepened as it picked up speed, making the hairs on my neck and arms stand up, and when it smacked into the tower it was a relief to have it ended. The hover broke up into four or five large pieces, each crashing down to the earth again, and the tower began collapsing in slow motion: A loud cracking sound like a gunshot and the tower was leaning crazily to one side, falling so slowly it might have been my imagination. Outlined against the silvery night sky I saw one figure jump, arms and legs moving wildly as he plummeted. When it was almost perpendicular to the ground, the tower shattered into dust, and then the ground leaped beneath my feet, a huge cloud of debris and sand billowing up from the ground.

Orel fell, swallowed up by the shadowy dust storm.

For a few heartbeats we all just stood there like assholes as silence swallowed everything again and settled in. *So much for our volunteer Spooks*, I thought.

Movement at my elbow made me jump. The blonde I'd snatched the rifle from was standing next to me. She glanced my way and we shrugged our eyebrows at each other. I opened my mouth to say something smart, then snapped it shut as a loud scraping sound made the ground shudder again. Leaning forward slightly, I squinted through the darkness, then looked around. I was in the midst of Grisha's morons, which suddenly looked exactly like a bull's-eye. If I were Orel, a group of dumbfounded Techies standing with their mouths open and their rifles at their sides would look like fucking lunch.

I turned and started running hard, heading sideways to escape their gravity well of stupid.

When the scraping noise suddenly ceased, I twisted my head around without stopping, just in time to see a chunk of the toppled guard tower shoot up out of the settling dust, soaring twenty or thirty feet into the air on a lazy arc. I stumbled and sat down on my ass, the rifle I was still holding on to for reasons my hands refused to explain skittering away from me like a piece of kindling. The hunk of rock was twenty or thirty feet around, jagged on the edges but smooth on the sides, and for a second it was suspended in the air like a newly acquired moon.

The Techies didn't move. They just stood there, staring.

It's hard to adjust, Marin whispered in my head, unwelcome. *The first time you really have to deal with a first-class Psionic. They break all the rules, and it takes some time to adjust.*

The hunk of building screamed down at them, three seconds, two heartbeats. The split second before it hit, my little earbud crackled to life for a blink.

"Holy—"

And went dead. The impact was so massive I was tossed into the air a few inches, falling back down onto my ass again as a little extra bonus on the evening. A wave of sandy soil hit me with force, carpeting me in a thick layer, getting into my mouth and nose and making me cough and heave.

Gasping, I flipped myself over and got moving. My head was swimming, so I crawled. I needed to *move*, to build up some momentum.

"Avery?" Grisha's voice in my ear. "Avery? Where are you?"

Translation: *Are you under that fucking building right now*? I didn't even try to respond. I pushed myself up onto my feet and managed a stumbling, crazy-legged jog, trying to simultaneously clear my windpipe and suck in air. I made for the low remnant of the old dorm wall, poor cover but cover nonetheless, with the yawning elevator shaft behind it as a final retreat. I reached it, my head pounding, the faint outlines of my dimmed HUD pulsing like they'd been burned onto my retinas, until with one final pulse the HUD snapped back into bright clarity. I skidded around to the other side, intending to drop down and try to spot Orel from my hiding place.

Then I heard it: steady, heavy footsteps, right behind me. Too heavy for anything but an avatar...or a Monk. I kept running and yanked my Roon from its holster again, trying to clear my mind.

When he came, he came too fast, fucking *fast*, zooming

up from the shadows, coming at an angle. I squeezed the trigger but the shots trailed him as he traced a wide loop around me, coming at me from the side, flipping me onto my back and pinning me. Orel weighed about eleven fucking million pounds and I sank slowly into the loose dirt beneath him.

His face was the standard grinning Monk face, limited in expression, always, somehow, cheerful and blank at the same time. He'd lost his shades, and his tiny insectoid camera eyes dilated as they focused on me, his smile static and automatic, forgotten, unintended.

His artificial voice was like melted rubber.

"Ever been Taken, Avery?" he said, calm and unhurried. "Traveled into?"

XXXVIII

EATING MY BRAIN ONE TINY BITE AT A TIME, TUNNELING

I froze for a moment, hearing Grisha's words: *Like some-one worming into me.* I remembered every time I'd been Pushed, and wondered which was worse: being made to do things you didn't want, or having someone just *push you aside* and do them with your body while you sat inside your own head, screaming.

I struggled to bring an arm up, but the Monk chassis was too strong. He went still and I struggled harder, heaving against him, his alloy bones and hydraulic tendons, my legs flopping uselessly like they were part of some other asshole entirely, delighted with the show so far. I heard shouting, then the weak, distant *pop pop* of gunfire, too distant to do me any good.

And then I felt it.

It was like pressure in my thoughts, a sudden and urgent new focus, like someone had whispered something to me that I had no choice but to think about immediately.

The pressure grew and grew and I stopped flopping about, my whole body going stiff with strain as I tried to break free and think about something else, anything, *anything* that was not this huge balloon of nothing, this black hole growing in my head.

And then, without warning, the mental bubble just shattered, and I was in control again, my legs picking up their useless flopping without missing a beat.

Orel screamed, a metallic warbly screech that hurt my ears, and he sailed up off me as if some huge being had reached down from the sky and plucked him up. I sat up, panting, and watched him stagger backward into the old basement, beating at his own head with his hands.

"Ah, *fuck* you and your mutant fucking *brain*," he bellowed.

I scrambled along the low wall until I found a shallow indentation in the loose ground that provided a little shelter. I fumbled with the Roon, trying to check it over with shaking hands, my head pounding. I felt like I'd been chewed. I risked a quick pop up to make sure Orel wasn't moving. He was still standing there, cursing and shaking his head.

Your fucked-up brain gave him the fits, Marin whispered, sounding amused.

That is an unauthorized jailbroken Mark I chassis. It should be deactivated immediately.

I blinked, shaking my head. I didn't hear from Dennis Squalor often, and I didn't enjoy it when I did. *Good luck with that*, I thought back at him. Usually when I communicated with him he fled like a frightened bug.

This is unacceptable. This unit is operating outside my network.

I stole another glance at Orel and snapped the Roon shut. *Shut up*, I thought. *I'm fucking working here.*

Squalor ignored me. If he could even *hear* me.

We must apply the shutdown code set.

Anger flared up in me as I tried to ignore the suddenly chatty voices in my head and listen for Orel's approach. He couldn't see me where I was hunkered down, so he couldn't put me in the air. If I timed it right, I might put a shell or two in him when he came for me.

We don't have *the shutdown codes, shithead*, I thought. *Orel's got them.*

Not the antimutiny codes Richard created for his own network, Squalor said slowly, calmly. *My codes. I cannot tolerate someone operating one of my units outside the faith. It must be deactivated.*

Suddenly, Marin was there too. Marin was still talking. *Will it still work?*

I shut my eyes and clenched my teeth. Years now I'd had these ghosts in my head, and *now* they decided to start chatting. I was fucking cursed.

Yes. These codes are part of the Bootstrap subsystems. It is unlikely in the extreme that any hacker trying to subvert a unit would be capable of even discovering their existence.

"This doesn't fucking matter," I hissed, unable to stop myself from vocalizing. "Unless you think I'm going to stand up and shout fucking hex code at him while he *shoots me to death.*"

For two seconds, there was blessed silence in my head. Then, Marin was back.

Dolores, your people designed these augments poor Avery's got rotting in his head. They transmit, yes?

For a second I thought Salgado wasn't going to answer. I'd never had all three acknowledging each other before—never had them having a three-way conversation without me. Having them all talking to each other was maddening, like tiny people living in my head, eating my brain one tiny bite at a time, tunneling.

Yes. Short range, but they had to ping back to their CO's implant.

Any way we can use Avery's augments to transmit Dennis's shutdown codes?

I went still. Years. I'd had these assholes in my head for years, and the thought that they might actually be *useful* was fucking astonishing. It made me think, for a moment, that the cosmos did have a fucking plan for me after all.

Ye-es, Dolores whispered, sounding hesitant. *I doubt Avery received the level of training required to customize his beacon.* There was silence. *Avery...perhaps I could take direct control over your augment interface in order to accomplish this.*

I opened my eyes. I could still hear Orel muttering; only a few seconds had passed. "You can *do* that?" I hadn't meant to speak out loud, and froze up instantly, horrified.

We're you, Avery, she responded. Immediately, my HUD began flickering and a stream of text prompts began scrolling by in a tiny corner of my vision, too fast for me to pay attention to.

I chose to ignore "we're you." If I started thinking about things like that, my list of people I needed revenge against would get so fucking long I'd have to Monk-up myself to get to them all, end of the fucking world or not.

You'll need to buy us some time, Marin added.

"I've bought you all *years*, dammit," I hissed before I could catch myself. "You're all *dead*." In the silence that answered me, I realized Orel had stopped his crazy whispering to himself.

I launched myself to my left a second before the heavy Monk body landed right where I'd been huddled. I threw myself down and rolled, letting gravity pull me down toward the dark pit of the collapsed basement and the elevator shaft, hoping it took me out of view fast enough to prevent Mickey from snatching me up in his little invisible hands; when I was in shadow again I scissored my legs manically and turned myself around without rising up, putting the Roon on the upward slope I'd just traversed.

A second later, Orel landed almost perfectly between where I'd been and where I was and paused for an angelic moment, looking for me, and I could pick my shot. You could penetrate the armoring around a Monk's abdomen but it wasn't easy, and anything but a head shot was usually just an inconvenience for them. I'd had plenty of experience gunning with Monks, and I was aiming to slow the motherfucker down, make him less mobile. If I could stop him from leaping and running, it was a start.

I aimed for his feet, filled with delicate hydraulics and servos, tiny parts giving him balance and speed. Trying to stop my hands from shaking, I squeezed off four rapid shots, kicking up dust around him and then finally, in one perfect moment, shattering the hard outer casing of his right ankle. He made a strangely subdued, almost calm noise as he lost balance and fell over.

I struggled up, trying to race. When I finally got my

legs under me and looked up, the bastard was gone again. I stood for just a second, looking around, and found him again by the easiest method possible: He landed on me, cackling, the Monk's fake voice box struggling hard to approximate the braying laughter of Canny Orel. The impact pushed me down a few inches into the ground, suffocating me, but before I could ponder where I'd place "strangling on sand at Chengara while Canny Orel stood on your back" on my list of worst ways to die his cold, dead hands took hold of my arms, bending them back behind me and lifting me easily out of the shallow trench we'd created. Blood, warm and gritty, ran down my chin, and I poked my tongue through the new gap in my mouth where my front teeth had once been.

Handsome as ever, Avery, Dolores whispered. *We're almost there.*

Orel lifted me up, holding me in front of him like I weighed nothing. His bright white face was cocked in a blank, soulless smile, his eyes just pools of shadow. Monks in the moonlight were fucking terrifying—they *glowed*.

"This was too fucking easy," he said, making it sound like *aisy* and cocking his head the other way and smoothly putting his auto against my temple. "Avery, I had higher hopes for ya. Maybe Wallace was right about you."

I managed to jam the Roon into his belly, but his gun flashed down instantly, knocking it away as I fired, the shot going wild, my hand going numb as the gun fell away. Just as quickly, his gun was back against my head.

"G'bye, Avery."

I shut my eyes, my mind racing, and suddenly my HUD filled with angry red text, scrolling along so fast it was a blur, and Dennis Squalor, long dead but still a tiny god in his own way, spoke silently inside me.

You are cast out.

Still grinning, Orel went still, and then collapsed, dragging me down with him.

XXXXIX

HAD MET ME BEFORE AND
HAD A GRUDGE

I pushed myself up and stared down at Orel. His face was still frozen in a grin, the gun was still clutched in his hand. But he was absolutely still.

Looks like you're a genius, Dennis, Marin whispered cheerfully.

I am implacable and absolute. I am the guardian of that which I have created.

"You are boring as fucking hell," I said hoarsely, my throat filled with sand. I broke into shuddering coughs and dragged myself over to Orel. Numbness had spread up my arm and I dragged it behind me, useless. I tried to breathe deeply, but my chest kept clenching up and twisting me into fits of dry, joyless coughing, my HUD—back to normal now—flickering with each blast.

I pulled myself up onto the Monk chassis and straddled it, staring down at its head. Still glowing, still smiling. I had a sudden moment of panic, certain that Orel was playing with me, that this was yet another extended joke—I half expected Belling, not really dead, not really maimed, maybe younger and even more improved than ever to step out from behind a rock, or rise up out of the elevator shaft just a few feet away from us.

Nothing happened.

Awkwardly, I reached across myself and pulled my second gun with my left hand. It felt strange and heavy there as I slipped off the safety.

Nothing happened.

Dreamily, my own breathing loud and harsh in my ears, I pushed the auto down at Orel's face, pushing the barrel into one of its eye sockets, pushing and pushing until I was leaning on it, supporting myself on the gun. Still, nothing happened. The wind scattered sand around us. I wondered if I was the last of us left alive. I stared down at my hand, the gun, Orel's inert face, feeling empty.

"If you can hear me, Mickey," I whispered hoarsely, feeling like I'd never catch my breath again, "and I fucking hope you can, I hope, for the first time in forever, you're fucking *terrified*."

I spent a second or so trying to jam the gun's barrel even farther into the socket, concentrating too hard, forgetting my own basic rules of survival. I heard the steps a second before I got hit, and then I was on my ass and Grisha was on top of me, pinning my arms with his.

"No!" he hissed, his rasp echoed in my earbud. "It is too dangerous. We need him alive."

I opened my mouth to shout at him, but as I did so he was torn from me and sailed up and over the old dorm wall, completely silent, his face just a pale expression of shock. Then he was gone, like he'd never been there.

Orel was moving.

I take it back, Marin hissed. *You're a hack and a fruit-cake, Dennis.*

The unit remains off-line, Squalor whispered back serenely. *He is manipulating himself using his ersatz mental abilities.*

The monk jerked, first this way, then that, twitching itself into an upright position. I watched, mesmerized, as he puppeted himself erect, swaying and jerking, over-balancing and then overcorrecting. When he suddenly steadied and raised one arm in a familiar, in-control gesture, I decided I'd seen enough of the magic act. I put the gun on him, couldn't think of anything clever to say, and squeezed the trigger. And got a dry click as my reward.

He turned his head and looked at me. After a second, the smile on his face broadened by thick degrees, and I tried to imagine the level of telekinetic control required to tug every tiny fake tendon, every microscopic bit of that face into the exact expression he wanted. I wondered if he was running the whole unit, pumping the coolant and greasing the gears. I wondered how long his brain would survive in there with the juice cut off.

Too long, I figured, was just about my luck.

I started backing away as I dropped the spent clip and tucked the gun under my armpit, my right hand still hanging limp at my side. It was prickling with pins and needles, pain bleeding back into it, and I could move the fingers a little—coming back to unfortunate life bit by bit. Reaching back across myself, I felt in my coat pocket for a fresh clip just as Orel leaped toward me in a sudden, viciously fast move—landing a foot short and falling over onto his side. He didn't say anything, or grunt, or make any noise at all, and was back up on his knees immediately, and then back on his feet, wobbling a little as he gathered himself for another spring. He was off kilter and rough, though, and I timed him pretty easily—he was so fucking fast he almost clipped me anyway, but I managed to duck down and roll under him as he sailed through the air. I rolled to a crouching position and slapped the clip home. Orel popped up just in front of the elevator shaft and I realized I'd put him between me and my final retreat. Before I could do more than blink at this dumbly, the invisible fist I was so fond of mushroomed out of thin air and slammed into me, knocking me back on my ass.

I forced myself to sit up, gun ready, but Orel was sprawled on the ground again. As I watched, he jerked upright, startling me, and I wasted two shots that came nowhere near him.

"What's the matter, Canny," I muttered to myself. The silence was creeping me out—he wasn't giving me the needle like Mickey always did, and he wasn't making *any* noise at all. "Can't puppet yourself and smack me around at the same time?"

I steadied myself and took careful aim at his head. He shot toward me, crashing into me like a cannonball—the motherfucker had *thrown* himself at me. For a second he was on me, pushing me back down into the sand, and then he rocketed away before I could pull out the gun on him again. I'd managed to push myself halfway up onto my elbows when he smacked into me again, just hurling himself like a fucking boulder, taking me square in the chest and knocking the breath out of me, then zooming off. I stared up at the dark sky above, thinking that this was never how I thought I'd go, pummeled to death by Canny Orel using himself as a battering ram.

Every nerve screaming, my heart pounding as I thought about him being out there somewhere, silent and floating, driven by the power of his mind, I forced myself to stay down, listening. My HUD, still bright and clear, dialed up my hearing suddenly, a minor blessing as my old rotting augments suddenly worked as intended for a change. Above the hiss and spit of ambient nothing, I heard him—a quick scrape, the fluttering noise of something moving through the air. My hand was tight and white on the butt of my gun. I counted in my head, using instinct to time him—and sat up suddenly, back complaining, raising the gun, as he was still ten feet away, and firing twice.

In midair, Orel veered and spun awkwardly, lost balance, and tumbled backward, skidding into the loose ground like an undetonated shell. He bounced once, twice, and then sailed over the slight lip and into the elevator shaft like something had yanked at it from below.

I sat there, gasping, the cold air burning my throat as it went down. I closed my eyes and dropped the clip, fumbling with a shaking hand for a fresh one and slamming it into place. As I pulled the slide, I felt a hint of an invisible touch, and then a giant iron fist made of nothing at all grabbed me and yanked, and the elevator shaft came at me like it had met me before and had a grudge.

SIT ON THIS ROCK FOREVER NOW PLAYING WITH OUR BONES

I banged up against the side of the shaft and pinged off it, slamming into the other side and repeating the process twice more, my teeth jumping in my head each time, my HUD dimming and brightening up like a loose wire was being knocked back into place. The air rushed by me with a sizzling noise, like hungry static eating me alive.

I shut my eyes and stretched out my arms, letting my gun drop away. The ladder rungs slapped into my left hand, and I flexed it, my fingers slipping through three, ten, fifteen rungs before I got some purchase. I clamped my hand as hard as I could, and with a searing, tearing pain my arm was dislocated and I slammed into the wall like I'd been fired from a cannon at short distance, smashing my nose on the ladder as an extra kiss from the cosmos. My HUD flickered and was gone again, giving me a split-second of red across the board before fading away completely.

As fresh sweat popped up all over me, I thought, *Well, shit, this feels like just about the right level of fucking nightmare for my jobs.* If Remy were alive—or Glee—I could have told them that nothing ever went as planned, and you had better expect to be hanging from an access ladder at least once.

Thinking of Remy and Gleason, I gritted my remaining aching teeth and sucked in the dank, black air. My face was hot and swollen, slick with blood and sweat. Anger bloomed in the pit of my stomach, a sour infection—everything had been swept into the past and there was not a fucking thing I could do to change any of it, and I wanted to just tear down the whole fucking shaft, pull it down with me and bury me and Orel forever. With effort, I moved my right arm, still feeling weak and numb. Gritting my teeth against the strange, numb pain—like pain from my future, reverberating backward along time—that spiked down from my shoulder and into the rest of my body, I swallowed blood and felt around my pocket until I found the thin little grenades Grisha had provided us. I pulled two free and toggled them active awkwardly, my fingers feeling thick and stiff. I counted to three in my head and let them drop, grabbing onto the ladder with both arms and hooking one elbow into the rungs.

I counted to three again in weird, cold silence, just my own wet, ragged breathing and the creak of the rusty ladder for company.

There was a silent, bright flash below me, the whole bottom of the shaft lit up and outlined perfectly, kind of pretty. The ladder began trembling and I swung gently from side to side, sweating and breathing hard, concentrating on keeping my grip. When the blast of hot air smacked into me, it felt kind of good for a split-second and then turned into a searing agony, hotter and hotter as air rushed past me. I shut my eyes and clamped my mouth shut, unable to breathe through my nose as heat and air roared past me, pushing at me, making me regret just about every decision I'd ever made in my entire fucking life, each one wrapped up in the complex tapestry that had brought me to this fucking spot in the time-space continuum. I hated my past selves intensely as I felt my skin blistering, melting, and running off my face like wax.

With a faint, sudden popping noise, it was over and the air felt ice-cold again, just like that. My HUD came on bright as day as my vision began to dim and—

I was still falling, so I knew I'd been unconscious for only a split second. Then the floor came up to say hello; I ducked my head under my functioning arm at the last second and tried to twist myself around. I landed on my side and my teeth jumped in my mouth again, my gun biting into my side and leaving, from what I could tell, a permanent impression of an automatic in my skin. Scissoring my legs, I pushed myself up into a sitting position and slid my hand into my pocket, seeking a gun, my eyes everywhere, blind in the gloom. My augments, it appeared, had finally shit the bed for good.

I could see Orel pretty easily, though. He was on fire.

His clothes had burned away, leaving just the sickly white skin of your standard Monk chassis. It burned with a blue-orange flame that licked and caressed him, his whole body and his face—eyes, nose, mouth—outlined in flames, everything else perfect shadows. I stared for

a second. I remembered I'd dropped my gun on the way
down, and I thrashed around the scorched, debris-littered
floor feverishly trying to locate it, until I realized *I* was
on fire too—at least my coat was. The yellowish flames
licked at me lazily, like they had nothing better to do,
jumping and creeping along the synthetic fibers.

The hallway was charred and filled with thick, black
smoke. Patches of fire clung to the walls, everything
burned down to the clean metal. I looked at Orel's fiery
outline as I backed away on my ass, sweeping my hands
around me as my legs pushed me along. My hand miracu-
lously found the butt of my gun, and I grasped it weakly,
unable to close my fist very well or very firmly. I wondered if my hair was on fire, and I decided I didn't need to
check. I'd know soon enough.

Orel stood with his hands in front of him curled into
fists, his elbows bent. The Psionic fist slammed into me
without warning and knocked me backward, my finger
spasming and sending a bullet into the air as I traveled. I
hit the wall of the elevator shaft and was pinned there as
if someone was holding a thick log against my chest—my
arms and legs dangled free.

I stared at Orel's silent, burning outline. My hand tightened as best it could on the butt of my gun; my other arm
dangled numb and useless at my side, the arm slightly
longer than it should be as it hung free from the socket.
Anger filled me up and spilled over into my blood, my
heart pounding its crazy, off-beat rhythm in my chest,
all the pain suddenly burned away. Orel had fucked me
a million times over, pushing me around like a piece
on a board—I'd thought I was on the cosmos's Rail all
these years, trapped on a path, but it had been *Orel*'s rail.

Remy's death was on Orel's hands. Glee's death. Kev Gatz, Rose Harper, Krajian, millions of fucking people in the Plague—all because Orel had pushed me onto the board, pointed my toes in a direction, and then awaited results.

I forced the hot, acrid air into myself, took it in deep, and closed my eyes, seeking the imaginary glass shield I'd used to keep the voices at bay. I forced calm into myself like caulk, pushing the rage and fear aside, filling myself with beige numbness. *Patience*, I thought. It was the lesson Canny had taught me. For years he'd been teaching me. Patience. Wait for your moment and don't move until it comes.

Orel took a stiff, unnatural step toward me, his hands skeletal, all the fake skin burned away, leaving the impervious alloy bones beneath.

I relaxed my grip on the gun. I had use of my arm; he didn't have me wrapped up tight. Hard enough to keep his body upright and moving while he did other things, hard to multitask when you'd just been blown up and were on fire. Kev Gatz had had a lifetime to get to know his Push and hadn't figured it out before he died; Orel had had just a few years.

I stayed limp. Anger bubbled over the edges of my imposed calm.

"I hope you enjoy the fucking *graveyard*, motherfucker," I rasped. I had to shout or twitch, so I shouted. "You got your Monk body. You got it without anyone pulling your strings, and you got your fucking God Augment. You get to sit on this rock forever now, playing with our bones. Well fucking played. You are a *fucking genius*."

Silently, the burning Monk stepped toward me, like it

was dragging itself behind itself, the heavy alloys of the Monk chassis reluctant. The pressure on me increased, pushing me into the hot wall, crushing, making it almost impossible to breathe. A yellow pulse started filling my vision in time with my off-kilter heartbeat.

He took another step; he was only about eight or nine feet away. Able to just bend my elbow, I brought the gun up in one quick, jerking motion and squeezed the trigger once.

He had to choose which Push to keep up—he wasn't experienced with it to begin with, and now had the strain of operating his entire physical being with his mind and using it on me. Instinct made him dive to one side, landing on the bubbling floor awkwardly; the invisible log disappeared from my chest. I dropped to the floor, staggering once and then launching myself forward, sprinting, my dislocated arm flopping at my side. I had to keep moving, keep coming at him and not let him concentrate.

The smoke made it hard to see, my eyes stinging and blurring, but the flaming outline of Orel as he rolled on the floor was clear enough, and I pushed myself at him, giving it everything I had. Jumping for it, I sailed down and landed on his back, fire leaping up around me for a second and then snuffing out. I leaned forward and snaked my arm around his neck, my gun still clutched loosely in my buzzing hand.

He tried to snatch me away with his telekinesis, my legs snapping up into the air, pain shooting through my body, but I hung onto him, my arm feeling weak and sore. I hung on with everything I had as he whipped me this way and that, trying to peel me off. When my arm felt tired and loose, sweat dripping from my face, I thought, *Shit, he's going to beat me. He's going to shake me loose and*

throw me against the fucking walls until I'm dead, and I
hated him. I realized, suddenly, that I'd never really hated
anything before. I'd despised people, I'd *killed* people, but
I'd never hated anyone until this exact moment, standing
in the ruined guts of Chengara with a *thing* responsible
for every bad moment of the past few years.

I pushed my legs down around his sides and squeezed
while I loosed my arm a little, enough to get some play as I
tried to angle the gun in toward his face, into his mechanical jaw.

He suddenly went limp. A second later, we both shot
into the air and slammed into the charred wall, me pinned
between it and the Monk, then bouncing off, spinning
around, and slamming into the opposite side. Something
stabbed into my shoulder, then sliced down toward the
middle of my back—

"Motherfucker!"

—as we were scraped away and spun so I was upside
down, then smashed down onto the floor. Wet pain soaked
into my clothes. I shut my eyes and pictured Remy on the
soldier's back, hanging on no matter what and certain,
certain I was about to free us, to take him off that truck
and save him. Fucking certain.

With a grunt I moved my arm and jammed the gun's
barrel into the hollow where his cheek had once been,
now burned away to the bare gray skeleton. The angle was
hard to judge, but I immediately knew there was a chance
I'd shoot myself as well if the bullet passed through. I hesitated. I thought of Grisha. I heard him: *Your winning or
losing determines whether the entire human race withers
on the vine. I must be sure you understand that you* must
take him alive.

I pictured Mickey's face on the hover, leaving me behind in this exact spot. Mickey always had a deal. Mickey always had connections, always had a plan, a fall-back position. I thought of Remy. I thought of him watching me turn and put a gun on him. The cold, numb feeling from my arm seemed to spread rapidly, pumped through my body by my stuttering heart, settling in and removing all the fire, the pain, and leaving behind just an empty certainty.

I thought,

Avery Cates, Destroyer of Worlds

and pulled the trigger.

EPILOGUE

I STARED AT THE HEAD. THE HEAD STARED BACK.

My steps echoed off the buildings as I walked down the cobblestone streets, twisting this way and that, barely wide enough for two people—if there was anyone else around—to pass. The buildings on each side were three or four stories high and cut off the sun, making everything dark and chilled, and there were occasional tin roofs stretched between the sides, cutting you off from the sky completely.

Toledo was deserted.

It was in good shape, though. It didn't look like the city had taken any bombings or serious tank actions during the civil war. None of the blocks I'd walked past had sported empty lots filled with rubble, and the streets weren't chewed up and churned into muddy pits. Mainly what I noticed was the lack of bodies; Toledo looked neat as a pin, as if everyone had just packed up their necessities and bugged out one evening, walking slowly and chatting, remarking on the weather.

I paused under another one of those simple roofs stretching a few feet over me. Vines grew on it, twisting under and around themselves, creating a canopy of green with purplish flowers. I stared at it. My back ached, tight and swollen, and my shoulders throbbed under my rough shirt. I stared at the canopy for a long time, swaying there on my feet, thinking about nothing. It had been months, but I was still not used to the absence of my HUD; there wasn't even the flickering shadow of it that I'd lived with from time to time. It appeared to be permanently shut down.

Blinking, I looked around. The silence was an anesthetic. I could close my eyes and there was nothing but wind and my own breathing. I'd been walking. Sometimes there were towns or camps with people in them, but mostly it had been open air, abandoned settlements, and silence. Sometimes I just closed my eyes and walked blindly for a while, opening them later with a faint sense of excitement to see where I'd ended up, if I was still alive.

Some of the camps and towns still tried to convince me to stay, to pay me off, to make me their sheriff. It was amazing. People never gave up, even when they'd been given up on.

Blinking, I turned and examined the building to my left; they were all connected, attached, like one huge sinuous building stretching the entire length of the street. A wooden sign hung by one short chain, the other side broken so the sign was on an angle. I turned my head slowly until it looked right-side up to me and read it: LA ABADÍA. The doors were thrust inward, the tiled floor barely visible for a few feet before being swallowed by darkness, but I could make out the edge of an old wooden bar. I always investigated bars. It was a policy.

There were a few overturned stools and tables inside, but otherwise it looked neat and orderly. It smelled dry and dusty. The ceiling was low and reminded me a little of the basement of Diocletian's palace, thick stone columns and rough stone walls. The floor was wood, much abused but still in decent shape.

I set the shredder against the wall and unslung my pack, relief sweeping through my muscles for a second, replaced immediately by a buzzing, humming ache that settled in like it knew my muscles well and liked it there. Dropping the pack on the floor, I adjusted my hip holsters and walked slowly around the bar, keeping my eyes open and turning around steadily as I went. I didn't know why I bothered, except that old habits were good habits.

The floor behind the bar was covered in broken glass that crunched under my boots as I walked its length. The shelves behind and under the bar were bare except for a couple of huge mechanical rat traps with the skeletal remains of their victims still clenched inside. Someone had already been through here looking for booze. Mixed in with the shattered glass were a dozen or so credit dongles, all useless now that the cops had gone into hibernation without Marin's codes. I kicked at them a little, studying the floor. I kept at it, walking back toward the center of the bar, and sure enough located the telltale outline of a trapdoor. Pushing glass aside with my boot, I cleared the area until I could see the thin outline of the door's edges.

I dropped to my knees and felt gingerly around the edges, trying to avoid tiny shards of glass in my fingertips. I found the well-hidden indentation that allowed me to get three fingers under the lip and lift the trap up, revealing a dim, shallow pit in which a stack of paper yen, a pile of credit dongles, and two gleaming bottles of... something sat like a present from the cosmos for my years of service.

I took one of the bottles and held it up. No label, a vaguely cloudy amber color. Could be booze, I thought. Could be rat poison. I took the bottle back around the bar and sat down next to my pack and set the bottle between my spread legs as I undid the straps. I pulled out Mara's head, eyes still open, still gleaming with artistically rendered life. I set the head gently on a nearby wooden chair so she was staring at me, and then picked up the bottle.

"What do you think?" I asked the head.

Mara kept her opinions to herself. I knew it was Orel in there, a copy of him, but Mara's not-quite-pretty face made it impossible to imagine the hateful old spider, so I thought of it as Mara.

You've finally gone crackers, Marin whispered. *That's what* I *think*.

No one's talking to you, I thought, dismissing him as I twisted the cap off the bottle. I sniffed the contents— sweet and sharp, definitely alcoholic—and tipped the bottle up for a swallow. It was surprisingly good, light and fruity with a distinct bite I enjoyed, the familiar burn of booze. I took a healthy swig and paused for a breath before taking another, a pleasant warmth blooming immediately in my middle.

Setting the bottle on the floor, I winced a little as a sharp tearing sensation rippled up my back. I stuffed one hand into a coat pocket and pulled out the sheaf of folded paper I'd been marking my progress on. There was no power for handhelds, no signals in the air anyway, and no hard-copy maps anywhere I'd been able to find. So you wandered. I'd found Toledo using ancient signs still planted here and there, and some luck. I scanned through the lists of street names I'd already walked through, taking sips from the bottle, and finally wrote *Calle de Nunez de Arce* on the bottom of the list.

I stuffed the papers back into my pocket and stared around the empty room. The light was failing, and I thought I might see if there was a good defensible room somewhere in here, just stay where I was for the night. Plenty to burn. If there was booze hidden away, there might be food, too. And Toledo was, as far as I'd been able to tell, about as deserted as any place in the world. And there were plenty of deserted places.

After a few more minutes I stood up and took the bottle on a tour. The place had a crazy layout, small rooms linked by narrow hallways, all still furnished with the peculiar wooden chairs and tables, most still in place. Everything looked ready for business, like the vampires were coming later on in the evening to have a few cocktails. I found a winding, darkened set of stairs heading upward and it led me to a larger second floor, more or less one open space with two large windows on the back end, the orange sun streaming in hot and dry. It felt empty, although there were some boxes and some gray sacks piled here and there: a storeroom. As I entered, a platoon of large black rats scrambled out of the way, and I made a mental note to reclaim a few traps to set up around me as I slept.

Between the two huge windows a man sat spread-eagled, his hands flat on the floor on either side of him.

He was tall, had oriental features, and wore a nicely cut black suit and overcoat, black gloves, and the shiniest black shoes I'd ever seen. His trousers had ridden up to reveal black socks and an inch of his tan calves. He stared straight ahead, his head tilted back slightly and resting against the sill of the window.

Setting the bottle down, I unsnapped the holster on my left hip and rested my hand on the butt of the gun as I walked over to the windows. I stopped directly in front of him and studied him for a moment; he looked perfect, fresh and supple, and my underbrain kept screaming to pull the gun and shoot the avatar before he gave up this game and leaped for me.

I forced myself to take my hand from the gun and knelt in front of it. I glanced down at the floor; the cop had placed his gun and badge there between his legs. I picked up the beautiful leather wallet containing his badge and flipped it open. The silvery template inside was dim and lifeless, the hologram's battery juice dried up. Captain Emil Yodsuwan. I flipped the badge shut and dropped it back at his feet. He'd seen it coming, the shutdown, and he'd found a place of relative privacy to wait for someone to recrank the servers and wake the cops up.

I picked up the gun, a nice chrome-plated auto, pre–civil war. Full clip. I slipped it into my pocket and set about going through his pockets. I found a credit dongle and dead handheld, a spare clip for the gun, and a battered old data cube. I held the cube between my thumb and forefinger for a moment, studying it, and then pushed it into my inside pocket. There was no way to read it, but it might be fun to try.

Satisfied, I turned and walked back down to the front bar, reclaiming the bottle as I passed it. Everything was exactly as I'd left it, only darker. I'd have to break up a table and chairs soon to get a fire going if I was going to avoid having to work in the pitch black the night had become everywhere, but instead of getting to work I slid down to the floor again, stiff back complaining, and sat in front of the head. I stared at Mara for a moment, thinking, but there was nothing to say to her.

A sudden noise made me twist halfway into a kneeling position, hands flying to my holsters. I stayed that way for a few jumpy, irregular heartbeats, sweat breaking out cold and slimy on my face, and then sagged back down to the floor. There was no one there.

I stared at the head. The head stared back. I thought of Grisha, who I'd found half buried in dry, loose sand a half mile or more out in the desert, his hands curled into claws, beetles roaming over his body. I thought of Marko, who I'd never found any sign of. I liked to think he'd crawled away, made his escape, but I couldn't know that. I thought of them all, in turn.

I could hear nothing except the wind pushing its way through the vines on the canopy, and the light was failing fast. I stared at the head and the head stared back and I felt a familiar weary heaviness inside. I shut my eyes and thought grimly, *There will never be anyone there.*

APPENDIX

Superstes per Scientia

Confidential Memorandum

To: Baklanov, G, DIC

Fr: McKie, Andrew, ADM

cc: none

RE: *Zadravec Diary*

Dear Grisha,

As you know I have been depressed of late at our lack of progress. I know you understand the seriousness of our situation, but you and I may be the only ones in the directing committees who do; I won't sling mud in writing but I find myself more and more frustrated at the attitude of those who oppose your efforts to salvage what can be salvaged of this disastrous world.

Grisha, my little professor, where are you? Your absence is terrifying. I know you well enough to know you do not waste time, but I am selfish enough to wish you here. I send this to you hoping it finds you, somewhere, that our courier teams are still intact and functioning.

It is like I can feel the world constricting around me. Every day, fewer of us left. Noise on the line where there used to be voices.

As per your instruction of two weeks ago, we secured and explored the small settlements near Split that you marked. We found no one alive in any of them, though all showed signs of recent habitation. We searched thoroughly and took away several items of possible interest that will be cataloged and digitized according to our usual protocols. One item, however, was of significant interest and I am reproducing portions of it within this memorandum in the hope that it finds its way to you. I suspect you will garner great intellectual pleasure from its contents, if I know you, and it may shed some light on your current mission.

The item is a diary, a journal. It is unusual in that it is written by hand, in ink, and not simply a recording or other digital artifact. It is written in an old script; we had to dig through the archives to find a study of it. To think that someone has been passing this down for decades, perhaps a century—I am unclear when we're agreed that the practice of handwriting like this died out. But I am digressing.

You know I love my digression, my little professor.

I will not reproduce the diary in its entirety here. Much of it is extremely prosaic in nature, and some was impossible to decipher, as it appears to have been written when the author—whose first name is unknown—was extremely inebriated. I trust, however, that you will find the chosen excerpts instructive, if perhaps depressing. But then how can one be depressed in this world. Depression was decades ago, burned away. Now we just observe, and note, and sleep dreamlessly, waiting.

Zadravec Entry One: This morning something is different. I sat out in the garden and wished for coffee as the sun rose, but there was, of course, no coffee. Also no police, so I did not complain. I have distrusted this peace, this quiet. Ever since the Little Captain shot himself all those years ago and we were without an SSF Field Officer for the first time since my parents' time, others have rejoiced, others have celebrated. When no more police came to take his place, people became incautious, believing everything changed. There has been excitement ever since the bombing, the night that was bright as day years ago.

For a while, it seemed to be true. We heard nothing from the police, nothing from the Joint Council, nothing from the army. Nothing. Some celebrated, but the silence was frightening to me.

I remembered when the Little Captain shot himself in the head. He made a strange speech about the future, about there being none. Then there was nothing for a few months. Then the army came. Then the police again, strutting around, an army, too. Then they left again. And nothing since. Except the sunrise at night.

Zadravec Entry Two: I wish I knew why Henri has left; without word, without me.

* * *

Zadravec Entry Three: Today the strangest thing has happened. A meeting had been called; Carl the provost proposed that we send emissaries to other settlements nearby and negotiate trade agreements, diplomatic exchanges. Cooperation and mutual defense. And also, though this was unspoken, to inquire about their children, if they had any, and if they did, to spy on them and speculate why we were, to a person, barren. Although I think Carl often thinks too much of himself and his title, bestowed upon him because he thought of it first, this was a sensible suggestion and I was willing to be patient.

In the middle of the meeting, the first meeting that has been of any value in months, old Victor shuffled into the square. This was surprising, as Victor does not often leave his house, even now that the Vid Screens no longer function. We all paused in surprise, but he said nothing, simply appeared, and then, suddenly, Marik and Antoine stood up, swaying drunkenly, and started walking. They also said nothing. The rest of us stared after them. I thought it was a prearranged meeting, although Victor did not often socialize or even speak to anyone, preferring to autoscan channels on his Vid rather than to speak to any of us. They walked past the old man, though, who continued to stare at us unblinkingly. I noticed he was not wearing shoes.

Then Victor also turned away, and left.

We attempted to continue the meeting, but nothing came of it. We had, of course, been in regular contact with the other villages before, but the networks were down and did not seem to be coming back up, although

Zukov performed a scan every few weeks just in case. He sometimes finds transient, mobile networks within range, but so far they are all encrypted and not public. At any rate, we broke up and went home.

Zadravec Entry Four: Today we were assaulted by brigands, a hungry group of women armed with shredding rifles pilfered from somewhere. We offered no resistance. They strode into the square without fanfare and had a long list of demands, but we had very little to offer them. They beat Carl terribly and issued their demands again, threatening to kill many of us if we did not meet them. I did not think they would; if they had ammunition for their guns, which I was not sure they did, it would be too precious to waste on us. It did not matter; we had already given them what we had to give.

When they left us, taking a meager haul of food and other supplies—Zukov lost our last chargeable battery— I noted several people missing and went searching for them, but they were nowhere to be found. As I searched, I ran into Victor down near my house, walking stiffly. I tried to hail him, to stop him, but he ignored me and acted as if he could not see me at all. I attempted to take his arm and guide him back to his house, but he refused— without words, without gestures, simply by not moving when I urged him to. He stared past me down the street and I turned to follow his look.

Several of the younger men were walking toward us. At first I thought they were coming to aid me with Victor, that we might carry him bodily to his house and deposit him safely, but as they approached I became uneasy. They moved stiffly, and stared as Victor stared, and when they came near none of them responded to me, although I knew their families. They moved silently past and kept walking, no matter what I said. They ignored me, and in moments I was alone with Victor again, feeling discomfited.

Then Victor began shuffling away, still silent. I let him go. I went back to my house and felt very alone.

Zadravec Entry Five: I am frightened; this morning Zukov is missing. The whole village suddenly seems empty, and I wonder how many people have simply stood up and walked away, glassy-eyed and silent. Carl woke me from a deep slumber with the news. I had to invite him in for a glass of my precious whiskey to steady him and get the whole story, which wasn't much to tell. Ever since the invasion, we'd set up some simple alarms consisting of trip wires and piled pots and pans in nettings, and everyone took turns standing guard at the main approach. It was Zukov's turn this evening, and when the wire was tripped the noise brought Carl running, old hunting rifle in his hands. He found Zukov simply walking into the woods, silent and unresponsive. He became angry and attempted to stop Zukov, but he said that the man was insensible, not reacting to pain or any obstruction, just walking and walking, implacable, silent.

I asked Carl if Victor was anywhere nearby, but he said no. He'd seen no one else.

I insisted we search the village. We found Victor in moments, striding about naked, apparently unaffected by the chill. But as I'd expected, we didn't find many others. I started running from door to door, banging and shouting.

None of the chimes worked anymore, of course, just as none of the escalators functioned inside. I made as much noise as I could, and when everyone had assembled to discover what had driven me insane, it was a shockingly small number of people.

We were childless, all of us, and absences were simply not noticed right away. We had been a village of a hundred souls, and now barely thirty stood in front of me.

"Victor," Carl said before I could intervene. "That old bastard is behind this."

It was terrible, and I could not stop it. Crazed with a sudden terror, they hunted poor old Victor and tore him from his house, where he was sleeping. He appeared normal, now; at first outraged that we would invade his house, then alarmed and peevish, and finally terrified as several men took hold of him and dragged him outside.

A drum trial began. We had much experience of these from the various army occupations that took place, all of our younger folk pressed into the army, the rest fleeing the Press Squads. I witnessed many instant trials, all performed with mock dignity and faked diligence, and ours was no different. They thought, perhaps by killing poor old Victor, everyone would return and all would be well again. He was convicted and sentenced, and everyone but me took up stones and surrounded the old man. It was clear that he did not understand what was happening. I wept as he stared around at us, at people he had lived his entire life with, blinking and twitching, demanding in a timorous screech that we explain ourselves.

And then they stoned him to death.

It was over far more quickly than I would have imagined; the first stone hit him in the chest and he collapsed under it, wailing, and within seconds he was silent. I turned and ran, feeling helpless and angry, and shut myself in my home. Poor Victor. I did not like him. I had never liked him. But now I mourned him. For so long, with the Little Captain watching us, with the hovers at his command, we cursed the police and said to ourselves that if we were able to run our own affairs, things would be better. We are running our own affairs, and everything is much worse, and I wished a new Little Captain would arrive to issue commands and stop us from ourselves.

Outside, there was no noise. I wished for Henri, his voice, his disdainful manner. I wanted company in the house.

Zadravec Entry Six: Someone buried Victor. I don't know who, but his frail, bruised body was gone the next day. I spoke to no one. Carl attempted conversation, but I ignored him, and no one else tried to speak to me, everyone going about with their eyes downcast. I would have left, but where is there for an old woman like me to go? After getting water I stayed inside again. Some time in the evening someone rapped on my door, but I ignored them, and a few minutes later they abandoned the effort.

Zadravec Entry Seven: I ventured outside in need of food; my slim larder has shrunk, and my tin of N-tabs is almost empty. I think I will starve soon. There is no one left to worry about me, and since Victor, we are not a village anymore. We are a collection of combatants choosing our moment. I do not have any desire for death, but I do not wish the slow, inside-scraping fade of starvation. I will struggle until the end, but if the end comes I will slit my wrists and close my eyes, dream of Henri.

I saw Carl immediately. He was standing in his night-dress, staring at me. At first I paused, thinking he was surprised to see me, but slowly I realized he was vacant, still. He was our new Victor.

I approached him and made some effort to speak to him, but he was lost, as Victor had been. Alarmed, I wandered the village, but my worst fears were confirmed: I could find no one. Every house was empty, every path abandoned. I walked freely into every building, shouting, but no one answered.

When I found my way back to my own abode, Carl was gone as well. I stood shivering in the wind. I thought, *Well, now there is food enough for a while, if I can raid everyone's hidden stores for myself.* The thought made me feel tired, and I did nothing about it, letting it sit there unopened, a rock in my mind. I decided I will wait. I decided I will see if anyone returns. Then I will decide what to do. When the world has returned.

ACKNOWLEDGMENTS

As with all of these novels, a cast of thousands labors behind the scenes to make me look good, or at least marginally better than I actually am. To my team of Booze Acquisitionists, who managed to locate a bottle of Mackinlay's from the North Pole Shackleton camp, thank you from the bottom of my heart, and for the last time, no, you cannot have any. To my team of makeup artists who transform me from Pudgy Middle-Aged Man to Man Who Is Definitely Not Drunk Right Now, Why Do You Ask? you perform miracles every day, and no, you do not get a raise. To my team of Fixers and Cleaners, who magically transform every public humiliation and potentially jailable offense into publicity triumphs, I can truthfully say that I don't know how you do it. Because I never remember anything the next day.

To everyone at Orbit Books—Tim, Devi, Alex, Jennifer, Jack, and Lauren—I thank you for, well, everything, from expert editorial advice to amazing covers, enthusiastic promotion, and friendly, liquor-laden support. Plus, y'all paid me for my books, and thus you have purchased my heart as well.

The kids at Fine Print Literary Management have more hijinx in their little fingers than most people accumulate throughout an entire lifetime, and somehow use alchemy to transform said hijinx into sage career advice and royalty checks. My eternal thanks to Janet Reid, Agent to the Stars, and her cadre of minions.

My friends and family, although I don't see any of them often enough anymore, remain inspirations and comforts: my wife, Danette, the Greatest Wife Ever in the History of Wivery; my brother Sean and my Sainted Mom, who still admit to being related to me for no known reason; Ken, Jeof, and Misty, who haven't defriended me from Facebook despite plenty of reason to; Sean Ferrell, who drinks a lot, god bless him.

Finally, where would I be without Lili Saintcrow? Years ago she taught me to read and write while we were both in a mysterious prison in an unspecified location, beaten daily and forced to subsist on rats and runoff; needless to say these books would never have been written without her. Every year she mails me a small pebble; someday I know that pebble will be black, and then it all begins. Until then, I abide.

extras

orbit

meet the author

JEFF SOMERS was born in Jersey City, New Jersey. After graduating from college, he wandered aimlessly for a while, but the peculiar siren call of New Jersey brought him back to his homeland. In 1995, Jeff began publishing his own magazine, *The Inner Swine* (www.innerswine.com). Find out more about the author at www.jeffreysomers.com.

introducing

If you enjoyed THE FINAL EVOLUTION,
look out for

EQUATIONS OF LIFE

by Simon Morden

Samuil Petrovitch is a survivor. He survived the nuclear fallout in St. Petersburg and hid in the London Metrozone—the last city in England. He's lived this long because he's a man of rules and logic.

For example, getting involved = a bad idea. But when he stumbles into a kidnapping in progress, he acts without even thinking. Before he can stop himself, he's saved the daughter of the most dangerous man in London.

And clearly saving the girl = getting involved. Now, the equation of Petrovitch's life is looking increasingly complex.

Russian mobsters + Yakuza + something called the New Machine Jihad = one dead Petrovitch. But Petrovitch has a plan—he always has a plan—he's just not sure it's a good one.

I

Petrovitch woke up. The room was in the filtered yellow half light of rain-washed window and thin curtain. He lay perfectly still, listening to the sounds of the city.

For a moment, all he could hear was the all-pervading hum of machines: those that made power, those that used it, pushing, pulling, winding, spinning, sucking, blowing, filtering, pumping, heating, and cooling.

In the next moment, he did the city dweller's trick of blanking that whole frequency out. In the gap it left, he could discern individual sources of noise: traffic on the street fluxing in phase with the cycle of red-amber-green, the rhythmic metallic grinding of a worn windmill bearing on the roof, helicopter blades cutting the gray dawn air. A door slamming, voices rising—a man's low bellow and a woman's shriek, going at it hard. Leaking in through the steel walls, the babel chatter of a hundred different channels all turned up too high.

Another morning in the London Metrozone, and Petrovitch had survived to see it: *God, I love this place.*

Closer, in the same room as him, was another sound,

one that carried meaning and promise. He blinked his pale eyes, flicking his unfocused gaze to search his world, searching…

There. His hand snaked out, his fingers closed around thin wire, and he turned his head slightly to allow the approaching glasses to fit over his ears. There was a thumbprint dead center on his right lens. He looked around it as he sat up.

It was two steps from his bed to the chair where he'd thrown his clothes the night before. It was May, and it wasn't cold, so he sat down naked, moving his belt buckle from under one ass cheek. He looked at the screen glued to the wall.

His reflection stared back, high-cheeked, white-skinned, pale-haired. Like an angel, or maybe a ghost: he could count the faint shadows cast by his ribs.

Back on the screen, an icon was flashing. Two telephone numbers had appeared in a self-opening box: one was his, albeit temporarily, to be discarded after a single use. In front of him on the desk were two fine black gloves and a small red switch. He slipped the gloves on, and pressed the switch.

"Yeah?" he said into the air.

A woman's voice, breathless from effort. "I'm looking for Petrovitch."

His index finger was poised to cut the connection. "You are who?"

"Triple A couriers. I've got a package for an S. Petrovitch." She was panting less now, and her cut-glass accent started to reassert itself. "I'm at the drop-off: the café on the corner of South Side and Rookery Road. The proprietor says he doesn't know you."

"Yeah, and Wong's a *pizdobol*," he said. His finger drifted from the cutoff switch and dragged through the air, pulling a window open to display all his current transactions. "Give me the order number."

"Fine," sighed the courier woman. He could hear traffic noise over her headset, and the sound of clattering plates in the background. He would never have described Wong's as a café, and resolved to tell him later. They'd both laugh. She read off a number, and it matched one of his purchases. It was here at last.

"I'll be with you in five," he said, and cut off her protests about another job to go to with a slap of the red switch.

He peeled off the gloves. He pulled on yesterday's clothes and scraped his fingers through his hair, scratching his scalp vigorously. He stepped into his boots and grabbed his own battered courier bag.

Urban camouflage. Just another immigrant, not worth shaking down. He pushed his glasses back up his nose and palmed the door open. When it closed behind him, it locked repeatedly, automatically.

The corridor echoed with noise, with voices, music, footsteps. Above all, the soft moan of poverty. People were everywhere, their shoulders against his, their feet under his, their faces—wet-mouthed, hollow-eyed, filthy skinned—close to his.

The floor, the walls, the ceiling were made from bare sheet metal that boomed. Doors punctured the way to the stairs, which had been dropped into deliberately left voids and welded into place. There was a lift, which sometimes even worked, but he wasn't stupid. The stairs were safer because he was fitter than the addicts who'd try to roll him.

Fitness was relative, of course, but it was enough.

He clanked his way down to the ground floor, five stories away, ten landings, squeezing past the stair dwellers and avoiding spatters of noxious waste. At no point did he look up, in case he caught someone's eye.

It wasn't safe, calling a post-Armageddon container home, but neither was living in a smart, surveillance-rich neighborhood with no visible means of support—something that was going to attract police attention, which wasn't what he wanted at all. As it stood, he was just another immigrant with a clean record renting an identikit two-by-four domik module in the middle of Clapham Common. He'd never given anyone an excuse to notice him, had no intention of ever doing so.

Street level. Cracked pavements dark with drying rain, humidity high, the heat already uncomfortable. An endless stream of traffic that ran like a ribbon throughout the city, always moving with a stop-start, never seeming to arrive. There was elbow room here, and he could stride out to the pedestrian crossing. The lights changed as he approached, and the cars parted as if for Moses. The crowd of bowed-head, hunch-shouldered people shuffled drably across the tarmac to the other side and, in the middle, a shock of white-blond hair.

Wong's was on the corner. Wong himself was kicking some plastic furniture out onto the pavement to add an air of unwarranted sophistication to his shop. The windows were streaming condensation inside, and stale, steamy air blew out the door.

"Hey, Petrovitch. She your girlfriend? You keep her waiting like that, she leave you."

"She's a courier, you *perdoon stary*. Where is she?"

Wong looked at the opaque glass front and pointed through it. "There," the shopkeeper said. "Right there. Eyes of love never blind."

"I'll have a coffee, thanks." Petrovitch pushed a chair out of his path.

"I should charge you double. You use my shop as office!"

Petrovitch put his hands on Wong's shoulders and leaned down. "If I didn't come here, your life would be less interesting. And you wouldn't want that."

Wong wagged his finger but stood aside, and Petrovitch went in.

The woman was easy to spot. Woman: girl almost, all adolescent gawkiness and nerves, playing with her ponytail, twisting and untwisting it in red spirals around her index finger.

She saw him moving toward her, and stopped fiddling, sat up, tried to look professional. All she managed was younger.

"Petrovitch?"

"Yeah," he said, dropping into the seat opposite her. "Do you have ID?"

"Do you?"

They opened their bags simultaneously. She brought out a thumb scanner; he produced a cash card. They went through the ritual of confirming their identities, checking the price of the item, debiting the money from the card. Then she laid a padded package on the table and waited for the security tag to unlock.

Somewhere during this, a cup of coffee appeared at Petrovitch's side. He took a sharp, scalding sip.

"So what is it?" the courier asked, nodding at the package.

"It's kind of your job to deliver it, my job to pay for it." He dragged the packet toward him. "I don't have to tell you what's in it."

"You're an arrogant little fuck, aren't you?" Her cheeks flushed.

Petrovitch took another sip of coffee, then centered his cup on his saucer. "It has been mentioned once or twice before." He looked up again, and pushed his glasses up to see her better. "I have trust issues, so I don't tend to do the people-stuff very well."

"It wouldn't hurt you to try." The security tag popped open, and she pushed her chair back with a scrape.

"Yeah, but it's not like I'm going to ever see you again, is it?" said Petrovitch.

"If you'd played your cards right, you might well have done. Sure, you're good-looking, but right now I wouldn't piss on you if you were on fire." She picked up her courier bag with studied determination and strode to the door.

Petrovitch watched her go: she bent over, lean and lithe in her one-piece skating gear, to extrude the wheels from her shoes. The other people in the shop fell silent as the door slammed shut, just to increase his discomfort.

Wong leaned over the counter. "You bad man, Petrovitch. One day you need friend, and where you be? Up shit creek with no paddle."

"I've always got you, Wong." He put his hand to his face and scrubbed at his chin. He could try and catch up to her, apologize for being . . . what? Himself? He was half out of his seat, then let himself fall back with a bang. He stopped being the center of attention, and he drank more coffee.

The package in its mesh pocket called to him. He

reached over and tore it open. As the disabled security tag clattered to the tabletop, Wong took the courier's place opposite him.

"I don't need relationship advice, yeah?"

Wong rubbed at a sticky patch with a damp cloth. "This not about girl, that girl, any girl. You not like people, fine. But you smart, Petrovitch. You smartest guy I know. Maybe you smart enough to fake liking, yes? Else."

"Else what?" Petrovitch's gaze slipped from Wong to the device in his hand, a slim, brushed-steel case, heavy with promise.

"Else one day, pow." Wong mimed a gun against his temple, and his finger jerked with imaginary recoil. "Fortune cookie says you do great things. If you live."

"Yeah, that's me. Destined for greatness." Petrovitch snorted and caressed the surface of the case, leaving misty fingerprints behind. "How long have you lived here, Wong?"

"Metrozone born and bred," said Wong. "I remember when Clapham Common was green, like park."

"Then why the *chyort* can't you speak better English?"

Wong leaned forward over the table and beckoned Petrovitch to do the same. Their noses were almost touching.

"Because, old chap," whispered Wong faultlessly, "we hide behind our masks, all of us, every day. All the world's a stage, and all the men and women merely players. I play my part of eccentric Chinese shopkeeper; everyone knows what to expect from me, and they don't ask for any more. What about you, Petrovitch? What part are you playing?" He leaned back, and Petrovitch shut his goldfish-gaping mouth.

A man and a woman came in and, on seeing every table full, started to back out again.

Wong sprang to his feet. "Hey, wait. Table here." He kicked Petrovitch's chair leg hard enough to cause them both to wince. "Coffee? Coffee hot and strong today." He bustled behind the counter, leaving Petrovitch to wearily slide his device back into its delivery pouch and then into his shoulder bag.

His watch told him it was time to go. He stood, finished the last of his drink in three hot gulps, and made for the door.

"Hey," called Wong. "You no pay."

Petrovitch pulled out his cash card and held it up.

"You pay next time, Petrovitch." He shrugged and almost smiled. The lines around his eyes crinkled.

"Yeah, whatever." He put the card back in his bag. It had only a few euros on it now, anyway. "Thanks, Wong."

Back out onto the street and the roar of noise. The leaden sky squeezed out a drizzle and speckled the lenses in Petrovitch's glasses so that he started to see the world like a fly would.

He'd take the tube. It'd be hot, dirty, smelly, crowded: at least it would be dry. He turned his collar up and started down the road toward Clapham South.

The shock of the new had barely reached the Underground. The tiled walls were twentieth-century curdled cream and bottle green, the tunnels they lined unchanged since they'd been hollowed out two centuries earlier. The fans that ineffectually stirred the air on the platforms were ancient with age.

There was the security screen, though: the long arched

passage of shiny white plastic, manned by armed paycops and monitored by gray-covered watchers.

Petrovitch's travelcard talked to the turnstile as he waited in line to pass. It flashed a green light, clicked, and he pushed through. Then came the screen that saw everything, saw through everything, measured it and resolved it into three dimensions, running the images it gained against a database of offensive weapons and banned technology.

After the enforced single file, it was abruptly back to being shoulder to shoulder. Down the escalator, groaning and creaking, getting hotter and more airless as it descended. Closer to the center of the Earth.

He popped like a cork onto the northbound platform, and glanced up to the display barely visible over the heads of the other passengers. A full quarter of the elements were faulty, making the scrolling writing appear either coded or mystical. But he'd had practice. There was a train in three minutes.

Whether or not there was room for anyone to get on was a different matter, but that possibility was one of the few advantages in living out along the far reaches of the line. He knew of people he worked with who walked away from the center of the city in order to travel back.

It became impossible even to move. He waited more or less patiently, and kept a tight hold of his bag.

To his left, a tall man, air bottle strapped to his Savile Row suit and soft mask misting with each breath. To his right, a Japanese woman, patriotically displaying Hello Kitty and the Rising Sun, hollow-eyed with loss.

The train, rattling and howling, preceded by a blast of foulness almost tangible, hurtled out from the tunnel mouth. If there hadn't been barriers along the edge of the platform, the track would have been choked with mangled corpses. As it was, there was a collective strain, an audible tightening of muscle and sinew.

The carriages squealed to a stop, accompanied by the inevitable multilanguage announcements: the train was heading for the central zones and out again to the distant, unassailable riches of High Barnet, and please—mind the gap.

The doors hissed open, and no one got out. Those on the platform eyed the empty seats and the hang straps greedily. Then the electromagnetic locks on the gates loosened their grip. They banged back under the pressure of so many bodies, and people ran on, claiming their prizes as they could.

And when the carriages were full, the last few squeezed on, pulled aboard by sympathetic arms until they were crammed in like pressed meat.

The chimes sounded, the speakers rustled with static before running through a litany of "doors closing" phrases: English, French, Russian, Urdu, Japanese, Kikuyu, Mandarin, Spanish. The engine spun, the wheels turned, the train jerked and swayed.

Inside, Petrovitch, face pressed uncomfortably against a glass partition, ribs tight against someone's back, took shallow sips of breath and wondered again why he'd chosen the Metrozone above other, less crowded and more distant cities. He wondered why it still had to be like this, seven thirty-five in the morning, two decades after Armageddon.